21.3.17
Nicks

SoV

Books should be returned or renewed by the last
date above. Renew by phone **03000 41 31 31** or
online *www.kent.gov.uk/libs*

Libraries Registration & Archives

CUSTOMER
SERVICE
EXCELLENCE

CSE

Kent
County
Council
kent.gov.uk

D0682901

Also by Maggie Ford:

The Soldier's Bride
A Mother's Love
Call Nurse Jenny
A Woman's Place
The Factory Girl

A Girl in
Wartime

Maggie FORD

EBURY
PRESS

1 3 5 7 9 10 8 6 4 2

Ebury Press, an imprint of Ebury Publishing
20 Vauxhall Bridge Road,
London SW1V 2SA

Penguin
Random House
UK

Ebury Press is part of the Penguin Random House group of companies whose
addresses can be found at global.penguinrandomhouse.com

Copyright © Maggie Ford, 2016

Maggie Ford has asserted her right to be identified as the author of this work
in accordance with the Copyright, Designs and Patents Act 1988

This novel is a work of fiction. Names and characters are the product of the
author's imagination and any resemblance to actual persons, living or dead, is
entirely coincidental

First published in the UK in 2016 by Ebury Press

www.eburypublishing.co.uk

A CIP catalogue record for this book is available from the British Library

ISBN 9780091956660

Typeset in India by Thomson Digital Pvt Ltd, Noida, Delhi

Printed and bound in Great Britain by Clays Ltd, St Ives plc

Penguin Random House is committed to a sustainable future for our business,
our readers and our planet. This book is made from Forest Stewardship
Council® certified paper.

MIX
Paper from
responsible sources
FSC
www.fsc.org   FSC® C018179

*In memory of those caught up in WWI
and the East Enders for whom war was brought
to their own door steps.*

*Also to my son John and my daughters
Janet and Clare.*

Chapter One

June 1914

Louise Lovell glanced over her sixteen-year-old daughter's shoulder as she passed the kitchen table; in her hands were several large spuds which she would peel and cut into chips to go with the cold roast lamb left over from Sunday.

About to tell her that she'd have to clear the table ready for that evening's dinner, she paused, gazing fondly at what the girl was doing. She was wasted working in a factory making cardboard boxes.

'Wish I'd been given your gift, love,' she remarked. 'That's really lovely.'

Connie looked up from the pencil drawing she was doing. 'You think so, Mum? Thanks.'

'Ran in me family, drawing, y'know, but passed me by, didn't it?'

'Maybe it's in you too, Mum, somewhere,' Connie said absently, returning her attention to the country scene she was copying from a black-and-white picture she'd found in an old newspaper.

Later she'd colour it in, using her own imagination for the hues from the cheap box of watercolour paints she'd got for her twelfth birthday four years ago. The little pallets of bright colours were hollowed from much use. Soon they would be all gone but when she'd be able to afford a new box was anyone's guess. Dad said she was too old for such soppy childish things.

'Time you got out of them kids' toys,' he'd said. 'You're sixteen now, and in work. It's about time you started acting your age.'

Dad didn't – or wouldn't – understand how essential they were to her. Drawing and painting were her life. She had a gift, as Mum said. Even at twelve she'd been able to look at a person's face and draw it well enough for people to instantly recognise the owner. Under her bed in the back bedroom she'd once shared with her sisters, both now married and moved away, were pencil portraits of the current silent screen stars, men who'd made her heart go pit-a-pat: Maurice Costello, Charles Ray, James O'Neill, each a perfectly recognisable likeness.

Alone, she'd dream of one day meeting one of them, becoming his adored lover, showered with gifts, envied and rich, though chance would be a fine thing. It was only a fantasy. In the real world she worked in a factory, standing at the assembly line for hours on end turning the cardboard edges of boxes into place and dabbing them with sticky paste as they passed, and it looked as if she'd be staying there doing it until, like her sisters, she got married and became a housewife.

'Come on, love, best clear away,' her mum said. 'Your dad'll be home soon, and you know he likes to sit straight down to his meal.'

Obediently, if reluctantly, Connie got up from her chair and began carefully to collect all her bits and pieces, the two pencils, the India rubber, the nearly completed drawing on its sheet of off-white paper she'd smuggled out with a thin stack of similar sheets from her workplace – for how could she afford proper parchment on factory wages?

Carefully she rolled up the landscape drawing so that it wouldn't crease, and, with her arms full, went out of the kitchen and up the dark, windowless stairs of her terraced home in Cardinal Row, Bethnal Green, to stash all her stuff away under her bed.

Soon she would be vacating this room, with its cheerful sunshine coming in first thing in the mornings, for the back room downstairs. It wasn't a prospect she looked forward to. She had no option but to comply with the wants of her family.

This house being two-up-two-down like all those around here, she and her two sisters, Elsie and Lillian, had shared this room for as long as Connie could remember; the other bedroom was occupied by her parents. But since her sisters had left to get married, Elsie the year before last and Lillian just a few weeks ago, she'd had the room all to herself. And lovely it had been too, but not for much longer.

Her brothers, George, Albert and Ronald, had slept in one bed in the downstairs back room since they were kids, two at the head and one at the foot. But now they were grown men: George twenty-one, Albert – Bertie – nineteen and Ronnie seventeen. So, as from next week, they'd have her room and she'd have the downstairs back room. No more privacy, just the curtain around the bed behind which she'd retire after everyone had gone up to their rooms around ten o'clock.

Of course, if they were home late they'd go straight upstairs, so there was no fear of her being bothered. But there'd be no more lingering at a window to gaze down into the neighbouring backyards, or the pleasure of having the early morning sun pour through the window on to her face.

Her mother's voice calling up the stairs interrupted her thoughts.

'Hurry up back down here, love, I need you to lay the table while I dish up your dad and brothers' dinners. It's getting late and they'll be home any minute now, hungry as blessed hunters.'

Connie couldn't see why they'd be hungry as hunters, except Dad, who was a coalman delivering heavy sacks of coal to households by the hundred and needed lots of sustenance. The boys had far less energetic jobs as far as she could see.

Ronnie was a packer in a sweet factory while Bertie was a milkman, which meant admittedly he was up early, but it was not exactly hard work. As for George, he was a law unto himself, doing casual work on and off but he was more than decently involved in his Free Church pursuits, which were held in a small hall half a mile away. Its pastor was his mentor, and he hoped to be one himself one day.

He was always going on about it to his family and how enlightened a person would become if they joined.

Not that there was anything wrong in that, except that it got a bit tiresome sometimes, none of the others being all that religious. It was more that he wasn't in proper work as often as a young man should be. How he'd ever be able to save up to get married, much less support a family, was beyond her.

'Connie, love, the time's getting on.'

'Coming, Mum,' she called back. Dismissing her meandering thoughts she hurried downstairs.

Arthur Lovell opened his paper, and being a bit politically minded more than usual these days, made a point of scanning the headlines before turning to the sports pages to see if there was anything on his local football team, Tottenham Hotspur, not that there'd be all that much, it being Monday.

This evening, though, it was the headlines that caught his attention, making him pause in shovelling his dinner into his mouth. Letting the still full fork fall back into the bowl, he let out a deep, irascible growl as he squinted against the June evening sunlight that slanted through the kitchen window directly on to his newspaper.

'Gawd – I dunno what's wrong with this bloody world! What with that bloody Ireland making trouble and them perishin' suffragettes causing even more bother! I don't know what they expect to gain. What do women know about politics, I ask you?' He eyed his family but they knew better than to respond.

His bushy eyebrows met in indignation, his large moustache bristling.

'Now it says 'ere someone's gone and shot some archduke in the Balkans. That's going to cause trouble,

5

you mark my words. Always trouble somewhere on the continent, countries squabbling among themselves. Thank Gawd we live in England.'

Peering closely at the smaller print while Connie and her mother paused to gaze at him, though his sons continued eating their dinner, he went on, 'Some damned upstart or other wanting to prove a point, I suppose.'

Dad loved shouting politics each time he opened his paper. Having now got this bit off his chest, he turned abruptly to the sport pages, the newspaper rustling noisily. His wife gazed at him for a moment or two, the bread knife paused in the act of slicing bread.

'Never mind, love,' she said quietly, not all that interested, before resuming slicing the loaf. 'Finish your dinner, there's a dear, before it gets all cold and horrible.'

Chapter Two

July 1914

'Wouldn't be a bit surprised if this don't develop into a perishing full-scale war,' muttered Arthur Lovell, glancing up from his paper. 'So long as it don't involve us.'

Connie glanced at her father from where she was sitting at the kitchen table, covertly sketching his likeness on a bit of paper, one hand shielding it in case he noticed what she was doing and made some mocking remark.

He wouldn't get that annoyed but she would feel an idiot as he tossed his head and tutted – that to her was as good as ridicule. Mum, on the other hand, would smile and nod, might even voice her pride, which would make him shake his head even more and ask lightly whether she hadn't got better things to do, again inadvertently making her feel a fool.

'Goin' out tonight, love?' Mum asked her now, though it was obvious, Connie having already changed into nicer clothes than those she wore for work.

She was meeting a couple of friends, Cissie and Doris, and the three of them were going Up West to gaze in all the big London shop windows for an hour or two and dream about wearing the lovely expensive garments they saw displayed there that they could never afford. It was a pastime of which all three never tired.

Later they'd come home to hang around for a while by the shrimps and winkles stall outside the Salmon and Ball pub under the railway arches to laugh and chat and maybe flirt a bit. Connie was tall for her age and boys often made a beeline for her, even though her friends were just as pretty.

She brought her mind back to her mother. 'Meeting Doris and Cissie at half past,' she replied.

'Then you'd best be off, love, or they'll be wondering where you are.'

Connie got up from the table, folding the paper with her drawing and tucking it into the pocket of her hobble skirt, already thinking of the evening ahead: the bus they'd catch, boarding it as ladylike as possible with her tight hem hampering her ankles. If any man watching dared smirk, she'd be ready to glare at him as haughtily as she could until he finally pulled a straight face again.

There were several more bits of blank paper in her Dorothy bag along with a couple of pencil stubs, for, if she got the time, she intended to quickly sketch one or two of the garments that most caught her eye. Later she'd have a go at running up something similar on Mum's sewing machine, the material bought locally and far cheaper. This was how she kept up with the fashion, to the envy of friends and workmates. To her mind the talent for dressmaking was another art, going hand in hand with that of drawing.

Giving Mum a quick kiss on the cheek and her dad a peck on the top of his slightly balding head – to which he growled, 'Get orf!' – she was away to enjoy her evening of window shopping.

'Let's just hope our government keeps its own nose clean and stays out of it – all this squabbling between Germany and Russia and now France. Ain't none of our business, and besides, this country can't afford to dabble in other people's wars.' Connie heard her father growl contemptuously from behind his *Daily Mail*.

Tension was beginning to mount daily, the newspaper full of this growing unease in Europe. Connie could see it in her own parents' faces as foreign governments began glaring at each other across borders.

These last few days there had been reports of Austria breaking off diplomatic ties with Serbia; Serbia mobilising its army; the Tsar warning Germany that he couldn't remain indifferent if Austria invaded Serbia.

Recent news had been of Austria declaring war on Serbia and of Russia ordering the mobilisation of a million troops, then, as July turned into August, came reports of the Kaiser warning that if they didn't cease within the next twenty-four hours, Germany too would mobilise. That deadline ignored, Germany had declared war on Russia.

Connie could see the concern on Mum's face, but all her father said was: 'Bloody storm in a teacup!' as he turned to his beloved sports pages.

But Dad's words, meant to reassure himself as well as those around him that in no way would Britain let herself be dragged into conflict, held a note of anxiety and for once Mum didn't lightly change the subject by asking if he wanted the window opened wider on this hot evening or did he fancy another cup of tea. She merely stood looking at him, her round face blank, her mouth slack, her plump shoulders slumped, the tablecloth she was still holding, limp and only half folded.

Connie, in the process of getting ready to pop over to Cissie's house, felt the tension her father's comments had brought to them all: Bertie on the point of going outside to light a cigarette, Mum not minding pipe tobacco but hating cigarette smoke; Ronald, his younger brother, about to follow him out, their older brother George doing nothing as usual. Having finished their tea of ox tongue sandwiches, her three brothers had their minds more on going out to find girls, or whatever young men did when well away from the house of an evening.

Bertie was already courting: a pretty, fair-haired, easy-natured girl, Edith Kemp, or as he called her, Edie. He'd brought her home to meet them all earlier this year and it was recognised that come next Christmas the two of them would get engaged, both sets of parents happy for that to happen.

Young Ronnie said he'd be seeing a few mates this evening but beyond that gave no more away. George was off out to yet another of his odd chapel meetings, saying he was taking part in helping organise a fete for August. To Connie it seemed he hardly ever went anywhere else but there. In a way it touched her as being just a bit unhealthy but she said nothing and carried on getting ready to go off to Cissie's house. Their friend Doris would be over too and they'd probably play gramophone records and giggle over one thing and another.

'Well,' Connie heard her dad burst out. 'Didn't think we'd be foolish enough to end up being dragged into this war too.'

No one responded to the irascible remark as they all crowded around the morning paper which was spread out on the parlour table, its headline staring up at them: *Britain Declares War with Germany*.

Yet as they read, Connie felt she detected more a sense of euphoria than dismay among her brothers at least, a feeling of pride more than fear. Germany would quail before the might of the British bulldog and, before it knew it, they would soon have Germany on the run, tail between its legs. The Government was already saying it would be over by Christmas, although Lord Kitchener was declaring vehemently that the Government was wrong, that this could prove to be a far more drawn out process than they imagined – or at least were trying to convince the country.

It was hard to credit how swiftly everything had moved on in a matter of days. Three days ago Germany had asked France, Russia's ally, to remain neutral, but France had declared that impossible, leaving Germany to demand the right to send troops through neutral Belgium so as to invade France. Yesterday Belgium had refused, while Britain warned Germany that if it did march on to Belgium soil, she would have no choice but to stand by an old treaty with Belgium and declare war on the invader. In the small hours of this morning Germany had

11

Maggie Ford

ignored the threat and now every newspaper carried the headline in huge letters that Britain was at war.

Beyond the front-room window, even in this small side street, Connie could already see a more than usual amount of people passing, mostly men, each with a set look of fierce determination, or so it seemed. Her first instinct had been to find paper and a pencil to sketch that look she saw. But there were other things to think about. As they had finished breakfast, both her sisters had come knocking frantically on the front door in a panic. Now they sat around the table, straight-backed with fear.

'I've had a busting row with Harry,' Elsie was saying, her face taut as she sipped agitatedly at the cup of tea Mum had handed to her. 'As soon as we read the paper he started going on about how it was his duty to sign up as soon as he could. I ask you, where are his brains? We've got a little'un now. He can't go and leave us. What if he got killed, and me left on me own with just me and a little kiddie?'

She'd had the baby just before Christmas. They'd named him Henry after his father, for all he'd always been called Harry.

'I told him, point blank,' she went on, her voice rising, 'if he went out that door and signed up, he'd never see me again. I'd leave him. I would.'

Her words made Connie shudder involuntarily. If her brother-in-law did join up, how easily those words could prove true.

'My Jim's saying the same,' Lillian put in. 'And me having just discovered we're going to have a little'un of our own. How would *I* cope if he got killed?'

12

'It won't come to that, love,' Mum said, sipping her own tea as if her life depended on it. 'We've got our regular troops and the Government is already saying it'll all be over by Christmas.'

'That Lord Kitchener don't think so,' Elsie put in harshly, 'says it could go on for years. He's already talking of calling for ordinary men to volunteer. Harry says they're already opening up recruiting offices .all over the place and expect thousands to enlist. But I don't want my Harry to be one of them.'

'If I was younger, I'd be there, up front like a bloody shot,' their father said, his voice grating with harsh determination. Now that the inevitable had happened, her father had been the first to change his tune about the war.

'Then bloody good job you aint!' her mother burst out, sharp for once, even to the extent of uttering a swear word, which she rarely did. Dad shut up and she turned to Connie's sisters.

'You two had any breakfast? I could make some. The baby'll be fine in his pram. You can take him in the other room when he wants feeding – give you some privacy. Though your dad'll be off to work as soon as he's finished his breakfast. The boys aren't home. Bert's already off finishing his milk round, and Ron has to be in work by seven thirty. Neither of them has seen the paper yet. George was here but as soon as he read the news he was off to have a chat with that minister of his, so he said. So I don't know when he'll be coming home.'

Connie wasn't interested in her eldest brother's pursuits but her sisters' words had set her thoughts working, and deeply concerned thoughts they were. Ron and Bert would have seen the newspaper placards on the way to work or heard the news from their colleagues. Had either of them already gone to see if they could enlist? Mum had said the country already had professional soldiers: the British Expeditionary Force – the BEF – proper soldiers who'd soon have Germany on the run, and the war would indeed be over by Christmas, if not sooner. And Lillian and Elsie's husbands and the boys, all full of impetuous eagerness with no idea of what fighting could entail and what could happen to them, wouldn't be wanted. At least that's what she hoped.

She shuddered, imagining her brothers and brothers-in-law fighting in a foreign land, maybe killed. Mum and Dad – their sons gone . . . Hastily she turned her thoughts back to the present.

'I'd better be off to work too,' she said. 'They'll be wondering where I am, and be upset with me if I'm late.'

She made to leap up from the table but her mother countered, 'I don't expect many people will get to work on time on a morning like this, love. It ain't exactly a normal day, is it? Same with your dad, I think.'

Glancing up from the newspaper he was still reading, he looked as if struck by lightning. 'Good Gawd, I forgot all about work!'

He glanced at the ornate mantel clock over the fireplace as though it might bite him. 'Look at the bloody time! I should've been on my rounds an hour ago. War or no war, housewives expect their coal to be delivered.'

'I don't suppose anyone'll be fretting over late coal deliveries on a day like today,' his wife said, murmuring somewhat absently, turning her attention to her eldest girl. 'Look, love, I'm sure if you go home and have a quiet talk to your Harry, without getting all riled up and starting another row, I'm sure he'll see sense and not go galloping off like a wild bull.' She looked at Lillian. 'You too, love. Go off and have a proper talk with your Jim. At the moment everyone's running about like headless chickens, doing things they might regret. If we give ourselves time to calm down, we'll all be better off.'

Anxious about what her employers would say to her for being late, Connie rushed out of the house even before her sisters left.

From the short street where she lived, she turned on to Bethnal Green Road only to find herself caught up in a hurrying mass of people, most of them heading in one direction – westward. Some were on foot, others on bicycles – loads of bicycles – the buses that passed her crammed full. They usually were, but today everyone looked obviously bent on joining those already gathered in front of Buckingham Palace or Downing Street. There they would be cheering themselves hoarse, she imagined.

Resisting the urge to join them, she crossed the road as best she could towards Dover Street, where her firm was situated. Inside she was met by almost complete silence, hardly a soul to be seen except the foreman she saw striding towards her – a heavy-set, stern but fair man in his forties. One hand was raised as if waving her away.

'I'm so sorry I'm late,' Connie began automatically, half expecting to be handed her cards.

'You're not late. You're one of the few who's bothered to come in and you probably won't be working at all today. Everyone's too riled up. Bet they're all cheering like mad up the West End, I shouldn't wonder. You might as well go back home or go and join them. Tomorrow it will all calm down and when you come in, see that you're on time. The company can't put up with any more of this.'

His tone had sounded agitated, but she guessed it was more from a sense of excitement that had caught the whole country, it seemed. Sighing, thanking the war itself for giving her a day off, even if it would be unpaid, Connie turned and left, remembering to say a polite thank you as she went.

What to do now? Back in Bethnal Green Road, she decided at first to resist following the crowds, but moments later found herself joining them. In her jacket pocket were some scraps of blank paper and the stub of pencil she always kept handy, together with a piece of India rubber. She would spend time drawing the expressions on people's faces, maybe a crowd scene, maybe Buckingham Palace itself. And if Their Majesties came out on the balcony to show themselves to the cheering crowds, she would sketch them too, as best she could from where she guessed she would end up, standing at the back of the vast throng.

Excitement at the prospect caught at her. Those drawings would be something to add to her scrapbook. As she walked with the crowd she silently thanked her school teacher who'd taken her under her wing when she'd been twelve, recognising her talents, and had given her art lessons when she should have been outside at playtimes and lunchtimes.

'You've a rare gift,' Miss Eaves had said. 'When you leave school you must protect that talent, nurture it,

16

practise it at every moment you can spare. Then one day you will become a good artist and even make money from it. And please, don't let it drop once you leave school, thinking it all a waste of time. Make quite sure to do as I say, won't you, my dear?'

Overawed by such dedication and earnestness, she had nodded and, to this day, that tutor's words still rang in her head. But how did a factory girl like her go about becoming a real artist? She didn't know. Yet she was sure that one day it would come about. Until then all she needed was faith and dedication. Dad and her family – except Mum, of course, who showed such pride in her – could say what they liked, make fun of her if they wanted. At this moment her heart was filled to the brim with determination.

Chapter Three

September 1914

In Connie's place of work, Sybil Potter, who stood beside her at the slowly moving conveyor belt, said, 'Ain't it just wonderful, the news this morning? Ain't it wonderful?'

Connie kept her eyes on the small cardboard box whose ends she was folding with nimble fingers, quickly dabbing glue around the edges ready for Sybil to press together before the conveyor belt bore the object onwards. Her eyes already moving towards the next box approaching to be dealt with, she said, 'What news?'

She'd been too pre-occupied by her own thoughts this morning, her mind full of the drawing she had done – a really successful one of baby Henry when Elsie and Harry had come round last night. No one but Mum had noticed her in the corner working away, the small piece of paper supported on an open book, everyone probably assuming she was reading. But Mum had cast a few sly glances towards her, her eyes full of secret pride.

The drawing had become a perfect likeness of the child and as she made her way to work this morning her mind was on mounting it in a sort of framework of black, sticky passé-partout to make it look as professional as it was possible to be and giving it to her sister and her brother-in-law as a sort of present. They'd be delighted, at least so she hoped, and it would be her first ever presented portrait of someone, if only of a baby. She just hoped that they'd see it for what it was and hold on to it as a keepsake. Thinking all of this as she walked, head down, she hadn't looked up to notice the news placards.

'*What* news?' Sybil mimicked as she stuck down the ends of yet another box. 'What . . . You must have heard the newspapermen yelling it out on your way to work?'

'I'm sorry,' Connie said. 'My mind must have been elsewhere.'

'Oh, you!' Sybil spat derisively.

'Well, what news?' Connie demanded, suddenly feeling just a little shirty.

'Why, we're winning, of course!' Sybil went on as if quoting, 'The BEF and the French have already pushed back the German troops, almost back to where they started. And the BEF have only been over there a few weeks. Like the Government said, it'll be a quick war. And you never noticed the news on all the placards on your way here?'

'I was thinking of other things,' Connie cut in – all she could think to say, but already her heart was thumping with relief.

Wonderful news! Why hadn't she noticed? It meant that the ordinary man in the street wouldn't be required to fight, wouldn't be told it was his duty to volunteer. Last night at home there'd been such a ruckus – her sisters were still upset, Elsie about her Harry and Lillian about her Jim. And then there was Mum crying her eyes out because Albert, only nineteen, had told them of his intention to enlist, with Dad going off at him saying he was a bloody fool and to wait until he was called up, not go rushing off like a silly sod to get himself killed and what would his Edie have to say about that.

Young Ronnie had added to their father's anger, saying he intended to follow his brother.

'No you don't,' Dad had warned. 'You're still under age.'

'Then I'll just tell 'em I've just turned eighteen,' Ronnie had shot back at him. 'All my mates are going to do it and I don't want to be the one what's left out. No one's going to question whether I'm old enough, and I do look eighteen, maybe nineteen, because they'll need all the men they can get if it comes to finishing off the enemy in double quick time. And I'll be eighteen in a few weeks' time anyway, so what's the difference?'

Dad had risen up off his chair in his anger. 'You bloody well listen to me, you silly sod! You want to see that eighteenth birthday of yours? Well, if you get yourself killed, you'll never live to see it, will you? You ain't going to no recruitin' office, and that's that. Till you're eighteen, you come under my orders and you do as I say. After that I can't stop you.'

Sitting back down abruptly into his chair, he had leaned forward to grab his pipe off the mantelpiece and thrust it into his mouth, reaching for his tobacco pouch and stuffing some of its contents into the pipe's bowl.

The others had watched as though mesmerised as he reached into his pocket for his matches, striking one, applying it to the bowl, noisily sucking in as the tobacco ignited, to puff smoke all around his head like a grey halo. Connie recalled the smell of the smoke as she had never done before, while everyone fell silent, struck by his outburst, except for Mum, who could be heard snivelling quietly.

Now, from what Sybil Potter had just told her, she couldn't have heard more wonderful news if she'd looked for it. It meant that her brothers had been saved from their mad impulse to join up; that her sisters would stop quarrelling with their husbands over this talk of volunteering, and that this country could return to peace as soon as the enemy was beaten back by the French and the wonderful British Expeditionary Force – back to their own country to lick their wounds. That would serve them right for thinking they could push other countries around.

The Battle of the Marne it was being called. The Germans losing all the ground they'd captured, Paris now breathing a sigh of relief as the enemy found itself pushed back. Its only course, the papers were saying, had been to dig in and hope for recovery. Open warfare on what was being called The Western Front was a hopeless task. In six weeks all it had done was to march through Belgium with only a fraction of French soil gained and now lost.

But now the papers were reporting that with the enemy forces firmly entrenched, French and English troops were finding it hard to dig them out and had decided to dig in as well so as to stop the casualties it was causing. As autumn passed, the front line seemed to have suddenly become a stalemate.

'It 'aint right!' Connie heard her dad burst out as he crumpled up his evening paper in a fit of frustration. 'Soldiers are supposed to stand up and fight, not cower in bloody trenches.'

'Maybe there's no other way,' Mum said mildly as she poured yet more tea into the quarter-full one sitting within reaching distance on the parlour table beside him.

Taking his ease after a day hauling hundredweight sacks of coal on his back to one customer after another, Dad now sat with his feet on the fender of the fire which blazed away against an uncomfortably chilly September day that had rained non-stop since early morning.

'Well, I can't see it being a short war if they're goin' to carry on doing that,' he answered her. 'Someone's got to give way in the end, then they'll have to fight like proper soldiers. This sort of lark could go on for ever 'n' ever as far as I can see.'

Connie sat at the table gazing into the fire and occasionally at Dad's boots, idly wondering how long it would take for them to start smouldering and Mum to say as she always did, 'Watch them boots of yours, love, before they catch fire,' and him moving his feet to stare at the boots before returning them to their usual position.

Connie had arranged to go down to the library with Doris but she wasn't looking forward to the prospect in weather like this. Umbrella or no, she'd probably return home looking like a drowned rat.

In fact a drowned rat was coming through the front door even now, the door closing with a loud bang. There stood Albert, dripping wet but on his face an expression of triumph mingled with defiance.

Going straight through to the kitchen to take off his sodden topcoat and boots, he came back into the parlour to plonk himself down on an upright chair just by the curtain that shielded Connie's bed.

From there he surveyed his parents' faces, first his mother's. 'Sorry I'm a bit late coming home, Mum. Been out with some of the blokes. Me tea in the oven, is it?'

She nodded. 'I'll bring it in here for you, love.'

As she disappeared, he turned his attention to his dad. 'Well. I've done it!'

'Done what?'

'Signed up.'

There came a gasp from his mother, who was coming back with his dinner, a cloth shielding her hands from the hot plate as she stood there stock still.

His father glared at him. 'You've what?'

'Signed up. Took meself into the recruiting office and volunteered.'

His father took his feet off the fender, almost falling out of his chair.

'You bloody fool! What the bloody 'ell for?'

While his mother, like some automaton, put the hot dinner plate carefully on the cloth-covered table, his father, half out of his chair, leaned belligerently towards his son.

'You bloody, silly fool! What about your girl? What about Ada?'

'Edith,' Albert corrected calmly. 'Edie. I'm telling her tonight, when I see her.'

His mother had sat down, limply. 'Oh, Bertie, love! You should've told us what you intended to do. You should've spoke to Edie first – warned her. And what about you, love, say if you get ki . . . hurt, wounded?' Her voice faded, choked into silence by stifled tears.

He looked at her affectionately. 'I'll be all right, Mum. I'll make sure of that. But I had to,' he added firmly. 'Everyone's doing it. You can't be the odd one out, standing back and watching them go and you do nothing. It's not right.' He gave a shrug. 'So I've done it, and there's no going back.'

Connie watched her father still sitting forward in his chair as if turned to stone, then abruptly he got up and stalked out, passing his son without a glance at him.

'I'm going down the pub.' His voice drifted back to them from the kitchen.

Moments later he reappeared in his overcoat and cap as he stomped down the narrow passage, heading for the front door, his wife's voice calling out, 'Don't be too long, love,' but the door had already slammed shut.

There was silence for a while then she said to her son, 'Your tea's on the table, Bertie, love. I think I'll have an early night.' So saying, she moved away, going slowly up the stairs, shoulders hunched as though her clothes were now a heavy weight, too heavy to bear.

Connie too got up from where she'd been sitting by the window with its curtains closed against the miserable weather outside.

'I've got to go out now,' she informed Bertie, who had taken himself over to the table to begin his dinner. He nodded without speaking.

'I won't be all that late,' she added. She didn't know what to say about her brother enlisting. She was proud of him, she guessed. Proud and a little afraid. 'I'm off to the library.'

Somehow the thought of braving the bad weather for the bright, warm lights of the library seemed now strangely enticing.

The parlour was deserted when she got back home, Mum already in bed as she'd promised, Dad not yet back from the pub. Albert had mentioned going round to see Edie, and Ron hadn't yet come home from wherever he was. And George was no doubt at his church. Connie settled down in the silent cosiness of the parlour to start on the book she had borrowed from the library: *Sons and Lovers*. She'd taken a fancy to it, while Doris had got herself a light, humorous book, peeking into it and laughing out loud until the librarian had frowned at the two of them.

The library had been practically empty, most people no doubt preferring to leave it until a day when the weather might be kinder. Now, back at home with the place to herself for once, she was looking forward to at least an hour or two before Dad and her brothers came trooping in.

Settling back in Dad's empty fireside chair, absorbed by the story, she didn't know she'd fallen asleep until the sound of a key fumbling in the lock brought her awake with a start, her book having fallen to the floor.

Quickly retrieving it, she leapt out of the chair, thinking it was her father coming home; by the sound of the fumbling key, he was a little the worse for wear from drinking with his mates. Or perhaps it was Ron, equally tipsy, he too no doubt having met friends.

25

The street door opened and Connie could make out someone trying to creep quietly along the passage, in his effort making more noise than he intended. Connie heard her mother's tired voice call down from upstairs. 'Love, try to be quiet, you woke me up, dear.'

It was Bertie's voice that answered, a tiny bit slurred. 'S-sorry, Mum – didn't mean to wake you.'

'Albert?' Connie called. At the sound of her voice, the parlour door opened. Albert peeped around the door, a foolish expression on his face as it moved into the room followed by the rest of him.

'Sorry to disturb you, Con. Was you asleep?' No doubt she looked like she had been, but she shook her head.

'I was reading.'

'Won't keep you, then,' Albert began, but in seconds had started to expand on his remark. 'Just come back from Edie's. Had to tell her what I done . . . enlisted . . . you know.'

So saying, he flopped into Dad's now vacant chair. 'I'm sorry, Con, I had a couple of glasses while I was round there, Dutch courage, I guess.'

'How's she taken it?' Connie asked cautiously.

'Not sure,' he muttered. 'But it's done now. No going back. Have to hand me notice in at me firm tomorrow. Give up me milk float, say goodbye to poor old Jinny, me horse. Been good to me, Jinny, pulled me milkfloat ever since I started the job, never ever got skittish. Now I'm going to be whipped off to be a soldier and Lord knows where I'll end up. Don't s'pose I'll ever see poor old Jinny again.'

'So how did your Edie take it?' Connie repeated in an effort to make him talk more sensibly. She feared she

26

knew the answer – as if his Edie would take his news with smiles and cries of good luck, well done, he not even consulting her before doing what he had. Where were his brains?

Albert grimaced. 'Not too happy, I'm afraid.'

'Did you expect her blessing?'

'Lots of blokes are going off to war with the blessing of them that love 'em. It's our duty.' He looked as if he were about to cry.

'How much drink did you say you've had?' she asked abruptly.

'A couple of beers, maybe a couple of whiskies. She had a port and lemon. Her mum and dad went to bed – said we needed to be left alone. We was glad, we needed to talk proper about things. Embarrassing with them there.'

'Is she all right?' Connie asked, wide awake now and thinking of Edie faced with this sudden revelation. What would she herself have done if she'd got a young man who'd gone and signed up out of the blue without a word to her first and expecting her to take it lightly and with a smile? Maybe one of these days she'd have a young man and find herself faced with some awful news or other. She hoped that when she did find someone her life would be smooth and lovely.

'She had a bit of a cry,' Albert said. 'Well, in fact she burst into tears, said I'd gone behind her back, why didn't I tell her what I'd intended to do before I did it and ask what she thought. She said I could get myself killed and what would she do then? She also said she loved me. She's never really said that before, not like that. Then she just fell into my arms and said she never wanted to

27

lose me, then all of a sudden she stopped crying and she said, "I know you had to – you had no option." And kept saying she loved me over and over again and then we cuddled and she said she respected me for what I'd done, and that she'd wait for me and . . .'

He stopped, looking suddenly sheepish. 'I don't know why I'm telling you this, Con. It's sort of private, like. Do you think I'm being daft, telling you all this?'

Connie shook her head, her heart going out to him. But for the beer and the whiskies he might never have opened his heart to her, for fear of embarrassment or that his sister might have laughed in his face.

But embarrassment on his part seemed to dissipate as he went on, 'She loves me, Con. And I love her. She said she'd wait for me,' he repeated. 'And I know she will. We've been going out together for months and now I know she'll be waiting for me – when I come back, we'll be married and—'

With this he broke off, lowered his head to hide sudden tears while Connie sat looking at him, her own not far away. One day she hoped her own tears would be for some wonderful man, and that he would love her as much as Albert clearly loved his girl. But for now she just felt sad: sad that her brother was going away to fight and that the future for all of them was far from certain.

Chapter Four

October 1914

As young Ronnie burst into the house, his face aglow as if in triumph of some sort, his mother got up from her chair, glancing questioningly at him.

'Bit late home tonight, love? Doing a bit of overtime?'

'No, I left on time,' he answered, plonking himself down at the table in readiness for his evening meal.

He grinned at Connie, she halfway through her own dinner, while their mother went out to the kitchen to bring in his plate, which she'd been keeping warm for him.

'Where's Dad?'

'Extra shift, Mum said,' Connie replied, her mouth full of sausage and mash. She glanced over to where George sat on a chair in the corner having finished his own food with almost indecent haste. She resisted the urge to comment: no work yet, then?

When was the last time George had worked? There he sat in his nice suit, his nose in that blooming Bible – well, not exactly a Bible, a sort of coloured book with a picture of the coming of Salvation, whatever that was. It was a wonder he didn't take his bed to that church of his – which was more of a bleak wooden hall than a proper church, sitting well back from a tiny row of houses in Three Colts Lane.

He'd go there most days, all over that minister of his or pastor or whatever he was called, and then come home to spout the odds about this wicked world and if people stopped to listen to what the Lord was trying to tell them, it'd be a far better place – da-di-da-di-da – until they were sick of hearing it. Usually when he started up in the evenings, Dad would get up, tell them he was off to the pub, leaving the rest of them to suffer. Much as she loved her brother, Connie couldn't help but feel it wouldn't do George any harm to pray less and work more, be an asset to the family instead of driving them barmy with his religious outbursts.

That George hardly worked got up all their noses, especially Ronnie and Albert, though when he did the odd casual job, he'd give nearly all of it to Mum, and when she asked how he was fixed for money, he usually said something like 'the Lord will provide'.

Currently, he was so engrossed in his reading, he'd hardly spoken to her, much less Mum. He seemed to live in a world of his own. It shouldn't have but it got on her nerves sometimes, and this evening she felt glad to be getting out of the house, meeting some friends of hers. The three of them were going to a young persons' club they belonged to in Old Gosset Street to have a laugh and a joke with a few boys, enjoy a soft drink or two.

'What's made you so late, then?' Mum's question to Ronnie cut through her thoughts as her mother came in with his dinner, all steaming hot from the oven.

Connie saw him grin. 'I've been stuck for ages in a blooming great queue, everyone there looking to sign up.'

About to take up Connie's now empty plate to bear it off to the kitchen, his mother turned back to stare at him. 'Sign up?' she asked. 'What for?'

Dad, who had just come into the room, stopped short. No one had heard him enter the house. He was in time to catch his wife's last words: 'Sign up? What for?' Now he stood there glowering. 'What you mean, sign up?' he growled.

'For the army,' Ronnie said calmly as if explaining in monosyllabic words to a child. 'You should've seen the size of the queue there.'

Connie saw her father's bushy brows come together, his generous moustache twitch. 'You can't sign on. You ain't eighteen yet.'

'I will be in November.'

'That's still five bloody weeks away.'

'They don't ask questions so long as you look old enough.' He started back a fraction as his father came to stand over him, still in his coat and cap, his face black from the sacks of coal he'd delivered all day to endless households.

'Go and wash up, love,' Connie heard her mother say anxiously, but he took no notice of her plea.

'I don't bloody care what or who they want. You go back there and tell 'em you still only seventeen, and I'll come with you to make sure you do.'

Ronnie looked his father straight in the eye.

31

'I'm a man now, Dad. I signed up as one. I'm a man –
a soldier. It's done. I leave on Friday – for Aldershot.'

Albert was still stationed at Aldershot, approaching
the end of his six weeks training. 'I might meet Bert.
We'll be together. They do put brothers together, and
close friends and sometime whole streets or neighbour-
hoods, if they sign up at the same time, all in the same
regiment whenever possible. It's good for morale.'

'Then I'll tell 'em you're under age,' his father raged,
obviously not listening to a word of what Ronnie had said.

Connie's mother remained hovering in the doorway,
her hopes of her husband leaving the matter to go and
clean himself up for his evening meal forgotten.

It seemed to her that Mum had still not taken in the
full significance of what she had been hearing. 'Oh
Ronnie, love, what've you gone and done?' she asked
unnecessarily.

'I'll tell you what he's gone and done,' Dad bellowed.
'He's gone and bloody well buggered up his life, that's
what he's gorn and done. And I'm going back there with
'im to undo it. He's underage.'

'They're taking lots of blokes underage,' Ronnie cut
in, only to have his father swing round on him.

'Then I'll tell 'em, it ain't going to be my son! Not
'till he's—'

'Can you hear yourself, Dad?' Ronnie interrupted.
'You don't tell the army what's what. And as far as I'm
concerned, it's done, finished, and there's nothing you
can do about it.' His tone moderated. 'Don't worry about
me, Dad. I'll be all right. But you do see that I've got
to go. The country needs every man it can get. In five
weeks I'll be eighteen and I'll have to go then. A few

weeks, what does it matter? There's nothing you can do, Dad.'

He leapt up from the table, startling Connie as well as her mum. 'I'm off to see a couple of mates of mine. We joined up together, we'll be going off together and that way we'll probably stay together.'

Connie saw him turn to look at George, still apparently absorbed in his Bible as if oblivious to the argument going on around him.

'What about you, George? You going to sign on too? We all need to pull our weight for this country.'

His mum gave a gasp. 'Not all three of you! If all of you was to get—'

'What about it, George?' He cut through his mother's words. 'You ain't even mentioned the war since it started except to preach against it. You can come along with me if you want, what d'you think?'

Connie turned her eyes to her eldest brother to hear what he had to say, but he hadn't even looked up. It seemed to her that he feared to meet his youngest brother's eyes.

Finally he said, 'I think too many are panicking, doing things on the spur of the moment that they could regret later on.'

'What d'you mean?'

'I mean, maybe best to wait a bit, think about what we're doing. Men killing each other is not the way out. I mean—'

'Then what bloody way out do you mean, George?' Ronnie broke in savagely. 'You mean sit here on your arse while Germany marches across Europe without a by your leave – that what you mean?'

George's gaze remained trained on his Bible. 'Talk is what we should be doing,' he said. 'We should talk, discuss our differences, peaceably.'

'Talk?' Ronnie was obviously having a job to hold his temper. 'They're not going to talk! Not now! Not any time!'

George's voice remained steady. 'Our Lord said, "If a man smite thee, turn the other cheek . . ."'

'Sod you, George, and your bloody other cheek!' Ronnie burst out. 'If you're too scared to go and fight for your country, say so!'

'That's enough, love.' His mother's voice was trembling. 'There's too much going on out there without our own family fighting each other.'

His father grabbed the parlour door and flung it wide open in a temper. 'Come on, you, we're going down there to sort 'em out right now.'

'You're not washed, Dad,' Connie cut in. 'You can't go like that.'

'And I ain't going nowhere,' Ronald cut in. 'Except with me mates. We're all going out tonight.'

Before anyone could move, her brother was out the door, grabbing his coat off a coat peg in the passage as he went, the door slamming behind him.

It seemed, having handed in his notice to his employers, that they, instead of displaying annoyance at the loss of a worker, had given Ron their blessing, seeing him off with their good wishes and saying that when the war was over his job would still be open for him. A week later he was in the army.

'Measly job like that?' Connie scoffed. 'When this war's over and he comes back he'll be worth more than some old packing job!'

In reply, her dad, having now resigned himself to his youngest son going off to fight, glanced up from his morning newspaper.

'Ain't it about time you started looking for a better job?' he growled. 'There's loads of jobs goin' in the vacancy columns. With men all goin' into the forces and no one to fill their jobs, they're lookin' for women to fill 'em. And there's you, still fartin' about in a factory making boxes when you could be doing something towards the war effort.'

Connie felt irked by her father's low opinion of her, but it was food for thought.

Chapter Five

Her seventeenth birthday had come and gone and been
hardly noticed. Christmas had also come and gone and
already it was February. Nineteen fifteen, her two
brothers in the army though not yet sent to fight, and
just as well, judging by the awful news from the front:
men bogged down by wet winter weather since
November. Trenches full of mud, it was said, yet giving
little cover from pitiless enemy shellfire; thousands
being sent *over the top* at the mercy of enemy rifle fire,
thousands already killed and the war only six months
old. It was said that freezing weather was causing even
more misery. How long before Bertie and Ronnie were
sent over there? The prospect hung over the family's
heads like the Sword of Damocles, dulling any joy of
a new year.

Her two sisters and their little families, Lillian with
new baby James and Elsie with little Harry, both named
after their fathers, had enjoyed Christmas dinner round

Mum's. Both of them still had their husbands at home, but for how much longer?

Connie found her mind turning to that as she made her way to work through a wet February morning. From what the newspapers were saying, instead of calling for volunteers, the Government was beginning to contemplate general call-up of all able-bodied man not in a crucial job. It was frightening. Two months into nineteen fifteen. They'd said the war would be over by last Christmas. Now there was this threat of conscription whether a man was willing to fight or not.

And George – still at home, still sitting on the sidelines hugging his faith to him like a safety belt. If there was a general call-up he'd have no choice but to obey. Lately a feeling of contempt for him had begun to steal over her, one she tried vainly to stave off, but what about her? She too was guilty of doing nothing. At school she'd reaped high marks for English, history, geography, drawing, especially drawing, praised by her teachers. So why was she hanging on to some mundane job in a box-making factory? She'd been there over two years since leaving school at fourteen. It was time she bettered herself.

Ever since Christmas, Dad had been on about women doing war work, so maybe she should begin looking for something more rewarding than just standing at a conveyor belt?

That morning, instead of going directly to work, she bought a local newspaper, turning to the job vacancies pages. Standing at the corner of Bethnal Green Road and Shoreditch High Street, she scanned the more interesting list of job vacancies, pausing at one which had caught her eye. It wasn't anything to do with the war effort but a small Fleet Street newspaper – a vacancy for a filing clerk. That had to be easy, surely. Filing things didn't call for much more brains than gluing boxes together. And working in an office would be a luxury after factory work. She nipped quickly home to get her school report before returning to the bus stop.

Folding the newspaper at the page the advertisement was on, she glanced up in time to see a bus going in the direction of the firm. Newspaper tucked under her arm, handbag held firmly, hobble skirt only slightly impeding her, she joined the queue of those boarding it, thankful she'd not had to wait for ages; the cold brisk wind threatened snow and played with the upturned brim of her hat.

Standing outside the tall building scanning the several firms marked on the front of the building, she felt her heart sink. What made her think herself capable of office work? Even so, she summoned enough courage to step into the cage of a lift to the second floor.

Knocking lightly, she waited. A girl in a smart, narrow-skirted suit answered, smiled and said, 'Just come in, dear – no need to knock.'

Five young women sat on chairs against the wall, each with that tense about-to-be-interviewed look on their face, each clearly dressed in their best, which was so much better than her own clothing. Each obviously with far more intelligence than she imagined herself to have – girls who knew about offices, not factory girls used to standing at some conveyor belt for hours on end for a pittance, girls no doubt with a high school education.

She'd never gone on to high school despite her excellent marks. 'We ain't got that kind of money for uniforms and books and things,' her father had decreed. 'Your sisters didn't, nor your brothers. Wastin' time for another couple of years when you could be earning honest money. Makin' out you're posh when you aint.'

So she'd never been given that privilege.

Handed a form to fill in: her name, previous employment, schools she had attended, any additional education she'd had. She took a seat at the end of the queue.

As the next hour eased along and the first chair was vacated, in turn occupied by another hopeful, her confidence began to fade. Against all those still coming in and those that had been before, what chance did she stand?

Finally it was her turn. The inner office door opened to disgorge the previous applicant and Connie got up at a signal from the young lady at the desk, who said that Mr Clayton would see her now. She was a little more encouraged by the fact that being quite tall she might look older and more efficient than she felt, as she tried to stop her eyes from watering.

A man in a grey suit sat behind a desk. He looked somewhat debonair and had a nice smile as he gestured to the chair on the other side of the desk to where he sat.

'Please, sit down, er . . .' He broke off to consult the form. 'Miss Lovell.'

Obediently she sat.

He looked up at her. 'Are you working now?'

She nodded.

'References?'

She shook her head.

'A school report?' He had a nice voice with a certain deep ring to it.

Pushing the thought aside, she nodded and quickly produced it, glad to have had the forethought to nip back home after she'd seen the advertisement. Now she watched him scan it, her heart thumping fit to burst as she waited. He murmured, 'Hmm,' several times, which screamed, 'Sorry, but we're looking for only high school or college-educated applicants.' After a third 'Hmm,' he looked up.

'I see one of your tutors thought highly of your art skills, especially portraits, enough to help you. Have you kept it up?'

'All the time,' Connie burst out with more enthusiasm than she had intended. 'I really love sketching and drawing and painting!'

He sat looking at her as she closed her mouth in embarrassment, already feeling a fool and wishing she could run far away. He was leaning back in his chair and watching her closely, making her fidget uneasily under his stare.

Finally he said, 'I'm so sorry, my dear, but as it stands, I'm afraid that you wouldn't be suitable for the vacancy as advertised.'

What had she expected? This was only the first job she'd gone for and maybe she should concentrate on war work after all and do her bit. All she wanted now was to get out of this place. Nor was she comfortable with the way he was regarding her. Almost as if she was being flirted with, but she said nothing.

He had brought his hands together, the tips of his fingers to his lips as if studying her. There was a sparkle in his eye.

'However, if I may I'd like to set you a little task – with your consent, of course.'

There followed a long drawn out pause while she wondered what she would be asked to do, all the while feeling herself to be under a sort of microscope, making her feel deeply uncomfortable. He hadn't said test, he had said task. What on earth did he have in mind? She was about to ask when he spoke again.

'This may sound a little odd, Miss Lovell . . .' He gave a brief, self-conscious laugh before continuing. 'Would it sound too preposterous if I were to ask you if you could do a small sketch of one of my colleagues for me? Would you be able to do that? I've just had a sudden idea, you see.'

Bewildered, she found herself nodding in agreement, not quite understanding why. She was beginning to feel even more uncertain. Had he been elderly or imperious, she'd have walked out, but as he was youngish – she judged in his late twenties – not at all high-handed and being so nice, maybe he had something in mind for her that might get her a job here after all.

'Our Mr Jonathan Turnbull,' he said, 'sits in the next office. What I'd like to ask you to do, if you don't mind, is sketch our Mr Turnbull's likeness as near as you can manage. Would you do that for me? Please.'

Again she nodded. She found herself suddenly eager to show him that she was more skilled than he seemed to imply, and he could laugh his head off once she'd left this office.

'Well, if you will excuse me just one moment,' Mr Clayton said, getting up from his chair and walking out of the office, leaving her alone with her thoughts.

She could not help but wonder why a man of his age should still not be in uniform when men were out there fighting for their lives and the honour of their country.

Minutes later he returned with Mr Turnbull, a rather plump, middle-aged man who, smiling awkwardly, sat down on a chair on one side of the room. Mr Clayton laid several pencils and a rubber on the desk where Connie was sitting, together with three or four sheets of high quality cartridge paper. It was then he saw the look on her face.

'Please, Miss Lovell, I'm being very serious about this. When you have finished drawing our friend here, I'll explain. This isn't a joke. If you wish I'll leave the room?'

Connie merely shrugged, determined to prove her talent as an artist even if not as a filing clerk. But she didn't want him looking over her shoulder. To her relief, he walked off, leaving her alone with her chubby sitter, who smiled awkwardly at her and said, 'Sorry about this, miss, but he doesn't do anything without reason.'

Feeling more at ease and with a sudden surge of excitement, Connie took up one of the pencils and, studying the man's podgy face, became lost in a world that she had always enjoyed.

The man was decidedly embarrassed and it showed in his eyes. Connie always thought that the eyes made a person, brought them to life, bared their soul as no other part of the face could. And as Connie observed Mr Turnbull she could see that there was more than just embarrassment in there. Her pencil seemed to fly, hardly any need for the rubber. It was only a quick sketch but right out of the blue she felt inspired. This sometimes happened and in no time at all it was finished. She put the pencil on the desk together with the completed likeness. 'It's done,' she announced firmly.

The man got up and stretched. 'Never could sit still for too long,' he said quietly, seemingly over-awed. 'Hope it was worth it. Can I see?'

'Come and look,' she said, feeling suddenly proud of the likeness she had captured, almost having forgotten where she was.

She watched him bend over the drawing, stare at it for a moment, then straighten up. She heard him whisper, 'Good God! It's me. No doubt about that. But I look worried out of my life – sort of haunted. I never thought . . . I didn't think it showed.'

His last words caught her attention. 'Why should you feel haunted?'

He looked at her for a moment or two, then seemed to collapse in on himself, his voice fading to a whisper.

'My son-in-law was killed last week. My wife and I, we don't know what to say or how. Our daughter is beside herself with grief, and we don't know how to help her. We feel helpless. We feel—'

The door opened, cutting him off mid-sentence as Mr Clayton came in.

The man instantly straightened his shoulders, becoming a different person as his boss enquired, 'Is it finished? There are a lot of applicants still waiting.'

As if it were her fault, Connie bridled inwardly, beginning to feel on edge as he picked up her drawing and studied it a moment, comparing it to the sitter.

'Good God! You look—' he began, but Turnbull cut him off mid-sentence, saying, 'Thanks, old man, but I've got work to do,' and promptly waddled back to his own

43

office. Mr Clayton watched him go with a crooked smile that Connie could only interpret as completely cordial.

For a long time it seemed, there being other applicants waiting, he surveyed her drawing until she was on the point of asking if he was done with her as she had work to go back to, then he looked up at her and said quietly:

'As I said, Miss Lovell, Constance, you're not really suitable for the job of filing clerk, but, if you don't mind, there's something I really would like to put to you which you might be interested in. I have to make a few enquiries and it's a bit of a long shot. Hopefully I'll be in touch. But we'll just have to see.'

Chapter Six

On the bus back to Shoreditch High Street she couldn't get Mr Stephen Clayton out of her mind. The way he'd regarded her was unsettling, though she couldn't quite say why, only that it had set a strange churning in her heart. Suddenly she wanted desperately to get that job, though it didn't look all that likely now. But he'd said he'd something else in mind. What was it? She knew her father would think the worst of his interest in her, given the difference in their ages and social standing, but she felt sure that Mr Clayton was an honourable man more interested in her artistic skills than her pretty face.

He had said before she left, 'It often occurs to me that cameras can be a little intrusive. The moment people find themselves in the camera's eye they instantly pose or try to hide, depending on circumstances. The result, a precious second of truth lost. A cameraman busily setting up his camera may fail to catch that illusive expression, a fleeting second of shock or devastation on a grief-stricken face. But no one notices someone with a pencil and a scrap of paper. An expression you seem to have caught on my colleague's face. A camera can't always do that.' He had smiled at her, a charming smile that lit up his face, making her heart race.

Walking home along Bethnal Green Road, too excited to return to work today even if it meant she got into trouble, she recalled that smile he'd given her after studying her drawing, even more than those words he'd spoken almost to himself. 'Uncanny, quite uncanny, the expression you've caught. Could only have been there a second yet you've captured it and held on to it.' But the more she thought of his smile, the more her heart began to race all over again.

'I've an idea,' he'd said, his smile fading, suddenly becoming serious. 'But first I need to ask you: how long does an expression stay in your head?'

The question had surprised her. 'It stays with me,' she'd said. It felt quite normal to her that it would, so why had he needed to ask such an odd question? Surely something seen lingered in everyone's mind, didn't it?

It was then he'd mentioned that he might try and put an idea of his to the powers-that-be, as he termed it. It had sounded very mysterious and when she asked he'd answered with a lovely smile and 'We'll just have to see.' He'd not expanded on it and now here she was, still blank as to what he'd had in mind – if he'd had anything at all, though it did, she was sure, have something to do with her being asked to sketch that Mr Whatever-His-Name-Was. He had promised to notify her one way or other, though it would take a little time and he had asked her to be patient.

As he'd remarked with a wry grin, committee meetings seldom settle anything quickly and even then a proposition can be thrown out. But he would put his idea forward and see what would come of it.

'If not . . .' He'd shrugged. 'It'll be my loss. I'm good at facing up to loss.' He'd ended with a look that made him strike Connie as someone who had faced some tragedy in his life. But she could still remember that whimsical smile he'd given.

The question was, how long would she have to wait for a decision? Should she stay in her present job or carry on looking for another one where she'd be of more use to the war effort? Her mind on this, she finally turned into her street. There was no point going back to work now. She'd tell them tomorrow that she hadn't been feeling very well.

Her mum answered the door to her knock, and the first words to come spilling from her mouth were, 'What you doing home? Are you poorly?'

'I went looking for a job,' she said as she passed her in the tiny hallway. 'Like Dad suggested.'

'Did you find anything?'

Hanging her hat, scarf and coat on a hook, glad of the warmth of the house, she said, 'I don't have enough schooling. The man interviewing me said he might have something else in mind but not to count on it. So I shall wait. I don't know how long for. Could be a waste of time and it was too wet to go looking for anything else. Maybe tomorrow.'

'You'll have to go to work tomorrow or you'll lose the job you've got. And you don't want that. Anyway, I've made dinner, so you might as well sit and have it with me.'

Mum always cooked dinner at midday, eating hers then and reheating the others for when the rest of the

47

family came home from work. Bringing in the meals, she went to the stairs and called out, 'George, dinner's ready.'

'Be down in a minute,' came the faint reply.

As her mother came back into the room, she said, 'He's bin out.'

'Looking for work or signing up?' Connie asked tartly as she sat down to eat. Her mum gave half a sigh, torn between love for her son and loyalty to Dad.

Her dad had made no secret of his feelings towards George: a mixture of anger, disgust, contempt and not a little embarrassment. She understood how he felt, but like Mum, she loved all her brothers and sisters. Though she was closer to her brothers, sometimes she felt as if her sisters looked down on her a little, maybe because she was the youngest, and sometimes it hurt. But they looked down on George more. Surely, he must know what they all thought of him after Bert and Ronnie had practically fallen over themselves to enlist, while he hung back, still quoting that same old phrase: *Thou shalt not kill!* He seemed quite impervious to others' opinion of him, and sometimes Connie felt hardly able to look at him let alone speak to him.

Her thoughts went suddenly to the man who'd interviewed her today, Mr Clayton: good looking, healthy, of fighting age, she'd judged. So why wasn't he in the forces? Was journalism an exempt role? She didn't think so. Had he even attempted to volunteer as her brothers had done? To believe such a thing would destroy these feelings he had conjured up inside her, feelings that even now were unsettling her.

Hastily she turned her mind away from speculation. What the man did was nothing to do with her. She had her own life to worry about. He had at least made her think more seriously about this artistic talent she had.

Dad called it messing about. For all that her eldest sister had liked the portrait of baby Henry, mostly she and Lilian sneered at her efforts and said it was about time she grew up. Her two brothers had no opinion and for that she was glad. Only George showed any interest, taking her drawings seriously, and for that she loved him and tolerated him more than the rest of the family. Mum, of course, was proud of her talent – said it came from her side, although none of it had seemed to come down to any of the others. Now she prayed that she'd get this wonderful opportunity, whatever it turned out to be, to use it. All she could do was keep her fingers crossed.

Upstairs George heard his sister come in and vaguely wondered at the reason for her being home so early from work, though his thoughts were elsewhere. Since his two brothers had enlisted, Dad kept calling him yellow, scared. He'd talked about it with his minister, Joseph Wootton-Bennett, who in his strong, assertive voice had advised him to trust his Bible that said emphatically, thou shalt not kill.

'It says exactly what it means, my boy, and you can't get away from that for it comes from the very mouth of God Himself. You are one of my most dedicated parishioners. Surely you would not go against the teaching of Our Lord and look to slay your fellow man? Yes, they are wrong to walk into another's country, but ending a

49

man's God-given life will not solve the situation, my son. All you will succeed in doing is cutting short that man's life – a man who may have been given no choice but to obey his superiors – and cause his parents to grieve for the son they had probably brought up tenderly, with love, in the hope of him living a long and useful life, marrying, begetting children, until God Himself called him. Condemn his wife to be a widow? Orphan his children? And why? Because this country says you must go against God's Law and kill your fellow man, a man you have never met. You know it is wrong, my son.'

Yes, it was wrong. He trusted his pastor implicitly. A non-conformist, Joseph Wootton-Bennett may have been at odds with the sentiments of most other churches, but his aim was to help the poor, the sick, the needy, expecting members of his congregation to do the same. How then could he go against such a man whose teaching made more sense than orthodox religion, which looked on those willing to go off to kill their fellow man with pride? Now, with his brothers having rushed off to join up, he was beginning to find himself in disgrace, his beliefs misunderstood.

'You're scared!' his father had mocked after another argument at Christmas. 'Bloody scared out of your pants while your brothers are fightin' for their country.' Well, they weren't yet but Dad saw it as if they were . . . 'And 'ere's you, wetting yourself in case this country finally gets you in its grips. There's already rumours that we could end up with military conscription by next year if we're still at war. Then you'll 'ave to go, won't you, whether you like it or not. Then we'll see. I'm bloody ashamed of you, that's what I am.'

So saying, Dad had turned his back on George since then and had hardly spoken to him. But Dad was not going to turn him from his beliefs.

His minister would hand him pamphlets, booklets that he'd written, sometimes in the form of poetry, exquisite poetry that went straight to the heart: gentle patience, control over anger, the ability to turn the other cheek. They made him wish that others could read the message they held, that if all men could understand, there'd be no wars. He'd agreed to hand them out to people, but when he did, all he got were snide remarks and ridicule; usually people tossed the pamphlets to the curb – or back in his face – as they walked off. It was soul destroying, really. But it hadn't shaken his faith and never would.

Chapter Seven

March 1915

There'd been no word from the newspaper that had interviewed her. So much for talk, getting her all excited. So much for expectation! What had she expected? A factory girl with just an ordinary education . . . Not even reckoned clever enough to master a filing job. Better to stop dreaming of wonderful things and resign herself to what she was. Besides, she now had much more to think about.

At the weekend Ronnie and Bert had appeared on the doorstep, on twenty-four-hour leave. But excitement had changed moments later to deep concern and, from Mum, tears, as they heard that the two were finally being sent abroad. This was embarkation leave.

Young Ronnie, eighteen just four months ago, now looked so much older than that, as if his youth had been stripped from him overnight. But there had been something else that had disturbed the family, at least her. Hardly had they stepped into the house to be fallen upon by Mum and have their hands mightily shaken by Dad.

George made the excuse that he'd planned to be away that weekend with a friend of his and had vanished upstairs to appear a few minutes later with an old case, briefly wishing his brothers well and disappearing out of the house.

Nothing was said, which made it all the more obvious, and painful. And there was no need to guess what they were all thinking – that he had no guts, no guts at all, not even to face his brothers with his so-called beliefs, but had made that pathetic excuse of having made plans. Connie had felt ashamed of him, at the same time deeply embarrassed, and that embarrassment was still with her now.

The thing was, one couldn't go more than a few steps without seeing the recruiting posters on every available wall. Especially the eye-catching one with the handsome colonel with the wonderfully huge moustache and those steady eyes looking into those of everyone who went by, and that steadily pointing finger as if directed at the passer-by personally; underneath the words YOUR COUNTRY NEEDS YOU.

How could anyone see those posters and ignore the call? Already it had prompted thousands more young men to volunteer, so the newspapers were saying, including her two brothers-in-law, who had now signed up with the wives' understanding, even if they feared what would happen.

And then there was George . . . But she would not think of George. It made her unhappy to think about him.

He had tried to explain, so he said, but Dad would have none of it and she couldn't blame him. In fact as soon as George walked into the room, Dad would get up and walk out, usually muttering something about him having something else to do; more often than not it would be down the pub.

Mum would be left there, slack-faced and ill at ease. Any attempt of George explaining his beliefs, or any attempt on his part to follow her and explain how he felt, would have her hurrying away to do some household chore or finding some shopping that needed to be done.

But he had explained his reason to Connie, and she found herself feeling for him. Part of her admired the fact that he was prepared to bear the ridicule of his family for something he believed in so strongly. In the current patriotic climate it was far easier to join up than say no and stick to those beliefs. However, she did still feel that it was his pastor who was exerting undue influence on him. Hopefully one day George would see it.

For a long time the atmosphere in the house could have been cut with a knife. But since the boys had left, weighed down by their gear ready to be sent off to France, the house had felt like a mausoleum, even though they'd been stationed away from home for months. The knowledge of their being sent abroad to fight had felt more ominous.

When it was time for them to leave, Mum had been in tears, clinging to them as if she alone might stop them; Dad had solemnly shaken hands with them but looked as if he too wanted to hold them tightly.

Elsie and Lillian, who'd come on the Sunday to say goodbye as though that might be the last time they'd see them, took turns to throw themselves into their brothers' arms, while their husbands shook Bertie and Ronnie's hands, telling them to look after themselves and come back safe.

Connie had dissolved into tears at being held close by each of her wonderful brothers, while Bertie's fiancée, Edie, an engagement ring now on her finger, had stood quietly back, dry-eyed but ashen-faced, too numbed to cry. She'd have her moments of tears standing with her Albert on the railway platform to see him off in privacy, or with as much privacy as any railway station can afford with hundreds of men bidding goodbye to their wives and sweethearts.

Three weeks had passed since they had left, and Connie had been working next to Sybil at that rotten conveyor belt, always with her mind on the hope that maybe tonight a letter from the *London Herald* might be awaiting her to say she had a job there. Some hope!

'It says in the paper,' Sybil yelled above the rattle of conveyor belts, 'it says women are being asked to do war work, taking over from the men what's gone off to fight.'

Connie nodded in her direction, one eye on the box coming along. 'I've read that too.'

'You know, I think I might have a go at that,' Sybil shouted hoarsely. 'Anything's better than this bloomin' dead-end job. I'm sick of it. But there was never a choice before. But now there is and despite me dad saying I should hang on to the job I've got, I think I'll take tomorrow off and go and see what's on offer.'

'I might come along with you,' Connie said on the spur of the moment. She too was sick to death of this unending, soul-destroying job. She was just wasting her time away waiting for those newspaper people to contact her. It was time to take her life in her hands and look for something more rewarding than sticking boxes together.

But with war work, she'd heard that you had to work where you were told: maybe at some machine or other, taking over where the man who usually operated it had left off to join up. She might just be exchanging one factory job for another. Though some women were now delivering milk like her brother had, or doing a post round – though that wouldn't be so bad. It was being said that women were now working as bus conductors, even bus drivers. But she could end up in a factory sewing parachutes or making bombs – hard, dangerous jobs – did she want that? And once in war work it was like being in the army – you wouldn't be allowed to leave just because you didn't like the work.

Not only that but by following Sybil she'd be giving up any chance of accepting any situation the newspaper intended for her. Not that it seemed likely after all this time – if there was a situation at all. That man, that interviewer Mr Clayton, had just been offering her a pipe dream, stupid man! Getting her hopes up like that.

She went home that evening not so much upset as resigned. Why be upset when there'd been no job in the first place? She should have known from the start that an opportunity to use her drawing talents was too good to be true.

It had started to rain, not much, but arriving home, letting herself in by the back door after popping into the loo first to save having to go out there later when it really began to come down, she found her dinner waiting for her on the table. Dad was already halfway through his, but of George there was no sign.

'Letter came for you around dinner time,' said Mum as she sat down to eat. People round here saw midday as dinner time even though they often had their main meal in the evening, calling it teatime. Apparently better-class people always called their midday meal lunch, their evening meal being dinner.

She stopped eating. 'A letter? For me?'

Her first thought was that one of her brothers had thought to write a note to her personally and a surge of excitement caught her. Where were they, the two of them? How were they? If they'd had time to write home, they couldn't possibly have been put in any danger.

'Who's it from?' she asked stupidly.

'I don't know, love,' her mother said mildly. 'It's your letter.'

But when had she ever had a letter from anyone? They were usually addressed to Mum or Dad, usually Dad, and they were usually bills. If her sisters needed to get in touch, they popped round, being only streets away. So would her friends.

The envelope had an English stamp and postmark. There was also a printed name on the left side: 'The *London Herald* Newspaper'.

Excitement shot through her, which was instantly dulled by a defensive reaction. A letter finally telling her that she was not suitable for any situation at the paper. What had she expected? Putting it to one side she took up her knife and fork and began to eat her meal that suddenly seemed to have no taste in it.

Chapter Eight

April 1915, somewhere in France

It was the smell that hit Albert first as, along with this new intake, he and Ron clambered down into the already crowded, narrow trench that in the half-light of dusk could be seen zigzagging endlessly into the distance.

They'd been brought by bus, ordinary London buses that to his mind made the fighting at the front almost farcical. But not for long as, alighting at their billets four miles behind the lines, they could plainly hear explosions of shellfire and see the flashes even from this distance.

Given just time to deposit the belongings they didn't need and gobble down a long-awaited if meagre meal, the new intake formed up to march towards the shellfire. Albert's heart was thumping, his stomach going over the nearer they got, knowing his brother felt the same, knowing that each man in their company felt the same, though no one said anything, looking straight ahead as they marched, faces set. All that travelling, on top of a four-mile march past fields of winter mud that had once been ripe for crops, they had been almost glad to reach their destination, relieved to find a temporary lull in the gunfire.

Passing through the ruins that had been the fine town of Ypres, Albert had become aware of a strange odour that seemed to hang in the air.

'What's that smell?' he'd whispered to Ronnie beside him. 'Can you smell it?'

Ronnie had nodded, keeping his voice down. 'No idea. Ain't never smelled anything like that before. Gas d'you think? Hope it's not.'

'At least we've got gas masks. No one had any gas masks earlier on. Some say they'd piddle on their hand-kerchiefs and put that to their noses – that's supposed to stop gas getting inside a bloke.'

'Shut up and eyes front!' came a harsh command from behind. They shut up and looked to their front, glad to be finally halted. The smell had become even stronger as they'd neared their destination.

'Smells like something died,' Ronnie muttered. 'Dead horses?'

But no one answered as something other than dead horses dawned in the mind of every man, their expressions tightening as they clambered down into the already crowded trenches that seemed to go on and on. Albert followed the rest, the clinging smell coming up to hit him, making him want to gag. He was to discover its source the next morning. But tonight he slept, worn out, half-sitting for want of room, hardly out of his kit before his eyes closed. Ronnie was already snoring despite the occasional explosion of enemy shelling. Neither realised how lucky they were that no one would be ordered over the top tonight and they could rest.

Waking up stiff and parched as dawn came up, Bertie peeked over the parapet in the half-light and finally began to make out strange humps dotted here and there across the churned-up mud. As the light grew, he saw they were bodies, unretrieved bodies. Horrified, he asked why of the thin air.

'You can't go out there collecting 'em, sonny,' answered a gruff voice behind him. 'More than your life's worth with Jerry lookin' on. Try doin' that and you'll end up joining 'em.' The sergeant smiled sadly at his stunned expression. 'I know, son, they deserve to be buried, decent and proper like. But who's gonna do it, and what's the point? They don't know they're dead and gone to heaven, sonny, so what's the point getting yourself killed just to get 'em back?'

Without waiting for Albert's response he moved on.

Ronnie groaned himself awake and stretched his cramped limbs. 'What'd he want?' he asked. To which Albert muttered, 'Don't know.'

Waking up had brought the return of the smell: the poisoned and burnt mud mingled with that cloying stink of rotting corpses. The odour of men crowded together in a narrow space had another smell all of its own: controlled fear, body sweat; control deserting a man, a bowel emptying itself unexpectedly, and stale vomit of those who, on the last onslaught over the top, had seen the limbs or the head of a comrade blown clear from his body, a man cut clean in half. These stricken witnesses did not weep, but they had a special look of their own. There was a vacancy about them, in their stare, in their silence.

Hastily, Albert turned to peep again over the parapet at the churned-up stretch of mud, interlaced with barbed wire and pitted with shell craters. News reports at home bore no resemblance to seeing it first hand as they had marched.

'Christ!' Ronnie had cursed when they'd been first ordered down into the trench, which was narrow and already crowded. Albert had not replied – couldn't. That single word exploding from his brother's lips said it all. Minutes later his boots and several inches of puttees had disappeared under the muddy water, despite the duckboards. As he lifted one foot clear, a man already there, squatting on some firing steps, had grinned up at him.

'Wouldn't bother, mate. You'll get used to it.'

'Used to this?' Bert had shot at him, too shocked to grin back. 'Pigs couldn't get use to this!'

The man stopped grinning. 'Then fuckin' don't. Anyway you'll soon be dead, so don't fuss your fuckin' self about it.'

So saying he'd got up to plough his way further along as the intake of raw young soldiers piled into the trench in the dark.

The only relief Albert had felt was that everything had been relatively quiet – none of the bombardment he'd been expecting, just the occasional crack of rifle fire that seemed to come from a distant direction. He was knee deep in mud and water. He'd turned to a staff sergeant who'd been busily getting this new intake to move along. 'How do we stay dry, Staff?'

The man hadn't even glanced at him. 'You don't. Don't have time to worry about that – been under bombardment for days. Bit of a lull now. Keep your heads down, cos it'll probably start up again at some time or other. Them over there's forever takin' pot shots at us.' With that, he'd moved on.

A young lieutenant who was coming up to Bert from the other direction had explained in a quiet, cultured voice, 'There are a few dugouts that are relatively dry back there where they lay down the wounded. Some manage to get a wink or two of sleep there when they can.'

'Where do the others sleep?'

The man had given a weary smile. 'When you're under fire, old chap, you sleep standing up the second it ceases. Cat naps. One hardly realises one's drifted off. Beneficial in its way, I suppose.' With that he had turned back the way he'd come.

Now fully awake, Albert thought of the lieutenant, a cultured voice amid the coarse cursing of working-class men waking up, stiff and sore from lying awkwardly.

But he thought more of something to eat as he took a swill from his water bottle. How did men eat in this place? Moments later he found out. Someone coming along, keeping his head down, poured a thin gruel into the mess tin he had hurriedly found and held out. It wasn't half bad and he gobbled it down, feeling a little more satisfied as he stowed away the empty mess tin.

At that moment, the bowels of hell seemed to break loose as a terrific bombardment opened up from somewhere behind the German lines, which, he realised, were hardly more than fifty yards away.

Instinctively he ducked and cowed against the running wet walls of the trench he was in, grateful for its cover. Lying beside him was his brother, Ronnie, swearing like the devil. The noise was deafening, yet he could hear himself saying over and over, 'Keep us safe, dear God, keep us safe!'

Further along the trench, a deafening explosion sent sandbags and mud up into the air, knocking him off balance. It could have been no more than sixty feet away. A few minutes later, although it seemed an eon, the bombardment ceased as suddenly as it began. Men were running to where the shell had exploded. Bert automatically ran with them, as much as mud and water allowed, Ronnie close behind. Anyone who had been in that spot would have stood no chance.

What met him was devastation, bodies, parts of bodies, strewn in what was left of this section of trench, half-buried by collapsed walls and sandbags, the wounded crying out in pain, others lying inert, unaware of a leg or an arm gone or dead. He felt his stomach heave.

'Don't just stand there, Lance-Corporal!' bellowed a voice behind him. 'Get that body out the way so the wounded can be got out, before someone bloody well falls over it! And look lively!'

Controlling his heaving stomach, Bert glanced to where the sergeant had indicated to see the young lieutenant with the nice accent.

He looked exactly as if he was asleep, one arm lying casually across his stomach, the other arm across his chest, eyes gently closed. He was stone dead. Blood oozed from where a piece of shrapnel had penetrated his right temple, no doubt lodged deep in his brain. He couldn't ever have known what had hit him. Bert found tears had begun to cloud his eyes and run down his cheeks. He continued to regard the graceful recline of the dead man, a man that just a few minutes ago had been—

'Stop gawpin' like some silly bugger!' The sergeant's voice boomed in his ear. 'Make yourself bleedin' useful. You and that soldier there, get that poor sod out the way—'

'That soldier's my brother,' Albert cut in idiotically as the sergeant pointed to Ronnie, who stood transfixed, eyes wide, face frozen by shock.

'I don't care if he's bleeding Beelzebub himself!' the sergeant grated. 'Both of you, drag the poor sod out of the way so's we've got room to get the wounded somewhere. And you two . . .'

He turned on a couple trying to help others clear the wounded. The men were half-dazed, like Albert and Ronnie, having only fifteen minutes ago arrived with the new intake.

'Get that soldier there into the dugout. Leg's gone so take it easy with 'im – if he ain't bled to death by the time you get 'im to first aid. And you other two . . .' He turned abruptly to his original quarries. 'Stop playing silly buggers and get on with your job!'

As Albert obediently took the dead lieutenant's shoulders, Ronnie the feet, and they lifted the body tenderly as if the man might still feel discomfort. He had a strange thought that suddenly made him want to laugh, if it hadn't been so very sad. 'Here endeth the first lesson.'

But he didn't laugh. Instead, the tears streamed down his face. They weren't for himself. They were for the well-spoken young man whose life had been swept away. Had he lived, what would he have been? A lawyer, a doctor, a teacher, a professor? Who knows? Yes, indeed, here had ended Bertie's first lesson, his first day at the front.

But this was not the time for thinking. Thinking could send a man crackers. It was a lesson he was going to have to learn pretty sharp.

Yet the thoughts ran like ghosts through his head: how many more months would this death and destruction last before the war ended? And in any one of those months he or Ronnie could be injured, crippled for life, even killed. It didn't bear thinking about. And it was not something he or Ronnie could ever put into their letters home.

Chapter Nine

That evening, the letter had lain unopened on her pillow.

'Ain't you going to read it, then, love?' her mother had asked as Connie put it to one side to get on with her dinner before going out for the evening with some friends.

'Later,' she said offhandedly. 'I know who it's from. It don't matter.'

'But it looks official, love. It says the *London Herald*.'

'I know.' Connie had shrugged. 'A job I went after ages ago but they said I wasn't suitable. It's just a letter confirming it, that's all.'

With a drawn-out 'Oh' her mother had gone off into the kitchen to make another cuppa, leaving Connie to slip the unopened letter under the pillow on her bed.

When George came in from wherever he'd been, he would go directly up to his room, having it all to himself since his brothers left home. It seemed rather unfair that she still had to put up with the parlour alcove with only a curtain for privacy. A girl needed privacy. A man didn't, not all that much anyway. But if – when – her brothers came back on leave, they'd need a place to stay.

But each time Connie thought about George having this space of his own, coupled with the fact that he was still not in uniform, it filled her with contempt.

This evening, wearing a new skirt she had made – one that followed this year's new fashion influenced by the war, being much wider round the hem now and shorter by several inches, giving more freedom to walk normally – she had met Cissie and Doris for a jaunt up the West End. Hating to spoil their enjoyment, she'd forced herself to be bright and cheerful. Besides, had they noticed her low spirits, she would have had to explain why she was feeling down, and she didn't want to go into detail on the failed interviews. But now she was home.

Alone in the parlour, having washed her face clean of face powder at the kitchen sink and cleaned her teeth, she undressed slowly, got into her nightie, turned down the gas lamp and clambered into bed. Mum would be first up in the morning, waking her with a cup of tea. She'd be obliged to dress quickly, concealed by the curtain, before Dad came down. All so easily avoidable and again she felt a twinge of annoyance towards her eldest brother.

Lying there, she held the unopened envelope between her fingers. It was hard not to resist a temptation to tear it in half and drop it on the floor, its contents unread. But she needed to read it, and braced herself to its bad news. Sitting up suddenly, the bedclothes slipping down to her tummy, she leaned forward and ripped open the envelope to pull out a single sheet of headed notepaper.

It was too dark to make out what it said. But relighting the gas lamp might alert Dad, always a light sleeper, noticing the glow under the door on one of his frequent trips in the night to the privy in the backyard. He'd be especially hard on her given they'd all been warned to be very careful about too much lighting since January when German Zeppelins had dropped bombs on Yarmouth and King's Lynn, the towns fully lit at the time but now, of course, like London, swathed in darkness. Three cottages utterly destroyed in one raid; several people killed including a small boy and his little sister; pictures of cottages flattened, utterly unrecognisable as once having been people's homes, had sent shivers down her spine. This was what devastation truly was, those same towns, and others, shelled by German warships.

So with relative darkness outside, being a dirty night, any glow would have had Dad opening the parlour door to find why she'd relit the gas lamp, and she wanted no intrusion. Drawing the window curtains was dangerous too. Dad always pulled them back before going to bed – to let out the smell of cooking, he said, and get a bit of fresh air into the place, for all the windows stayed closed in cold weather. Trying to pull them together would inevitably cause that rustle and squeak they always made when being dragged along the rusty metal rail, loud enough to catch the alert ears of a sleepless man.

But with the letter now open, she needed to see what it said. Creeping out of bed she found a small stub of a candle in a holder in the small table drawer, lit it with one of Dad's matches and took it back to bed with her. By its fitful light she began to read, knowing that she'd tear the letter to bits in frustration and fury after having read it.

It wasn't the terse response she'd expected – more or less saying thank-you-but-no-thank-you – but a longish, hand-written one, the writing small and neat.

Dear Miss Lovell,

First I apologise for the time it's taken to let you know the outcome of my approach to the management with my idea. But at last I've had a response. They've decided to give it a shot. A long shot, maybe, but it could work out well. If it doesn't, I promise to give you a really glowing reference so you'll be able to get a job anywhere. After all, during the time you do spend on the paper, even if it doesn't work out a success, you'll have learned a lot and will be able to make use of it. Would you reply telling me what you think? My reputation's on the line too over this idea so I need to make this a success. I'm willing to give it a try if you are?

Please tell me what you think. Don't leave it too long.

Mr Stephen Clayton,
Editor

P.S. Moving heaven and earth to get them to take you on, I've a strong feeling about this. Really looking forward to seeing you if all goes well.

Stephen

In the light of the spluttering candle, she stared at the single name. Stephen! He'd signed the postscript Stephen!

As if . . . had he felt a small tinge of attraction? Her heart had gone pit-a-pat but what if he had felt something too? No, she was just being silly. Better to forget it.

Tomorrow she'd promised Sybil she'd go with her to the labour exchange to see about volunteering for war work. Here there'd be no question of laying her off. It would be a steady, long-term job, at least until the war was over. By that time she would have become a skilled worker, hopefully a still needed skilled worker. Was she ready to sacrifice that solid chance for this slim one? And what would the job entail? Mr Clayton must think that he had told her what she was engaged to do, but she still didn't know. She wasn't so sure about the job now. And what would Sybil think? Talk about burning one's bridges. But Stephen . . .

There was no sleep for her tonight. She was still awake watching a rainy dawn come up when Mum brought her a cup of tea.

'Your dad will be up soon so best hurry and get dressed, love.'

She was dressed, her face washed, her teeth cleaned, and eating her breakfast of porridge as he came downstairs.

'What was goin' on last night?' he muttered to her across the kitchen table. 'I could 'ear you movin' about for ages.'

Yes, the walls, floors and ceiling were thin in terraces. One could hear everything the people next door said when they raised their voices just a fraction. There'd be bumps and bangs every second of the day, and a child crying was like a siren piercing the ears.

*

At eight o'clock Connie was on the corner of Ellsworth Street where Sybil lived and Bethnal Green Road. What was Sybil going to say when she told her of her news?

'I can't come with you today,' she began as they met. 'I think I've got that job in Fleet Street – there was a letter waiting for me when I got home last night.'

'That one you told me about all that time ago? That was a couple of months ago.' As Connie nodded, Sybil said, 'That's really marvellous!' Her round face creased into a huge smile. 'And you thought they'd forgotten you. You lucky cow! But why did they take so long?'

No disparagement, no offhanded shrug, but a huge smile of genuine joy for her. Connie felt a twinge of regret; Sybil was such a nice person, a good friend at work and out, and now hearing her news she was just happy for her.

'My interviewer, Mr Clayton, Mr Stephen Clayton,' Connie went on with a need to state his full name, at the same time with a stab of excitement at the prospect of seeing him again. 'He had a job persuading them.'

'We will see each other still, when we can, won't we?' Sybil asked, her smile faltering.

'Of course,' Connie replied warmly. Yes, she wanted that more than anything. No not quite anything. She wanted this job. She wanted to prove to Stephen Clayton that she was capable. She wanted to see him again, feel her heart thump like it had that first time, something she'd never experienced before – a strange and wonderful feeling. But she kept her face straight as Sybil said with some disappointment in her tone that she had to be off.

'Perhaps we can see each other this Saturday,' Connie said quickly by way of compensation. 'If you're not doing anything?'

'I'd like that,' Sybil said, bucking up to grin. 'Still, must be off. Good luck, Con. Can't wait to hear how you get on and I'll tell you how I did.'

And she was off, running for the bus that had drawn up several yards down the road, a crowd of workers already waiting to get on.

As the bus drew away, Connie, her somewhat tatty umbrella shielding her face from the spattering of rain, made her way to the bus stop opposite to wait for the one that would take her to Fleet Street, and, she hoped, her future.

Hurrying through the main foyer, up the stairs to the second floor, folded umbrella dripping water, she found the *London Herald* with no trouble. The young woman who opened the frosted glass door was the same who'd opened the door to her that first time, but this morning as she entered the outer office, no line of hopeful applicants met her, for which she was grateful.

'This way, Miss Lovell,' the lady said, her tone far more courteous than that first time. 'My name is Miss Cranwell. I'll take your hat, coat, and your umbrella. I expect you would care to freshen up.'

Leading the way to the cloakroom, she waited outside while Connie hurried in to relieve herself and hopefully soothe away some of her nervous tension. Afterwards she washed her hands and touched her lips with just the faintest trace of lipstick her father had no idea she owned. Running a hasty comb through her wavy hair that her hat had left flattened, she stood back from the narrow mirror to stare at herself.

What would Stephen Clayton see? A mature-looking young woman, she hoped. After all she was seventeen now, but her height meant that she could pass for much older and she only hoped Stephen Clayton would see a mature, composed young woman, not a childish bag of nerves.

The secretary was waiting for her as she came out, refreshed and hopefully calm. The woman's smile seemed to confirm it as she led the way to the office Connie had entered the last time she was here. As the secretary tapped lightly on the frosted glass, Connie suddenly felt her nerves begin to flutter.

The secretary looked to be in her early twenties: tall, very sure of herself, trim and beautiful. How could she, at seventeen, for all she already had all the feelings of a woman, dare to think of herself as being competent enough to take on the job being offered, whatever it was? She was a fraud. She would finally betray herself, come out with something stupid and have to admit she wasn't up to this job, that Stephen Clayton had been misled. He could blame her, not himself, for being so gullible in that new idea he'd excitedly but misguidedly conjured up.

She wanted to turn and run but was already being ushered into his office, the secretary smoothly withdrawing as he hurried round from his side of the desk to greet her with a hearty handshake. His flesh felt warm.

'I'm so very glad you've decided to go along with this venture. Seeing your talent for drawing, I knew immediately that we would have to put you to work in some capacity. I am still thinking exactly what that capacity might entail.' He paused, regarding her, and then taking a deep breath, said, 'I need to be honest with you, Miss Lovell. I never mentioned this in my letter but you will have to undergo a trial period.'

'A trial period?' she burst out. There was a catch to all this good news? A few weeks and it would be 'Sorry, we don't think you're up to this.'

She saw him draw in a deep breath. 'I've had the devil's own job to convince my superiors that this idea could really lift off. That's why it's taken so long. I needed to be certain.'

'But you're still not certain,' she cut in, disappointment making her bold, anger making her forthright. She'd given up a secure job to take up this position, turned down the chance of war work too. And he'd still not asked her to sit down. He seemed on edge. 'And perhaps I am wasting my time coming here.'

He turned sharply to look at her.

'No, of course not! This will be a trial period of a few months, see how it works out, but if it doesn't, if they feel it's not working and cut it short, I will make sure you have a job here – in a few months you'll have learned something of how a newspaper works and I will help you all I can towards a career in the print. Are you willing to give it a go, Miss Lovell – Constance? May I call you Constance, by the way?'

Hearing him address her by her Christian name sent an excited tingle up her spine. As she calmed herself and nodded, he brightened, his next words tumbling from his mouth.

'That's great! We're going to make things happen, Constance, you and me.'

Impulsively she heard herself blurt out, 'Connie.'

'Connie,' he repeated, as if savouring her name. He indicated for her to sit while he returned to his side of the desk.

She made her way home full of the wonderful news on how her day had gone. Starting Monday week, she'd be gradually integrated into the world of newspapers, though still some way off being sent on small assignments with a photographer and a junior reporter.

She arrived home around four o'clock, having accepted Mr Clayton's offer to take her to lunch so as to discuss his plans with her. He'd asked if she had any questions but then chimed in energetically the moment she tried to oblige.

There was one question she did manage to ask, though she now wished she hadn't, one that had been niggling away at her ever since she'd met him. Her two brothers and brothers-in-law had been among thousands who'd so far volunteered for military service. While Stephen Clayton spoke of the job, her mind had wandered, playing with the feeling that he, like George who was hanging back, evading the call, had also suffered qualms about putting himself in danger. Maybe he saw his job as more essential; maybe he was scared; or maybe he fostered more or less the same principles as her brother? Was he, as she suspected of George, hiding behind his beliefs? Suddenly it had seemed of vital importance that she know.

She'd come out with it before she could stop herself. 'You're still a civilian, Mr Clayton?' Seconds later she could have died.

He'd broken off from what he'd been saying and for a while regarded her, his expression bleak. Finally he said, very slowly, 'I did try, several times. But, you see, I'm partially deaf in my right ear – scarlet fever as a child nearly finished me off, but left me, as I said, deaf, and I am afraid the military rejected me because of it.'

'I'm sorry, I should never have asked,' she said, still mortified. 'It just came out. I'm so sorry, Mr Clayton.'

He'd asked her to call him Stephen, giving her a vague impression of almost flirting with her. But him being older, a different class and her boss, led her to find it improper to use anything other than his formal name. Nor had it warranted her asking such a personal question of him.

Coming home she still felt the embarrassment of it crawling through her being. How could she have dared to ask such a question? At lunch she'd sat rigid, wanting to apologise but totally unable to find words suitable enough. He had, however, cheered up immediately, returning to discussing the project he had in mind, as if the question had never been voiced.

Still cringing at her audacity, at the same time relieved that what had been troubling her had been laid to rest, she let herself into her house. Despite her embarrassment, she was bubbling over with her wonderful news, but there was only Mum to tell.

The place these days had an empty air to it, with Ronnie and Albert gone. Even the few times in the past when she'd come home before them and Dad got in from work, the house had always felt alive. Now the empti-ness seemed to brood. Dad coming in later would make it feel better, of course, he filling the house with his larger-than-life presence, as always, and she blessed him for it.

Turning the key in the front lock, she opened the door to find her mother standing waiting for her as if she'd been standing there for hours. But instead of asking how she'd got on, she held out a sheet of notepaper.

'Oh, Connie, I'm so glad you're home.' Her voice sounded strained.

'A letter's come from Bertie. Oh, Connie, he says they're still all right but that they've been sent to the front, still together, though.'

'The front – where the fighting is?' Connie cried stupidly, her own news forgotten. It was three weeks since their twenty-four-hour embarkation leave.

'You'd best read it.' Her mother was holding out the single sheet of scruffy notepaper to her, Connie taking it to stare bleakly at her for a second or two before lowering her eyes to read:

Dear Mum, Dad and Con,

Just writing to say me and Ronnie were conveyed here yesterday. So far all is quiet, well, almost, but I want to tell you we are both doing well. Blokes say it can be like this with nothing really happening apart from an exchange of rifle fire every now and again, so it don't seem so bad. But it's not all that comfortable what with this blooming weather. Ain't stopped raining since we've got here and the trenches have got about a foot of water in them. It don't drain off and some blokes who've been here longer have got what's called trench foot. Hope we don't get it. Makes them really miserable. But the rain just keeps making the walls of the trenches cave in and our job at the moment is to keep shoring them up.

But I don't want you back home to worry. We're all right. By the way, Ronnie sends his love. That's all I can say for now. Write again soon as I can. Thanks for the letter you wrote, only just got it, and the photos of you and Dad. Bit faded but keeps us in touch, a bit of home. That's all for now, run out of paper. Love to all and to Connie as well. Tell her to take care of herself.

Bert & Ron.

P.S. By the way, I've been made up to lance corporal. And Ronnie's bloody jealous, bless his little cotton socks! Love, Albert.

The letter, dated just over a week ago, revealed how long the post took to reach its destination. Then came the dread thought: how long would it take to be notified of the death or injury of a loved one? Connie dismissed the thought instantly. Her brothers were going to be fine, she had to keep believing that.

Looking up, she saw her mother nibbling at her bottom lip and realised she had been watching her the whole time she'd been reading, as if going over her son's words with her. How many times today, all on her own, had she gone over and over what her son had written?

As she caught her eye it seemed to break the spell. Mum drew in a long, audible breath, and then let it out again in a long, tortured cry. 'Oh, Connie, I pray they'll both stay safe . . .' The next instant she reached out and took her in her arms, the two of them weeping silently as they held tightly to each other, each striving to draw comfort from the other.

By the time Dad came home they were composed. 'Had a letter from the boys today,' Connie's mum said in a controlled tone. 'Read it yourself. They've been sent to the front, together, just over a week or so ago.'

As Connie watched her parents' faces, saw her mother's mouth crumple, her father's eyes become filled with a haunted gaze as he read, as if he was already being notified of a loss, she let a silent prayer rise up inside her.

Please, God, keep them safe, make this war end soon and bring them home, unhurt, please.

Chapter Ten

May 1915

Three weeks she'd been at this job. In that time nothing seemed to have progressed. She was a junior filing clerk in this noisy newsroom: people moving about, typewriters clacking, telephones ringing, voices raised in discussion. But at least she now knew what went into each file, how to find its place in the filing cabinet and retrieve it again when needed.

During her trial period she'd several times been asked to sketch this and that person's likeness so that the results could be studied and discussed. Tests, she supposed, but either she could do it to their satisfaction or she couldn't, and several times she had to stop herself coming out with that very remark, but it was better not to antagonise these people.

It still had not been properly specified what she was doing; all she now seemed to be doing was sitting at a desk filing various bits of correspondence. Either she could do the job she'd been hired to do, or she couldn't, and it was about time they made up their minds about that. She said little of this to her parents, who now saw her in a new light – their youngest daughter in an office earning far more than she'd done sticking boxes together in some factory. Mum was proud of her, Dad too in his way.

'How'd you get on today, love?' Mum would ask each time she came home from yet another trial day. And what could she say? She herself was not being told anything much beyond that they would study her drawings and let her know the moment they came to a decision.

'Not bad,' she would lie, with no idea whether she'd done well or not.

Dad hadn't been much help. 'You want to tell 'em to stick their bloody job up their you-know-what if they're goin' to go on messing you about.' She had ignored that advice. She needed to keep this job.

But in all this time she'd not once been asked to seriously prove her worth outside of the office. There was, it seemed to her, a distinct doubt that she would ever be an asset to the editorial department. Today as she sat idle, her present spate of filing done, she took up a pencil and a sheet of clean cartridge paper and gazed around the department for a likely subject to sketch.

Stephen Clayton was having a word with John Carver, one of the editorial staff, who was seated at his desk a few feet from hers. With her eyes darting between the pair and her sheet of paper, she'd began to sketch, her pencil moving with decisive strokes. It wasn't so much the seated man, but the one standing that interested her. Seldom did she have an opportunity to do a sketch of Stephen Clayton; he was either half-obscured behind the glass of his office or moving at a brisk pace through the editorial department on his way to somewhere or other. But now was her chance to catch his likeness more seriously. She could feel her heart tightening with hidden excitement as she drew his face; she felt almost heady. She needed to be on her guard though in case the two men noticed what she was doing. It was so easy for one of them to look up and catch her.

Her pencil moved swiftly over the white surface of the paper, her eyes glancing up briefly, then looking down, her brows drawn into a frown of concentration. Soon a sketch of Stephen Clayton was forming, conjured up by a strong sense of excitement – a sensation that made her breathing quicken, her senses whirl – a feeling she realised was far stronger than that which she'd been vaguely aware of for a long time. She was in love: secretly she was in love with Mr Stephen Clayton.

But he wasn't in love with her. He couldn't be – he was her better and elder. And even if that weren't the case he was most likely married. He'd never mentioned a wife and, of course, she could never ask him. But one thing she was determined to do was to show him her completed sketch of him and John Carver, provided he stood there long enough for her to finish it. That he was half turned towards her was an asset. His face, seen at a three-quarters angle, was perfect; his expression was faintly animated, though she had no idea what the two were discussing. She had completed the sketch just seconds before he suddenly looked up in her direction.

Seeing her concentrated look, he smiled. Pencil still in hand, it had to be obvious what she had been doing and she felt her cheeks colour. Hastily she dropped the pencil on to her desk, but there was no time to hide the paper. She sat gazing back at him in the way a guilty felon would. But moments later he had said something to John Carver and turned, walking back to his office without another glance at her.

Connie sat gazing down at her sketch. Then she came to a decision. If she didn't do this now, there might never be another opportunity. Quickly she got up from her desk and hurried towards his office, tapping on the slightly ajar door.

'Come in!' came the light voice.

Peeking around its edge in response to his request, she was met by a huge smile at seeing her that almost stopped her heart.

'Connie! Everything all right?'

'Yes,' she managed. 'I needed to see you.'

It sounded utterly feeble, and unable to find anything more intelligent to say, she thrust the sketch across the desk, feeling oddly desperate. She watched him pick it up.

'I did this a couple of minutes ago while you were talking to Mr Carver,' she explained hurriedly.

Experiencing a moment of desperation, she decided that if she detected the least sign of interest on his face, she'd pounce with her query, 'Is that good enough for you to think about trying me out properly on something worthwhile?'

Instead she stood dumbly watching him scrutinise the drawing. He seemed to be taking a long time about it. Finally he looked up. 'How did you manage to get an expression like this when I was nowhere near you, talking to Carver?'

83

'You were only a few feet away,' she said meekly.

She saw him catch the corner of his upper lip between his teeth, like someone coming to a decision. Suddenly he looked up at her and for a brief second she saw a look that would have been perfect for a sketch, but one that made her draw in a silent breath. If she had paper and pencil to hand now, she would have depicted a look that was akin to something far, far deeper than a mere decision. She felt her heart skip a beat but was she wrong? Had she misconstrued his expression? Was she just a silly lovesick girl merely seeing something she wanted to see? But this talent of hers said no. She, who could retain a person's expression in her mind long after she'd seen it, would retain this one for all her years to come.

He felt something for her, she was sure. But was it only her wish for him to be in love with her that had fooled her artist's eye? But no. She was sure that look had been there, perhaps only for a moment, but it had definitely been there.

Even as she debated with herself, he began to speak again. 'I can't get over the way you do this. It's amazing. Now look, I'm sorry things have been moving so slowly. I do intend for you to do more than just filing. I'm going to tackle the management again, insist you be sent out with one of our junior photographers.' He suddenly sounded so eager, like a small boy contemplating an exciting outing. 'I'm going to move heaven and earth to get you recognition, Connie, my dear. I'll tell them, let it be a trial run. What can they lose? I really do want you to make sense, more than anything, show them what you're made of. I'll make them see you could be a great asset to the paper.'

84

Taking a hold of himself he drew a deep breath. When he spoke again he was very much more controlled. 'I hope, Connie, that you're what this paper's been waiting for, something to draw our readers in. I've a feeling, Connie, that you have the power to attract so many more readers than we now have.'

In their short conversation he had called her Connie three times, and she treasured it as she nodded and withdrew, her heart feeling it was about to fly away like a bird.

It was four more weeks, four more long weeks, and now it was the end of May, a whole month without hearing anything, four weeks that seemed to crawl, a lifetime, as things seem when waited for.

As for what had passed between Stephen Clayton and herself during that fleeting moment . . . She wondered now whether she'd imagined it; certainly no more had come of it. He now seemed to be avoiding her. She in turn hadn't set foot inside his office, scared to push herself forward again in case she was met with a hostile glare. Clearly he'd thought better of her going out on assignment. Though at times she also wondered if perhaps he'd felt guilty about that shared look; had he decided to distant himself from the temptation of a former factory girl, one who was clearly beneath him?

She should have drawn some comfort in that he was purposely avoiding looking at her, that in itself proving there had been something to that brief moment a month ago, that what had passed between them in his office that day couldn't be denied.

It was Mr Carver who brought the message over to her little filing desk. 'Mr Clayton told me to tell you that you'll be going out with one of our junior photographers.' She looked up at him, startled, but he had more to say. 'He says take a notebook with you – says Mr Mathieson has sanctioned it.'

Mr Mathieson was the *London Herald*'s chief editor. She wanted to leap up and bound into Stephen's office to thank him, but she curbed the desire, instead keeping her voice calm to ask Mr Carver when.

The reply came swiftly. 'Now.'

She couldn't wait to get home to tell Mum and Dad about her day. Told to accompany a photographer and an interviewer, she'd been required to hover to one side, sketch pad and pencil in hand, unseen, unnoticed. What she was to do had been left up to her, but she'd faithfully sketched the pride on the face of the interviewed woman whose son had just been awarded the DSO.

It was a start and she felt Stephen Clayton's hand in it. Gratitude flooded out of her. Mum and Dad would be so proud, would tell Albert and Ronnie in their next letter. She'd write too and tell them. And George – he'd be pleased for her. Her sisters would be surprised – they'd always made it clear they thought she'd never be more than a factory worker like them, before finding a nice man and marrying him.

But the thought that Stephen Clayton, editor, had been working for her good made her feel on top of the world. She needed to prove herself to him, increase his esteem of her, and after a while . . .

She dared think no further than that but her heart pounded at the thought that he'd done this out of something more than just regard for her skill, something she felt sure he was trying to hide from her, though why, she had no idea. It had begun to plague her until she wondered if she was going a little mad – a lovesick seventeen-year-old pining after an older man, her boss. As she went into his office to say a formal thank you for what he'd done for her, it seemed to come out of its own accord after she'd voiced her thanks.

'Not at all,' he responded, getting up from behind his desk and coming towards her. 'It was just that I felt you could be an asset to the paper.' He'd come to stand just a foot away from her.

'Not because you felt something for me?' she blurted out before she could stop herself. He gave her a sharp look then turned, moving away from her as if embarrassed. 'I'm not sure what you mean, Miss Lovell.'

He had resorted to using her surname, which he'd not done since first calling her Connie, except when in the outer office with other people listening.

Before she could stop herself, she blurted out, 'Are you married, Mr Clayton?'

Immediately she wanted to bite off her tongue as he swung round to glare at her, the look instantly fading as he regarded her, alarming her to see pain in his eyes. As silence between them stretched, she saw a depth of emptiness in those eyes that would stay with her the rest of her life. Moments later, he lowered his gaze and gave a small shake of his head. 'I'm afraid I lost my wife two years ago.'

'I'm so sorry,' she heard herself exclaim. It sounded so wrong. She stood silent, at a loss for what else to say.

After a long pause, he spoke again as if miles away. 'I was twenty-four when I married her. She was twenty-one.

Neither of us knew it then, but she had cancer. Six months later, I lost her.'

Connie suppressed a gasp. That made him twenty-six, nine years older than her, yet he looked so young. But there were still nine years between them and that made her realise what a child she still was. Why would he want her?

His words so matter of fact, coupled with a shrug that, had she not seen the expression in those blue eyes of his, his flat tone would have fooled her as it no doubt fooled others.

'My parents are dead too,' he went on, as though carrying on a normal conversation, 'my father recently, of a chill, my mother when I was fifteen.'

Without a break he straightened up, executing one of his charming wide smiles as if nothing sad had passed his lips. 'Good to know things are working out okay for you, Connie. Your chance to make the most of it.'

Not knowing what else to say, she said, 'Thank you.'

Last night there had been a zeppelin raid over London, one of several this month: homes bombed indiscriminately. This morning Connie was at one of the devastated sites. No one noticed her standing a little apart from her paper's interviewer and its junior photographer. She could have been a bystander, ignored by those whose lives had been torn apart. She sketched: an elderly woman, her daughter and her daughter's two children, one eleven, one seven, standing in front of what had been their home while soldiers did what they could to help get their possessions to safety before looters stole away whatever they could.

The women's faces betrayed their sense of loss; they were desperately trying to keep it private and it tugged at Connie's heart. It was painful to see but she had a job to do: to commit to posterity that look, that need to hide their grief, that sense of loss in front of strangers. While all the interviewers displayed sympathy, the photographers busy with their cameras, it would only take a small thing to slip for the older woman to burst into tears and shriek at them to go away. For a few hours earlier she had watched her husband die. He had escaped injury, being outside in the street with them and most of their neighbours as they watched the huge airship glide across the inky sky, glowing silver, caught in the crisscross of searchlights – a sight to see. But the shock of the blast had keeled the man over, and there on the safety of the pavement he had passed away of a massive heart attack.

Connie gathered that only a week before, her daughter's husband – her son-in-law, her grandchildren's father – had been killed at Ypres. And now the last man of the family was gone, not from the bomb that had demolished their home, but definitely related.

That empty look in the eyes of these people pushed out all other thoughts as she sketched, her pencil moving rapidly back and forth, up and down, outlining, shading. By the time she'd finished she was totally exhausted. Her work done, she tucked the drawing away out of sight and stood staring along the road, not wanting even to glance at the bereaved little family in case she burst into tears, making a fool of herself. Minutes later a taxi pulled up, no doubt hailed by a neighbour; the two women and the children clambered in to be whisked away to relatives and privacy.

Maggie Ford

Back in the office she laid the sketches on Stephen's table for him to see. For a moment he stared at them as if mesmerised. Then slowly he said, 'Good God!' before taking a deep breath. 'This they have to see!' he burst out and hurried from the office with them, leaving her gazing after him.

She was still there when he reappeared with Desmond Mathieson, their chief editor. She could hardly recall what he said other than she had the paper's permission to accompany photographers to whatever dramatic event presented itself. Her work, if suitable, would go on the appropriate page carrying that particular news item.

She felt her heart swell – a proper position at last, along with a rise in salary.

'It's a start,' Stephen said after Mathieson left. 'And I know it's going to be a damned huge success.'

His face had lit up. His blue eyes shining, he reached out, drew her towards him and planted a kiss on her cheek, startling the life out of her.

Chapter Eleven

She could hardly wait to get home and tell Mum about her promotion. Her mum listened intently, every now and again breaking in with, 'fancy that', and 'well, I never did', and 'wait till your dad hears', and 'I knew you'd do it one day'.

The one thing she did hold back was the kiss Stephen Clayton had exuberantly planted on her cheek, making her blood pound through every vein of her surprised body in a hot surge.

Mum was in the middle of even more exclamations when a knock came at the front door. As she went to go and answer it, Connie heard her give a little scream. Instantly she was out of the kitchen, making her way down the passage to the street door, in time to see her mother throwing her arms around the neck of a tall soldier, her son, crying out, 'Bertie! Oh, Bertie love!' All the while she was kissing first one cheek then the other.

Reaching the door, Connie could see Ronnie hovering behind him, his own face wreathed in smiles. It was then she realised how filthy both their uniforms were, that they had actually travelled home in that state.

As they came into the house, Mum having transferred her embrace to Ronnie, Connie took her turn to hug Albert, before noticing something moving on one of the shoulder-straps of his khaki uniform. She pulled away instantly. 'What on earth's that?'

He grinned down at his shoulder. 'Lice – they won't hurt you.'

Her mother gave a small horrified squeak, then, with a supreme effort, collected herself. 'For God's sake, love, go through into the backyard and take your things off, quick as you can. I'll get the bath down from the wall and boil up all me saucepans of water so's you can have a bath, both of you. Get you clean. To think the both of you was sent home like this!' She paused, head tilted questioningly. 'Why've you both come home without letting us know? You've not been hurt, have you?'

'We've been given four days' leave,' Albert said, taking off his battered army cap, and struggling out of his tunic.

His mother stared at him. 'Four days?' she repeated stupidly. 'You mean you've got to go back to the fighting in four days?'

He didn't answer. Instead he said, 'They give blokes some sort of leave every now and again – or they'd go barmy with all what's going on over there. Still—'

He was cut short by her cry. 'Oh, love! We do hear awful things of what's 'appening, and I get so worried and frightened for the both of you. In case—'

'We get by,' he cut in sharply. 'I don't want to see you worried, Mum,' he went on in a more gentle tone.

'Me and Ron look out for each other and we don't do so bad – we're pretty well fed and ciggies are free and every now and again we get sent back behind the lines to rest away from . . .' He let the rest fade away. 'Well, what about that bath, Mum?'

While the two had a good wash in the tin bath, getting into it together for a stand-up wash to be quicker, Connie and her mum stayed in the back parlour, the kitchen door tight shut.

Connie could clearly hear their deep voices through the thin walls: the laughter of fighting men free for a while of the fear and harassment of war.

She heard the back door open suddenly and a gruff voice give a startled exclamation followed by more laughter, voices raised in greeting. She could not help a smile, visualising her father coming in on such a scene of two naked men standing up in a tin bath with ten inches of water to wash in.

She and Mum listened as their voices – the boys' and their father's – came low through the wall, questions asked and answered: how it was over there, questions that couldn't be asked in front of women.

Eventually the conversation ceased, and there came the sound of clearing up, the bath being manhandled out to the backyard to be emptied. Moments later, Connie's father came into the room, his face still not cleansed of coal dust from his job.

'You can go out there now,' he told them. 'They're both decent. And they've 'ung the bath back on the wall and cleaned up after themselves.'

'They needn't have done that!' Mum burst out. 'If they'd left the water in the bath I could've soaked their uniforms in it before they went back. Them uniforms is full of 'orrible—'

'You couldn't, Mum,' Albert said, coming into the room in his civilian shirt and trousers. He looked shiny and human once more as if he'd never seen the sight of a uniform or a war; Ronnie came in close behind looking just as clean and bright. 'They wouldn't have been dry enough before we 'ad to put 'em on again to go back.' At the mention of going back his voice lost some of its exuberance.

'Then I'll buy some disinfectant,' she said. 'What we use to get rid of them bugs what come out in the summer from where they've bin breeding all winter, 'orrible little things! Most of us round 'ere 'ave trouble with 'em. Well anyway, that'll do the job,' she ended firmly. 'At least you'll go back cleaner than you arrived.'

Ronnie grinned. 'I wouldn't worry, Mum. It won't make much of a difference. Like them bugs, the bloody things'll be back in no time.'

In her mind, Connie could see her brothers crawling alive with ticks as they fought for their country. She saw tears glistening in her mother's eyes and knew she was seeing the same thing. But moments later Mum was herself again, her voice firm and authoritative.

'Well, you're both looking respectable now, and it's about time I got a decent meal ready for you. You must both be starving.'

'We are,' Ronnie laughed. 'A cheese sandwich on the boat and what passed for a cuppa tea – ditch water more like – nothing on the train.'

'Well, I've got sausages,' she said promptly. 'I'll do mashed potatoes, baked beans and fried onion. It's what I was going to do for Connie and your dad anyway. You both look as if you need feeding up. You're skin and bone, the pair of you. And there's apple pie and custard for afters.'

'Sausage and mash,' Albert murmured as she hurried out. 'Apple pie and custard. Sounds really great.'

To Connie it was as if they had both just come home from work.

The feeling continued as they sat down to their meal. None of them had touched on the war, the acute shortage of supplies with cargo ships being sunk by submarines, food getting harder to come by daily, resulting in soaring prices, though Mum did remark that the introduction of rationing might help to keep costs down when it came into force. To which they all nodded, the talk going on to other harmless subjects.

Yet beneath the easy conversation there was tension. It showed itself suddenly when Mum casually spoke of something she intended to do next week, her words fading as she realised that by then her boys would be back over there fighting the enemy, their lives at risk once more.

The look in each member of her family's eyes tore at Connie's soul. If she'd had paper and pencil she could have caught that bleak expression, but it would have been sacrilege to have done so. She knew it would stay with her for a long time to come and she had to swallow hard to avoid breaking into tears.

Her father was the first to stem the thoughts that had stolen into all their minds. 'Well, I'll be off to the pub in a while,' he announced heartily as he pushed away his empty afters plate. 'You two fancy a drink?'

'You and Ronnie go,' Albert said. 'I have to go and see Edie.'

Mum got up to make a cup of tea, Dad saying, 'Not for me – tea and beer don't mix.' His sons also shook their heads, preferring to be among men and surrounded by the warm smell of beer and the sound of deep voices.

They were making ready to leave when they heard the back door open then close. Seconds later George came into the room, and stopped sharply as he saw his two younger brothers standing there. He looked utterly stunned but before he could say anything, Albert spoke for him.

'It's 'orright, George, we're 'ome on four days' leave, 'ave to start back on Sunday evening. You do get 'em if you're in the forces, y'know, even if you risking your life fighting over there. But you wouldn't know about that, would you, George?'

The sarcasm in his words was inescapable and their mother's hand flew to her lips to stem a gasp while his father gave a warning cough.

George said nothing. He just stood there for a moment, then he said in a voice much too hearty: 'It's nice to see you both and looking well. But I . . . um . . .' He hesitated and drew himself up a little. 'Well, I've got to get ready to go out again. Sorry. A meeting I've got to be at. I won't need anything to eat, Mum.' He threw her a brief glance, speaking fast as if to stop any further remarks. 'I'll have something out after the meeting. It could go on for a bit so I'll probably stay with a friend afterwards. Maybe see you tomorrow, then, or if not, look after yourselves.'

It was all gabbled, giving no one a chance to say anything, but now Albert said, very slowly and pointedly, 'Probably too late by then, George. No doubt we'll be on our way back to Belgium, to the front. You remember that, do you, George – we're fighting them Germans over there?'

It was so obviously pointed that his mother drew in a sharp breath. 'Bertie!'

But George had already slipped out of the room, closing the door quietly behind him.

Connie felt her heart beginning to beat irregularly as her mind went instantly to Stephen, the way she had first misjudged him, much to her deep embarrassment. But George had no excuse.

George didn't leave the house immediately. It was early summer, eight o'clock, and still light despite being overcast. He'd spent all morning at his chapel and would do for most of this evening. But first he needed to take himself upstairs and tidy away his belongings. Albert and Ronnie would need to use the room and he didn't want any trace of himself to be evident.

Clearing done, he quickly went very quietly down the stairs and let himself out into the street, closing the door gently behind him. For him, not going to war had nothing to do with being too scared. 'If it felt right, I'd volunteer, instantly,' he told himself. But it didn't feel right.

The words of his minister drummed in his brain as he hurried away from the house. *Though shalt not kill.* Yes, he believed that wholeheartedly and nothing was ever going to change it.

True, he'd recently had his share of white feathers being thrust at him by silly women, but with the teaching he'd received he knew he was strong enough to ignore their condemnation. Let them shower him with white feathers. Christ had been subjected to ridicule, pelted with vile rubbish, made to drag His cross to His place of execution, beaten all the way, but His resolve had remained strong. He was a lesson to others. And so He had died refusing to defend Himself, knowing He was right. And so did he, George Lovell, know he was right to take his stand in turn against evil.

How many times had he heard that old comment: 'If you saw your wife or daughter being violated by your enemy, or your children with a loaded pistol held to their heads, you'd soon change your mind.'

But they were wrong. Even as he leapt to their defence, his loved ones would be slaughtered, leaving him bereft and a traitor to his beliefs.

This his preacher had told him so many times. And he was right. But it didn't ease the shame he felt at his inability to face his brothers, ready to die for their loved ones, their country. Was he merely a coward after all, using his lay preacher's doctrine like a shield? He had to know; needed reassurance that he was doing the right thing for the right reason.

The first drops of a summer shower began to fall, making him lengthen his stride, setting his face towards the small hall where his mentor, Brother Joseph Wootton-Bennett, preached the word of God to his little congregation, the Followers of Christ.

He just hoped not to meet anyone on the way, especially a woman who, seeing a young, fit-looking man in civilian clothes, might easily get the wrong impression. He'd never had the courage to stand up and declare his beliefs, unlike Brother Joseph, who would have blazed away at any accuser, in his booming voice arguing anyone down with his beliefs, a strong-willed man others could look up to. He admired Wootton-Bennett immensely, at the same time trying not to acknowledge that the man was in his fifties, way above being called to war.

The rain was becoming a steady downpour, hopefully keeping people indoors. He felt grateful for the rain. He was running late and increased his speed, thrusting the episode with his brothers behind him.

Brother Joseph was alone when he got there. He was a smallish, thick-set man, slightly balding, with large ears, snub nose, thin lips and pale grey eyes that would widen alarmingly when he was wrapped in the throes of a fierce sermon. He was sitting at the table from where he preached, reading his Bible and jotting thoughts down in a little notebook. He looked up as George entered.

'My dear man! Our meeting ended minutes ago. I thought maybe you were unwell, though you seemed well enough at this morning's meeting.'

'My brothers came home on leave,' George excused himself. 'I felt I had to stay and talk to them.' It was a small lie – hardly a word said to them, in truth, before slinking away. 'This is why I'm here now. I need to speak to you.'

'You are harbouring doubts, having seen your brothers?'

George nodded, already feeling a traitor to this man's teaching. 'I'm not frightened of being killed or injured,' he burst out in his own defence, 'it's just that—'

'You are horrified that you may be robbed of your belief by the words and deeds of others, to whit, your brothers. So you have come here to be given strength to maintain your beliefs. But you already have that strength, my brother, believing in what the Bible tells us of our Saviour.'

'Yes, of course.'

'Then have no fear,' his mentor continued. 'Read, then read again the teachings of the Commandments that thou shalt not kill. And in Exodus, chapter twenty, verse thirteen of your Bible, it is said "thou shalt not kill". And in the gospels of St Matthew and of St Luke, our Lord during his Sermon on the mount uttered that very same law. How many more times need it to be said: Thou shalt not kill!' His grey eyes opened wide. 'May I also remind you, dear man, that St Matthew, chapter five, verse thirty-nine, tells us our Lord said: "Whosoever smite thee on thy cheek, turn to him the other also". And yet again, St Luke six, verse twenty-nine, Jesus said: "and unto him that smiteth thee on the one cheek offer also the other". Take heart, my son. Be you strong and believe in what you know is right. Those who doubt your motives, stare them in the face, just as our Lord Christ did before those who mocked him.'

He waited while George took several deep breaths to compose himself, then went on, 'Good man. Remember the words of the Old Testament and of Our Lord. They'll keep you strong when others mock you, call you coward.' He stepped back. 'Now off you go and face them all with good heart and strength of will, knowing you are right. God bless you, my dear man.'

With that he shook George by the hand before returning to his Bible and jottings, leaving George to walk from the hall, buoyed up to face whatever might come. No matter what others might say to him, he would never weaken again. A wonderful person was Joseph Wootton-Bennett, and tomorrow morning he would be back here to pray and sing with the others of the congregation.

After George had gone, Connie helped gather up the empty plates, taking them out to the kitchen.

Her mother was filling the washing-up bowl in the sink with boiling water from the kettle, cooling it to hand temperature with cold water from the tap. Connie took up a teacloth to dry the crockery and put it all neatly away as she always did. They'd usually chat as they worked, but this evening she said little, her mind on that kiss from Stephen Clayton.

'You're quiet tonight, love.' Her mother's voice startled her.

'Just thinking, Mum.'

'What?'

'Oh, nothing much.'

'Private?' Her mother laughed, but Connie didn't rise to the challenge.

'I might pop across to Cissie's,' she said, quickly changing the subject. 'Ask if she'd like to go to the pictures tomorrow night.'

Why had he done that, kissed her on the cheek like that? It wasn't the sort of thing a girl expects from her boss. In that brief peck she had felt the warmth of those lips against her skin, making her whole body tingle.

For him it might not have meant anything at all – a brief display of appreciation of her work, carrying him away for a second. He had probably considered it just a mere gesture. And he had not long been widowed, and was probably still grieving his loss.

But for her it had gone deeper than a mere gesture. She was in love with him. But what would such a man want with a girl like her?

Hurriedly she brushed the silly thoughts from her mind and, hanging the teacloth back on its hook by the door, went from the kitchen to comb her hair, put on a coat, and went back to say a final goodbye to her mother before she went to knock on Cissie's door.

Albert had already gone out, leaving while they were washing up, poking his head around the kitchen door saying apologetically that he was off to surprise his Edie.

'Don't mind, do you, Mum – you and Dad, I'm only just home, and—'

'Course we don't mind,' she'd said. 'You go and surprise her, love.'

His going had apparently given Ronnie food for thought. Ron had got up, stubbed his cigarette out in an ashtray and announced he might look some girl up whom he used to know, rather than going to the pub.

As Connie came into the room, she heard her dad say, 'And don't 'ave no truck with them seein' you're in civvies and coming funny. Tell 'em if they want to see your uniform it's bloody runnin' alive wiv bloody lice from the front line. Tell 'em they can put that in their bloody pipe and smoke it!'

'I will, Dad, don't you worry,' Ron laughed as he let himself out. The very second he'd gone, Mum picked up the ashtray to empty it, her nose wrinkling. The aroma of pipe smoke was far different, smoother, comforting even, much nicer than what the boys smoked. Connie couldn't help but smile.

Chapter Twelve

Edie's father answered the knock on his street door, amazed on seeing Albert standing there. 'Good God! Albert! Come in, son! Come in!' Raising his voice, he yelled over his shoulder: 'Edie, someone for you!' As they stood in the narrow passage, he asked, 'How come you're home, son?'

'Four days' leave,' Albert began, but there was no time to say more as Edie appeared in the passage.

Pulling up in shock at seeing him, she galvanised herself into action, almost throwing herself at him, the two clinging to each other, her father retreating, her mother's voice heard calling from the kitchen, 'Who is it, Edie?'

But the two had no interest in any other than themselves, lips locked in a long, hungry kiss.

'I had no idea you were coming home, darling,' Edie gasped as finally they broke away, breathless. 'I thought you were still over there.'

'Got leave,' he said, grinning. 'Four days – got to be back on Monday, got to leave here Sunday night to be back on time. You didn't get my letter?'

'No.'

'Soon as I was told I was being given leave, I wrote you one to tell you. Didn't want to give you a shock when I turned up.'

'It's a lovely shock, darling, it really is, the best shock ever.'

But this was no time for talking. Pulling her to him, he kissed her yet again, lingeringly, she hungrily returning his kisses while he murmured against her lips, 'I love you, my darling.' And she saying, 'I love you too.'

Having let himself out of the house, Ronnie stood wondering what on earth he should do. He'd so looked forward to going out for the evening, an evening of freedom, not stuck in a trench for forty-eight hours at a time; hemmed in by his comrades in arms while the artillery gave the enemy a good pasting; a constant bombardment that became hardly noticeable after a while; whistles ordering men over the top. Thank God he'd come back each time in one piece after every aborted advance.

Here in the street, all silent and still, the bombardment he'd become used to seemed now to be echoing in his head in the quiet night. There was no one to look up – all his mates were gone, joined up – and this sudden realisation that his evening could be spent alone. There was no one he knew any more.

He'd told Mum and Dad that he was going to look up a girl he knew. Some hope! He could possibly go for a drink in the Salmon and Ball, the big and usually busy pub under the railway arch in Bethnal Green Road. But what was the point of drinking alone, with no friends?

Besides, he wasn't in uniform. That still hung, filthy, in the backyard, Mum having hung it up on a hanger in the hope that the clean air would rid it of infestation. He'd forbidden her to try to wash off the dried mud, and he didn't want her handling it too much with the lice it held. In four or five days' time it would be just as filthy and lousy.

He'd heard of people mistaking any man seen in civvies for a coward, never stopping to find out whether he was home on leave and glad to be out of uniform for a while. All very well wearing one's uniform with pride, as many a serviceman did, but not what he'd come home in. No, not to go to the pub.

But where else? He suddenly thought of a girl he used to know. Dorothy Bacon.

She'd be about eighteen now, a few months younger than him. He used to like her a lot. Maybe he could ask her out if she was still around.

Hoping her family hadn't moved away, he took himself to where she used to live and tentatively knocked on her door. What if they'd moved? But it was she who answered, gazing down at him from the top of the two steps that led up to the house, her expression one of surprise.

'Ronnie? Is that you? What you doing here? But I thought you'd joined up ages ago.'

'I did.' He felt just a tiny bit rattled. This blooming business of must be seen in uniform or else. 'I'm in France, in the thick of it.' Why in God's name did he need to justify himself? 'I've been given four days' leave. They do that sometimes after you've had a dose of fighting at the front.' Justifying himself again! 'I've got to go back there. Leaving Sunday night, but while I'm 'ome, I thought I might look you up, see 'ow you are.'

Her face had broken into a smile. Was it relief? 'Well, you'd best come in. Me parents are down the pub. They always go there on Thursdays.'

Inside, he said, 'I thought you might like to go dancin' somewhere. It's not late. And it's still a bit light out there.'

She pulled a face. 'It's not that, Ronnie. It's lovely to see you. But with you not being in uniform . . .'

'I 'ad to leave it at 'ome,' he said quickly as she led the way into the front room. He was offered a seat on the rather dilapidated sofa and she sat herself down next to him. He went on talking. 'It's filthy – couldn't wear that here.' He made a feeble attempt at a joke: 'You'd've taken one look at me and shut the door in me face!'

To his joy, she laughed. 'No I wouldn't have.'

No, of course not. Filthy and lousy, he'd still have been wearing a soldier's uniform and she'd have looked proud instead of that sceptical look she had first offered him.

'I saw a bloke a couple of days ago who wasn't in uniform,' she went on. 'He was buying something in the shop where I work. Some customers began calling him a coward. Then one of their wives went and stuck a white feather in his breast pocket. The way he slunk out of that shop made me feel ever so embarrassed for 'im. He never said a word, just slunk out. I mean, who knows, he might have been in the forces, like you, on leave and just wanted to get back into civilian gear. Or he might not have been fit enough to be taken in the forces, though he looked 'orright to me. I think I've heard that some soldiers put on special armbands to show they're on leave when they put on civvies.'

The wind was spilling out of his sails with every word she spoke and he wished he hadn't come round here at all. But she was still talking.

'I know you wouldn't have slunk out like that, Ronnie. You'd've walloped into one of 'em. I think you're a real hero, joining up like you did, and you still being underage when you did.' He was aware of her gazing sideways at him as she sat there beside him. 'I often think about you and wonder how you got on and where you are,' she went on in a soft, dreamy tone. 'I've not seen you for such a long time but I think about you a lot. Always did, right from school when I first knew you.' She leaned against him a little. 'I hoped you might come to see me before you left. But you never did.'

She sighed deeply, then turned to him, giving him a lovely smile, changing the subject self-consciously.

'Whyn't you take off your jacket? It's ever so warm in here. It's been a really close day, despite the rain, and we always keep the windows closed of an evening, especially when me mum and dad go out. They get worried in case someone gets in. You never know, do you? You might as well take it off. I'll hang it up for you.'

It *was* warm in here. Obligingly, he slipped out of his jacket, which she took and hung up on a hook behind the door, coming back to sit next to him again, her arm touching his. Through his shirt sleeve he could feel the warmth of her skin and something stirred in him, a feeling that instantly had him on his guard. He had no right to feel like this about her.

'It was such a surprise seeing you after all this time,' she murmured, 'and ever so nice seeing you on your own. We was always with lots of friends and it's nice

107

just to be just the two of us. It's ever so early still and Mum and Dad won't be 'ome till the pubs shut. That's hours away yet.'

Her sitting so close to him was beginning to heighten that sensation inside him and he compressed his lips to control it as she went on. 'I was really upset when I heard you'd joined up. That's when I realised I'd fancied you for years – ever since we left school. It sounds silly, but it's true. I always wanted to tell you that but when you went and joined up, that was when I really wished I had. Ain't that silly? But now you're here and it feels just right to tell you. And you did have a soft spot for me, didn't you, Ronnie?'

Yes, he had. At school she looked older than him, as girls often do, and his eyes would follow her slim, lithe figure. Fifteen, sixteen, always with groups of mates, other things to do, but he'd all but forgotten about her until this evening. Now, with her hand on his knee, the sensation it provoked growing ever stronger, he turned and kissed her. It was like magic as she placed her hand behind his head, preventing him from pulling away, and returning his kiss with such strength that he had to fight to stop himself pushing her down beneath him on the sofa. Seconds later, he pulled away from her, almost fiercely.

'I'm sorry, Dorothy, I didn't mean to do that.'

She'd sat back, not looking at him, her lips forming a little pout.

'I'm sorry too,' she said. 'I thought . . . Well, I thought . . .' She let her words die away, then began again: 'I just . . .' Again she lapsed into silence, leaving them both sitting in silence.

He was about to say that he should go, when finally she said, 'I feel a real idiot, telling you how I felt.'

'Don't feel like that,' he said lamely.

'But I shouldn't've come out with it like that. It must've sounded so daft and so embarrassing and so forward.'

'It wasn't.' He needed to say something else. 'I've always liked you, Dorothy. More than liked . . .' It was hard to explain how he was feeling. 'The way you say you felt about me,' he began again. 'I think I feel the same about you. But what with the war and me going into the forces, I put so much to one side. Then I thought of you this evening and suddenly I wanted to come to see you, see if you still lived here. And you do. And I'm so glad. And I really want—'

He broke off, realising he must sound a complete idiot. Then he heard himself saying, 'Can I see you again? I'd like to. Before I go back Sunday night.' He found himself out of breath in pent-up anticipation, and looked quickly at her to glean her reaction, saw those liquid brown eyes of hers, that shapely face, dark hair bobbed in the new style, and he knew: this was the girl he'd like to be with for the rest of his life.

She was gazing at him. He found himself waiting for a rejection. But instead she said, 'On Sunday? What time?' It was a simple question.

'Let's make it early,' he said, his heart racing.

On Sunday, they'd have the whole day together until six when he'd have to leave. They could have dinner out somewhere – get to know each other better. He would ask if he could write to her and if she would write to him. And who knows . . .

'I'll call for you about ten o'clock?'

'Lovely,' she said and leaned her head on his shoulder. It was just as if they'd been together for years.

'You're my bloke now, aren't you?' she said suddenly. The way she said it made him feel he could have sailed on the clouds. 'I know I'm seeing you on Sunday, but would it be all right if I come to the station and see you off?'

The request was so poignant that it felt they'd been together for years rather than just an hour or two. The next leave he got, whenever that would be, he'd be straight round to her house; he'd meet her parents and gain their blessing for her to be his. Meantime he'd write to her and she'd write to him. In time he would propose to her, buy her an engagement ring, and when this war was over they'd get married, find themselves a little place to live, settle down, raise a family. With the war over, please God, life would be golden. Such a wonderful dream. He found himself determined to make it a reality.

Sunday morning he took her behind a park shelter, and she in turn, not having intended to, gave herself to him with tiny squeaks and sighs.

'I must let Elsie and Lillian know that Ronnie and Bertie are home,' Mum said early Sunday morning. The two boys were in bed still, taking advantage of luxuriating between clean sheets and a soft mattress, with no need to rise too early and no George to get under their skin.

Telling Dad where she was off to, she hurried away immediately after breakfast, first to Elsie's, then on to Lillian's, Connie going with her for want of something better to do.

For Connie, Sundays always seemed to drag, these days. It had become a joy to get back to work, to see Stephen, to catch glimpses of him in his office, to have him come and speak to her.

'They'd be so upset if we didn't tell them,' Mum was saying as they hurried the few streets to convey the news. 'There ain't much time. Albert's out with Edie this afternoon and Ronnie said he was seeing someone he'd not met for a long while and they're having dinner out. So it's this morning or nothing. Four days' leave doesn't give anyone time for anything,' Mum gabbled breathlessly as they hurried back home with the girls. 'So much time already taken up them getting home, and they've got to leave at six to be back by Monday. Today's the only time you'll get to see them. They'll both be out this afternoon cos Albert's taking his Edie out, and Ronnie says he's taking some girl he's met out for Sunday dinner and they 'ave to be back on the ship on time or they'll be in trouble.' Connie saw tears in her mother's eyes as she hurried on explaining.

They hadn't needed to be told twice. Elsie had snatched off her apron as soon as she heard, leaving her husband Harry in charge of little Henry, dragging a comb through her hair, grabbing her front door key and banging the door shut behind her, following Mum out to go round to Lillian's house two streets away to convey the news to her. Lillian handed over baby James to her husband Jim and bustled out behind her sisters and their mother.

Back at home, Connie stood by as her sisters threw themselves at their brothers. It was a strange, unsettling morning, filled with bursts of emotion. She found herself dreading the final farewells: Mum's eyes glistening,

111

trying hard not to shed her tears; Dad clearing his throat and blowing his nose. Even now her sisters were clinging to the two boys as if they would never see them again, giving their emotion full volume.

They were in full flow as Albert made ready to go to meet Edie, the only chance they'd have to be alone to say a private goodbye. Later Edie would go with him to see him off on the train, but those goodbyes, with other servicemen saying farewell to their own families and loved ones, wouldn't be private. They needed their time together now.

Of George, there had been no sign all day. He'd not come home this morning after staying overnight at a friend's house. When he finally appeared just before his brothers were due to leave, his excuse for not returning earlier was that he'd had to stay and help his pastor get ready for the eleven o'clock service and for conveni-ence's sake had accepted his friend's offer of dinner before the afternoon Sunday School. He hoped Mum hadn't minded but Sunday was a busy time. She didn't reply, merely got on with making sandwiches for the other two on their journey. Leaving at six this evening so as to be there the following day, George only had hardly half an hour with them, thus escaping any drawn-out awkwardness.

His mother, her mind more on seeing her gallant sons off, chose not to even acknowledge him. His dad seemed to have forgotten he even existed. Not that George made any effort to address him. On the only occasion he did, he was met with a 'Humph!' and a dismissive shrug.

Seeing it, Connie could hardly ignore a feeling of contempt coupled with bewilderment. How he could so lightly sidestep his duty when his own brothers were out there fighting and dying for their country . . . No! Not dying. She felt herself cringe. If that ever happened, she would curse him for the rest of her days, even as she silently and fervently prayed that nothing so awful would happen to them.

As for George, one day she promised herself that she would sketch what she saw on his face, if, unable to help herself she suddenly asked why he'd chosen to detach himself from what was every young man's duty in these desperate times.

In a way, however, he was not getting away with it lightly as far as Mum was concerned. For some time now he'd had the bed he and his brothers had shared all to himself. But that night, after the boys returned to war from leave, Mum had put her foot down.

'I don't see why he should be comfortable with a room all to himself when Ron and Bertie returned home with lice,' she said to Connie. 'He can sleep down here and you can use the boys' bedroom upstairs while they're away.'

It was wonderful: a room all to herself, if only temporarily while Ronnie and Albert were away. George, compelled to obey Mum, was getting no more than he deserved.

Chapter Thirteen

July 1915

It had been over a month since they had returned home from leave, but Ronnie couldn't get his brother George out of his mind.

He wanted to think of Dorothy, dwell on how they'd made love behind the park shelter, of the long letter he'd written to her and how long before hers to him arrived.

Instead all that kept invading those thoughts was the way his brother George had stood in the doorway back at home, grinning like a Cheshire cat. 'Sorry, didn't mean to disturb.'

And Albert saying coldly, 'What makes you think you're disturbing us, George?'

'Meant to be home earlier but a lot's been going on.' George either hadn't noticed the sarcasm or had chosen to ignore it. 'It's been a real busy day.'

'Too busy, George,' Albert had sneered, 'for a farewell chat to your brothers before they go back to fight for their country?'

George had winced. 'At least I'm here in time to say cheerio.'

'In time to save you suffering from a guilty conscience, eh?' Albert had grated.

Ron had felt himself cringe. He too felt nothing but contempt for his eldest brother but would never have shown it like Bert had. But the more he thought of the incident, the angrier he was growing, because the memory kept pushing away thoughts of Dorothy and those last exquisite moments together.

He'd thought of what he was going back to while George stayed at home, protected by the shield of his so-called beliefs. How could a man shrink from being a man yet still endure the scorn of those who had gone to fight? Was that a kind of courage? If so, it wasn't the courage Ron wanted to have.

Lying on an unforgiving army bed next to Albert's in a billet some miles behind the front line, Ron tried not to think of tomorrow. Orders were that their unit wouldn't be going back to Ypres where they'd been supporting the Belgium troops, but would march all the way down to Loos in France to fight alongside the French there. He fervently prayed to survive, to return home to Dorothy, alive, unhurt, pick up where they'd left off. To lose out now horrified him more than the carnage of a front line trench.

He'd not told his parents about Dorothy; too early, despite their frantic union behind the park shelter. Telling Mum he'd met someone would just have her saying, 'You shouldn't let yourself get too involved with any girl, love, not the way things are.' But he had told Connie and she had grinned and said how happy she was for him and that she'd make friends with her so that she wouldn't feel out of things. 'In time I'll ask her if she'd like to come and meet us all.'

Sitting at her desk, Connie's mind was miles away. Ronnie had a girlfriend now. Albert had Edie. She had no one. Would Stephen Clayton one day be hers? She doubted it. But in December she'd be eighteen. Admittedly he would be one year older too, but as time went on, nine years' difference wouldn't be seen to matter so much.

This morning he'd sent her out with a photographer, Kenneth Fenton, to record the devastation from a zeppelin raid last night. She'd stood a little removed, unnoticed, sketching the scene being played out a little way off but not so far off as to be unable to record the expressions on the faces of those whose homes had been destroyed, whose treasured possessions had been smashed, whose lives had been wrecked. It was heart-breaking. Wars took place elsewhere. British soldiers faced the enemy in distant corners of the earth, not here, not civilians here, not on British soil.

Several newspapers had been there, popping cameras being met by blank expressions of half-concealed anger at being exposed to the cold press. That was where she could score over the camera, her silent pencil catching the real soul of those devastated people. Nothing else could do that and she had silently thanked Stephen Clayton for his belief in her and her talent. But it went deeper, she was certain – in the way he would look at her of late, the way his vivid blue eyes lingered, to switch away abruptly as their eyes met.

Now she gazed down at a sketch she'd surreptitiously done of him a few moments ago. He seemed to have liked the ones she'd done of those poor people this morning and was now with his chief editor showing them to him – he himself having taken a deep breath from wonder and excitement as he viewed them.

She curbed the thrill that passed through her, aware that it came at the expense of the misery of others: homeless, everything they'd owned now swept away. Where would they go? Worse, who had they lost? Not a thing to rejoice about on her own account.

The zeppelin raid had been around midnight. A couple of miles east of where it had let loose its bombs, she, Mum and Dad and half the street had come out of their tenements to stand on the pavement watching the thing glide past overhead, low in the sky. There'd been more than one, but that one had passed directly overhead, with all those beneath it holding their breath. At what seemed a snail's pace, its ghostly shape gave out a low throbbing that vibrated inside her chest. Searchlights swept the black sky, seeking to trap it in a criss-cross of light and bring it down with shellfire. Impervious, it glided on over the rooftops. Mum had whispered, 'Hope it don't decide to drop its load on us,' and Dad had replied, 'Expect they're aiming fer the City, more like.'

But there had been one small moment that had made her smile, that made her smile now as she thought back on it.

Standing in the dark street alongside their neighbours, most having left their beds lest a bomb fell, hurriedly slipping a coat over pyjamas, feet into slippers to come out and stare up at that gliding instrument of death, her mother had given her a nudge with an elbow, inclining her head towards where several neighbours stood together. 'Take a gander at old Wilkins over there,' she'd hissed.

And there was old Wilkins, well into his eighties, bent of knee, bow-legged, standing in nothing but his vest and long johns, his long, wispy-haired chin jutting out as he gazed upwards. It had been hard to suppress a giggle, the spine-chilling zeppelin forgotten for a moment.

Connie smiled now at the recollection. But watching the thing go over always carried a weight of anxiety, and as it continued to glide on its way to another part of London, a sigh of relief had been heard all round.

Speculation broke out on who would get it. Old Man Wilkins had toddled back indoors. After a few good-nights, an exchange of hope that nothing crucial would be hit, everyone had melted back indoors to bed, the danger past, but maybe not for those further west.

Going back indoors to her bed, she had heard faint explosions, shivered at the thought of devastation for someone and had said a little silent prayer that lives had been spared on this occasion.

Then this morning, Stephen Clayton had approached, laying a hand on her arm, its warmth penetrating the long sleeve of her summer dress to send a thrill coursing through her veins, and leaning close with a broad grin to tell her he'd managed to arrange for her to go with young Ken Fenton to one of the bombed homes and do some sketches.

'You don't know how much I am banking on you, Connie,' he'd said, a thrill rushing through her as he had not called her Miss Lovell. 'This could be the making of you. Would you care to have dinner with me this evening, somewhere nice, where we can talk about your future here on the paper?'

Her future, here on the paper. Hadn't that already been decided? She felt she was doing well, and he wouldn't take her out to dinner to censure her. She'd hardly been able to answer; she had merely nodded instead, felt him squeeze her arm lightly, saying he intended to show her sketches to Mr Mathieson, hopefully to gain his approval for them to appear in tomorrow's *London Herald*.

'Fingers crossed,' were his parting words, but all she was aware of was the warmth of that somewhat intimate pressure on her arm which she could still feel.

Now he was back, triumph spread across his handsome face. 'We've got Mathieson's approval! In fact he said you're a marvel. He said this sort of thing could get the paper selling like hot cakes as our readers get to see more. What do you think of that, my dear?'

His excitement transferred itself to her but began to dim a little as common sense took over.

Asking her to have dinner with him, it could only have to do with work. And here she'd been kidding herself that it could be something more. Even so, her heart racing, she kept imagining being seated opposite him in a lovely restaurant, the two of them drinking wine, eyes on each other . . .

Stupid fool! Her mind snapped back, the cigarette-smoke-filled news office seeming to slap her in the face: the clacking of typewriters, the ringing of telephones, deep male voices talking shop, every now and again a female voice – three women working here beside herself, taking the place of men who had joined up.

Her old friend Sybil had written saying she was on a factory line filling shells with explosives. 'Paid men's wages,' she'd written, 'thirty-two bob a week, three quid for nights, work round the clock to keep up with demand.'

Connie pulled her mind back to Mr Clayton. Could she dare think this dinner date was more than just business? He squeezing her arm – it could have been merely a hopeful outcome to his negotiating with his superior. But asking her to have dinner with him – just to discuss how her talent could best serve his paper? That could have been done in the office, surely? There were other signs: the times she'd noticed him studying her from the window between his office and the newsroom. If she met his gaze, he'd turn away to his desk, leaving her to wonder why he'd been looking at her.

It should have raised her hopes. Instead it only served to confuse her. But this invitation had come right out of the blue; dare she bring herself to believe it to be anything other than about work and how her future career would go? But what if it had to do with something else, something she would love to happen? As to the chief editor's acceptance of her sketches, she could hardly wait to get home to tell Mum and Dad her good news.

Letting herself into the kitchen by the back door, she saw the girl sitting at the table; Mum was standing beside her. The girl had her head bent but Connie could see she'd been crying, was still tearful, in fact.

'This is Dorothy,' Mum announced, her expression grim. 'Her and our Ronnie met when he was home on his last leave. Been writing to each other every week, she says, since he went back.' Connie instantly was alarmed that something had happened to her brother, but taking a fortifying breath, her mother went on, 'He's said nothing to us about it but it seems she's missed her monthly since he went back and her people 'ave turned her out, don't want nothing to do with her. Her own mother – I ask you! She come 'ere 'cos she was desperate.'

The girl looked up, her tear-stained face defensive, her voice small and shaky. 'I didn't know where else to go.'

Mum glanced down at her. 'I'm not going off at you, love.' Then she looked at Connie. 'I couldn't turn her away. I left her 'ere and went straight round to her people and gave her mother a good piece of my mind.'

The thought of her mother giving anyone a good piece of her mind made Connie smile. Even though on the whole she was a quiet-tempered person, her mum could have her moments. But she kept a straight face, feeling for the distraught girl. She nearly came out with, 'It is Ronnie's?' but thought better of it.

'So what're you going to do?' she asked instead.

'Take her in. What else can I do? She ain't got nowhere else to go, poor thing.'

Connie made to ask where she'd be sleeping but her mother got there before her. 'She can 'ave the boys' room while they're not here. I've got to ask you if you'd have the bed down here again until we sort something out.'

'What about George? Where will he sleep?'

'He'll have to put up with the sofa in the front room,' said her mother, adding with a wry smile, 'when he's home. He's hardly ever here anyway.'

George more usually stayed at one of his chapel friend's homes.

So that was it, down in the back room again, and for how long this time? Mum was always ready to help any

121

poor soul in trouble, and this poor soul claimed that she was carrying her first grandchild too. 'What about when the baby arrives?' she asked, to which Mum shrugged. 'We'll come to that when it happens.'

'Does Ronnie know?' she asked, not caring that the girl heard.

'She wrote telling 'im and he wrote back saying he's over the moon, though he's not mentioned it in his letters to us.'

'How does he know if it's his?' That was cruel, but she felt angry, at the girl and at her Mum for being so gullible.

Her mother's sharp voice startled her. 'He'll know. She's missed her monthlies and says she's always so regular. She has other signs as well, and it's been since our Ronnie and her got together, so that adds up. She'll 'ave it around March and if that don't prove . . .' She let the rest go unsaid.

Chastened, Connie put that aside. 'What about Dad?'

'I'll deal with your dad,' came the reply, and the look on her mum's face told Connie that Dad would knuckle down once he'd let off steam. Mum was a quiet woman but when she wanted her way she got it.

The girl had stopped crying. Looking from one to the other, she offered Connie a small tremulous apologetic smile, and in that instant Connie found herself liking her.

Heavy barrage began making itself heard miles before they ever reached their destination, having already done a hundred or more miles from Loos. 'Don't sound too 'ealthy, do it?' Ronnie hissed to Albert marching beside him.

'I think it's ours,' Albert whispered back, keeping his eyes on the soldier in front, hoping he was still moving in a reasonably straight line and not meandering all over the place in his weariness, to which his brother muttered, 'Just 'ope so, that's all.'

'All I want is to lie down and put me feet up. Boots are killin' me.'

'Mine too,' sighed Ronnie.

What had started as a brisk march had become little more than a trudge after two days of it. Even so it had been a relief to be told to report for this journey and for a while at least escape this endless round of slaughter. Though what they would meet at the end of this trek was now beginning to announce itself from the energetic power of the distant heavy gunfire.

They hadn't exactly been told where they were going, but south had been the general direction, and finally the name Somme had been uttered, to which they were drawing ever closer and to another battle area.

'Be glad when we get there, that's all, barrage or no barrage,' Ronnie added and fell silent, concentrating on his painful feet in his sweaty boots and stinking wet socks.

Despite the days of walking through the heat of summer, it had been an indescribable relief to be ordered away from the devastation that had been Loos: the unending confusion of enemy bombardment, snipers, being ordered over the top time after time only to retreat, some in one piece, some not at all – God knows how he and Bert had survived, hardly a scratch except from tangled barbed wire, while all around men went down writhing, screaming, their agonies ignored in the orders to get back, while others went down without a murmur to lie silent in death.

Attempt after attempt to reach let alone overpower the enemy had proved little more than a blood bath.

Suddenly their company had been ordered out, no reason given, told to return to their billets five or six miles to the rear to pack and make ready to march. It had been a relief – one that had stayed with them for most of the trek south. But the noise of heavy gunfire up ahead was starting to shatter that relief. Yet in another way, it would be a relief to get there, throw themselves down in a new billet and get some proper food down them.

'I could sleep for a week,' Bert muttered as they queued for the mash and bully beef that was sending out such appetising smells to set every stomach rumbling.

Ron grinned. 'Sleep – you'll be lucky. I bet we'll get just enough time to drop our stuff and then march to the front.'

'Not after two days of bloody footslogging. I could sleep till the cows come 'ome.'

Ron sighed. 'We'll see.'

But Bert was right. Given decent if hard beds to flop down on, most lost themselves instantly to fill the barrack with snores and grunts.

That night was bliss. They were oblivious of the continuous bombardment some five miles away, five miles they'd be ordered to cover, taking them to the front line. *What we'll find there, God only knows, but I can guess*, was Albert's last thought before he fell into a deep sleep to dream of walking arm in arm with Edie by the Serpentine on a bright, sunny, London summer's day.

Despite desperate weariness, Ronnie hadn't dropped off straight away. He laid awake, thinking of the letter he'd had just before leaving Loos. Had they left one day earlier, Dorothy's letter wouldn't have got to him, might never have reached him, or not for weeks, months maybe. By then he could have been . . .

Hastily he turned from that thought and concentrated instead on the wording of her letter, and especially on the way she had begun: 'My darling Ronnie . . .'

In it she'd expressed how much she'd loved being with him, that she hoped it would go on for ever and ever; had been thinking of him every minute of every hour of every day. He'd written as often as he could, scrawling notes to her between going over the top or helping clear the trench of cigarette ends, matches and other debris soldiers dropped at their feet while cooped up in a man-made, narrow, twisting ditch that went on for ever, hundreds of men to each section.

In obedience to the shrill whistles ordering them all over the top into that nightmare of insanity, he'd find himself repeating her name: Dorothy, Dorothy, Dorothy . . . as bullets flew, praying none would find him and end his hopes of ever seeing her again. Each man had his prayer; his was to see her again. But now he had her letter saying she that she was pregnant, that it was his. That leave, it could only be his.

His eyes slowly closed, that thought of her filling him with love, that she was his and he was hers, that she would wait for him and that she was having his baby. She'd written that after her own mother had thrown her out as a strumpet, Mum had taken her in. To Ronnie, it felt as if they were already married. As soon as he was given leave, they would make it official.

Chapter Fourteen

August 1915

It had been three weeks since the zeppelin raid, and the results of the paper's chief editor's opinion of her sketches had reaped benefits – Connie had found herself sent out three times this week.

Today Stephen had handed to her a small pile of her sketches, cut from different editions, his handsome face wreathed in smiles as he laid them before her on her desk, standing back to see her reaction.

'Looks like your name will soon get known,' he whispered, leaning towards her so only she could hear him above the sounds of the office. He was leaning so close that she could feel his breath on her cheek. 'I think our readers will start to look for your sketches,' he went on, as she felt her own pride well up, knowing that at last she was being looked upon as possessing some degree of usefulness.

It was all she'd ever wanted – to be a success at something. She might even get a wage rise, and be able to give more to her mother. She'd had a lean time of it of late, with her sons away bringing in no money. And George – no one counted on George any more as he existed on casual work so it wouldn't clash with his chapel attendances. Refusing to heed the calls for young men to defend their country, he continued to hide behind the shield of that so-called religious belief of his.

But his time was coming, she thought with a tiny prick of satisfaction. Military conscription had now come into force: single men between eighteen and forty-one who'd not previously volunteered had been ordered to register. But George was still defending his right to have nothing to do with war, fiercely declaring his beliefs and causing the worst family upheaval she could ever remember. Even Albert and Ronnie volunteering hadn't had the impact this one had. It was Dad who'd put his foot down just three weeks ago.

'Beliefs, be buggered!' he'd exploded. 'Too bloody scared to go and fight for his country, he ain't no son of mine and if he insists on cowering be'ind his bloody silly religion, then he can find somewhere else to live – 'e ain't living 'ere no more. An 'e ain't no bloody son of mine!'

Mum put in that he was their flesh and blood no matter what, but her entreaties hadn't moved him. Connie had never heard her father speak so strongly but George had moved out without argument. No one asked where he was living, maybe with a like-minded companion, though he'd left a forwarding address if any letters came to him. No one had attempted to contact him. Mum might have but for Dad being so adamant that he was no longer a member of this family.

'We've two sons fighting and we can hold our heads up and be proud, and I ain't 'aving that coward pullin' this family down and showin' us up!'

George's absence meant that, now with Dorothy staying with them, the house didn't feel so full. Dorothy was a constant presence, helping out whenever she could, but wary and quiet whenever she was in the same room as Connie's dad.

Connie turned her thoughts back to the present. She gazed at the cuttings Stephen Clayton had handed her; she couldn't wait to show them to her parents. And tonight she would be having dinner with him. It was to have been weeks ago but had been cancelled due to some work that had come up. It was probably only to do with her work, her future here, nothing more. Even so it was exciting to know he was taking such interest in her, if only under orders from his boss. She told herself not to get too carried away by excitement. Strictly work, nothing more.

It had been about work, though not entirely.

It was arranged they go to dinner straight from the office. Connie's main concern had been letting Mum know in case she worried. She had rushed home during her lunch hour to say she was going out straight from work with a couple of friends.

At home she had quickly changed into a nicer frock, with Mum asking, 'Somewhere special, then, love?' to which she'd answered that they were going dancing, a little group of them from work. Mum said protectively, 'Well, take care of yourself, love, don't let any boy take you away from your friends. You keep with 'em. Safer like that,' as if she was still fifteen, not coming up to eighteen. 'And if there's a zeppelin raid, you take cover quick smart.'

'I will, Mum,' she'd said, giving her a kiss on the cheek before rushing off to get back within her hour's break.

Now she sat opposite Stephen Clayton in her best frock but feeling it far from suitable as she cast glances around the posh restaurant. Leaving him to choose from the expensive menu, she sat with eyes trained on the spotless white tablecloth, embarrassed with herself.

'You look very nice, Connie,' he'd said as he helped her off with her coat to hand to the young lady behind the grand-looking cloakroom desk.

Until then she'd not been able to find much to say to him at all, other than make brief responses when he'd said, 'I've ordered a taxi for us' and 'Thank heaven it's a decent evening, warm for once, and no rain' and 'I think you'll like this restaurant – a favourite of mine.' Out of the office she was unable to find any suitable reply that wouldn't make her feel stupid.

Having him tell her that she looked nice – her in this ordinary frock while all about them were people in what looked like evening attire – had the instant effect of raising her spirits, making her feel more hopeful that this invitation might actually have nothing to do with work after all.

She'd grown a little more relaxed as he'd advised her on what to order from the menu the waiter handed them.

As they waited for their meal to arrive he ordered red wine to go with the main meal and a sweeter wine with the second course. He seemed so at ease as he chatted lightly on this and that. She listened, intrigued by the light sound of his voice as he mentioned the way food shortages were affecting restaurants.

'But a good high-class restaurateur usually knows how to come by the *odd* luxury.' He gave a chuckle at the word 'odd' and she found herself laughing with him.

In that moment he became suddenly serious, regarding her closely. 'You know, Connie, you've a lovely rippling sort of laugh . . . and a really wonderful smile.'

Instantly she felt her cheeks flush, grow warm. Unable to respond, she clutched her wine, unused to it, sipping it a little too fast, feeling it catch in her throat.

They ate in relative silence. She had not tasted anything like the meal he had ordered for her in her life, yet it was hard to eat for nervousness until she finally pushed it away only half eaten.

'You've eaten hardly anything,' he observed, to which she hurriedly said, 'That starter filled me up, it was so good.' He laughed, pushing away his own sweet, unfinished.

As the waiter removed the plates, Stephen sat back in his chair for a second then leaned towards her.

'Mr Mathieson is finally coming round to my way of thinking – that you're an asset to the paper and that your sketches have been part of the reason why our circulation is increasing. However, he's a cautious man, is our chief editor, so – against my advice – rather than making you a fully paid-up member of the editorial department, he wants to continue with the trial period for a little longer.'

Connie felt her heart sink. So this *was* purely a business dinner. Mr Clayton had no interest in her other than seeing her as an asset to his paper. A weight settled on her heart but she managed to smile.

She wanted to hate him but her heart was crying that she loved him, silly fool that she was. And now she would have to sit here, opposite him – pretending to have enjoyed her dinner, sip at the brandy he'd ordered, which bit at her throat, and smile as if no other thought had ever been in her head. She could hardly wait for this evening to be over so she could go home to bed and cry herself to sleep. Stupid!

She hardly heard Stephen as he spoke of his beloved paper, of the big things he had in mind for her. 'I intend to have them send you out on lots of assignments,' he ploughed on, 'not just the dramatic ones but pleasant ones as well. Once Mathieson gets used to the idea of a woman doing such a job, he'll let me have full rein on the assignments I give you. I'm sure that this could be a big seller – I can definitely see it lifting off.'

It was a deep relief to finally leave. He had insisted on seeing her home in the taxi, even getting out to help her down, the touch of his hand sending a stupid thrill through her entire body. She was about to say a stiff goodnight when she realised he was still holding her hand.

'Connie,' he began as she hesitated. 'Would you care to have dinner again next Friday?'

As she hesitated in surprise more than anything else, he hurried on.

'Say no if you don't want to. I'll understand. But Connie, there's something I need to say to you. It's nothing to do with work, something much more important, personal, to do with you and me.'

As she made to reply, confused, he held up a hand. 'Not now. Leave it till next week. I hope to have your answer then. But I hope—' He broke off suddenly,

131

adding, 'Let's leave it till next week. This is the wrong time to say what I need to say, what I need to explain, before you . . .'

To her surprise he leaned towards her and taking her lightly by the shoulders, touched her cheek with his lips, only for split second, his breath sweet. Then he hurried back into the taxi, it clattering off leaving her standing alone on the pavement.

Her parents were still up, and so there was no chance to go to bed in the corner to think on what had transpired moments ago.

Instead, saying she needed to concentrate on some sketches she'd done for her employers, she made for the front drawing room, which was seldom used except for some special party or visitors.

In its cold, clammy atmosphere she gave herself up to quiet tears, even now uncertain whether she should believe what Stephen had seemed to be intimating, yet wanting so much to believe that he really must love her.

Connie sat opposite Stephen in another wonderful restaurant, the low babble of other diners lost in conversation. Their second date – if that's what it was. Many in uniform, Stephen wore a special armband declaring him exempt from military service.

The meal was delicious. If her parents could see what had been placed in front of her, they'd have a fit. She'd meant to make the most of it yet found herself able to eat only half again, unused to such fine food. Maybe also because her insides felt all jangled being out with the man who'd occupied her private thoughts these last few months. Yet all they talked about was work.

With food shortages, even bread had gone up to almost twice its previous price; shops had little to sell; the Government was still threatening military conscription; all sorts had been drafted into the forces, even women to work in munitions factories and on farms helping the war effort.

She became aware Stephen was talking to her. 'Sorry, I didn't mean to start talking shop. I just want to take you out, Connie, somewhere nice. So what about seeing a show? What do you fancy? A play, drama, comedy; vaudeville; plenty of singing and dancing, comedians thrown in, that'd cheer us both up, how about that?'

He smiled as she shrugged. 'We'll do vaudeville, then, shall we?'

She nodded. She had to admit she enjoyed it. Stephen laughed at the comedian, joining in with the singing of topical songs: 'Pack Up Your Troubles', 'Take Me Back To Dear Old Blighty' and 'Keep the Home Fires Burning'. And he held her hand. He also bought her a small box of chocolates, though how he had managed to find them in these times, she'd no idea, nor did she ask except to thank him and say how nice it was of him.

Going home in the taxi, she half expected him to take her hand as he'd done in the theatre but he sat very still beside her, not touching her at all as he mostly gazed out of the window, she finally doing the same on her side, her mind in turmoil. She had looked forward to this night, expecting a wonderful evening, but it had become a sham. After last week, the way he'd touched her cheek with his lips – was that after all just friendliness? Though to her, the kiss hadn't seemed at all like that. And the words he'd murmured . . .

When finally he did find something to say, it was simply to mention how important it was for the *London Herald* to keep up the morale of its readership. Then he'd lapse into silence, one that Connie didn't feel she could break.

'Shame about young Ken Fenton going.' His voice came out of the gloom.

Kenneth Fenton was the young photographer she'd often accompanied, and the two got on well together, much better than the paper's older men, who seemed so often to take exception to a young woman being with them. Ken had finally decided to sign on.

'We're going to miss him. He was a damned good photographer,' Stephen continued as if they were talking at her desk.

'Was?' she said tartly. 'You make it sound as if his life has already been written off.'

'I didn't mean it that way, Connie,' he said like a small boy who'd been reprimanded. 'That's what I find so wonderful about you, Connie. You're sensitive, kind; you worry about people.'

Faintly embarrassed, she didn't reply and felt him sit back to resume looking out of his window while she returned to gazing out of hers. They could have been strangers.

Recognising the corner of her street coming up, she sat up ready.

Sensing the movement, he turned to her and leaning forward, tapped on the little window that divided them from the cabbie. 'Pull up here, please.'

As he did last time he said goodbye some doors from her home. She didn't have a front door key yet, not until that recognised age of twenty-one. He'd taken her arm and it felt so nice as they walked along the street in silence. Then he stopped and took her hand.

'Connie,' he began, 'There's something I need to tell you. Please don't take this the wrong way, but I've . . .' He paused then began again. 'It's that I've had feelings for you for some time – well, right from when you first came into my office, but I didn't truly heed it then and you were so young. I even rebuked myself for it.' He took a deep breath before continuing. 'I found it nigh on impossible to get over losing my wife. When you came for your interview that day, I was still grieving, after over two years. Then you were shown into my office and something changed. Like a breath of fresh air, though I didn't recognise it at the time, but it felt as if the grief I'd been clinging to seemed to melt away.'

Again he paused. She waited, silently. 'Since then,' he continued, 'my feelings for you have mounted but I've found it hard to convey what I feel.'

His voice faded; his hand let go of hers to transfer itself gently to the back of her neck and just as gently eased her face towards his.

She let it happen, felt his lips close very lightly on hers, no sudden passion, just a gentle pressing of his lips against hers and when she didn't pull away, the pressure grew more certain and she knew then that this wasn't something that had suddenly come upon them, that it had been growing over all these months, each unaware of the other's feelings. Now suddenly she wanted to taste the fruit, certain that he did too.

Behind them was an alley: little more than a gap, one of several that occasionally broke the line of tenements

135

in this street, a mere footpath by which homes could be entered by the back door. Just a small movement backwards would take them out of sight of any prying eyes.

She felt her heart begin to pound as together they eased towards the dark, narrow space. A sudden fear caught her: she thought of Dorothy and her predicament, and felt her body tense. He must have felt it too and instantly broke away.

'Connie, I'm so sorry. I wasn't thinking.'

His voice faded as they stood apart now. It felt like the aftermath of a dream that had threatened to turn into a nightmare: waking to find only the empty stillness of a deserted room.

'Forgive me.' His voice had become a whisper. 'I had no intention . . .' He broke off then slowly added, 'I'm deeply sorry.'

'You mustn't be,' she said quickly, her love for him almost overflowing. 'But I'm glad—'

'I'm horrified I've ruined things between us,' he cut in. 'I want us to be friends – more than friends. I know you're young but it really doesn't seem to matter. I just want to know if you still feel anything for me . . .'

On impulse she leaned forward and kissed him, cutting off his words. For a moment he stood with his arms at his side; the next moment he was holding her to him, returning her kiss, gentle now, controlled, but it was wonderful.

The next day, Connie stood outside a general store, in Smithfield, watching women coming and going, listening to housewives on meeting each other and pausing for a chat. Their talk was all about how the war was going, but no mention of loved ones in France or fighting in Turkey. No one asked after a neighbour's son or husband, lest they be told of someone lost or injured. They spoke of mundane things: cost of bread, the lightweight Christmas table they would have this year, the mess so-and-so's street was still in after that zeppelin raid a month ago and when the authorities were going to clear it up.

They spoke lightly; they smiled. But behind the gossip, voices were flat, and behind the smiles there was a stubborn refusal to be defeated. Even so, she'd see that expression betraying despondency, despite a refusal to be conquered by it. To her, it revealed the spirit of these people. It broke her heart as she sketched, secretly, her sketchbook hidden by the open book she held in front of her, appearing to be reading.

Back at her desk on Monday, she faithfully copied on to larger sheets of paper what she had quietly sketched: women's heads thrown back in laughter at some joke or other, animated as they exchanged recipes. She'd purposely left out that look she saw in every eye, that expression on every face. It would be up to her chief editor to decide what would go into the next edition. She guessed what he would decide on. This time the underlying despair was for her eyes alone.

First she showed them to Stephen, watching his eyes grow thoughtful as he surveyed them, maybe thinking of his wife or even maybe he saw what she'd tried so hard to keep out. 'I'm in awe, Connie,' he said. 'I'll get these up to Mathieson, and if he rejects them, I'll half kill him.' Then in a whisper: 'Love you, Connie.'

Chapter Fifteen

December 1915

'I don't know what to do.' George gazed appealingly at his pastor for help, for advice, though before the man opened his mouth he knew what that advice would be. 'It wasn't so bad when it was just a case of being free to volunteer. I felt justified keeping well away from it. But with this rumour of enforced military conscription, I don't know what to do.'

There was a long silence as Joseph Wootton-Bennett regarded him. Finally he said slowly, 'All you need, my son, is to remain strong. God will guide you. Trust Him.'

'But I'm beginning to feel isolated, as if I'm the only one.'

'You are not the only one,' came the reply. 'Look around you, my boy: everyone in this little community of ours believes that life is sacred, held only in the hands of the Lord until He knows when it is right to gather his creatures into His arms – not for man to decide as and when he feels a need to slaughter another – a man in whom God put as much into making as He did into you. Would you then take His decision into your own hands, even if that man came at you with murder on his mind?'

'I don't know. I've always followed our faith, but—'

'But now you are in a quandary. You feel as if God has deserted you. But He hasn't. It is the Devil speaking to you, whispering in your ear so that you think it is your own mind pushing you. Cast aside that evil whisper. Listen instead to the clear voice of God Himself, who is ever beside you.'

'I do listen, but when I see what's happening all around me, it's hard to—'

'The Devil flits hither and thither as the whim takes him,' his mentor broke in, 'leaving you with the agony of indecision. The Devil has no care how you feel beyond rejoicing at what he does. His sole aim is to destroy your faith in God's word. But our Lord is forever by your side and He will never leave you. Listen to His words, George. Listen and take heart.'

'They're talking of forcing conscientious objectors to fight and sending them to jail – hard labour – if they refuse to drop their beliefs.'

His minister's expression had grown sad. 'Then you must face that inevitability with a strong resolve, my son, as Jesus did when nailed to the Cross. He is your example. He died for you. In your own small way you owe Him this sacrifice. If you are thrown into prison, made to slave harder than you ever imagined in your life, survive on slops, be deprived of sleep, think of Him – you choose to suffer to preserve His great sacrifice, God's great lesson by sacrificing His Only Son for us all, your friends and your enemies alike.'

He paused to give George an encouraging smile. 'That thought alone will give you strength to endure, my son. And endure you will, because I know your belief is very strong. So take heart.'

As he listened to that quiet, authoritative yet under-standing voice, he began to feel his resolve growing by the second. What a truly marvellous man his minister was; one who would himself endure what he preached – against killing a fellow human, albeit an enemy looking to kill oneself.

Except that he was well above the age of conscription, but George felt certain that if called to fight, the man would resist unto death.

It had been some months since Stephen had taken Connie to dinner and then the theatre. At her door afterwards he had spoken of how he felt about her, raising her hopes.

Since then, there always appeared to be one reason or another to take up his time. Connie had become deeply confused. It was as if he was holding her at arm's length in case she had read more into it than he'd intended.

But he'd opened his heart to her, hadn't he? That night he'd kissed her. Then what he said afterward, and that day, not long afterwards, when he had whispered that he loved her. . . .

So why did he now seem to have stepped back from her? She couldn't bring herself to ask. One kiss, a small indiscretion instantly curbed, a promise to have dinner the following week, which hadn't happened, he having been called away on some private business – what did that constitute?

She had felt let down after he had raised all her hopes. She'd made a fool of herself. She knew she was in love with him, but as time went on she was indeed beginning to feel like a fool.

Whenever he approached her on office business she'd force herself to treat it casually, not looking at him, even if he tended to hover.

True he was busy, they were all busy, the war saw to that. Every day news was gathered on the war's progress. Even though the Western Front appeared to be in the throes of stalemate, neither side seemed to gain or lose ground. People wanted to know, to read every scrap of information that might bring some encouragement to the heart.

But at home more zeppelin raids had meant her being sent out more often for her pencil to depict what she saw. Yesterday was the sixth time she'd been sent out.

'Mathieson's saying how pleased he is with what you're doing, Connie,' Stephen said, making her jump.

Engrossed in sorting out her filing, still doing that job between times, she'd not heard him approaching her desk.

Recovering her composure, she forced a smile. 'I didn't hear you come up. You made me jump.'

'Sorry,' he said quietly. 'I just needed to tell you what Mathieson told me, that he thinks you're proving an asset to the paper, against all his prior reservations. He says it's beginning to draw readers' attention and he thinks before long they'll be looking for your sketches more and more. It's something totally different and, so he says, brings something more human to the paper than cold photographic images, though we still need them.'

He paused to draw breath, then continued, 'There's something else I need to tell you . . . ask you. I'm so

141

sorry about the time that's passed since you and I went to dinner together – it couldn't be helped, but everything's okay now. A bit of private business, and I apologise. But it's all sorted out now and I'd like to ask if you'd care to have dinner with me again this coming Saturday.'

Her first impulse was to voice an offhanded no thank you. Instead she found herself almost leaping at him, mentally, striving to modify this sudden joy she felt. In a steady voice, she said, 'That would be nice, a nice change.'

'To humdrum filing,' he laughed.

Despite herself, Connie laughed too. A silly joke, but it bore more joy than he could ever know, in one instant releasing all her doubts. Her heart warmed as he gave her a lovely smile and, turning, went back to his office, not looking back.

Through the glass separating his office from the rest of the area, she saw him sit at his desk to bend his head over whatever he'd been previously working on. He should have looked up at her and smiled, but he didn't.

It felt as if they had been here for ever. All Albert could do was pray that he and Ronnie would come out of it in one piece. Going over the top in the small hours of this morning, a bullet had seared across the flesh of his upper left arm as he ran blindly towards the enemy lines, the darkness split only by the unpredictable and blinding flashes of chaotic shellfire. The bullet had ploughed a deep gash; blood soaked the sleeve of his stained and filthy uniform. Fortunately it had missed the bone, but God, it hurt! A second of numbness then, whoosh, the pain had hit him.

He wasn't sure if he'd yelled out or not. Ronnie hadn't appeared to have heard or seen anything in the chaos of the charge. Moments later they'd been forced into a retreat as men fell all around, an officer frantically signalling back those on their feet but staggering almost to a halt. Hope of gaining the enemy line was utterly dashed; common sense had been the officer's only option.

Ronnie, seeing all that blood, had been in a panic when they'd finally tumbled back into their own trench, demanding to know how bad it was and what should he do to help. But a medic had taken one look at the wound, grinned and nodded. 'You were bleeding lucky there, son,' he'd muttered as he pointed him in the direction of the first-aid field tent. 'A bit further right, you'd have had your chips – hearts and bullets don't mix, y'know.'

To Albert's disappointment – in a way – he'd merely undergone first aid; his wound was stitched and bound, and he had been pronounced fit enough to return to his post.

Had the bullet gone deeper, smashed the bone to smithereens, he'd have been sent back to the field hospital for a while to escape the madness of war, the soul-shaking reverberations of shell blasts, that wall of rifle fire, death and pain all around.

It might even have meant the arm having to be amputated and he'd have been sent home invalided – safe at last, who knew? Except that he'd have been forced to leave Ronnie behind in this hellhole, and that he didn't want.

He thanked his lucky stars his was no more than a flesh wound. Six months here, so far he'd been lucky, so damned lucky. Thousands and thousands had been killed just in that short time.

'You all right?' Ronnie opened his eyes to ask as he slipped back down into the trench beside him.

'I'm fine,' Albert answered, sliding down to a sitting position beside his brother. But Ronnie had closed his eyes and was already snoring again.

Taking advantage of a lull in the fighting, most were dozing, legs out-stretched or tucked beneath them, their heads cradled in some muddy niche in the trench wall where it felt most comfortable. They were miles away in dreams of home, no doubt, and loved ones, others lost in a precious letter from wives, sweethearts, parents back home; or absorbed in writing to them, lost to the war for a while.

He thought of Edith and began searching his kit for a bit of paper and pencil. Crouched over a scrap of paper, stub of pencil in hand, one knee crooked to support his letter, oblivious to those next to him, all of them packed so closely that to try to walk even a short distance meant stepping over legs and hunched bodies.

Edie wore his engagement ring and wrote almost daily, letters filled with love and concern, though half of them were so delayed they often came in one batch and he was never sure which to start on first. They lay now all together in his kit, went with him into battle. Men were sent over the top in full kit and it always felt to him as if she was with him; her love shielded him from harm.

Even so he looked forward to those couple of weeks away from the front line, men given this break now and again to rest up and regain their sanity. Without it a man could go mad. There were some to whom that actually happened: they just went crazy, did daft things, their bodies shaking from head to toe; some who shot themselves in the foot looking to be invalided home; some who went berserk and attacked their officers or just stood staring about them with wild eyes, ignoring orders; some who just stood up and walked away. Such men were caught, arrested and, so it was said, shot as deserters.

He just hoped this flesh wound of his would be the only one he would ever get; he prayed – he who'd never been one given to praying – that when this war was over, as it had to be one day – it couldn't last for ever – that he be returned whole to Edith. There were times just before being sent over the top that he would glance at Ronnie and see his lips moving and know that he too prayed.

He prayed Ronnie would come out unscathed in this war, that he'd continue to have good luck smile down on him, just as Albert felt it was smiling on himself at this moment while, his arm bandaged, he bent over his letter of love to Edith. Before too long they'd hopefully be granted a few days' leave and sent home to rest. And he intended to enjoy that to the full with Edie.

Tenth of December, Connie's birthday. Being a Friday she was at work. Tomorrow Mum had planned a little family get-together for her.

Her parents had given her slippers first thing this morning – not a huge present, but most things were hard to come by with all the shortages these days. Unless of course you had pots of money – then you could buy any luxury you fancied. But for ordinary people such things were out of reach.

Today she and Stephen were having midday lunch together. He had wanted to take her to dinner this evening but Mum and Dad were expecting her home. Stephen wouldn't be at her party because she'd so far not told her family about him – something made her cautious: his age, hers; he an editor, she nobody, really.

He still saw her home, dropping her off a few doors from where she lived so that he could kiss her goodnight properly while the taxi's engine throbbed noisily as it waited to bear him away.

He said he loved her and his kisses did linger but no more than that; they might as well have been mere friends. He'd never spoken of his previous marriage or of his deceased wife since his first mention of it, nor of having any relatives. Connie felt it best not to probe but where his past life was concerned, he sometimes seemed to be like an island in the middle of an empty sea. He had a flat but had never asked her there.

Nor could she ask anyone at work about him, for he seemed to prefer to keep his private life to himself, especially where his previous marriage was concerned, and he certainly seemed to want to keep their relationship quiet as well. Yet he was attentive to her in his own way. Passing a florist on the way to lunch he had slipped in, telling her to wait outside, and had emerged with a bouquet of pink chrysanthemums for her, saying, 'Happy Birthday, Connie.'

Now in the little restaurant he pushed an expensive-looking red velvet box across the table towards her.

'Happy Birthday,' he said again as she stared at it. 'My real birthday present to you. Hope you like it. Open it, Connie.'

146

Her hands fluttered excitedly, as she did so, and she gasped as she pulled out the lovely silver bracelet that was nestling inside.

No one had ever bought her anything so beautiful, and so obviously expensive. The outer edge was inlaid with a curved leaf design; it glinted and shone. She had never seen anything so gorgeous.

'For me?' she cried stupidly.

'Who else?' He laughed. 'Look on the inside.'

She lifted it from its box and peered at where he'd indicated. There inscribed were the words, *All my fondest love, Stephen*.

Fondest love! Not undying love, not enduring love. Like a gift from a friend or a relative. A little of her joy dissipated but she smiled and said, 'Stephen, you shouldn't have done that – this must have cost a fortune. It's so lovely.'

'Glad you like it,' he said quietly. 'It's given with more sentiment than it says there.'

And looking up across the table, she, who had the gift to fathom what a person was feeling, read deep love in his eyes, and with a huge leap of her heart, she knew she was his. She had to be.

Head bent, busily sorting out some bits of filing, Connie looked up to see Stephen standing at her elbow. She hadn't heard him approach. But then the office was always so noisy.

'Sorry, Connie,' he blurted as she started. 'I'm disturbing you.'

'No,' she said as her heart did a tiny leap of elation. These days it happened every time he came near. She

147

wished it wouldn't, yet she also wouldn't have wanted it any other way.

'Everything all right?' she asked needlessly.

'Yes . . . Fine.'

He seemed edgy. She heard him clear his throat nervously. 'Christmas not far off now,' he began. 'I'm told we need something to cheer our readers up.'

The second Christmas of the war, with still no end in sight. She knew what he meant about people needing to be cheered up. But how did one do that when there was nothing to cheer up about?

'I had a talk with Mathieson,' he said, 'and he agrees we need to interview a few people having a good time – if we can dig up any.' He gave a wry smile. 'Get a few pictures if we can. Only on this occasion you're being asked to go out without a photographer, maybe just an interviewer, to depict people being happy, or trying to, depending on which way you look at it. It might make a good scoop. A photographer might end up making people look self-conscious. But no one will realise what you're doing . . . you know what I mean, Connie? And afterwards . . .' He paused and she heard him draw in a deep breath, letting it out slowly as if to control some inner conflict. 'Have dinner with me? We need to talk about your sketches before they go to print – go over things very carefully, because God knows, there's little enough to cheer anyone up these days.'

That was true – there was always dire news of the fighting on the Western Front, and from Turkey as well, and it did nothing to raise one's spirits; the food shortage was growing worse by the day despite rationing; wives were being widowed, children being orphaned, and families

148

bereaved by the thousand; in every street more than one window, often several, with curtains drawn, each announcing a loss. The total of men being killed in these last three months was some two hundred and fifty thousand, that on top of the thousands killed this year alone.

Mum had received letters from Albert and Ronald saying they were both well and hoping to get leave before Christmas. At least letters were being delivered and loved ones getting them within a few days – the authorities were making sure of that. Reading Ronnie's letter had panicked them all when he'd said that Albert had got a wound in his arm, but it was only slight and he was fine.

Even so it had made them worried. Next time the wound could be worse, much worse. On top of that there was still talk of military conscription, of married men being put on a register. Both Elsie and Lillian worried for their husbands. They would get into a terrible state every time the question was raised, but now they were slowly coming to terms with the fact that they might have to survive without their men. What else could they do? And Dorothy was putting on a brave face, and trying not to get in anyone's way. She had only a few months to go, and was blooming, the sickness of the first three months long gone.

One thing, the zeppelin raids seemed to have given up; the last one had been in early November with none since. It should have helped to make people feel better – but enough to be cheerful? Connie wasn't all that sure. There was no guarantee they wouldn't start up again – a dreadful experience with war brought to the very door of ordinary people, civilians being bombed from the skies – that was something no one could ever have visualised a year ago.

There had seemed no end to it – those incredibly long, slow-moving, cigar-shaped craft gliding low, almost majestically, terrifying those on whom they'd dropped destruction. Large guns were brought over from France, mounted on the back of army trucks and shook the area, but the zeppelins just glided on like monstrous predatory ghosts.

But Connie couldn't forget the faces of those whose homes were totally destroyed, whose loved ones had been injured or killed. Sent out to sketch what she saw, those faces still played on her mind and at times haunted her. She'd find herself waking from sleep to lie there in the darkness, feeling the dream still with her: the stark faces, eyes a simmering mixture of grief and outrage. Even children in this war had become victims. A war on children – how could an enemy be so callous, uncaring? It was nothing short of pure savagery, worse than beasts, newspaper headlines, even hers, proclaimed in outrage, her sketches printed alongside to add weight. Mathieson swore it sold more papers.

War seemed to have turned ordinary people into beasts too. Just before the zeppelin raids had ended so abruptly, Connie had been with a group of others – it hadn't escaped her attention that people needed to watch, whether out of self-preservation or in the desperate hope that no bomb would drop in their area – when a zeppelin, caught in searchlights, had suddenly burst into flame. It was reported later that a new kind of bullet had done the job. As it had slowly descended, burning from end to end, those around her had broken into yells of triumph, not one with any sympathy for those burning to death inside.

Stephen Clayton's voice brought her back to the present. 'Our Mr Mathieson keeps on about the way you catch an expression – says it's quite uncanny. But you look all in lately. Is it worrying you? We can talk about it over dinner this evening.' There came a pause. She saw him catch his lip with his teeth. Then he added, 'If you want to – talk about it, I mean.'

Eyes were the window of the soul, it was said, and it was true – eyes could shine with hidden amusement, hidden disdain, or even hatred without the lips ever moving; could dim, turn blank, become dull with despondency, fill with anguish, despair, disgust, no matter what their owners strove to conceal.

Over dinner his clear blue eyes seemed to be devouring her even though his conversation was concentrated mainly on business. He was concerned for her even though their talk was of when she'd be sent out to record people enjoying themselves. Connie felt her heart swell with joy that he loved her enough to be concerned for her well-being.

Chapter Sixteen

February 1916

As Connie came in from work, taking off her snow-covered shoes, her mother handed her a letter. 'It's George,' she said. 'Been arrested for fighting.'

'For fighting?' Connie's tone raised in incredulity.

'In the street – arrested for causing a disturbance, it says.'

Sitting at the kitchen table, Dorothy, her stomach big now, the baby expected late February or early March, glanced up. 'Hope I hear from my Ron soon.' She sighed. 'Seems ages since I had a letter from him.'

Mum looked at her in sympathy. 'Should get one soon, love. I just hope both my boys are all right.' She turned back to Connie. 'But George – don't know what your dad will say when he comes in tonight and reads this.'

He'd left to do his coal deliveries well before the post had arrived. In normal times it would get delivered about seven thirty, another one around eleven, one in the afternoon, and the last one around teatime. But the war made deliveries erratic; sometimes one post was missed out altogether.

Connie's father had no sympathy for postmen – nowadays more often post-woman. 'Wouldn't 'urt 'em to get a bit more of a move on,' he would grumble if his football coupon was late turning up. As for Mum, every time the letterbox clattered, she'd hurry to collect it, hoping it was from her boys. Letters from the fighting forces had priority and were delivered as regular as possible, but sometimes a delay would have two arriving at once.

'My George in prison!' she said, unable to believe it, while Connie read the letter to herself.

Short and to the point, it confirmed the arrest had been for fighting in the street and disturbing the peace. She'd have smiled at the word 'peace' had it not been for the consideration to send him to a long-term prison for the duration of the war for declaring himself a 'conscientious objector'.

Connie handed it back to her mother not quite knowing what to say except, 'Dad will be home in half an hour.'

Her mother began carefully to fold the official notice, running her thumbnail repeatedly along its edges, folding and folding until it refused go any smaller. Connie took it from her and put it on the mantelpiece for her father to read when he came in.

Mum, in an obvious fluster, had hurried out to the kitchen to get the meal she'd been heating up.

Ill at ease, Dorothy got up too, awkwardly waddling out to help the woman who had so unselfishly taken her under her wing, for which she had hardly stopped thanking her, as well as for all her kindness.

'Don't let it worry you too much, Connie,' she said as she went out.

Connie nodded but said nothing. It was good to have another girl in the house, pregnant or not. Who cared? Lots of girls making the most of their men's leave were ending up pregnant – in war it didn't seem so much of a crime, and it gained more sympathy than recrimination – though some were still prim about it. Maybe they had nothing better to do, was Connie's thought. She found Dorothy a lovely person. Ronnie was a lucky man. When this war was over and he came home, they'd get married. And please God let it be soon, she prayed.

Swiftly she ate the stew Mum had managed to cook up for their evening meal, for all there was very little meat in it. She was seeing Stephen tonight but told Mum she was seeing a couple of friends she worked with.

Stephen was taking her to see a play and would be at the end of the road with a taxi. But her mind wasn't on that. Rather it was on him seeing her home afterwards. Maybe they would linger out of sight in that narrow passage between the tenements, but only briefly. He would kiss her gently, then urgently, and always she willed for him to take it further, to fondle her, but he always checked himself, saying that he couldn't, he mustn't.

Asking why not reaped no response at all, other than a few mumbled words about not thinking this to be the right time. And as they moved apart she would stand a little away from him, wanting to demand if he was serious about her or not. But she was never able to bring herself to do so, dreading a row that might have him saying it best they parted for good. What in heavens name would she do then, having to work with him knowing what he meant to her? And would he feel the same?

*

154

Changed and ready for the evening she was on the point of leaving when her father came in, making for the kitchen sink to wash off the coal-dust.

'Tell your dad about the official thing we got, Connie,' Mum said without turning from the stove where she was dishing up his stew.

'What official thing?' he growled.

'The one about our George.'

'What about 'im?'

'Tell him, Connie.'

'George has been arrested. We got a note from the police.'

'Arrested? What for? Fer not signing on?'

'No, for fighting in the street.'

Her father swung round, his face dripping soapsuds. 'Gawd's strewth! I'll kill 'im! Him, perfessing not to strike the other cheek and all that soddin' rigmarole, and—'

'I've got to be off, Mum,' Connie said, glad to be away from her dad's raised voice. Stephen would be waiting. And tonight she so hoped he might do more than just kiss her in that dark little alleyway when they said good-night, but judging from all the other times, she didn't think so.

There'd come a time when she must introduce him to her family, and there lay the problem – that difference in their ages. She could almost hear Dad bellowing: 'No, you find a boy your own age!' And Mum with her fingers to her lips, sighing, 'Oh Connie, love. He's far too old for you, love. When you're sixty he'll be nearly seventy – an old man. No, love, your dad's right.'

And then having to tell them he'd been once married . . . Pushing away the thought, she hurried on.

He was waiting by the taxi – few cars were allowed petrol as it was in short supply. He took her in his arms and, for once, kissed her lingeringly in view of all those passing. Maybe tonight he would prove his love for her – maybe not going all the way, for she knew he would honour her welfare and good name – but well towards it. Who knew?

Only then would she know that she was really his.

The play wasn't a long one; it finished early, but instead of bringing her back home, Stephen had requested the taxi go a different way.

'Where are we going, darling?' she asked. Just lately she had made a point of occasionally addressing him as darling, at first just the once and as he hadn't objected, a little more often. Though so far he'd not reciprocated, which worried her even as she strove to ignore it.

'I thought you might like to go back to my place,' he said in a low voice so that the driver wouldn't hear. 'For a nightcap before I take you home, if that's all right with you?'

It was perfectly all right. Her chest tightened with excitement and, oddly, fear, considering she'd so long wanted him to prove his feelings for her.

In a wide mews, she waited while he paid the driver, then followed him to a door leading into a spacious hallway, up a broad staircase to his second-floor flat; she stood aside as he unlocked the door to be led into the loveliest sitting room she had ever seen. He turned on the light to reveal soft beige furnishings, a deep carpet in a soft pattern, gleaming coffee table and a side table on which stood a gramophone.

As he helped her off with her coat, she noticed the sideboard. It held two large photographs, and on a side table there were another two, each of a young woman – a pretty young woman – smiling into a camera. Connie instantly knew it to be Stephen's wife, his deceased wife. Suddenly she felt as if her world was about to collapse. Why bring her here when his wife was everywhere?

Invited to make herself comfortable on the settee, she watched him pour a gin and tonic for her and whisky and soda for himself. 'Gives us a chance to relax,' he said lightly and came to sit beside her, 'before I take you home.'

Suddenly those expectations of him making love to her fled. How could she let it happen with his wife watching them, if only from a photo frame? What had he been thinking?

But he merely came to sit beside her, no arm around her, no kiss laid on her lips. In fact he hardly spoke at all.

She could stand it no longer. 'Stephen!' She shot it out. 'Stephen, do you really love me? Do you?'

He sat away from her and studied her. 'My dear darling, I love you,' he said slowly. 'I've loved you from the moment you came into my office all that time ago. But I came to recognise it so slowly and you seemed so young and I tried to make myself dismiss it as the stupid reaction of a lonely man. I'm so sorry.'

Suddenly it felt as if her heart was floating – she was floating. She leaned forward and kissed him, ignoring the frowns she imagined on the face of that woman in those photographs. It was lovely to have him put his arms round her, kiss her, have him tighten his grip; through her blouse she could feel his hand on her breast

157

as his kiss strengthened; she felt herself being borne slowly back on to the settee. It was more than anything he'd ever done in that dark passageway.

Suddenly his lips left hers. He took in a deep breath and sat up, she only just managing to collect herself enough to straighten up too.

'What is the matter, Stephen?' she heard herself demand.

For a second he didn't reply. Then he said, 'This is all wrong. I'm so sorry.'

'What do you mean, all wrong?'

He looked chastened, his eyelids drooping over his blue eyes. 'I can't. Not here.'

Instantly she knew what he meant and all the anger went out of her. It was here of course that he and his wife would make love, would couple in the room behind her where the closed door hid the bedroom. How could she think he could make love to her here? Why bring her here at all?

'I think it best I go home now,' she said in a monotone.

He nodded in agreement. 'Maybe that would be the right thing to do. I'm sorry.'

'So am I,' she said with more sharpness than she'd intended. She waited as he gathered up her coat, helped her on with it, watched her as she adjusted her hat with its turned-up brim, tucking her short hair beneath it, all without either of them saying another word. In the taxi they were equally silent.

Helping her out as the taxi drew up at her destination, Stephen kissed her, lightly, on the cheek; she turned and walked quickly away, aware that he was watching her as she went.

She only just managed to wipe the tears from her cheeks and summon up a bright smile before her dad opened the door.

'Bit late, ain't we?' she heard him growl. 'Gel your age should've bin 'ome a damn sight earlier than this.'

'Bus broke down,' she lied tersely. 'I was with my friends, so it was all right.'

'Well, make it decent time next time,' he growled as he closed the door. She made for the parlour, which was now in darkness. Mum was already upstairs and Dad went on up to join her.

Gently, Connie closed the parlour door, wishing she had a proper bedroom in which to give vent to the misery that seemed to be threatening to overwhelm her.

Was it over between them? If it was, to have to go into work and see him there was going to be unbearable.

All night she tossed and turned, unable to sleep for thinking, every now and again finding herself breaking into tears, silent tears lest Mum or Dad hear and came to find out what the matter was.

Morning found her unable to eat her breakfast. Mum wondered if she was sickening for something. Going off to work was agonizing, sitting on the bus wanting only to jump off at each stop and go . . . go where? Anywhere but work.

Entering the building as if going to the scaffold, she climbed the staircase rather than take the cranking lift, avoiding having to meet anyone. Reaching her desk she saw Stephen in his office look up, then look away.

Gathering up the filing that had been left in her tray, she began to busy herself.

Her nerves leapt as she felt someone come to stand behind her. Stephen.

'Are you all right?' he asked.

She forced a smile. 'Yes.'

She wanted to say blithely: *Why shouldn't I be?* But she couldn't. Her lip was beginning to tremble. She caught it tightly between her teeth to stop it. He was regarding her closely, his own features grave.

'Connie,' he began, then hesitated. He whispered in case anyone overheard, though she wondered why that should matter any more. 'I need to apologise for last night. It's just that I don't want to treat you less than you deserve. I love you, and I feel I have to . . .'

He broke off then began again. 'Connie, I don't want to lose you. I've never been all that good at making love. Maybe because my wife—' Again he broke off. 'Can we still see each other? I don't want to lose you, Connie. Can we start again?'

For a moment she sat looking up at him, then looked away and nodded. She heard him take a deep breath, exhaling in a trembling sigh of relief. 'Tonight?'

'Yes,' was all she could say.

Everything seemed to be happening at once.

On Thursday second of March Dorothy gave birth to Ronnie's baby, it having taken two full days to come into the world. Mum wrung her hands as the midwife worked on the mother, and Connie felt just as anxious until finally a beautiful little girl made her appearance. An exhausted Dorothy decided to call her Violet in Ronnie's absence.

That same day the Military Service Act came into force. Stephen went straight to the recruiting office, which frightened the life out of Connie, even though her heart swelled with pride for him. He returned to say they'd decided the deafness in his right ear was too profound for them to take him. But he'd at least done his duty, unlike her brother George, who was in prison still, still refusing to bow to military service, and would be transferred to a place of detention until such time as the war was over or he changed his mind.

Three days after the baby arrived, Ronnie and Albert were given five days' leave. Their arrival had preceded their letters and the place was in instant turmoil.

'Where're we going to put the two of 'em?' Mum asked Connie in a state of confusion. What with the anxiety of the birth, a second-hand cot needed to be bought to go upstairs in the boys' room, where Dorothy was nursing her baby.

'They'll have to have your bed in the parlour, love, and you use the sofa in the front room. It's only for a few days before they go back.'

'Can't Albert have the sofa and Ron go upstairs with Dorothy?' It made sense but Mum looked as if she'd been struck by a fist.

'Connie, they're not married!'

Her voice sounded so aghast, especially given that they now had a little daughter, that Connie had to curb a smile. So that was it. She was to use the front-room sofa for a few days. It was a house full of people, her sisters popping round to see the baby and their brothers, Ronnie upstairs with Dorothy most of the time, despite the concern of Mum's prim and proper mind. Though three days after giving birth, what would they be expected to get up to? And with Albert bringing his Edie home at all odd times too, with no room to sit, Connie was glad to get back to work – and Stephen.

Chapter Seventeen

August 1916

Squatting by the field where he'd been digging seed trenches along with another group of prisoners – conscientious objectors like himself – George ate his meagre meal in gulps. He had only fifteen minutes to eat before he had to get back to work. They'd been marched off to work early this morning despite the drizzle. Taunted by other prisoners, who were hardened criminals, and bullied by guards who saw them only as cowards, each bore it with fortitude.

He had been in Dartmoor a few months now, brought here in April from where he'd been in a local prison, moderately fed despite being treated with scorn. Here, something they called a midday meal consisted of a small hunk of bread and a bowl of watery soup they called skilly. Exercise comprised of two twenty-minute sessions, walking round and round the seventy-five-foot-square high-walled courtyard, forbidden to speak to their fellow prisoners on pain of three days on bread and water. George's only outlet was forced labour outside the prison, and hard work it was too. These last few months he had been mending roads. Squatting by the roadside as he ate, his only consolation was that he was working with others who'd been imprisoned for the same beliefs as himself.

As he finished the last crumb of the stale bit of bread, having soaked it in the skilly, his thoughts went back to that day he'd been arrested. Having received his calling-up papers, his stomach had churned over as he gazed at them; he'd put them to one side in the mad hope that by ignoring them he might be overlooked. They'd sat there glowering at him from his friend's sideboard. Ernest, a member of his chapel who was about the same age as George, had taken him in when he'd left home. Ernest too stood firmly by their deep-rooted conviction that a man does not kill his fellow man.

'You've got one too,' Ernest had said, producing his own summons.

'I'm going to ignore it,' George told him firmly and his friend had grinned.

'You can't do that. They'll be down on you like a ton of bricks. Best thing is for you and me to go together, tell them our beliefs won't allow us to accept military service of any kind. And I mean *of any kind*!'

Next to the official letter there had sat another, from his mother. He'd read it but hadn't replied to it, not quite sure what to say. She'd wanted to tell him that his brothers were home on five days' leave and maybe he might like to see them. She'd said that Ronnie didn't look at all well: he seemed a little vacant at times, hardly talked, and she was worried about him. She'd said that she

164

missed him: no matter his convictions, he was still her eldest son and she loved him, no matter what.

It was the words 'no matter what' that hurt, stopped him from replying. It had nagged on his mind for ages afterwards and maybe it was that which had made him lose his temper the way he had.

Ernest's set expression had heartened him at the time but there'd been another question to settle. 'What if we're given the option of doing work of national importance, nothing to do with combat?' George had asked. 'Like market gardening or going into the medical corps?'

'We'd still have to sign the military oath, and that in itself makes us a traitor to our beliefs.'

Then something had happened that had entirely altered his thinking. All these months later, it still plagued him, disturbed his sleep, and even now as he stood up beside his brethren on a command to resume work, he couldn't stop thinking of it.

Surprisingly, he and Ernest Jarvis hadn't been marched off to prison for refusing to enlist; they had instead been given time to think it over, told that they would be summoned again and by that time they would have changed their minds and opt for non-combatant work.

It had sounded tempting, but a harsh talking to from his pastor had him thinking straight again. He would not consent to any sort of non-combatant work, and especially to signing the military oath.

For a long time he'd had to put up with jibes and taunts, even face-to-face accusations of cowardice from those he'd pass in the street or whilst sitting on a bus or entering a cafe. There'd been times when he had even been refused service. He'd managed to rise above it, walking away straight-backed from the cafe or after being ordered off the bus or when a white feather had been thrust into his hand.

That day in February his mother's letter had still been on his mind, that and the awareness that he'd not had the courage to go and see his brothers while they'd been home. He'd just been to a particularly harrowing service where he'd listened to all sorts of horrors one could inflict upon another under the orders of an army officer, he himself who'd maybe never even yet soiled his hands with the blood of another man. He had come away incensed at the wickedness men could inflict on others.

He was thinking about it as he'd made his way along Shoreditch High Street, having again to walk after being refused boarding a bus by a young conductress, no doubt having taken the place of a man who'd gone off to kill.

At the corner, he'd paused to light a cigarette. As he'd put away his matches, a young woman had ran up to him and, with one movement of her open hand, had swept the cigarette from his mouth, her voice a shriek, stopping other passers-by in their tracks.

'You ain't wearing an armband!' she'd screeched as he stood shocked. 'Why ain't you wearing a bloody armband?' she'd yelled, giving him no chance to speak. 'You're one o' them bloody conchies, aren't you? Feckless cowards, 'iding be'ind your bloody Christ's blooming coat tails, and my poor husband only this week reported missing believed killed, you stinkin' cowardly bastard!'

With that, she'd fetched a handful of white feathers from her handbag, obviously stored in there for this very reason, and had thrown the whole lot in his face.

In a sudden burst of unexpected anger, already upset by being unceremoniously rejected from the bus, he'd taken a step towards her without thinking what he was doing. She had instinctively leapt back, catching a foot on a jutting corner of a paving stone and had landed on her backside on the pavement.

Several had rushed to help her up, at the same time glaring up at him, but one man, a biggish lout, had come at him. In an effort to defend himself from a hefty blow, he'd shut his eyes and struck out with both fists. They'd landed on the man's jaw without him hardly being aware of it.

It was pure self-defence, but the force of that protective move had sent the man sprawling. Then, without realising what he was doing, he'd thrown himself on top of the sprawled body, his hands around the man's throat in a blind rage – blind, animal fury that had come from nowhere. It seemed to be someone else trying to choke the life out of the body beneath him, such was the rage that rose up from the soles of his feet. The next thing he knew, he had been yanked off his victim by someone, one arm twisted way up behind his back, causing such pain that he'd cried out. Moments later, his wrists were manacled behind him and he'd been bundled into a police van to be thrown into prison for assault.

There'd been no thought, no reason for it that he could think of now, and it haunted him that he, normally a mild-mannered man, a believer in turning the other cheek, should attack another with such a desire to hurt, even kill, as he had felt. And all because . . .

To this day he couldn't believe it of himself. But no matter how he tried to excuse himself from that moment of insanity, one thing still played on his mind: if he, with all his beliefs in *thou shalt not kill*, could feel such a surge of anger as to want to kill, how was it that he saw himself as above such things?

Often he'd recall with shame how his declaration in court that he was a conscientious objector was met with a storm of laughter. But sitting in that cell awaiting transfer to a longer term prison, into his heart there'd crept the realisation that still disturbed him: he who'd been so against killing his fellow man had tried to do just that, and not even in self-defence. Wasn't that what his beliefs were supposed to be about – that a believer didn't kill, even to defend himself or his loved ones from his enemy? Even when faced with death? Yet murder had been in his heart when he'd clamped his hands round his attacker's throat, propelled by blind fury, and he hadn't even been defending his country or his loved ones.

Realisation had slowly dawned on him that it was an automatic response to resist when threatened, despite all his high ideals of pacifism. Maybe he was wrong to have done what he did. But it had shown him how weak a man could be. He'd not appealed to his God, but had lashed out: every lesson he'd ever learned had fallen apart in that one short moment. Not only was he still ashamed of himself, he'd come to see that he was no better than the rest of them.

He stood now with his fellow prisoners, pickaxe in hand, ready to resume the work he'd been consigned to do, and wondered at himself. He knew that if his brothers or his parents were at the mercy of a loaded gun, he would strike, never mind all his high-blown beliefs.

For a moment he wanted to throw down the pickaxe, march towards his guards and announce before all his fellow prisoners that he had changed his mind. But those with him would view him as a traitor to his beliefs and he couldn't bring himself to face that.

He was a coward too.

The short break over, he retrieved his pickaxe and, bending his back beside the others, he suddenly understood that his duty lay, not in fighting, but in helping those wounded in their struggle for freedom. The realisation was like a heady shot of brandy. He could never take part in the killing of others but he could help those who had been ordered to and injured in the process. Maybe the medical corps would take him? Otherwise he would take any mundane job he was asked to do in an effort to help shorten this terrible war. And damn the preaching of Joseph Wootton-Bennett.

George stood facing the recruiting officer who was seated behind his desk, aware that the man was regarding him with some scepticism and not a little scorn.

'So . . .' he breathed, his thin lips twisting sarcastically. 'Why this sudden change of heart, man? What's made you alter your mind so damned suddenly?'

'I've been thinking a lot about it lately, sir,' George muttered, even more ill at ease than before. To his ears that sounded such an inadequate excuse, mumbled as it was, that his insides cringed.

The officer clicked his tongue impatiently. 'For God's sake, man, speak up! What was that?'

'I said I've been thinking about it a lot lately, sir,' George began again in a stronger tone.

'You've been thinking about it a lot,' the officer echoed in a mocking tone that made his victim squirm inwardly. 'In what way?'

The man was tormenting him, verbally torturing him for the bother and inconvenience he was causing by deciding finally to sign the military oath after all this time wasted, as the officer seemed to deem it. He was finding it hard to explain his change of heart, especially with his inquisitor gazing up at him with disdain written all over his narrow face. But he had to explain this change of heart, as the man called it.

'Since I lost my temper and hit someone, even though he was attacking me, I've come to realise,' he said desperately, 'that whatever a man thinks he believes in . . . I mean, not to retaliate . . . I mean . . .' Unable to explain his actions, his words trailed off. 'I'm sorry, sir, I can't explain it any more than that,' he heard himself saying, surprised at his own outspokenness. 'At the time I just lost control and hit out. It's weighed on my mind ever since and I finally realised . . . well, it's as I said. It's like we're all just people. No matter how much we think we're above lashing out, we are, well . . . frail, I suppose. And that thought's helped me change my mind about what I thought I believed in. And, well . . . that's all, sir.'

He knew he was talking like a fool; at any moment he would be told he was only trying to get out of prison. But the officer lifted his chin, gave a brief sigh and nodded.

'Very well – we'll get the ball rolling. But . . .' His eyebrows drew themselves together, he glowering up at George from beneath them in a warning gesture. 'I don't want you changing your mind at the last minute, man, or you'll find yourself in deep trouble – and I mean . . . *deep trouble*. D'you understand me?'

George nodded, finding it hard to breathe; it felt like it had on the day he had received his calling-up papers. His heart turned over – in fear? Was that all it had ever been, the fear of fighting itself and all that it entailed? But he'd committed himself and there was no going back.

'It will be in a non-combatant capacity, sir?' he asked bluntly, his tone surprising him, suddenly strong and direct. 'I still refuse to fight or kill anyone, you understand, sir.'

Was it this decision that was making him more direct than he'd ever been in his life?

The officer looked up, studying him closely. 'That goes without saying, of course. So, non-combatant, do you have a preference? Agriculture, maybe market gardening?' It sounded almost sarcastic.

'I'd like to opt for the Royal Army Medical Corps, if that's possible.'

'Hmm!' said the man, rubbing his chin as though this request were a dilemma for him. Then, taking a deep breath, he nodded. 'I don't see why not. Very well, I'll see what I can do, make sure you hear within a short while.'

As George half turned to leave, the officer stopped him, saying, 'I'd advise you to say little about this to your fellow inmates. For reasons you might well understand, being staunch conscientious objectors, they might not see things in quite the same way as yourself. You are dismissed!'

His words were so filled with sarcasm that it left George feeling a little sick as he took himself out of the room to those waiting to conduct him back to prison and more work mending roads; for how long he had no idea.

He hoped it would be sooner rather than later, for the pure reason that he had little stomach for facing his fellow prisoners, their conviction to keep their faith as strong as ever. He felt even more like a traitor as he was taken back to prison.

Chapter Eighteen

September 1916

Connie stood in the kitchen, reading the letter her mother had handed her. 'It's from George.'

Sitting at the kitchen table as she suckled her six-month-old Violet, Dorothy gazed up at the two of them. 'Hope I get a letter from my Ron soon,' she said quietly. 'Last one I got was all of two weeks ago. Ain't seen any of the growing up of our little Violet. She won't know him time he comes home.'

'Maybe he has no time to write,' Mum said, a tense look on her round face. 'I just hope him and my Albert are all right, way things are right now.'

Albert's last letter had mentioned being transferred to somewhere in France called the Somme. Now the papers were full of reports of fierce fighting there, huge casualties, fearsome onslaughts. If her boys were in the thick of it, it didn't bear thinking about. She turned back to Connie, changing the subject.

'I don't know what your dad's going to say when he comes home tonight and reads that letter from George. *If* he reads it. I just hope he don't go off the deep end, that's all.'

She'd read this one through the once and in silence, and she was right – Dad would probably not be pleased, might even sling it aside unread. But for Connie, this single page of cramped writing sent a wave of disbelief through her.

I expect this will shock you all a bit, but earlier this year something happened that made me think and has been nagging at me ever since. I don't want to go into it but I now realise that one can automatically retaliate without thinking when one is threatened, no matter what I previously believed. Maybe some can still turn the other cheek, but I didn't, and I now see that blind fury can leap up and take anyone off guard. That's what happened to me and I've now come to see that I've no right to preach pacifism after what I did on the spur of the moment without thinking. But I feel I need to make amends, so I've signed the military oath, not to fight, because I still don't think I could deal with that, but I've been accepted for the Royal Army Medical Corps. They say I could most probably end up in France, collecting the wounded and getting them to safety behind the lines. I reckon I'll be a bit close to the fighting but I won't be taking part in it. I could never do that, not even now. But doing this will help me conquer this guilt I keep feeling over what I did. I just felt I needed to tell you and Dad. That's all. Hope you're well. Love, George.

When her father came home, Connie expected him to toss the letter to one side, maybe even tear it up and fling it into the empty grate.

'It's from George, Dad. It's very important – you need to read it.'

The urgency in her tone arrested him on the verge of screwing up the single sheet. And now she watched as he smoothed it out and unfolded it.

Her mother was keeping out of the way, busying herself with dishing up her husband's dinner to put on the kitchen table for him, the back parlour for Sunday meals only. But he always went in there for his pipe and a quick smoke while he waited for his dinner to warm up. She was no doubt waiting for his bellow to reach her ears.

Connie watched as he began to read as if against his will, and saw his expression begin to change to one of disbelief. Yet there was no pride in his face, not the pride he'd exhibit when he read letters from his other two sons – brave sons in France, still in the thick of the fighting.

He was silent as he refolded the letter and quietly placed it back on the mantelpiece as if that was the only place for it. What his thoughts were, Connie could only guess. Surely from that anger and humiliation he'd felt over George's refusal to follow his brothers into battle, which he'd seen as sheer cowardice, there had to be some sense of relief that he could hold his head up again. But all she heard him growl as he stalked from the room to his meal was, 'Army medical corps, eh? Well, we'll see,' addressing no one in particular.

Left with her own thoughts, she found herself wondering how her brother would fare. But she knew he would fare very well now he was free of the rubbish that idiot Wootton-whatever-his-name-was, had put into his head. Men like that shouldn't be allowed, came the thought as she followed her father into the kitchen, from where the appetising aroma of stew was emanating. Maybe everyone was entitled to his own beliefs, so long as they didn't inflict them upon others.

But there were other thoughts on her mind. Half an hour from now, Stephen would be waiting with a taxi at the end of her road to take her to the theatre. She could hardly wait to finish her meal and be out of the house, and in the privacy of the taxi have him put his arm around her, bring her close while she savoured the warmth of his love for her.

Connie saw Stephen every day at work, but Friday evening and weekends were theirs alone. Whether it was having dinner together or seeing a show or even wandering together in one of London's many parks in the late summer sunshine, she dared to dream that one day she and Stephen would be married.

But there always lurked a feeling that it was all too good to be true. She'd still not told Mum and Dad about him. They'd have a fit. Mum was always voicing a hope that one day soon her youngest daughter would meet a nice young man and stop gadding about with all those friends she had made at work, as Connie had led her to believe.

The feeling was heightened by Stephen himself, his unexplained reluctance to take their love any further than a brief kiss goodnight, his arm around her in a taxi, or the occasional present that she kept hidden away from her parents. She tried to repress any memories of that strange evening in his flat, the way he had behaved.

She'd been in his flat several times since, but it was always the same, Stephen holding himself back from her as though fearing to openly declare his feelings. And those photographs, despite her reaction that first time, they were still there. She wanted to bring herself to remark on them but somehow never could. So many times she wanted to ask him point blank just how serious he was he about her, wanted to refuse any more invites back here until he promised to declare that he loved no one but her. Sometimes his attitude towards her struck her as more friendship than love, yet each time she found herself unable to refuse to come here after an evening out.

This evening, though, on his large comfortable settee, his arm around her, holding her closer than usual, their drinks on the coffee table before them being left where they were, untouched, her worries were too hard to ignore.

He'd put a record on the gramophone, soft music adding to the tranquillity of the room. She loved the sensation that the feel of his arm about her brought, though often interrupted by the gramophone running down, making the music slow to a tuneless drone, compelling him to leave her to wind the handle, and shattering any romance there might have been.

While he'd been winding up the gramophone she had been gazing across the room to the photos on the bureau and this time, as he returned to put his arm about her again, she drew away from him.

'What the matter, my love?' he said, a bewildered expression on his face.

177

She was about to say, 'Nothing's the matter.' Instead it seemed as if someone else was speaking for her. 'How long have we been coming here, Stephen?'

He was gazing at her as if not quite knowing why she was asking.

'How long?' she demanded again, trying not to let her tone sound brittle.

He thought for a moment, still frowning, perplexed, she imagined. 'A few months, I suppose.'

'You suppose,' she bit back. 'I thought you'd have known exactly how long.'

He was looking at her as if with no idea what she was talking about. Then he frowned, irritation beginning to seep into his expression. 'Do you?'

'Yes. Nearly seven months.'

'So why the question?' He was smiling now. But her lips remained tight.

'The question is, Stephen, how long is this to go on, you bringing me here, the two of us sitting together, you starting to get passionate then all of a sudden drawing away. What is wrong with you, with all this?' She swept out an arm to encompass the room, her voice rising, careless of what she was saying. 'I never go any further than this room. I follow you into the kitchen – how marvellous! But your bedroom door remains out of bounds. After seven months, Stephen . . .' She broke off, casting a glance around the room. 'And another thing: these photographs!' She wanted to add *of your wife* but instead she railed, 'If you really loved me, Stephen, I would have seen your bedroom by now, after all this time us being together.' Now she could say it. 'And you would have put all these photos away,

178

if you really loved me. So what is wrong with you, with us?'

Each photo showed such an amazingly lovely woman that it made her feel dowdy by comparison. A young woman smiling confidently – one a holiday snap, another a studio portrait, another on the small corner table of her and Stephen, his arm about her shoulders, his other hand holding hers, they smiling into the camera – a happily married couple taunting her, the woman staring at Connie accusingly, she felt.

He himself seemed blissfully unaware of his dead wife watching while he sat with his arm around her shoulder as they talked of their evening out, maybe a little about work, or telling her how fond he was of her, how he loved her. But all the time his dead wife would be looking on. It was more than uncomfortable, as if she was watching them disapprovingly.

Until now she'd not had the courage to ask him to remove the photos. How could she? It was his home. But one question persisted: was he still in love with his wife, if only with her memory, and where did that leave her?

Suddenly it was as if someone had thumped her on the back, forcing from her the words that had lain so long unsaid. 'Stephen, how do you really feel about me?'

For a moment he didn't answer. During her outburst he had leaned a little away from her, just looking at her, and she knew that she had messed everything up. Now he would say it was time he was seeing her home and she would get up, unable to answer, and allow him to help her on with her coat. She would adjust her hat over her short hair and have him lead her to the door, hail a passing taxi and take her home in silence. Maybe he'd peck her cheek as he left her, saying he'd see her on Monday morning at work. Instead he sat simply looking at her, his face a mask. She had to say something.

'How can you ask me back here, Stephen, and tell me you love me, yet you keep your wife's photos on show?' she said in a small voice. It sounded such a stupid question, like a plea uttered by a child. Yet she couldn't help herself, her mind reeling, her words tumbling out. 'Don't you know how that makes me feel? It feels as if she is still alive and I'm . . . just your bit of skirt. I feel—'

She wanted to say cheap but broke off, her heart thumping like mad, her eyes beginning to brim with tears. She watched as he got slowly to his feet, ready to coldly offer to take her home, she knew it. Instead he stood looking down at her. 'I'm so sorry,' he said quietly.

She was about to say in the coldest voice she could muster, 'I'm sorry too,' but he'd already turned away, going towards the sideboard.

She watched him pick up the two photos, very gently, one after the other, and lay them face down, just as gently, reverently, then go over to the small corner table and do the same to the photo there, again so gently and so reverently that a sudden sadness for him caught in her throat.

Coming back to her, he stood gazing down at her. 'Why are you crying, Connie?' he said as if he could hardly believe it. 'I'm sorry. I'm so used to them being there, I've never given it a thought.'

That didn't seem right. Of course he knew they were there. But he had moved closer to her, was reaching out, leaning towards her and, taking her by her arms, lifting her gently up from the sofa.

'Please don't cry, darling. It's in the past. I've done my grieving. And I love you now. Maybe I don't demonstrate it as much as I might, but you're still so young and I'm that much older than you and—'

'Eight years!' she blurted out, her tears drying, her eyes challenging.

'Nine,' he corrected gently.

'In December I'll be nineteen,' she countered stubbornly. 'That makes eight! Why should age make any difference? And I love you, Stephen.'

He looked at her for what seemed like ages while she returned his gaze, fearing to drop hers. It was then he said, very tenderly, lovingly, 'What do you know about love, Connie? I mean, about making love?'

She gazed up at him, shaken by his question. 'I . . .' she began, not knowing what to say to that.

But he answered for her. 'I imagine that, like all young women, even in their late teens, you are still an innocent. You feel love but you don't *know* love – don't know what it's about. No man has ever touched you *in that way*, if you know what I mean. I have never touched you – for that very reason. But to be perfectly truthful, my love, I long to—'

He broke off as though respecting her innocence, while she gazed back at him, not knowing what to say.

She'd never been properly told about physical love. Married women kept that to themselves. She shared giggles with friends on the petting they'd sometimes enjoyed, but whatever else happened, that was private too. She'd never had any boy *come it* with her as some of her friends called it. Stephen would kiss her, had once eased her down beneath him only to lift her back to a sitting position, apologising profusely. And somehow she'd felt cheated.

Now he was asking what she knew about making love. As she gazed up at him, strangely embarrassed, he smiled gently, his embrace tightening about her a little. 'No, of course you wouldn't. That's why I feel I mustn't take advantage of you, my darling. I love you. So very much. If you only knew how much. But I'd never take advantage of you. I want to marry you, Connie, if you'll have me. As soon as you're nineteen.'

His arms had tightened around her. His lips touched hers and then began to press hard. Automatically returning the kiss, she felt that familiar twinge inside her and, as always, instinctively felt that this was the love she had for him.

Suddenly he stepped away, releasing her as she tried to make the kiss linger. 'Now I must take you home, my love. But remember, I love you more than anything. And I'm so sorry about the photos.'

'It doesn't matter,' she said, her heart leaping in happiness. He really did love her. He had asked to marry her. She had meant to accept his proposal, sudden though it was, but his kiss had taken her words of rapturous acceptance right out of her head.

It was impossible to sleep. Stephen loved her, she was certain, he had asked her to marry him, but he had brought up their age gap. Was nine years' difference really a stumbling block to their happiness?

Then, as she lay staring into the darkness, came another thought: it could also be a stumbling block when Mum and Dad finally learned of the age difference between her and the man she had fallen in love with. Mum had often said, 'When you meet a nice boy, Connie . . .' no doubt visualising her daughter with some likely young chap. But Stephen was a man almost ten years older than her. Her parents would both be appalled. She could imagine their response: 'When you're forty, he'll be almost fifty. No, love, find yourself someone your own age. There are lots of boys around here.'

It plagued her and there was no one she could turn to. Maybe one of her sisters? Not Elsie, she'd scoff, rush off and relate it to Mum and Dad immediately. Lillian was more trustworthy: having been sworn to secrecy, she would delight in keeping it to herself until Connie found the courage to face them herself. She could trust Lillian.

'Well I never!' Lillian burst out on Sunday morning when Connie paid her a visit and, over a cup of tea and a cake, told her about Stephen and her fears about their age difference. 'If you love him, I don't think age would be that much of a barrier. Mum and Dad still live in the past but we live in a modern age and you can't just give up on a bloke just because they don't approve. It's your life, Con. Just go in there fighting. They'll come round.'

Connie didn't feel she was 'going in there fighting' but she'd gained a lot from Lillian's advice and felt strong enough to face her mother and father.

But not yet. Not quite yet.

Chapter Nineteen

November 1916

Seven thirty a.m., a grey November day, hardly light. The artillery barrage had ceased.

Orders shouted to fix bayonets, whistles blew the order to go over the top, men climbed out of trenches to begin moving across no-man's-land towards the enemy. They moved at a slow pace – every man moved half-crouched, as if that were any protection here on fearfully exposed ground, their only cover the smoke from exploding shells.

Gone was the lush grass of a peaceful countryside. Rain and shellfire had turned it to mud. Barbed wire, broken tree stumps, dead horses, bomb craters into which a man could fall never to get out again, slowly suffocated by the thick mud at the bottom, had done a complete job.

Very aware of their exposure, as was every one of a hundred thousand or so soldiers, Albert and Ronnie negotiated the shell holes weighed down by seventy pounds of equipment: wire cutters, entrenchment tools, gas helmet, groundsheet – though why one needed that, Albert had no idea – sandbag, haversack, two Mills bombs and two hundred and twenty rounds of ammunition. Each man gripped his rifle, and each man gave the same silent prayer: 'Please, don't let my number be up yet.'

The grassy meadows gone, churned-up mud clung to boots, impeding every step as each soldier had to drag each foot out by force. Barbed wire had barely been breached by the nightly barrage and had to be negotiated. Albert kept his eyes on the ground as he walked towards enemy trenches.

Then the machine-gun fire opened up and men began to fall. Instinct told him to lie flat, take cover, but that was against orders. Orders were not to dig in but to advance, and this they had to do. He looked across to Ronnie. Ronnie was bent double, ducking and flinching at each close wizz of a bullet.

'Dear God above – don't let him be hit!' Albert prayed.

Few, he was sure, would come back from this advance. Officers too seemed to think so. Yet another attempt to gain enemy lines failed, just as previous attempts had. Officers now yelled orders to retire. A mad rush back, tripping over fallen comrades, no time to help them as machine gun bullets tore past, scoring hits in every direction. It was a relief as he and Ronnie fell down into the relative safety of their trench; men were being hit on the very act of leaping in, even as they breathed a prayer of thanks for deliverance.

Albert uttered his own silent prayer of thanks. No one put thoughts into words as each man slowly got his breath back, not to dwell on the chance that the next advance might be their last. Trenches had become busy: the wounded tended, borne off to the field hospital just behind the lines, worst cases hopefully to be transferred for proper treatment later. The dead laid out, though most were out there still, it was said later some sixty thousand.

Stretcher-bearers were already collecting as many wounded as they could, an unwritten truce honoured by each side not to fire on them. When some trigger-happy sniper did, it would raise a furore from both sides condemning such practice. Stretcher-bearers for the most part were considered neutral, though they put themselves at risk of death each time. Brave men, Albert thought idly as he tried to settle his own jangling nerves, feeling suddenly dead tired. He looked around for Ronnie. No sign of him.

He felt his heart give a jolt, followed by a sick feeling of panic. Where was he? He'd lost sight of him following the order to retire. But he hadn't seen him fall.

'Ron! Ronnie!' His voice was urgent. 'Ron, where are you?'

'He's okay,' came a war-weary voice. 'Your brother's over there.' The man jerked his head to where the trench turned a sharp corner. 'But he don't look too well to me.'

A shell-burst overhead made everyone duck, but following the man's directions, he saw his brother crouched in the corner. Making for him as much as the crowded trench allowed, he burst out, 'Ron, you orright?'

He saw him shake his head, heard him mumble, 'Orright, just tired. Just wanna sleep.'

'You can't sleep. We could be ordered over the top again.'

'I ain't going.' The voice was drowsy as if he was already drifting off.

'What d'you mean, you're not going? Are you hurt?'

'Just get me pyjamas. Where'd you put 'em?'

This wasn't right. Albert shook him. 'Get a grip, Ron. You've got to pull yourself together.'

But all he got was, 'Stop shaking me. I just need a good sleep. Where's me pyjamas?'

'Where you going to find pyjamas here?' he tried to chide. No reply.

He felt goose bumps run across his skin and shook Ronnie violently. The last few days he'd become aware of a blank stare in his brother's eyes as if he was somewhere else.

'Pull yourself together, Ron,' he snapped now. 'You just need some rest. We all need some rest. Write to your Dorothy, ask how your daughter is. Maybe it'll stay quiet for a few hours.'

No need to be told to sleep. Ronnie had already dozed off. Albert would try and do the same, sitting beside his brother. But sleep eluded him and instead he found a sheet of paper in his breast pocket and wrote to Edith. The field post office sent letters off the very next day after the odd word had been pencilled out by their officer in charge of the censoring. There were no more calls to attack but no real chance to relax and sleep with shells from their own artillery keeping up a continuous bombardment. The full-throated scream of their own shells passing overhead and the resounding explosions over enemy lines did bring a sort of lulling effect until they seemed to retreat into nothing, hardly heeded. Huddled in his greatcoat, Albert slept, his letter to Edith only partly finished, the one to his parents laid aside. Most men slept, except those on sentry duty.

He hadn't even remembered falling asleep when he awoke to several men negotiating their way between the legs of the weary, bearing buckets of bread and hot soup from the kitchen bunker, the aroma waking men as instantly as if they'd been kicked.

Fishing for his and his brother's mess tins, he held them out as the cooks came abreast. Ronnie amazingly was still asleep, twitching and jerking every now and again as if in the midst of a disturbing dream.

Albert gave him a shove. 'Ron, wake up!' he said as the two mess tins were filled and two big hunks of bread handed out.

Ron stirred, groaned and opened his eyes. But what Albert saw made him go cold. Wide and staring, his eyes seemed to have no life in them, replaced with a sort of distant look as if he wasn't in this world.

Albert pushed the mess tin towards him. 'Ron – eat this! You need to eat! Come on now.'

The eyes slowly turned towards him but there was no real focus, no recognition. He seemed to be staring into the distance.

'Ron, bloody wake up, will you. Soup – better 'ave it while it's hot. And there's bread to soak it up with. Good, eh?' he said as if coaxing a child. But Ron wasn't a child. A sense of horror flooded over Albert. He'd seen men like this after a bombardment. Shell shock – the words sent a shudder through him.

Thinking back, there'd been indications of it after days under continuous enemy bombardment, but he'd assumed it to have been the normal reaction any man might display. But this was different.

Putting the mess tins on a sentry step cut into the trench between the wood shoring that helped support the mud walls, he took his brother by the shoulders and shook him. He seemed to come out of his trance, jerking to a sitting position to stare wildly about. 'We've got to go,' Ronnie burst out. 'This ain't right. We 'ave to leave. I'm going 'ome!'

Before Albert could stop him, he'd leapt up, knocking over one of the mess tins, and began to push his way along the crowded trench, tripping over men's feet to angry shouts, their food almost knocked from their hands.

Albert was after him instantly, yelling for him to come back. But Ron was already clambering up the roughly cut steps leading away from the lines and was quietly, purposefully walking off. Albert ran after him, up the uneven steps, yelling at him to stop.

Someone caught hold of him, gripping him by the shoulder, but he shrugged the hand away, running several yards before managing to bring his brother down with a rugby tackle. Ronnie fell flat on his face and lay there in the mud, Albert on top of him. But now he laid quiet and unresisting as if all the stuffing had been knocked out of him.

Someone was standing over the pair of them. 'Deserters, eh?' came a voice.

Without letting go of his brother, Albert looked up to see an officer, a major, immaculately attired, standing with legs slightly apart, against one of which he was tapping a swagger stick rhythmically. He might have

189

been on some parade ground, though fortunately for him the ground here leading away from the trenches sloped downhill, shielding him from enemy eyes.

'Deserters, are we?' he repeated as Albert got to his feet, dragging his brother up with him. 'Decided to leave the rest of your comrades while they lay down their lives for such as you?'

'Sir, not deserters,' came a voice. 'I told them if they wanted to shit to go well away from us in the trenches, while things are calm. There's enough shit down there already and the latrine's full, not been emptied, sir.'

'Then what were they doing lying on the ground, Lieutenant?'

'I saw this chap slip and knock his companion flat on his face. It is awfully slippery here, sir, the rain and slime, you know.'

The major thought for a bit while the others waited. Horror had taken hold of Albert. If Ronnie gave the officer the look he'd given him a short while back, one of half-crazed vacancy, the major would know straight away what Ronnie had been about, walking away from the fighting as if he had nothing whatsoever to do with it. Shell shocked? A mind snapped? A balance tipped over the edge?

The major thought for a moment, then an acid smile curved one corner of the thin lips. 'An extra few bits of shit won't make any difference, Lieutenant, I should imagine, to what's already there. Send them back, man, and let them get on with their . . . *business*.'

Pleased at his little pun, he touched his cap with his swagger stick, was smartly saluted in reply, and moved off to where a soldier was holding the reins of his horse just behind the shattered wall of what had once been a cottage.

He'd totally ignored the two soldiers who'd scrambled to their feet and, with an effort, at least on Albert's part, had come to attention and thrown up a salute. But the crackle of rifle fire a short way off caused the man's measured steps not to be quite so measured as he hurried to his horse.

'Thank you, sir, for not . . .' Albert began as he hauled his brother up to stand alongside him, anxious that Ronnie's face wasn't showing any sign of his previous odd behaviour.

The officer's face remained a mask. 'Get back to your post, Lance-Corporal,' he ordered, his eyes trained on Ronald. 'Take him with you and keep an eye on him. I'll not see any man put up against a post and shot for a deserter if I can help it. Now pull yourself together, man – both of you!'

'Yes, sir,' Albert said smartly, saluting while keeping a tight grip on Ronnie at the same time, in case he might let him down. Secretly he blessed the man for his understanding and quick thinking.

Back in the trenches, he stood over Ron, who'd collapsed against the trench wall, shoulders hunched. He was still staring into space, his body jerking and twitching every now and again. Others eyed him too, having seen the signs of shell shock before – some with futile concern, others with little sympathy for a man with so little control over his fears.

It hurt to the point of tears to know what others were thinking about his brother, and for the rest of the day, Albert kept a wary eye on him.

It was late in the day when their own guns opened up on the enemy. Everyone knew it heralded only one thing. After an hour it stopped as quickly as it began. And sure enough, all along the line, orders were being shouted. Men stood up, took up their rifles, awaiting the order to fix bayonets. Albert hauled his brother to his feet, thrust his rifle in his hand and held the fingers tight about the stock, putting the bayonet into his other hand. When the order came he would help those trembling fingers to fix the thing in case Ronald let it fall.

It was then he noticed the hands were not trembling any more. Ron's expression was fixed, his jaw jutting, lips tight, eyes steady.

There was no chance to heave a sigh of relief as the whistle blew. Men piled over the top, men who only this morning had seen comrades fall. It made no difference: each man was determined to give the enemy the full brunt of his fury, to give a good account for a slaughtered comrade.

Ronnie seemed in full control of himself. But if it came down to hand-to-hand combat, what would Ronnie do? Two things would happen, Albert thought as he walked at the required steady pace towards the enemy lines. Either Ron would go hell for leather at the enemy, hacking, yelling, his lust for blood controlling him, or he'd drop his weapon and cower.

He glanced over his shoulder. Ronnie was still there a step or two behind him. *Please don't have him turn and run*, he prayed. He'd be a perfect target. Was that why they were always ordered to walk, not run? Was it a sort of stealth? But already there was the crack of rifle fire, then the rattle of machine-gun fire, and now shells bursting into countless bits of shrapnel – did it matter if one walked or ran?

Some ahead of him, hardly visible through the now drifting smoke, had reached the barbed wire and forced themselves through the gaps a few at a time. In the night, brave men had wriggled out here to cut as much of the stuff as they could, often becoming targets themselves.

Those in front of him were visible enough in the half light to become standing targets. Any minute the call would come to charge the enemy trenches. But it wasn't happening. On every side, Albert could see men falling, so many men everywhere, falling to a storm of bullets. Officers' voices were calling to retire, the commands high-pitched with panic that a moment ago had seemed so positive.

He turned, saw Ronnie turn and begin to run. He ran too. Finally they were more of less out of danger, a few yards to their own trenches, to safety. Ronnie was just ahead of him.

In the fast-fading daylight the world seemed to have gone mad: enemy shells had begun bursting everywhere, one landing just yards from Ronnie's running figure. He saw his body leave the ground, becoming a semicircle in the air, then land. He heard himself cry out as more shells fell, though none quite as close. Ronnie had begun to writhe, to scream. Reaching him, he found his brother's right leg had been shattered, the foot completely gone.

Grabbing his brother's shoulders Albert made to drag him the last few yards, but in the dash of those trying to reach safety, lost his grip to be borne along with them. Falling headlong into the trench, he turned to rush back out to get Ronnie but someone grabbed his collar.

'You want to get yourself killed?'

Albert fought the grip. 'Me brother's hurt! I've got to go back for him!'

'No you don't! You stay here!'

Viciously twisting out of the grip, he clambered up to the trench lip. Enemy shelling had ceased. Everywhere he could hear cries of pain, cries for help, except from those already dead. Was Ronnie dead? In the gloom, he couldn't see his body, but out of the darkness he could hear someone crying in pain and was sure it was Ron.

'Help! Help me!' There were so many cries, but he knew Ron's voice well enough to know Ron was alive – he had to be.

Crawling on his stomach Albert reached his brother, found his shoulders amid all the equipment and began to drag him back towards safety. It seemed to take an age, all the time Ron screaming with each jerk. Finally gaining the trench he fell in with his burden on top of him. This time there was no cry of pain. Ron was silent.

In the fitful light of a flare someone, an officer, was staring down at the body. 'This leg's completely shattered. No good to anyone. Just one man when there's hundreds out there – you going to rescue them all, soldier? And who told you to go out there risking your life for one man?'

'He was my brother,' was all he could say.

The officer stared him in the face. 'What do you mean, *was*? He's just passed out, and just as well – going to lose that leg by the looks of it.'

Standing up, the officer signalled to a couple of medics tending other wounds, and left Albert to it, shouldering his way through the battle-weary as if they were a crowded Trafalgar Square throng.

Chapter Twenty

In the middle of the family dinner a knock came at the door.

'Oo the bloody 'ell's that on Sunday dinner time?' Connie's father burst out, slamming his knife and fork down on the table, which was laid with its best cloth. 'Bad enough 'avin' to make do with the stuff they call meat these days for a Sunday dinner without someone interrupting it.'

These days, the main dinner of the week was nearly always a family gathering, with what few seemed to be left: Lillian and Elsie and their children, both their husbands having been called up under the government's need for more men, married or single.

Now and again Connie's grandparents would turn up – her mother's mum and dad and Dad's father – each bringing something from their larders. Food shortages were growing evermore grim with thousands of tons of shipping being sunk around Britain's coast, and it was becoming good manners that anyone invited to dinner would contribute a little something.

This Sunday there was only Connie's sisters, and Dorothy with her baby, little Violet, on her lap. Ron's letters were always full of how proud he was of her. He wrote to Mum too, saying she would never know how much he appreciated her taking his Dorothy in after her own mother had spurned her, calling her a slut and asking her what would their neighbours think, and saying that they would never forgive her for bringing shame on the family. The girl must have felt it deeply but always put a brave face on it, never ever mentioning them.

That had turned Connie's thoughts to her own dilemma – her and Stephen. Then had come that knock at the door. As her father got up to answer it, she had felt her body tense, as though those thoughts of hers had been a sort of premonition.

As yet she'd not had the courage to tell Mum and Dad about her and Stephen. He'd asked several times if she had and when she shook her head, about to make an excuse that they weren't ready for that yet, he'd playfully half-threatened to come here one day and tell them himself. That had been last Saturday. Things had begun to become serious between them, yet she'd still not seen the inside of his bedroom, but his couch saw perhaps as much of their love as the bedroom might have – or nearly as much.

She was beginning to know what love really was as they lay together on his couch, Stephen kissing her, fondling her, until her insides screamed for him to complete what he'd begun. She would hear his breathing become excited, feel his body tensing, only to have him suddenly draw back from her, his voice laboured, saying, 'Not yet, darling, not until we are married.' It felt like a form of torture.

Last Saturday she had become angry, asking, 'When, Stephen? When do you intend us to marry?' wishing she'd asked it gently as he drew back to sit up, his expression tight.

He'd replied – 'I need to buy you a ring – an engagement ring' – only to spoil the sudden excitement that leapt in her breast. 'But I don't want you to wear it until we name the day.'

'Why?' she had demanded.

'I have to ask your father for your hand first. That will mean revealing the difference in our ages. He won't be happy, I know that. Any father would prefer to see his daughter marry someone her own age or very near it.'

She knew what he meant. A nine-year difference was a lot to ask her parents to accept. After a while, when they got used to it and once they'd come to realise what a gentleman he was, maybe they would resign themselves to it. But she didn't relish that first step – not the way her father was prone to bellowing at anything that displeased him. It meant nothing, she was used to it, he did no harm, but how would Stephen take it, he who'd been so well brought up?

But last week, sitting in a restaurant, he'd jokingly threatened to knock on her door and announce himself as her lover. Then, as she gasped, her eyes flashing, he'd grown serious, saying that her parents would have to know eventually. Was this unexpected knock him carrying out what had seemed to her a light-hearted threat?

Almost frozen to her chair while the others sat waiting with mild interest, she heard her father burst out, 'Gawd 'elp us!' A shocked pause, then, 'Come on in . . . fer Gawd's sake, come on in!'

'Hullo, Dad. I've bin given some leave.' It was Albert's voice but it sounded so tired.

Dad's voice grew louder. 'Whyn't you let us know, son?'

'Couldn't. I'm sorry,' came the reply. Father and son were now in the narrow passage. Connie felt faint from relief while still excited to hear her brother.

'Why not?' Dad asked, but there was no reply. Seconds later, he and Albert came into the room. Everyone was now on their feet, smiles of welcome falling away on seeing this gaunt figure standing there, his effort to smile at them frustrated by the heavy weight that seemed to have fallen on his shoulders.

He was in uniform, clean and smart, but it was the expression in his eyes that Connie noticed first: a haunted look, coupled as it were with one of despair.

She couldn't help herself from bursting out into a string of questions before anyone else could gather themselves. 'Albert – what's happened? Where's Ronnie? Is he all right? Has something happened?'

Albert's gaze centred on her was like someone beseeching help. Everyone else remained looking on in bewildered silence. When he finally spoke, his voice was totally flat. 'It's Ron.'

His mother gave a little scream. 'Oh, God! He hasn't been—'

'What about 'im, son?' his dad broke in, his hand sweeping out to hold his wife back as she made to rush forward. 'Somethink 'appened to 'im? He ain't—'

'He's all right,' Albert said quickly, but his voice sounded utterly worn out, as if he could hardly believe his own words. 'But he's bin injured . . .'

He broke off then began again, the words tumbling out in a rush. 'Got himself a blighty one.'

Everyone knew about blighty ones. It took a man out of the front line for good. It also spoke of being crippled for life: no good as a fighting man any more, flung out on the rubbish heap.

'How bad?' His father's words could hardly be heard.

'Bit of a leg wound,' Albert answered, trying to let them down lightly. Then, taking a deep breath as he knew they'd have to know the extent of his brother's injuries sooner or later, he went on, 'Truth is his leg's been smashed up pretty bad. He's still in France. They've got him hospitalised there. They couldn't save it – his leg. So they've had to . . . 'ad to amputate,' he went on in a rush. 'And there's a bit of shell shock too – he don't quite seem to know where he is.'

Sunday dinner was forgotten, Mum was near crying and she crumpled into a nearby chair, her two daughters staring stricken-faced, their children bleating, disturbed by their grandmother's reaction and not understanding what was going on.

Dorothy was sitting as though struck dumb, ashen-faced as she gazed down at her baby, one hand smoothing the little head, soothing her, for the child had no interest in what was happening. Only Dad was managing to hold himself together.

'All what matters is we've still got 'im – thank Gawd!' he growled. 'Once 'e's fit to travel they'll be sending 'im 'ome and 'e won't 'ave to fight any more and maybe even get 'imself killed fer this bloody country of ours. Thank 'eaven fer small mercies.' He gazed at his son.

'You look as if you've 'ad enough too, boy. You look all in.'

Connie heard her mother whisper, 'At least Ron's still with us, thank the Lord.'

She saw her sweep the back of her hand across her eyes in a determined gesture and felt her heart and her pride go out to her mother. No matter what this war might bring, Mum would continue to hold her family together, an example to them all.

Suddenly she was the keeper of the family again as she burst out, 'Oh look, we're all standing up and you must be worn out, love. Come and sit down, Bertie love, and I'll make you a nice cup of tea – make us all a cup of tea, this very instance.' She was speaking too fast, too much, revealing her own tension.

It might seem as if she had put her other son from her mind, maybe too painful to think of, but Connie knew it was there, in her eyes, hovering like a spcctre somewhere in her brain, waiting to escape and sweep over her. Then she would need all the cuddles and comforting one could give. But for now she was determined not to break down in front of her family, especially in front of Albert.

He had sunk down on a chair as if his legs had suddenly given way; Dad had also sought his own favourite chair by the low-burning fire.

Mum said suddenly and briskly, 'Does anyone want to finish their dinner?' to which everyone shook their head.

It was then a thought caught her and she looked towards her son. 'Oh, Bertie, I was fergetting. Look, love, I'll dish up a nice dinner, just for you. You must be ever so hungry after travelling all this time.'

He pulled a wry face and shook his head. 'I am a bit, but I couldn't eat just at the moment,' he answered. 'Maybe later.'

'Right then, love.' She looked at Connie. 'Help me clear the table, love, there's a dear. We'll all have a nice cuppa tea, and we might 'ave our afters later on – fer our tea, maybe. It's jelly and custard. But I'll sort you out a nice hot dinner, Bertie, which you can 'ave the moment you fancy it.'

He smiled, nodding his gratitude.

It had been just over a week since Albert had gone back to the front, and the house had an empty feel to it. It had been marvellous having him here, except for the news he'd brought about Ronnie. His presence had made the whole house come alive. Even when he'd popped out to see Edie, the place seemed to retain a sort of lingering warmth that had nothing to do with the fire burning in the grate.

He'd bring her back, the two sitting holding hands or he with his arm about her. The intimate way they talked together had made everything feel so comfortable. But having to watch them, Connie felt tormented, wishing it were her and Stephen, the family talking as easily to him as they did to Edie. Would they ever welcome him as they did her? She tried not to doubt it but was already imagining the tension there'd be.

It wasn't just that they'd see him as too old for her, but his background was also different to hers: his family was well mannered, well spoken; hers were working class with working-class ways, and working-class speech. They would feel uncomfortable, even resentful, she was

201

sure. Without having to think about it she could imagine the tension every time he came, whereas Edie and Dorothy had both been welcome, Dorothy fitting into the family so naturally and Edie already part of it. But they'd have to meet Stephen one day and she so wanted to marry him.

Only Edie had gone with Albert to see him off at the station, while the rest of the family stood waving him off from their door, watching his tall, upright, uniformed figure recede as he made his way down the street, turning several times to wave, pausing at the far end to wave one last time.

Connie had lingered, after Mum and Dad went back indoors, just in case he reappeared, backtracking to give that one final wave, just as she used to as a child when bidding goodbye to her grandparents after visiting them, running back to the corner time and time again to give them yet another wave.

But he hadn't turned. Albert had more on his mind than playing childish games. He was a man, a soldier, a fighting man having witnessed his brother losing a leg and who would be from now on a cripple on crutches, no use as soldier or civilian, for who'd give a crippled man a job after the war, so many of them returning maimed?

Hastily she turned from such dismal thoughts. This evening she and Stephen were going out to dinner. An early celebration of her birthday in three weeks' time, he'd laughed lightly. Nineteen, a wonderful age for a young woman to be. He had made it seem of great significance and she understood what he meant.

His twenty-eighth birthday, in June, had made him ten years her senior. Next month would see her birthday bringing the difference down to only nine years. Odd how just six months could make the gap in their ages feel so great yet come December it wouldn't seem half so bad. But she still feared Mum and Dad would not see it that way.

But it was Stephen she loved. He understood how things were and sometimes she wondered if he didn't speculate about what impact their difference in ages might have on his work colleagues. He seemed to strive not to give any of them any inkling of their relationship. Sometimes it made her angry, though she knew how he felt. But she suspected someone must have seen through those 'work' dinners they always had together.

Later that day, at dinner, sitting across the table from him having enjoyed as near a good meal as present government regulations allowed, she watched him dip his hand into his jacket pocket and draw something out.

'I've been thinking of this for some time,' he said quietly. 'It never seemed the right moment, but tonight I think it is.' He leaned towards her, taking her hand as it lay on the table by her empty dinner plate, still to be collected. Turning her hand palm upwards, he laid a small, square, dark blue box on it. 'For you, my darling,' he whispered.

But already her heart had leapt. The expression on his face told her what the box held before she even lifted the lid, and there as she did so, nestling inside was a ring with a single large diamond glinting and flashing in the low glow of the restaurant lights.

'I did intend to wait until you were nineteen,' he said, 'but I need to say it now. Will you marry me?' he went on as she continued to stare, adding, 'if you'll have me.'

If she'd have him? Dear God! Of course she would have him! Had there been just the two of them, sitting close together in his flat, his arm around her as she opened that box, he taking up the ring to gently, lovingly, place it on her finger, whispering, 'Will you marry me?' and in the hush of the room they'd have kissed, she would have breathed, 'Yes, oh yes, darling!' He'd have held her close, she his fiancée, his proper fiancée, and they'd have made love properly, for the first time, and afterwards she would have lain in his arms, dreaming of her life as his wife.

Instead, sitting in this low-lit restaurant filled with the quiet buzz of diners, how could she reply as she yearned to? All she could do was gaze down at the ring still in its little box, and suppress her joy. She loved him beyond anything in this world. Would she have him? Had he needed to ask? But how could she throw herself at him, fling her arms about his neck and cry out, 'My darling, of course I will!' with all these diners all looking on, grinning, making her feel like an idiot?

Instead, she closed the lid slowly, almost reverently, and held it out to him, already spoiling the rapturous moment, hearing herself saying, 'Not here, love – when we get home to your place and on our own.'

Home! She'd said home. Yet it wasn't home. Home meant having complete access to all parts of a place. After all this while together, she still hadn't – had still not seen the other side of his bedroom door.

She would, in time, break down the barrier her parents would put up in regard to the difference in her and Stephen's ages. But would she ever break down the one he himself had unconsciously erected in his heart?

The waiter had brought their sweet. She saw Stephen wave it away, heard him say abruptly, 'The bill, please; we need to leave.'

She watched the surprised man take up the plates, ask if everything was all right, saw Stephen nod, saying everything was fine but an urgent matter had come up. She watched him pay the bill and leave a more than generous tip. Moments later they were being handed their coats by the cloakroom girl, the restaurant door opened for them by a courteous doorman into whose hand Stephen dropped a second tip.

In the taxi home he did not speak the whole journey, nor did she. Nor did she speak as the lift took them to the second floor, nor as they entered his flat. Instead of pouring a nightcap for them both or putting a record on the gramophone, he came and sat close to her.

Drawing the little box from his jacket pocket, he took out the ring and, taking hold of her left hand, let it hover poised over the tip of her third finger.

She let it happen as if powerless. But as he paused, saying in a soft voice, the ring still over the tip of her finger, 'Connie, my dearest heart, will you marry me?' she found herself hesitating.

Flooding back that question of his ever-closed bedroom door. Why had he never taken her into that room to make love? Was it that in that room was the bed in which he and his wife had made love? Was it still a shrine to that time? If so, what was she doing here?

If he loved her, surely he would put his first marriage behind him. She didn't expect him to erase its memory. But to carry it like an emblem on his sleeve – what did that make her? All that was needed was for him to take her into that bedroom and make love to her on his bed. But this very gesture of reluctance to take her there made it appear to her that his dead wife stood between them and always would. She wanted to burst into tears and run out of the flat, away from him.

She couldn't help herself. 'Why do we only kiss and cuddle here on the sofa?' she said before she could check herself.

He sat back looking at her, the ring leaving her fingertip.

'Darling,' he said gently. 'I don't intend to make love with you until you and I are married. I would never be so selfish.'

That wasn't the answer she'd looked for. No, even though he'd made her cry out from that wonderful need she'd felt, which must have tempted him sometimes, he never took his own need to its conclusion, and she adored him for that, he a lovely, caring, thoughtful man. But she needed to be honest about how she felt.

'You've never once taken me to your bed. You've never even let me see inside that room, Stephen. Why?' When he didn't answer, she ploughed on. 'Is it because you hold that bed sacred to your wife's memory?' That sounded cruel, but she couldn't help it. 'Is that why I've never been allowed in there – because you still cling to your wife's memory?'

The way he was looking at her made her hesitate. She had said too much, had been cruel and careless. But her life was with him now and the question needed to be asked. How could she marry him if he still carried his wife's memory like a burden on his back? What sort of marriage would that be? True she could never ask him to lay the memory of his wife aside – that wouldn't be natural – but to have it come between them . . .

'I'm sorry,' she said, mortified.

'I'm sorry too,' he replied, and she knew this was the end. He would tell her it was all over.

Instead, he said, as if the previous conversation had never been, 'We must tell your parents the news: I've proposed to you and you've accepted. You do accept, don't you, my dearest? You want to marry me?'

'Oh, yes!' she burst out, her earlier hesitation forgotten. 'More than anything in this world!' And without effort this time, she put her fears aside as gently he eased the lovely engagement ring on to her finger.

Chapter Twenty-One

It was easier said than done – there were too many things on her parents' minds for her to worry them about the fact that she wanted to marry a man nine years older than her and previously married, for all that his wife was dead.

She'd promised Stephen she'd tell them on her birthday, as nineteen seemed to make the difference in their ages not so huge, but she couldn't. Nor would it be much of a birthday. The family already had so many worries: Ronnie, crippled for life and still in hospital in France; how would he fare when finally sent home? How would he find work to support his little family? And Albert could be killed at any time – hundreds of thousands dead, and for what? And here at home people losing heart at news of stalemate, men just killing each other. Here, food shortages, continuing raids over English cities. How could she add to her parents' problems?

It had been some days since she had accepted Stephen's proposal, and the ring he had given her remained unworn on her finger. Instead she wore it on a ribbon around her neck – close to her heart.

'I can't tell them about us, not yet,' she pleaded with Stephen, back at his flat one evening. 'Once Christmas is over, then I'll tell them.' But even she doubted her words.

One of the current tunes, 'If you Were the Only Girl in the World', was playing on the gramophone. Stephen held her hand, his grip tight. His kisses were becoming even more urgent, and suddenly his body was taking what hers was yearning to give him. But he'd forgotten to wind the thing and the music was already falling away, lower and lower, dying altogether as they'd sat in silence, each recalling what had happened.

'I'm so sorry,' he said in a low voice, silence now filling the room. 'I let myself get carried away. I'm so sorry.'

'It's my fault,' she said softly, her head against his shoulder. 'I let you.'

'No,' he said. 'It's my responsibility to look after you – I blame myself.'

She didn't answer but a thought was forming in her head. 'If I were to get pregnant,' she said slowly, 'they'll have to let me marry you.'

She couldn't help but think of Dorothy, cast out by her own parents, and Mum, good woman that she was, taking her in, looking after her, helping her with her son's child. And Ron, miles away in some French hospital. If her mum could care for a virtual stranger, as Dorothy had been when she'd come seeking help, surely she would break all the rules for her own daughter and the man she loved?

Stephen's voice cut through her thoughts. 'Becoming pregnant isn't the answer. I'd never insult you by my carelessness. I want us to marry with your parents' blessing, Connie, not their contempt. So you're going to have to tell them about us. I'll be with you and we'll face them together.'

'What if they won't let me marry you? Until I'm twenty-one, I'm in their charge. Could we run off and get married secretly?'

'Good Lord, no!' He leaned away from her a little, gazing at her with a preposterous look on his smooth face. 'But I'm not happy to wait until you're twenty-one. That's over two years away. Even if we wait until then, how much longer do you think you could keep our relationship a secret?'

She leaned closer to him, burying her head in his shoulder. 'Then what can we do?'

'We must tell them. But getting pregnant, especially deliberately, is certainly not the answer. You can't insult your own parents like that, Connie.' He gave a small derisive laugh at the thought. He paused then gently lifted her left hand on which she was wearing his ring, gazing at it for what seemed like ages, then said quietly, 'You've not yet worn this ring at home, have you?'

'I keep it round my neck – on a ribbon.'

He smiled, a sad smile that wrung her heart with guilt. 'I see,' he said, laying her hand down on her lap as gently as if it might break to pieces, the action making her feel oddly ashamed of her small act of subterfuge – that she should have flourished the ring in front of them and be damned what their reaction would have been.

'I don't want to hurt them,' she said quickly. 'They've enough to contend with these days.'

She saw him nod and knew he understood. Almost every family in the country had someone out there

210

fighting, fighting in Turkey too; almost every family had the constant fear of losing a loved one.

She wanted to let her body fall against him, have him kiss her again, his hands warm on her bare flesh, but all he did was put an arm around her and kiss her gently before moving away, murmuring that it was time he took her home before her parents grew worried.

So matter-of-fact after all that had happened, and now he was behaving as if nothing at all had taken place. All she wanted was to have that wonderful moment all over again, yet feelings of guilt had begun to steal over her. What would her mum and dad say if they knew their daughter was letting herself be made love to in a man's apartment? Stephen was right. She couldn't let herself get pregnant, disgracing the family she loved.

But it was more than just making love here on his sofa. It had begun to feel wrong – far from the sweet romance she'd imagined, it was beginning to contain an unhealthy quality to her mind, almost like illicit lovers taking furtive pleasure of each other in the secrecy of some dark alleyway. That bedroom of his, its door tightly shut as if it was sacrosanct, and she not cherished enough to share his bed. It had been so wonderful here on his sofa at first, but lately it was beginning not to feel right.

'I'm sorry, Stephen, for the things I said about getting pregnant,' she said, suddenly ashamed for even thinking of it. 'It was silly of me.'

But there was still this other thought plaguing her. If only he would take her to his bed, let her fall asleep in his arms. It would be so lovely; it would make her feel she really belonged to him.

211

Before she could check herself she had burst out, asking again 'Why have you never taken me into your bedroom, Stephen?' She was becoming angry. 'Is it because you still hold it sacred to the memory of—?'

She broke off, aware of him regarding her with an expression of sadness. She instantly read in it that she had gone too far; suddenly seeing it through his eyes without it needing to be put it into words. He and his wife had made love in that bed, she might even have passed away in it, a lasting reminder of the woman he'd loved and married, and not even she to whom he could make love on this sofa would ever be allowed near it.

Even as that thought came, she felt a twinge of rancour that despite making ardent love to her, there was a barrier between them, a barrier she felt she would never be able to tear down. All she could say was, 'I'm so sorry, Stephen, I wasn't thinking.'

He didn't smile. 'Taking you to bed, my dear, would be fatal, too easy to lose track of time, to wake up to find it morning, and what would your parents think, you being out all night? What excuse could you give, you who wear my engagement ring on a ribbon, hidden from them?'

It was said in such a matter-of-fact tone but she could feel the condemnation in that last question, realised how she was hurting him. Tears began to gather in her eyes – tears he had already noticed.

'You have to be honest with them, Connie,' he said gently. 'You have to tell them.'

She knew that now. To be honest with them was to honour him, though the thought of the possible consequences of telling them made her cringe.

*

Weeks had passed, and her nineteenth birthday had arrived and still she was hanging back from telling her parents about her and Stephen. He had given up asking her. He knew full well that she hadn't and it made her feel like a puppy terrified of its owner's anger; frightened too of his disappointment in her.

Her birthday fell on a Sunday. This evening he was taking her out to dinner to celebrate, somewhere very special, he'd said.

At midday she had been obliged to consume a Sunday birthday meal Mum had painstakingly cooked for the whole family and knew by the time she and Stephen had dinner, she'd hardly be able to find room for it.

Mum's offering had been a special birthday treat, a chicken she'd managed to get hold of – no one knew how. 'Your nineteenth birthday, love,' she'd said proudly, innocent of what had been planned for the evening. She'd have to apologise to Stephen as she pushed away her sumptuous meal, saying she was full to the brim.

She was meeting him at seven thirty, and had told her mum she was going with friends to a little club they knew to dance to a jazz band. Her mum had said, 'Well, don't let anyone lead you astray, love.' Connie knew her mother still saw her as an innocent, and was mistrustful of the effect this modern jazz music and jazz musicians might have on a young and impressionable girl like her daughter. 'Don't to be too late home, love,' she'd warned gently.

Connie hadn't known what Stephen had planned, other than being told to wear her very best clothes and nicest hat as they were going somewhere high class.

She guessed it was to be somewhere wonderful but in her wildest dreams hadn't even thought it would be the Ritz, the huge, electric-lit hotel she'd often walked past with friends. She'd never thought that one day she'd be setting foot in its sumptuous surroundings, conducted through the huge glass doors by those imposing, liveried doormen, and actually have a meal there.

It should have been lovely, drawing up in a proper chauffeur-driven motorcar Stephen had hired instead of a taxi, having a commissionaire open the vehicle door for them and another to open the hotel door to admit them into the most opulent surroundings she had ever seen, so hushed but for distant soothing music that she felt she dared not even speak lest she shiver the expensive atmosphere.

After handing her coat and hat to the cloakroom lady, she joined Stephen to be led to the sedate dining hall, the diners there looking as if they were worth millions, and she felt dowdy in her best dress. But Stephen threaded her arm firmly through his as they were conducted to their table.

She was gratified to find that the meal, though top class, was served in small portions so that whatever her lack of hunger compelled her to leave, wouldn't seem quite so noticeable. She'd expected to be overawed, but Stephen with his confident manner put her wonderfully at ease. Yet there was still that worry threatening to dim the wonderful evening, the delicious food bland in her mouth as she thought of her parents.

'I don't know how to tell them about us,' she said as they ate, and had him regard her across the beautifully laid table.

'I think you should let me come with you, you introduce me and let it go on from there.' He reached out across the table and took her hand in his; it felt so warm and comforting. 'It's got to be done sometime, my darling. It'll not get any easier by delaying it. You never know, your worries might be all for nothing, my love. When we leave here, I suggest we go straight to your parents and tell them.'

Gently she eased her hand away. 'I can't, not yet. They're already worried about poor Ronnie, and Albert's still at the front, and there's Dorothy pining for Ron to be sent home and see his daughter. He only saw her for just over one day after she was born. He's not seen her since. She'll be a nearly year old by the time he's well enough to come home. He'll have missed all the joy of seeing her growing up. I can't add to their problems, Stephen. Let's wait just a little while longer.'

He released her hand and sat back. 'Very well, darling,' he said like a man defeated. 'As you wish.'

But she knew her reticence to tell her parents about them was pushing them further apart. What if he were to grow frustrated by her continually deferring the matter and told her that it was all no use, it was all off and to call it a day? She couldn't have borne that. Yes, she would have to tell them – as soon as she found the courage. But she knew what their reaction would be and that terrified her. Telling them or not telling them, either way she could lose him.

Christmas bore all the signs of being a really miserable one, not only because it was getting harder to find anything, food prices having gone sky high, but because

215

Maggie Ford

of the bleak news of stalemate along the whole length of the Western Front, with thousands of men being lost daily. No one at home said much about it, but the tightness of Mum's lips, the anguished way she would twist her fingers together when she thought no one was watching, and her father's taut, grim face, told Connie of their fear for Albert's safety and anguish for Ronnie's future.

Dorothy was the one most noticeably affected, yearning for Ron to be finally sent home to spend the rest of his life watching his daughter grow up.

He was still in France, being treated for shell shock, they'd now been told – mild, they said, as if it were some sort of consolation – and for the ongoing treatment of his stump that wasn't healing as well as it should. Albert was still in the thick of it and who could say he wouldn't be killed at any time? How, then, could Connie burden them with news of herself and Stephen?

As for Christmas presents, it was fine for those with money who could afford any price, but ordinary people could only do their best. Everyone accepted with good grace that a kiss and a thank you for a humble gift was more precious than the gift itself, which was usually given with the comment: 'When this damned war's over, we'll make up for it!'

Christmas dinner would no doubt be festive, the family coming round with their tiny offerings, everyone trying to put a brave face on it, other than Dorothy, who without her own mother's shoulder to cry on, was using her future mother-in-law's instead.

Connie was already seeing Christmas as holding little promise for her, knowing she couldn't ask Stephen to be with her. What sort of Christmas would he have, alone

216

in his flat, no family to speak of, colleagues who'd probably have their own families to be with? But worse was the news hanging over her head that she'd have to tell her parents about him eventually.

Most of her time was spent going over and over what she would say, but it never seemed to come out right. She should have told them long ago and got it over with. At least she'd know by now where she stood with them.

She promised herself to tell them next week. Come what may, and have done with it, face whatever disparagement they'd aim at her.

Then came something that alarmed Connie even more deeply, making her feel certain that Stephen would be leaving her, even though it would not be his decision. She had been at work for a couple of hours when he had entered her department and came over to her desk, gazing at her as he held out an official document. 'My calling-up papers,' he explained bleakly.

It felt as if her heart had stopped. 'Oh, Stephen, no!'

'I never expected this,' he was saying as if she had not spoken. 'Perhaps they won't accept me. They didn't last time. The ear trouble, you see, I'd have thought they would have had all that on record. But that's the military for you.'

He spoke lightly enough and relief was flooding over her. 'Then it should be all right,' she said, 'once they've looked at your old files.'

When he spoke again it was as if to himself. 'The last time I tried to volunteer, that was. The time before I met you, at that time I made the mistake of telling the paper, and they were dead against it – said I was too much of an asset to leave them for any reason. I never realised they held me in such high esteem. They'd never admitted that to me before, but then they wouldn't, would they, in case I got above myself and sought a post with some larger newspaper or asked for a substantial rise in salary.'

He gave a whimsical smile seeming to be directed at himself.

Connie detected the irony behind the smile but her own heart was pounding. What if this time they took him? What would she do? The newspapers, even this one, were reporting carnage at a place called the Somme. What if something should happen to him? The idea did not bear thinking about.

'Maybe they'll reject you again because of your ear trouble,' she said hopefully. 'They've probably got their paperwork all mixed up.' After millions of men passing through the recruiting centres, mistakes were bound to happen.

'More likely they need men so badly,' he said, 'that they no longer care who they take. Most likely they'd take me, half-deaf and all.'

'They can't!' she burst out, but indeed they could. 'The paper might never find anyone as good as you; maybe they have to take on some elderly duffer who's past his prime. You're needed here. So many are being called up, you'll just be one of thousands. Surely they wouldn't miss one man.'

He made no answer and she let her tirade ebb away, her argument futile. But so many men were being lost, the recruitments centres were eager for more human fuel to replace them. But Stephen, a single man admittedly, but one who had been more than once rejected because of partial deafness when he'd gone to volunteer, surely they wouldn't have changed their minds? Now it was certain they'd take him despite his disability and his newspaper's need of him. It was out of his hands, out of theirs, out of hers too.

Her sisters' husbands were now on the front line and them each with a family and young children. Her sisters were feeling the strain. And even men previously deemed unfit for duty were being considered, or so it was rumoured. What chance did Stephen have?

The next morning he didn't come to work. She knew where he had gone. He returned several hours later, first having spent time talking to Mathieson, his chief editor.

When he returned to his own department, he went straight into his own office without glancing her way. She could see him from where she sat at her desk in the corner but could hardly get up and go barging into his office to find out the results of his time at the recruitment centre. That lunchtime he was out of the office interviewing someone for a story he was writing. She would have to wait until this evening. They'd be going to dinner together after work. He'd tell her then how it had gone. But it didn't look promising and the rest of the day was agony. Not once did he look in her direction and she was unable to concentrate on a single thing. Thankfully she would not be required to go out with a photographer on an assignment. Although there had been a zeppelin raid over London last night, the paper felt there had been too many depictions on its pages of devastated faces and their readership deserved a break.

219

That evening she and Stephen ate dinner in virtual silence. She was glad when they returned to his flat for their usual nightcap and she could tax him in private as to how he had fared.

After getting out of their outdoor things, she sat herself down on the sofa, but instead of sitting down beside her he remained standing, gazing down at her, his face as grim as it had been all day. She dared not ask how he had got on. Then suddenly it seemed to burst from his lips.

'I'm exempt – I've been rejected,' he said abruptly, but he didn't smile.

The terrible thought struck her: had he *wanted* to go into the forces? Had he been prepared to leave her after all, as easily and lightly as that, and now he was disappointed? She was being unkind thinking such a thing but couldn't help her thoughts from dwelling on it – she hated herself for even thinking it. But an immense wave of relief had flooded over her all the same, even though he didn't look at all happy.

'What's wrong, Stephen?' she managed to ask. 'They rejected you. You are exempt. So what's wrong?'

'I feel somehow ashamed.'

She frowned. 'How can you feel ashamed? It's not your fault. It was their decision.'

But he shook his head. 'I feel guilty.'

Instantly she leapt up, ready to put her arms around him, but he backed swiftly away, leaving her standing there. All she could do was entreat him.

'Why should you feel guilty? My darling, you're not guilty of anything.'

'I did something shameful,' he said in a low tone.

220

'What?' she entreated, alarmed. 'What on earth are you talking about, my love?'

He was nibbling at his lower lip as if unsure that he should tell her whatever it was. Finally he said, 'I tried to get them to overlook my affliction. I'm so sorry, my darling, but I felt I had to try and do my bit. I honour this country, same as other men, and that was why I volunteered at the beginning of the war. Now, of course, I don't want to leave you. All the same, I . . .'

He let the words die away as she stood wanting so much to hold him to her but frightened to do so in case he retreated even further away from her.

'I know we'd be torn apart,' he went on in a flat tone. 'But I felt I had to try and do my best. I went for the usual medical. The medical officer, an officious-looking chap, examined me thoroughly, and naturally in the course of his examination discovered the ruptured eardrum.' Stephen lifted his head challengingly. 'It was then I said a really stupid thing. I asked if he could overlook it and give me a clean bill of health. After all, other than that, I was fit and in perfect health. But he looked at me as if I had blasphemed – said haughtily that he was sorry but he was not prepared to allow himself to stoop – *stoop*, mind you – to passing any man A1 when he knew I was certainly not A1.'

Stephen turned from her and began pacing the room as he continued talking, seeming to be addressing the floor. 'He drew himself upright and said very slowly and deliberately, as if talking to some criminal, that he considered himself above such low practice, and should another medical officer examine me at some later date and find that I had been passed as fit by himself when

I was obviously not, it would most certainly reflect on him and his integrity as an officer – his words, uttered as if he were God Almighty – and he was not prepared for such to happen, not for anyone. He added that he didn't know me from Adam so why should I presume he would sink to what I was asking him to do for me, to lie and put his own career in jeopardy for someone he had never before set eyes on in his whole life? I've never had anyone address me in that tone, ever – the supercilious bastard! As if I were some wayward child. Then he officially filled in the medical forms, dismissing me as unfit for military duties.'

As Stephen's voice died away, Connie again tried to approach him, devastated for him even though her heart was singing with unbearable relief. But Stephen had more to say, his voice trembling with anger.

'He motioned me with his hand to leave, adding as a parting shot, I suppose, that I had insulted his integrity by even expecting him to bend the rules. I just wanted to crawl away. I've never felt that way before.'

Stephen wasn't even looking at her; it was as though he were speaking to himself as if trying to smother the embarrassment lurking within him.

'I do recall having heard about a move to recruit those with hearing difficulties but otherwise perfectly fit to fight – that they have a hearing officer who could issue orders – but the War Department threw the idea out as being suicide – the possibility of them walking unknowingly into a trap should their officer be otherwise distracted, to be mowed down by the enemy having not heard its advance. Even so, the way that blasted officer spoke to me made me feel like a worm, and I can still hear his tone, full of contempt at someone stooping to bribery, as he called it. It has left me feeling so bloody ashamed. I know I shouldn't be, but it's there.'

As his voice died away, Connie's heart went out to him and she whispered, 'I do know, my darling, I do know. It was so deeply unkind and unwarranted.'

And this time he didn't pull away from her as she came and held him close.

Chapter Twenty-Two

February 1917

It was the end of February and Ronnie was back in England. He had been admitted to a hospital in the west of London, not so much a hospital as a big house that had been taken over for treating shell-shocked patients. One of the nurses caring for him had sent a letter saying they had high hopes for him, he wasn't as bad as some and that his wound was clean and healing well. Connie saw her mother breathe a huge sigh of gratitude as she read, even as the tears fell from her face.

'Maybe he'll come home soon and then him and Dorothy can get married, make that little girl legitimate like, poor little thing.'

Legitimate. The word sent a shiver through Connie's body like an electric shock. Mum had been suffering all this time over her son's baby being born out of wedlock. What would she have done if her daughter had come home saying that she was pregnant? It would have killed her. Not that she and Stephen intended on taking chances but her need for him was growing beyond her. It was he who drew back, saying it was his duty to look after her, and she loved him for it, so very much.

She wanted to proclaim to the world that they were one, yet his ring still remained hidden from sight on the end of the ribbon around her neck. She wore it on her finger only when they were together. She was growing daily more angry with herself for her subterfuge and wanted to declare him to the world as her fiancé, whether it proved a disaster or not. Either way, she could never give him up now, even if it meant being thrown out of her family. Deep down she knew Mum would never allow that to happen, but even so . . .

She could see her mother's mind working towards getting Dorothy and Ron hitched as soon as possible to save the family's good name. So how could she give Mum, who was on tenterhooks about Ron and Dorothy, the smallest hint of how she and Stephen were behaving?

Stephen was not being helpful. 'When are you ever going to find a chance to tell them once your brother comes home? If you feel you're adding to their burden now, think what it'll be like once he is home. And to tell you the truth, Connie, I can't go on like this – all this secrecy, this hiding in corners. Something has got to happen.'

They were standing together at the end of her street before they said goodbye. To her it sounded like a threat and she shivered. 'I will tell them,' she burst out in desperation. 'I will!'

'When?'

'Tonight – I promise. Tonight.'

'How?'

She stood silent. Had she the courage to face them and explain why she'd not told them before? She could hear them asking how long she had known him. If she lied and said it was only a few months, they'd say it was too early to want to get engaged, that they needed to meet him and see what sort of boy he was. She'd have to explain about him, that he was no *boy*, that he'd been married before, and hear them say no, they wouldn't dream of her marrying a previously married man who was so much older than her.

He must have seen her anguished expression. 'I'll come with you,' he said abruptly. 'We'll face them together.'

Panic swept over her. 'No! No, Stephen. Let me tell them in my own way. I promise I'll tell them tonight – as soon as I go indoors.'

He looked at her sadly. 'I'll give you until Friday,' he said. 'I realise that you might need to find the right words to break the news to them. But darling, please tell them. For our sake, and theirs.'

'I promise,' she said again.

But it was easier said than done.

Connie wouldn't be seeing Stephen socially until Friday. By then she was to have told her family about their relationship. It was already Tuesday and at work yesterday he'd asked if she'd told them yet.

Forced to admit she'd not found the right opportunity so far with all their worry about her brother on the other side of London, and how he was coping with it – plus Dorothy was not bearing up at all well, worrying herself sick about it – Stephen had merely turned away without a word and returned to his office.

226

She'd felt devastated but could hardly go and plead with him, with everyone looking on. Some time ago her colleagues had become aware of something going on between Connie and Stephen and she hated that they now caught the hint of a tiff.

Today as she sat at her desk anticipating what she would say when he came to ask if she had done what she'd promised, she tensed herself to make yet more excuses. But he hadn't once come near her.

As soon as she'd had her lunch she was to be sent out on an assignment. Usually he wouldn't miss the chance to tell her himself, touch her hand like a secret embrace, but instead he'd sent one of his staff to tell her.

It felt very ominous and left her sick with worry. She promised herself that she would face her parents the moment she got home from work this evening. What other option was there? But what if, after she'd explained, they forbade her from having anything more to do with him? Or if he called it a day if she failed to act now?

She could see it coming and it horrified her even though it would be as much a wrench to him as to her. But she couldn't lose him. What would her life be without him? That was made starkly obvious at lunchtime. They usually had lunch together these days in a nearby cafe and she'd taken it for granted they would today, no doubt with him coaxing her to take her courage in both hands or suggesting being with her when she told her parents. And this time she resolved to have him with her and have them see him for the wonderful person he was.

Looking up from her desk as she made ready to go to lunch, she saw that his office was empty. Hurrying over, she spoke to Mr Turnbull. 'Is Mr Clayton around?'

He regarded her awkwardly. 'Gone to lunch, I think.'

It was like being hit by a steam engine. All she could say was, 'Oh, I see.'

She bought a cheese sandwich from a local tea bar, eating it at her desk. It was like sandpaper in her mouth. She put it to one side only half-eaten. With most of the newsroom gone to lunch, the place felt desolate. At least she'd be out of the office this afternoon with a photographer and an interviewer: there had been an accident in a factory filling shells – a faulty shell had exploded; one female worker was injured, another killed. She was expected to sketch the shock on the workers' faces. She did it automatically and much of her own anguish, she knew, also went into the sketches.

Stephen hadn't come back when she finally returned to the office. Her work had been taken up to her chief editor by Mr Turnbull to receive approval for it to go into tomorrow's edition. She didn't ask him where Stephen was.

It was the most awful journey home, sitting on the bus, shops and people passing by unobserved as she rehearsed how she was going to approach her mother, and worse, her father, and what she was going to say to Stephen when she next saw him. Now, she wanted so much for him to be with her when she told them.

The first words that greeted her as she came in were Mum's. 'They're sending Ronnie home. They say they're 'aving to make room for worst cases than him. Oh Connie, love, ain't that wonderful?'

There was no chance now to confront them with her own concerns and all she could do was clasp her mother to her and say it was the best news she'd heard in a long time.

It scared the life out of her going to work the following morning, sure he was bound to ask, rather than just ignore her. Her heart pounded seeing him approach her as she sipped her mid-morning cup of tea. He was smiling – that slightly sideways smile of his that always made her quiver inside with love.

She smiled up at him as he came to stand at her desk, but his own smile had vanished.

'Sorry to ask,' he began, 'but have you said anything to your family yet?'

The question sounded cold, as if he were addressing someone about business. She took a deep breath and tried to control the quivering in her chest, which was partly from love, partly from fear and anxiety.

'I was about to,' she began. 'I'd made up my mind to on the bus on my way home.' She was drawing out the dread moment. 'But Mum said they'd had a letter from the hospital, that they're sending Ronnie home. He's far from better but they need the room for worse cases than his. And Mum was all of a dither and Dorothy was excited and frightened at the same time, not knowing how he'll be and how she'll cope with him. I couldn't push my news on them at the same time, Stephen. I just couldn't.'

She was gabbling and he stood there listening to it all. At any minute he would turn on his heel and walk off – a signal that it was all over between them. Then what would she do?'

She heard him take a deep breath. Now he'd tell her that it was all over between them. But how could it be after what they had been to each other? How could he say goodbye to what they'd had together?

She heard him exhale slowly. 'Well,' he said. 'Maybe another time.'

What did that mean, maybe another time? In a small voice she posed the question and heard him reply quietly, 'We can talk about it over lunch. We need to get this cleared up, Connie, once and for all.'

Someone at his office door was beckoning to him. 'Must go,' he said tersely, but as he turned, his hand touched her arm briefly. That small touch spoke volumes: warmth and reassurance.

She couldn't wait for the morning to pass. Sitting at her desk, sorting out the filing which she would do between assignments, the next hours seemed to creep by.

It was wonderful sitting with him in their cafe, all the more wonderful seeing as only yesterday she was thinking that this would never happen again. But she could eat only little of the small lunch, toying with it as he ate heartily.

'Not hungry?' he asked at one time, as if nothing had ever gone on between them.

'I can't eat,' she said. This obviously spoke volumes as he put down his knife and fork and pushed away the plate to gaze at her.

'Right then, my love, I can see you're never going to be able to do this on your own. I know it's only Wednesday, and that I gave you until Friday to tell them, but I will come with you. We'll have this out with your parents together.'

Connie felt conflicted. On the one hand, it would be wonderful to have him with her, so her parents could see the kind of man he was. On the other hand, seeing them together would highlight the difference in their ages. 'No, Stephen!'

'Yes, Connie – before your brother comes home. We have to get this matter sorted. If not, I cannot see a future for us.' That frightened her more than anything, the tautness of his jaw muscles proof enough that he meant what he said.

Giving herself no time to think, she burst out, 'Friday, then!'

She saw his shoulders droop ever so slightly, revealing that he'd been going through just as much tension as she, and her heart went out to him.

'We'll see my parents together,' she repeated, though in her heart she trembled to think what their reaction might be: the shock on her mother's face, the frown on her father's. But they would have had to know eventually.

When she and Stephen had dinner together on Saturday, they would at least have lighter conscience, having their cards on the table and able to go on from there. But she was not looking forward at all to Friday.

The timing couldn't have been worse. After work, she came home to absolute turmoil. Some time mid-afternoon Ronnie had been brought home, completely out of the blue, by a Voluntary Aid Detachment person. As she entered, Ronnie sat in Dad's chair staring into the fire, his head jerking at intervals.

Seeing Connie, the VAD worker looked up from where he had been sitting close by him, talking to him in a quiet tone, while Mum and Dorothy sat at the parlour table not knowing quite what to do.

'I'm glad you're home,' the man said. 'I take it you're his sister.'

'Yes,' she answered, staring at Ron, not knowing what else to say.

'I am just waiting for your father to come home,' he went on. 'Then I'll have to leave. I've explained to your mother what is needed and I will also explain to your father. But the good news is that your brother is doing well, and I shall convey this to your father when he appears.'

Connie nodded as she took off her coat, laying it over the back of a chair, and placed her hat and handbag on the table on which empty tea cups resided.

'Shall I make some more tea?' she asked ineffectually.

She saw Ronald look sharply up at her and saw in his eyes the most startled look she had ever seen, as if he had suddenly been confronted by an enemy soldier. It made her blood run cold for a second or two.

She made herself smile gently at him. 'It's really, really lovely to see you, Ronnie. We've missed you so much.'

She watched the look slowly fade. During her time on the paper she had sketched so many expressions of trauma, but never one like this. She wanted to kiss her brother's cheek but instinctively knew that such an action would only make him flinch.

'Tea?' she queried again.

Mum's voice said, 'That'll be nice, love.'

She found herself glad to get out into the kitchen away from them all. It was there that she burst into quiet tears,

232

tears which continued to fall as she set about making the tea.

Not long after she'd brought the tea in for them all, little Violet began to cry from where she lay in her cot upstairs. Instantly Dorothy leapt up, which made Ronnie jump, although she didn't see it as she made for the stairs. Moments later she brought the baby down and then, doing something that surprised them all, she quietly moved towards her child's father and gently placed the baby in his arms. He automatically held out his arms to receive the little bundle. It was like watching a small miracle. Oblivious to everyone looking on, he held the child tenderly, bent his head and kissed her on the forehead.

Violet didn't cry. She was looking up at him as if she knew him, her wide blue eyes taking her father in. He lifted his head, still holding the baby very gently, and looked at them all one by one, with not one jerk of his head.

'She's absolutely lovely,' he said in a steady voice and Dorothy came forward to kiss him too. His free arm opened out to bring her closer to him – a little family united. It was as if he'd never been to war, had shells bursting all round him, had lost his leg to one, had become shell shocked by his experiences.

Although it didn't last. He finally had to release his hold on his precious little family and Dorothy took the baby from him, stepping back to the parlour table. On his own again, they saw his head jerk several times in quick succession; his eyes were closed, hiding from Connie any expression there might have been in them. The VAD man was smiling.

233

'I think he's going to be all right,' he whispered. 'But it will take time.'

He might have said more, but the crash at the back door heralded the entrance of her father and the onset of another round of emotional turmoil that would last long after the VAD worker had left.

Chapter Twenty-Three

It was two days until Connie and Stephen were to tell her family about their relationship, and the hours dragged by. Several times she wondered if she should at least drop a hint, but her courage always failed her at the last minute. It was all too easy to put a spanner in the works. Nothing must spoil her chances. And the sight of Ronnie sitting by the parlour window staring blankly out, head jerking, not speaking unless forced, only coming alive when Dorothy and the baby were with him, would have stopped her before she'd begun.

On Friday, as she and Stephen were getting out of a taxi at her door, she noticed how tightly he was holding her hand. Or was it she holding his?

It was a relief to see it was her mother who had come to the door and not her father.

'You're late—' she began then broke off once she saw Stephen. As Connie introduced him by name, adding that he was her boss, her mother drew in a startled breath. 'What's the matter, love?'

'Nothing's the matter.' Already she could feel the tension. 'No bad news. It's just that me and Ste— Mr Clayton, have something we need to tell you.'

Her mother stepped back. 'Well, don't stand there, come in.'

Dad's voice came from the parlour, where he was enjoying his pipe: 'Who is it?'

'It's our Connie and a young man, her boss.'

'What's 'e want?' Connie felt suddenly ashamed of her father's rough Cockney voice.

'We'll tell him ourselves,' she said hurriedly, letting Mum lead them into her humble parlour. At least the room would be clean and tidy; Mum was a house-proud woman, thank God.

It was all so different to what she had once dreamed about – she introducing Stephen to her family, he politely asking permission for her hand in marriage. That dream was so lovely in its traditional formality.

Now they stood in the parlour, her mother saying, 'This is Connie's boss who she works for. He says he's got something he wants to say to us, love.'

Connie was somehow strangely relieved that Ronnie wasn't here at the moment but in Mum's front room where he and his little family now slept, he no longer able to manage the stairs any more. How would it have been, Stephen seeing him for the first time, her brother hardly able to keep his head still as he gazed into space?

Her father had got up out of his chair to come towards his visitor with an enquiring stare. 'Ain't nuffink wrong, is there, Mr . . .'

'Clayton,' Stephen said readily. 'Nothing is wrong, nothing at all.'

'I'm sorry,' her father was saying. 'Don't mean to be rude, Mr Clayton, but if nuffink's wrong, why're you 'ere?'

Connie wanted to hold Stephen's hand and blurt out that they'd become engaged. Instead she stood at his side, inwardly cringing at her father's rough speech. Although she loved both her parents, she had always – perhaps unconsciously – tried at least to make an effort to speak as well as the sort of people she'd have liked to be. Not making a great job of it, but certainly better than her mum and dad.

'Nothing is wrong, Mr Lovell,' Stephen said. 'This is a personal thing. You see, I—'

'What d'you mean, personal thing?' her father interrupted.

Connie could contain herself no longer. 'Dad,' she burst out. 'Mum. Mr Clayton and I . . . Stephen . . . he's not just my boss, we've been going out together for quite a time now. And . . . well, there's this.' Pausing, she reached down into the neckline of the jumper she wore and dragged out the ribbon. 'I've had this for this some time. But I didn't want to—'

Mum came forward and took the ribbon in her hand to gaze at the ring dangling from it. 'A ring?' she exclaimed. 'A ring with a diamond.'

'It's an engagement ring, Mum. Stephen and I couldn't – we couldn't tell you. You see there were certain things I couldn't find the courage to tell you. But sooner or later I supposed I'd have to.'

'Engaged?' her mother repeated. 'And you never thought to tell us?'

''Ow long's this bin goin' on?' interrupted her father, his voice a deep growl, signifying an explosion at any minute. Connie felt her stomach tighten but Stephen spoke for her.

'I apologise sincerely, Mr Lovell, springing this on you and Connie's mother, but—'

''Ow long?'

'Several months.'

'So why now? You and 'er – you bin up to no good wiv 'er – takin' advantage of her 'cos she's employed by you? You ain't got 'er—'

'No I have not, Mr Lovell.' Stephen's tone was sharp. 'Connie was just worried about telling you earlier in case you forbade her from seeing me.'

Dad was glaring. 'What you mean, worried? What you got to 'ide?'

Stephen took a deep breath, putting a calming hand on her shoulder as she made to speak, aware that he knew it was he who needed to explain, not her.

'Because I am a bit older than Connie – by nine years – and because I was married before.'

Dad had grown angry even as he smirked derisively. 'Got rid of the little woman, did you? She slung you out or did you sling 'er out so you could get you 'ands on my daughter? Prettier is she, our Connie?'

'I lost my wife several years ago, Mr Lovell.' The quiet reply was low, steady. 'It was cancer. No one could save her.' Connie saw the fleeting look of pain cross his face. 'I met your daughter when she came to an interview but it was a long time before we became attracted to each other. I'm sorry that she said nothing to you in all that time but she was worried about what you would

238

say. I gave her the ring several months ago but she felt, as appears to be proving correct, that you wouldn't give permission for us to marry, and she insisted on keeping it out of sight. Mr Lovell, I want to marry your daughter. Will you give your consent?'

'Not till she's twenty-one,' was her father's flat reply.

Connie couldn't help herself. 'Then we'll go off somewhere and get married without your consent, Dad!'

Stephen's restraining hand on her arm again stopped her from saying anything more. 'If you feel that way, sir,' he said politely, 'then so be it. But—'

'No!' Her mother moved forward more briskly than Connie had ever seen her move before. 'No, she's old enough now to know her own mind, and if they've bin seein' each other all this time, then I—'

She stopped as the parlour door opened very quietly. There stood Ronnie, with Dorothy and the baby behind them. The room fell silent. Leaning on his crutches somewhat unsteadily, his head jerking more than Connie had ever seen in the short time he'd been home, he cut a pitiful figure. Staring fixedly at the floor, he negotiated his way awkwardly around the table to the upright chair by the window which in the short time he'd been home, he had silently claimed as his.

'We heard shouting,' Dorothy said. 'Woke the baby and Ronnie got all worried. So I thought we should come and see what was goin' on.'

Stephen might not have been here for all the notice Ronnie had taken of him as sat staring out of the window, his head twitching, painful to see, and embarrassing, Connie had to confess, hating herself for the thought.

239

But Stephen had started towards him, whispering, 'Beg your pardon, sir,' as he passed her father, who moved aside automatically. Approaching Ronnie, he held out his right hand. 'I'm sorry to have barged into the house like this, disturbing your small daughter. But I've come to ask for your sister's hand in marriage. I hope I've won your parents over but I'd like your consent as well, if that's all right. I promise to look after her, take every care of her, and you'll be my brother-in-law. What d'you think, Ron, about us being brothers-in-law?'

Connie saw her brother look up at him and give a faint smile; it was the first time since coming home that he had looked anyone straight in the eye, much less smiled, other than when gazing at his daughter, and she wanted to burst into tears. Glancing at her mother, she saw tears on her cheeks too.

Then a whimper came from the baby and all eyes turned to her, the sound breaking the tension. Then Ronnie's voice, clear as a bell, 'That- that's m-my d-daughter, Vi-Vi-Violet.'

In the few days he'd been home he'd not spoken a word. It didn't matter that his stutter was painful to hear – he had spoken and her Stephen had been the one who had prompted it. Even so, there was still no ready welcome in Dad's eyes and Connie felt that he resented Stephen for his sudden ability to break through – if only temporarily – to his son when he himself had not yet been able to. Connie felt her anger rise towards him. But Mum too was noticeably wary, nibbling at her lower lip as she looked from her daughter to Stephen and back again, as if she felt Stephen had taken advantage of the situation.

Connie felt the muscles in her stomach tighten in anger even as she smiled at her mother, keeping her father at bay, for if she won Mum round, her mum would make sure to bring him round in that usual quiet but dogged way of hers. But Mum wasn't on her side yet. She would need a lot of persuading – her daughter looking to marry a man who'd already been married once, albeit a widower, and he years older than her daughter, where she'd always expected – dreamed of – her bringing home a nice young boy of her own age.

She could see that Stephen had already sensed the tension. 'Maybe I had better go,' he said in a low voice, which made Connie start.

'No!' she burst out. 'We've come to get my parents' consent.' There was still this angry tension in her stomach. 'And if they don't intend to give it, then I'm ready to go away with you and we'll get married without it.'

She heard her mother's sharp intake of breath. 'Connie . . .' warned Stephen.

'No, Stephen, I mean it. 'Either we do that, or—'

She was about to add, 'we can part for good', but couldn't bring herself to say it.

But Dad with his usual lack of tact suddenly burst in, 'An' another thing – why ain't he in the forces, fightin' fer 'is country?'

She swung round on him. 'He's tried, Dad. But they won't take him. He had a serious illness when he was a child that left him profoundly deaf in one ear, and they won't have him.'

'Connie—'

'No, Stephen, I'm not having him accusing you of cowardice.'

241

But her father had more to say. 'Be that as it may, you're under age and until you're twenty-one—'

'It's wartime, Dad!' she flung back at him. 'It's not the nineteenth century any longer! Girls my age go off all the time the way things are to get married without their parents' consent – if they go to the right places and by special licence. There's no time for niceties any more.' She turned to Stephen. 'I love you. I want to marry you, and if I don't marry you, I shall never marry anyone, and I mean that with all my heart.'

The room had fallen silent. She could see Ronnie gazing at them, his head beginning to jerk again, his brown eyes looking a little wild. All the good Stephen had done him earlier on had been undone by a stupid, squabbling family.

'Ronnie!' she appealed to him. 'Ron – what would you do?'

He seemed to be trying to gather his wits. 'I . . . I w-w-would m-marry him if – if – if I w-was . . . was you.' His words caught in his throat as he said them.

She wanted to run to him and hold him to her, but common sense told her that if she did so he would dissolve back into the shell-shocked man he had become.

'Thank you, Ron,' was all she said. Then turning to Stephen, 'Come on, darling, let's go. We'll sort this out ourselves.'

With those few words she knew she was estranging herself from her family and it suddenly felt as if her heart was about to break. Why had she said them? But she was already out of the room, making her way towards the front door. Stephen was coming after her, calling her back, telling her to apologise, that she wasn't helping things by getting herself into a state unnecessarily.

She turned on him at that. 'Do you want to marry me, Stephen, or not?'

He stopped short. 'Yes, of course I want to marry you.'

'Then—' She broke off as her mother came hurrying from the room.

'Connie, love,' she began in a voice low enough not to be heard in the room behind them. 'Let me talk to your father. You ain't doing yourself no good going off in a paddy. You and Stephen – I like him, I have to say. I have to think he's the one for you, love, and it don't matter about him being, well you know . . . older.'

Dad's voice from the parlour called her name. 'What you doin' out there with them two?'

'I'm *talking* to them!' she called back, her voice firm enough to shut him up, and turned back to her daughter, her voice now an urgent whisper. 'It might be that him being older, he'll look after you more than some youngster with no idea – I mean some round 'ere I wouldn't give the time of day to. And you've got the promise of a comfortable life, a nice home, if I'm right. And a man what'll look after you.' She looked purposefully at Stephen. 'You go now. Let me talk to your dad. And sometime next week we'll see how things go.' She looked up at Stephen. 'Nice to've met you, Mr Clayton . . .'

'Stephen,' he said quickly, and she nodded.

'I pray everything works out well for you – for you both – but I know it will. Don't worry, you leave her dad to me.'

With that, she opened the front door for them, calling purposefully after her daughter as they went out, 'And don't be too late 'ome, Connie, love, there's a dear.'

Connie knew exactly what she meant.

Connie's mother had invited him to Sunday dinner this week even though as they left, she had given Connie her usual instructions not to be too late home, looking at Stephen as she said it in an unspoken warning to him to honour her daughter's precious state. He couldn't be off knowing exactly what she was alluding to and maybe it was that which made him suddenly do what he did.

In his flat, he'd kissed her tenderly and gently to the quiet music of the gramophone. She expected his embrace to become stronger as their needs mounted. Instead, he had drawn away from her and gently pulled her up from the sofa. She thought that he was about to hold her to him and dance in a gentle foxtrot to the slow regular beat of the music. Instead he whispered, 'I've made a few changes, darling, come and see.'

Taking her hand he led her towards the bedroom door, which he had always kept closed. To her surprise, still holding her hand, he opened it, leading her into the room, letting go only to switch on a small table lamp beside the bed.

Instinctively she looked around, noticing instantly how large it was and how sumptuously furnished, as she had always guessed it would be.

'I've bought a new bed, my love.' Had anyone else made such a bland statement she'd have laughed, but she understood. He'd finally put the past behind him. She was his now.

It was strange and a little terrifying undressing to her knickers and slip. She was going no further than that for now. As he too undressed, she had turned her back so as not to look at him as he slipped between the silken sheets. He pulled back the top sheets on her side for her to creep in, which she did, not daring to look at him, and turning her back to him in a silly effort for him not to see her in her underthings. He couldn't know that her heart was beating like a mad drum while her head told her that she should not be doing this, that it was far too sudden. She wanted to leap away, say it was so, but was too overwrought to even say that.

'I'll set the alarm clock for ten thirty p.m.,' he whispered as she finally lay next to him. 'In case we fall asleep.'

She knew what he meant, taking notice of her mother's pointed advice not to be too late home, the woman well aware that lovers could be carried away. She had to smile for it didn't take lying together all through the night for such a thing as she feared to happen. But she knew what Mum meant, and so did he. She was also confident that even in a bed he would continue to look after her.

Now as they lay together, she nestling into his arms, he said quietly, 'When would you like to marry me, Connie?'

Joy surged through her like a fierce flood and she leaned toward him, kissing his face. 'Oh, darling, you say. When?'

In the darkness she could feel him smiling. 'What would you say to September?'

'September?' She lifted her head a little to gaze into his face, only just able to make out its handsome shape against the small light of his bedside table lamp. 'That's only six months away. It takes much longer than that to arrange a wedding.'

'Things have to be done in double quick time when there's a war on,' she heard him chuckle.

'But the cost, it needs saving for. My parents don't have . . . They'd never save enough for a wedding in just six months.'

'They don't need to worry,' he said quietly. 'I'll pay for everything.'

But instead of gratitude she knew her parents would feel insulted by his offer. They had their pride.

'It's not just that,' she said, her body growing taut beside him. 'It could look as if it's being done in a rush and you know what people are like – I don't want to be the centre of speculation that I'm *having* to get married. It doesn't matter that they're proved wrong later on. The thought would still have been there.' She let her voice die away and he was silent for a moment.

'When would you think it the right time to get married, then?' he finally asked.

She felt herself relax, her voice falling to an easier tone. 'I'd like it to be a summer wedding . . . .' She broke off. 'Not this summer. That would be even worse. Or a spring wedding, say March or April, when the daffodils are out and buds are on trees . . .'

'That's a year away,' he broke in, sounding alarmed. 'How can I wait that long to claim you for my own, my sweetest? I can hardly contain myself now.'

She smiled in the dim light. 'What about December, then, near my birthday?'

He thought for a moment, then said whimsically, 'I don't think I can last that long.'

It made her laugh and with that laugh, she felt herself being gathered up into his arms.

'All right, darling,' she murmured. 'September, then.'

The next hour was bliss. As always he was careful, but to have him lie so close, little between them but her panties, easily discarded, then with the feel of the silk sheets caressing the two of them, she became his.

There was an hour to go before they must get dressed, tidy themselves and Connie taken home before her parents began to fret where she was. The last thing she wanted was for him to fall out of favour with them for bringing her home even half an hour later than he'd promised. Nothing must be allowed to alter her father's continuing suspicions of him for the worse.

She must have slept a little, awaking gently to the small disturbance of Stephen turning over. Moments later he was sitting bolt upright.

'Christ Almighty!'

She too sat up. 'What's wrong, darling?'

'The fucking time!' She couldn't remember ever having heard him swear, certainly not like that. 'Connie! For God sake, get up, get dressed!'

'What is it, Stephen?'

'It six thirty in the morning! The alarm clock didn't go off and we slept right through the night. Oh God! Your parents!'

It was then she became aware of thin daylight trickling through the drawn blinds.

Chapter Twenty-Four

How she got through that morning, she hardly knew.

Standing on the front doorstep at seven thirty, the sun only just rising, she and Stephen faced her mother. Connie's heart leapt with relief that it hadn't been her father who'd opened the door to them. He had already left home to pick his coal cart up from the coal company's yard.

But her mother's expression was no less intimidating than his thunderous one would have been. Staring down at her daughter, her expression of silent accusation pierced right through Connie's heart.

'It's not how it looks, Mum,' she began, but felt the grip of Stephen's hand holding hers tighten in warning.

'I'm sorry, Mrs Lovell,' Stephen said. 'We had dinner last night at a restaurant. There must have been something wrong with the food. After we came away, Connie was terribly sick.' He was talking fast as he continued. 'She looked dreadful. She would not get into a taxi to bring her home lest she was sick in the vehicle. I was so worried. She looked ghastly. So I suggested we try to

248

walk it off and I took her to back to my place where I let her sleep on the sofa until she felt better.'

Connie had never heard him lie before. To her ears he was far too glib, and she found herself looking at him as if he were a stranger. It came to her, suddenly and maybe unfairly – had he ever lied to her and had she, loving him, believed everything he said? The thought came and went in an instant but something had changed, if only subtly. Now she felt forced to go along with his lie.

'Can we come in, Mum? I still don't feel well,' she mumbled, hating herself, and him too, for making her do this.

Did Mum believe her, astute woman as she was? Connie found herself trying to look suitably wan, knowing her cheeks must be glowing with good health.

'I'm so sorry, Mum,' she bleated, aware her apology wasn't so much for the lie as for genuine sorrow for her own sense of betrayal – to herself, and to her mother.

The woman moved back from the doorway, slowly, as though with underlying suspicion.

'You'd best go straight up to bed then, love,' she said in a slow, quiet but commanding tone. 'Sleep it off while I 'ave a bit of a talk to your . . . to Mr Clayton, 'ere.'

What was being said, she'd no idea as she sat on the edge of her bed in the bedroom, hers now, her brothers away and Ron and Dorothy given the downstairs front room, he on crutches unable to use the stairs.

Finally she heard the front door open then close and knew Stephen had left. What had he said? What had Mum said?

She was only too glad her dad hadn't been here or there'd have been a real bust up, knowing him, but she knew that Mum with her quiet voice had won the day. What would Stephen tell her when she saw him? She wanted to see him so much.

She was still sitting on the edge of her bed as her mother came into the room.

'How you feeling, love?'

Connie shrugged and said nothing.

'You're lucky your dad wasn't here, love,' she went on. 'I'm not saying anything to him. He came 'ome worn out last night, humping coal to all them households. In this chilly weather people go through coal like a dose of salts. He went to bed early so he didn't know you wasn't 'ome. And this morning he left 'ome early. But I ain't saying nothing to him. But I warn you, love, you be careful what you doin' cos I don't want you bringing trouble 'ome 'ere. I got enough trouble with Ronnie and Dorothy and his little'un. And our Bertie and George at the front, and me worried all the time about their safety. So I don't want you bringing 'ome . . . well, you know what I mean . . . trouble.'

Mum was no fool. Connie felt chastened, ashamed, as her mother went on in her quiet, level way. 'I've 'ad a word with your Stephen and he knows 'ow I feel. I trust he'll honour you now with more concern fer your well-being. Cos there's many a slip, as they say, despite all the care . . .' She broke off, then said quietly, 'I trust you, love, not to let this family down. You seeing 'im later today?'

Connie nodded and said in a small voice, 'We'll probably go to the pictures this afternoon and then have something to eat.'

'Then don't go back for a nightcap, love. Tell 'im to bring you straight back 'ome. He can come in 'ere for a nightcap if he wants – nothing posh, just a glass of beer.' She gave a little smile at the humbleness of her own home. 'Then you can say goodnight and he can go on his way.'

'We hope to get married early September,' Connie heard herself burst out. It was earlier than the time she had arranged just last night, but she was sure that Stephen would be pleased.

Again her mother smiled. 'You can wait that long, can't you? You know what I mean, don't you?'

Connie nodded. Her mother briefly brushed her forehead with her lips and said she probably could do with taking a bit of a rest anyway and, leaving Connie to herself, gently closed the bedroom door behind her.

That afternoon Stephen called for her as if nothing was wrong. However, Connie could feel the tension between them. After leaving the cinema they had dinner but as they left the restaurant, he said, 'I think it best I take you straight home, my darling.'

She knew what he meant. Her mother had told her what she had said to him. But still she felt cheated. It wouldn't ever be the same again. That beautiful bed he'd bought just for them; it would be months until she would be able to lie beside him in it. Yes, she felt deeply cheated, hurt, even angry with him for honouring her mother's plea. She should have lauded him for it, but she felt let down, discarded almost. She said nothing, but it gnawed at her.

Connie had Sunday dinner at home with the family. Stephen was not invited. She didn't ask why – she could guess.

Monday at work was significant in that he didn't once come near her. She watched him as he moved about his office and several times she found him looking in her direction, turning sharply away every time she looked his way. She found herself doing the same thing when she caught him looking at her. Nor did they have lunch together; he was called to some meeting or other. It felt as if some invisible barrier had descended between them.

She was almost glad in the afternoon to be asked to accompany a photographer and reporter recording the disembarkation of a shipload full of the wounded – but only almost glad, because it was nearly always stressful, the sight of those being borne down the gangplank on stretchers or being gently assisted down between two helpers, arms about their necks, heads and faces swathed with grubby bandages, their gallant grins showing relief to be back on home soil but their eyes betraying the memory of what they'd gone through, and the fear they now held of what their future might be as men too crippled to be employable.

She recorded it all in pencil. The results, if approved, would be printed in tomorrow's *London Herald*, to the horrified fascination of its readers, while Mr Mathieson coolly enthused that it certainly helped increase the paper's readership.

Connie herself could only feel a deep sorrow for those whose eyes – the mirrors of the soul, she recalled again – she sketched. She felt something entirely different towards the men who gloried in seeing it selling more papers. At night the sights she'd witnessed often hung in her mind before she finally fell asleep, her last prayer at night always, 'Please God, keep my brother Albert safe and unhurt – and my brother George too.' Ronnie was safe now, but her prayers went to him as well. 'Please dear God, make Ronnie better, please.'

That night, her sleep wasn't a peaceful one, her dreams filled with her and Stephen quarrelling, he walking away, she running after him only to lose him as she turned the corner of God knows where, then searching for him, calling his name.

It was calling his name that woke her up. She hoped she hadn't cried it out for the whole household to hear. Lying inert, she watched the miserable March dawn filter through the curtains, heard her father stir in the next room, heard him cough – one didn't need to be a coal miner for the black dust to get down a man's throat; humping it through customers' doors was enough – heard him come downstairs, go into the kitchen, washing himself in the kitchen sink, spluttering and grousing. Mum followed him downstairs. Connie heard the dull clink of the kettle being filled and placed on the gas hob to make tea.

Listening to the sounds of morning, she lay in her bed, thinking of her dream. She would confront Stephen today and have this threatening estrangement out with him.

Did it matter what her parents thought? Did she care? She wasn't marrying them; once she married Stephen they'd have no more say in what she did and how she did it. Her life would go on with him. If she let it get on top of her now, she could lose him. What if they threw her out? Then she and Stephen would go off and live together, eventually to marry, and there would be little they could do about it.

Yet in the end she knew she couldn't do it. She wanted him so much but she wanted the love of her family too, their respect. But Stephen was the one she loved, and that mattered more than anything else. Thus she continued arguing with herself in the half-light while her parents set about a new day.

What did it matter if her parents felt she was getting up to something? One didn't have to sleep with one's boyfriend to get pregnant. It could happen in any dark alley in a few minutes or so, so why should Mum gasp at her spending a night with the one she loved so long as he took care of her? The awful dream she'd had in the night with him walking away, and knowing that she had lost him, made up her mind.

The next morning she strode over to his office. He was alone when she burst in without knocking. He looked up in surprise as she reached his desk.

'We have to talk,' she announced sharply.

'Are you all right?' he asked – too calmly for her liking. She hated Stephen's calm in the face of other people's ranting, especially hers.

'I couldn't sleep last night for thinking of you,' she went on without answering his enquiry. 'I dreamed we'd drifted apart. You walked off and I never saw you again. I tried but—' She broke off. She was gabbling. 'I don't want us to drift apart,' she resumed, trying to gain control of herself. 'I want to be with you, for ever. I don't care what my parents say. We're in love; that's all that matters. I know I'm only nineteen and still in their care until I'm twenty-one, but I don't think that matters any more with so many dying on the battlefields and . . .' Again, she tried to take herself in hand. This wasn't what she wanted to say. She began again. 'What I mean is half of those out there were just lads who did as their hearts guided, underage when they signed on whether their parents agreed or not. So I think I can go my own way without the consent of mine. I don't want us to be parted just because they got upset by us spending a night together. I want to sleep in that bed again, Stephen!'

What a stupid way to end her little tirade. She was out of breath. He gazed at her from his chair behind his desk. Why didn't he say something?

The door opened suddenly, the same time as the knock came. Before she had time to turn round, Stephen had leaped to his feet, his voice raised.

'Get out! I didn't say enter. Get out!'

'Sorry, I thought you—'

'*Get out!*'

Connie turned but the door had already closed. Stephen was staring at her, the blaze in his blue eyes still there. He'd not made any move towards her. Now she too would be asked to leave, he returning to whatever he'd been doing before she'd burst in on him.

Instead, he said, 'Connie, I'm so sorry.'

She knew it: it was the prelude to saying it was all over. 'I best go,' she said quietly. 'I didn't mean to interrupt you. I only—'

'No, Connie. Look, we'll have lunch together. There are things I need to say to you.'

That sounded like a death knell. 'What things?'

'We need to discuss our future.'

Maggie Ford

What could she say? She nodded, turned and walked from his office. Was it good or bad she would hear from his lips?

The rest of the morning dragged. Several times she looked up from her filing but Stephen hadn't once looked her way.

Towards midday she saw him open his office door and signal to one of the junior staff, say something to the boy, then close his office door to walk off in the direction of the lift, a sheath of papers under his arm. He looked very tense.

She too tensed as the messenger came over to her. 'Mr Clayton said he's so sorry, he's suddenly been called away to a meeting upstairs.'

'Didn't he say anything else?' she asked.

The young man shook his head.

All she could do was nod and watch him walk off. Why such a sudden meeting? Meetings were usually arranged days, weeks in advance. He must have known. Was he using a trumped-up meeting to get out of seeing her for lunch? If so, why even bother to make an excuse? He could have told her to her face. Unless he was trying to let her down lightly? She tried to believe that this impromptu meeting was genuine. Then why not come and tell her himself?

He didn't return to his office the whole afternoon. Having had lunch alone, she sat at her desk wishing she'd be sent for to go on an assignment, but the hours just toiled on until finally it was time to go home.

That night she dreamed Stephen had signed up for military duties, and she trailing him across a deserted no-man's-land, trying to catch up with him to tell him

256

to go home, finally finding herself on her own on a London street.

The dream had left her miserable all the next day. It had felt so real.

'Not seeing your Stephen tonight?' The question came from her mother as Connie sat at the parlour table reading.

Reading a book, any book no matter how boring, helped to dispel this . . . this sense of betrayal, she supposed it was. Stephen had been busy all week, dashing here, dashing there, out most of the time at meetings, appointments, some she thought quite unnecessary.

Yesterday he'd told her he had to be in Reading all day Saturday – he didn't say why – and he wouldn't get back until late so that they'd have to forego that evening's plans – the first time ever. Her immediate thought was: this could probably be the thin end of the wedge.

Her heart was sinking so low it felt as if it was about to leave her body. She tried to steel herself for the coming words: 'I don't think we should be seeing each other any more.' Stupid thoughts but she couldn't help it even as she put on a brave face and said, 'He's been busy. I'll probably see him tomorrow.'

He had said he would see her tomorrow, but it felt like a poor attempt to compensate for their missed Saturday evening together. And what would he tell her when they were alone on Sunday?

'Only probably?' Mum remarked, making her father look up from reading his evening paper.

'What gorn wrong between you two, then?' he asked, removing his pipe to puff smoke into the air before replacing it ''Ad a row, 'ave you?'

'No, Dad, we haven't had a row.' She wished they wouldn't pry so much. She heard him give a humph.

'Always said he was too much a cut above us.' He was back to reading his paper, now talking into it as if to himself. 'Always 'ad me doubts about that one, not being in the forces like. Deaf in one ear be buggered! They take anyone these days. Sort of makes you think of your George.'

He never referred to George as *our* George. It was always *your* George, directed at Mum, who herself used the word *our* all the time. Anger seethed through Connie. 'He tried, Dad,' she said, 'but they wouldn't have him.'

'So 'e thought fit to not ever try again.' It was so loaded, she wanted to leap up, confront him, but she refrained, nursing her unhappiness. But he had more to say. 'Well, don't suppose 'e'll 'ave much longer to worry about it anyway,' he sighed. 'Says 'ere, our boys out there've pushed them Huns back three miles at Arras and took eleven thousand prisoners. Got their own back after the buggers torpedoed that 'ospital ship of ours, all them poor wounded blighters drowned. Thinking about it must've given our boys even more cause to want to show the Hun what we're made of.

'Not only that,' he rambled on, still apparently talking to his newspaper. 'Now the Yanks've 'ad three of their ships sunk by German subs, they'll come inter the war and it'll be all over come end of this summer, you mark my words. Then we can all go back to sleepin' easy in our beds again – your bloke too, I don't doubt, feelin' himself bin let orf lightly.'

In all this Connie had sat quietly seething. Now she shut her book with a loud bang. 'I think I'll go out, Mum.'

'Where to, love?'

'Over to Doris's.'

'She's probably out wiv 'er mates,' Dad muttered into his paper. 'Chasin' boys, free as a kite, enjoying 'erself. No bloke messing 'er about.'

But Connie hardly heard as she left the room, seeking her warm coat, hat and scarf against a chilly evening breeze.

Chapter Twenty-Five

It was Sunday afternoon. Surely all her doubts were only in her mind, Connie thought as she and Stephen strolled beside Rotten Row, along which a few brave riders trotted their horses despite the cold, overcast afternoon, the Serpentine to their right bereft of Sunday boaters.

Yet even though they were together Stephen remained distant. Her arm threaded though his, Connie remembered last summer when, without need of a coat she'd thrilled to the touch of his free hand covering her bare arm. Today her winter coat made his touch feel distant, as he himself seemed – or was it just her overwrought imagination? If she continued feeling like this she could lose him for ever. She needed to tackle him about the worries she'd had all through last week about his odd behaviour. After all they were together now but he still seemed distant, his mind elsewhere.

'Darling, is everything all right?'

'What d'you mean?'

'I mean between us.'

He didn't look at her, his attention apparently taken by a couple of riders cantering by, their horses' hoofbeats dull on the soft ground.

'Why do you ask?'

She took a deep breath. 'Well, I've not seen you so much lately, you away nearly every day last week and then having to go to Reading all day yesterday. You never told me why.'

He was silent for a moment, then he said in a low voice, 'I had to go to a funeral.'

She hadn't expected that. Nor did he seem prepared to expand on the statement. She heard herself asking a little too sharply, 'Why didn't you tell me?' After what they had been to each other for so long, he could at least confide in her.

He was silent for so long that she was starting to feel shut out again, just as she'd been all last week. Then finally he said in a quiet voice, 'It was too close to my heart for me to say anything. I'm sorry.'

'I don't understand,' she burst out, fearing all sorts of climax to this.

'It was the funeral of my late wife's brother.'

Having said that much he appeared disinclined to say much else, leaving her to feel utterly excluded, yet not daring to breach it.

'He and I were very close at one time.' His voice resuming made her jump. 'But since . . . Well, we drifted apart somewhat. He was younger than my wife. But he went last week with the same thing as she had, cancer.' He seemed to be talking more to himself than her, as if attempting to comfort himself. 'Her mother died of it too. Who knows, it might have been hereditary, come out in any children we had and I'd have been doubly grieved.'

Hearing him, Connie felt as if she didn't belong here, as if she'd been intruding. She said nothing. But then he turned his head to her. 'So you see, I couldn't have told anyone without coming close to tears and making a fool of myself. I couldn't have stood other people commiserating. So I said nothing to anyone, not even you, my love. I couldn't.'

Suddenly her world soared, yet such sadness struck her heart that she herself wanted to cry. 'I didn't know,' was all she said, and felt his arm tighten against her hand.

She loved him so much and felt a deep respect for him too. She realised quite suddenly, perhaps for the first time, how like her mum he was – on the surface a seemingly quiet, retiring person, keeping his thoughts and feelings to himself, others getting the wrong impression of him. But maybe, like her mother, quietly having his way.

Mum, keeping her own thoughts to herself, nevertheless ruled Dad for all his blustering. And so Connie realised that she would never be able to get anything over on Stephen, just as her father couldn't her mother, and she loved him for that quiet strength, just as she honoured her mum for hers.

Stephen suddenly lengthened his stride and she looked up at him to see he was holding his head high. 'It's damned freezing out here. I suggest we go somewhere warm for a hot cup of tea,' he said briskly.

She expected him to say, 'Then I'll take you home.' Instead he said quietly, 'Then, if you like, we'll go back to my apartment – if you want to.'

If she wanted to! Oh, yes she did so want to.

*

It was wonderful lying in his bed again – their bed. But something else too, something she had never experienced in any of the times he'd made love to her. This afternoon, the miserable world closed out, she found for the first time how bringing love to its climax actually felt, and it was like no other feeling she'd ever imagined or would ever forget.

Knowing enough to realise he was looking after her, he would leave her at the moment of his climax. So it was that he moved away from her as always, this time much sooner, leaving her bewildered, but moments later he was holding her to him again, reawakening her senses. And this time his embrace was more urgent than she had ever remembered. As always the joy of him being part of her was wonderful, but this second time it felt somehow so different. Something was happening, something strange, almost unbearable yet utterly wonderful, her body being engulfed by it. She could hear herself gasping, crying out as it swept through her whole body, from the very top of her head to the end of her every nerve and fibre. Finally they lay together, very still, out of breath.

'Are you all right?' He whispered the question.

She nodded, then said, 'Yes.' Nothing more, but something had changed. Suddenly she felt herself a woman at last, knew this was what really formed babies. But he had guarded her against that, hence his moving away from her for a moment or two. Now she knew what making love was really like and it was marvellous.

He brought her home early. Mum was surprised to see them, smiling, but Connie could feel her watching her. Dad of course noticed nothing, instantly engrossing himself in his Sunday paper, purposely it seemed, after a brief nod to Stephen. But she didn't care any more. She and Stephen had been one, and would be again and again. And now she knew his nature was akin to her mother's, she felt she had never felt as comfortable with him as she did now.

Saying goodnight, he gave her a brief kiss by the open door before leaving. Her father was in the kitchen, she guessed, with his eyes on the two of them. She couldn't wait for Monday to come, when she would sit at her desk, knowing that when she looked towards Stephen's office, he, seeing her, would lift his chin, would smile, maybe lift a hand in a brief wave.

After work he'd see her home, but first they'd go to his lovely flat, make love the way they had today, and her world would feel complete yet again. And soon they would begin to set a definite date for their wedding day.

Just before she set off for work a letter arrived from Albert. It always brought mixed feelings: was he okay, was he ill, was he hurt? But he merely hoped everyone was all right; that he was; that he trusted they got his last letter; that he had got theirs and enjoyed reading it. His life out there was hardly mentioned, apart from wishing he was home, and that he was concerned as to how Ronnie was – was he getting better at all?

''E does seem a bit better,' Mum said as she put the letter on the mantelpiece for Dad to read when he came home, 'though I just don't know. Dolly can read it when she comes out of their room. She'll tell me what to say.'

It was Dolly now, Dorothy such a mouthful. She was a tower of strength to Ron. Not that he was much improved: he was still a bag of nerves, twitching, still tending to gaze into nowhere, saying little, then having to fight a stutter, but the way she stuck by him was a credit to her.

He was calm only when holding little Violet. Dolly couldn't have given him a finer present in helping him towards recovery, though it never lasted long. He seldom came out of their bedroom in what had once been the front room.

Leaving for work, Connie called out to them, 'I'm off now. Bye, Dolly,' getting a ready answer, then, 'Bye, Ron,' waiting for a while till she heard, 'B-b-bye, C-Con.' Ron's voice was laboured, early mornings doing nothing for his recovery. She only hoped, prayed, Albert would never be sent home like that.

Chapter Twenty-Six

May 1917

It didn't seem right being out here without Ronnie. Albert missed his brother terribly. He had mates, of course, but it wasn't the same. Mates came and went, sometimes split up by these meandering trenches, some killed, some injured and borne away to a field hospital, he never laying eyes on them again.

For all the time Ron had been with him, they'd never been split up. That was normal procedure for kin, for friends, even street neighbours. It helped morale, it was thought. Then Ron had got his blighty one, was back home on crutches, while he himself was still out here.

Stealing frequent cautious peeps over the parapet for any movement from the enemy lines as he'd been ordered, in the process inviting a bullet if he wasn't careful, was at least better than doing nothing. Doing nothing made him feel so utterly lonely – a feeling he just couldn't get over. Still, dinner soon, dolled out in the usual haphazard way but helping to take his mind

266

off loneliness despite the constant jostle of those moving around in the confines of a trench.

It was May and had been raining all night; was still raining now with no sign of stopping; had rained yesterday and the day before. Any further back than that he couldn't remember, each day melting violently into another. Water was above the wooden duckboards. Lots of soldiers had that rotting, stinking trench foot from constant immersion in water. It came right through the boots, the trousers always wet at least just past the calf, and one had to sit on firing steps or mounds of earth where shells had blasted away part of a trench, anywhere above the waterline. His feet didn't feel so good either.

Still, it was coming up to midday, and he could look forward to the usual meal, probably bully beef in gravy and a hunk of bread. It was filling and sufficient but after months of it, it was boring to the point of making a man feel weary just to look at it.

If Ron had been here, the pair of them would have made light of it, made a joke out of it . . .

'If you don't like it, give it to the cat!'

'What cat?'

'Lieutenant Smithers' cat. You've seen it – tucked down his trouser front. At least we hope it's a cat.'

Lieutenant Smithers, a bombastic little man, tended to scratch at his crotch from time to time whenever he spoke to anyone – a habit he probably wasn't aware of – and there'd been some who had sworn they'd heard it meow, unless it was him trying carefully to break wind.

But there was no Ron now to joke with about anything. As he waited for them to come along the lines filling mess tins and pouring draughts of water, he reached into his tunic breast pocket and drew out the letter Mum had sent him recently.

It said she'd heard from George again. He was on the Somme, further south in France, and his job often entailed going out into no-man's-land as a stretcher-bearer, collecting the wounded and taking them to a field hospital. It seemed that George, previously accused of being a coward, of being lily-livered, was now risking his life, expecting a bullet at any time, although there did exist an unwritten law between both sides that one did not fire on stretcher-bearers.

Even so . . . George a stretcher-bearer at the front, in direct line of fire? Who'd have credited it? He felt a new respect for his older brother. The man had come up trumps after all.

Albert's thoughts changed course – when this war was over he and Edie would rent a nice little house, settle down and start a family. They'd got married on his last leave – January – a brief affair with no wedding break-fast, no guests other than Mum and Dad, his sisters, Ron and Dorothy, Connie; they sat down to just an ordinary meal – no wedding cake though Mum, bless her, had managed to concoct something a bit special in its stead.

There was just time to scribble a note to Edie before the orderlies arrived with the usual bully beef stew, to tell her yet again that he loved her so very much and could hardly wait to be with her, for always. He'd hand it to one of the orderlies, who'd post it for him, along with dozens of letters from other men.

Holding out his tin he received his portion, hoping he'd have time to eat it. He became aware that the shelling had stopped, so used to it he was that he hardly noticed.

But the sudden silence meant that in a few minutes whistles would blow, sending them over the top into that hell that never seemed to end.

A hundred or so miles to the south George had worked through the night along the lines of the injured and dying at the field hospital, doing what he could to alleviate their suffering.

It wasn't much compared with what the doctors did but he worked hard and with all his soul. If he was going to do this right, if he was going to make up for his past misguided beliefs, he was prepared to spare nothing of himself; he worked long after others had done their bit tending the wounded. He was no medic; he had learned a little, but his job as he saw it was to stay beside wounded and horrified men in extreme pain, administering whatever aid and comfort he could while the doctors worked on the injuries: holding each man's hand, his grip painful as spasms of agony darted through that patient's frame. He'd often come away with fingernail marks embedded so deep into his own flesh that it bled.

He thought of that first leave, the way his father had spoken to him after all that time spurning him, accused of being a son to be ashamed of, refusing to greet him as his own flesh and blood. His words: 'Wonder you bothered to see us' had still held animosity.

Mum had intervened. 'You look well. How are you, love?' Neither of them referred to him now being in the forces or asked what he did.

'I'm with the medical corps now,' he'd supplied.

His father hadn't acknowledged that, but his mother had said, 'We got your letter telling us what you was doing. It worried me, though, how safe you was. You said you was training before you went, but I thought medical stuff took years to study, but I suppose in wartime things is different.'

She had gabbled on. Nerves probably. But what he'd really needed was to explain why he'd changed his mind about the beliefs he'd held. He'd turned to his dad. 'About why I did what I did, fooling myself all that time and—'

'Well,' his father had cut in, his voice a deep growl. 'Ain't much to be gained going over old sores.' His father's words left George feeling like an intruder in his own home.

His visit had lasted just as long as it took to drink the cup of tea Mum had made for him. Leaving, he'd tentatively held out a hand to his dad, who, to his relief, had taken it, not firmly, but had said, 'Take care of yourself, then,' which he felt meant more than the half-hearted handshake.

Dorothy with her little daughter had joined them but his brother Ronnie hadn't. 'Still not able to face the world properly,' she said, 'but he says he wishes you well.'

He'd never been back since, preferring to spend any leave he had in Paris, where he felt more at home these days. As for that chapel with its odd beliefs, he'd turned his back on that for ever.

He had stopped writing to his parents. It was futile, he felt, but his sister Connie often wrote, telling him all the family news. She'd told him all about her and this Stephen chap – a friendly letter that he'd answered, wishing her well, and she'd replied saying she hoped he'd be at her wedding – she was the only one of the family who had ever understood him.

Chapter Twenty-Seven

June 1917

Connie had been summoned to the chief editor, Desmond Mathieson's office. It was beautifully furnished and had a clear view of St Paul's Cathedral, its dome basking in the bright summer sunlight, catching her attention the instant she entered.

Why she'd been summoned she had no idea, only that he wished to see her, and now she was filled with concern that he might be considering dispensing with her services now that the date of her marriage to Stephen had been set to November and the news had been leaked out. She'd had lunch with Stephen half an hour before but he'd not mentioned that Mathieson wanted to see her. Surely he would have known, being the editor in charge of his department.

As she entered, Mathieson, who had been leaning back in his swivel chair like someone about to bestow a marvellous gift, had leaped to his feet and come round to conduct her to sit.

Maggie Ford

'Please, my dear, sit yourself down,' he chortled.

He seemed so full of camaraderie that it couldn't be the sack for her. Wondering what he wanted she let herself be helped to sit, after which he made his way back to his side of the large desk to seat himself in his own chair, all the while beaming across the desk at her.

'I expect you are wondering why I have sent for you, my dear.'

It couldn't be to give her notice; he was too full of smiles for that. She was sure she had given the newspaper satisfaction during the time she'd worked there. It had always been an odd sort of employment and she'd been well paid for it, had even earned a rise only recently.

Maybe he intended to talk to her about her coming marriage to Stephen. But that was months away yet, and would be a quiet affair anyway. After all, he having been married before, one shouldn't make a big do of a second marriage out of respect for the deceased first wife, and she'd been content with that.

Maybe he was thinking that she should leave the newspaper prior to the wedding. Before the war, women, once married, did not go to work, their task being to look after their husband, his house, and whatever children came along. It was no doubt that, despite him saying how indispensable her talent was to his newspaper, Stephen himself had no intention of her continuing to work after they were married, and why would she need to? He could give her all the things she'd never had – a nice house, a suitable allowance – something girls like her could only dream about.

Mr Mathieson leaned forward, the fingertips of both his large hands touching to form an arch beneath his

272

chin. 'I understand,' he began, 'that our Mr Clayton and you have arranged your wedding for late autumn.'

As she nodded he sat back in his chair, allowing it to swivel very slightly.

'Well, my dear, I've not spoken to Mr Clayton yet, but felt I should speak to you first in order to see what you might think about a proposition I have in mind, being that it mostly concerns yourself.'

She stared at him. For no real reason that she could find she felt a coldness creep below her flesh. Was he asking her to continue working for a good deal longer? Only this month, June the fourteenth, London had again been bombed after all that time of relief from attack. This time it hadn't been German zeppelins but German aeroplanes that had attacked the city.

Five days ago, in broad daylight, the East End had gazed up with wonder at the fine clean lines of the twin-winged aircraft, the German cross plainly visible on the tail and on each side of the fuselage. Someone had counted twelve aeroplanes; others said fifteen daring the barrage of anti-aircraft fire from the ground. But hardly had the realisation of danger gripped ordinary Londoners when the bombs had fallen. In an air raid lasting just fifteen minutes some hundred Londoners had been killed and four hundred injured; one bomb had fallen on a local school killing ten children – innocent kiddies who'd harmed no one; it was appalling. Another bomb had hit a train standing in a local railway station; there had been fatalities there too.

Connie had been sent with two photographers to one of the scenes to record the parents of the murdered children. It had been distasteful and sickening; she'd returned feeling a nervous wreck but her sketches had been praised by Mathieson.

She'd stood in his office receiving his praise, seeing his broad smile of satisfaction, hearing him exclaim with a note of unconcealed triumph that this would double – no, treble – their readership. But she had felt no triumph in this gift of hers. In fact, his praise had left her feeling contempt for him. Even now, several days later, she was still unable to get the scenes out of her mind.

Now, Mathieson was regarding her with a look of contemplation.

'My dear,' he began. 'If you accept my proposition, I will see that your salary is doubled, all your expenses paid, and the paper will make certain that you come to no harm.'

What was he talking about? She made to ask but he was already forging ahead. 'It may mean you and Mr Clayton putting your wedding back to the beginning of next year, say January. As I have said, I will see you are well rewarded.'

As she sat dumbfounded and a little bewildered, he leaned towards her as if to impart some wonderful news, elbows leaning on his desk, fingers linked.

'I have an assignment which I think will be the pinnacle of your achievements to date. Since you came to us, the *London Herald*'s readership has increased unbelievably. I am very proud of you and extremely grateful. Sadly, once you are married, you will leave this company. But one last assignment is needed before you leave for good. And that will be in a blaze of glory and triumph, of that I can assure you, my dear.' My dear! Not once had he used her name. 'And I for one believe that the *London Herald* will remember your name for many years to come.'

Then why wasn't he using her name at this moment? She wished he would get whatever it was off his chest and she shifted in her chair. Noticing her impatience, he smiled. 'Right, my dear, I expect you are wondering where all this is leading.'

She *was* wondering, and growing more suspicious by the minute, There was too much being said for this, whatever it was, to be palatable.

'Right, then,' he continued briskly. 'We have our war correspondents and photographers out in France and Flanders, and who are also making contact with those who have been hospitalised before returning to Britain. That is all very well, but others of the press are doing exactly the same thing. The whole of Fleet Street is at it. What we are looking for is a new slant, a crowd-puller if you like.' He paused for a moment, then said, 'This is where you come in, my dear. Your talent, your wonderful, exceptional talent, could help us increase our readership still further. What I am asking of you, my dear, is that we send you over to France. But nowhere near the front line, of course. You would be required to go round the hospitals, the wards, and sketch what you see, with your special talent for, shall we say, delving into the soul.'

All this time she had said nothing, but her heart had begun beating heavily. Now her back straightened as suddenly as an arrow striking its target. 'No!' It was hopeless to modify her tone. 'No, I can't do that!'

She thought of her brother, once a vibrant young man, brought home utterly destroyed by what he'd gone through, crippled for life and he not yet twenty-one. And Albert could also end up crippled or even killed as this endless war continued.

True, the USA had entered the war in April and people had been heartened by the news, seeing the Americans as saviours, adding weight to the ending of it. Others muttered – maybe unfairly – 'about time too'. But would that bring Albert back home whole, or not at all?

And then there was George, who'd never believed in war and the taking of another man's life for any reason, but who'd finally volunteered and was now endangering his own life to bring the wounded back to safety. He was maybe the bravest of all her brothers, for he had known full well what he would be facing when he'd opted to do the job asked of him.

And here was Mathieson, asking her to go over there and consign to paper the haunted, horrified, despairing expressions in the eyes of wounded, exhausted, devastated men. No! She would not do it. And if she got the sack for refusing, what did it matter? She would be leaving by the beginning of autumn for her wedding.

In her breast there had arisen a loathing for Mr Desmond Mathieson that must have shown on her face. But all he did was lean back in his seat, crossing his arms as he continued to smile at her.

'You will receive twice the salary you are getting now, my dear, plus the best of accommodation whilst you are there. Your travel expenses will be paid, plus whatever clothing you may need – you can name your own costs.'

He waited for her reply but it felt as though her tongue had cleaved to the roof of her mouth. This was practically a bribe. What else could it be? Her mind flashed to how she'd felt those few days ago, seeing the mothers of those children killed in such a depth of grief that it tore the heart out of any watching. Some had fallen to the ground, others had been transfixed by their grief, staring into nothing as a neighbour held them tight in their arms to prevent them sinking to their knees in utter despair at their loss.

'And your answer, Miss Lovell . . .?'

Mathieson's voice broke through her thoughts. It was the first time he had used her name since she'd entered his office.

Still unable to believe he was asking this dreadful request of her, she shook her head. 'I'm sorry,' she replied with what minuscule respect she could muster. 'I'll soon be leaving the newspaper, and all I want is to get married, to settle down, and start a family.'

She watched him unfold his arms and regard her with those intense blue eyes of his, they now suddenly becoming a hard stare, a brittle stare.

'My dear,' he said very gently, 'I cannot sack you for refusing to bow to my request, as you will soon be leaving anyway in order to get married. But your Mr Stephen Clayton will continue working here, will he not?' Not waiting for a nod of agreement, he went on, 'He has many, many years ahead of him with the *London Herald* – exceedingly promising years – perhaps finally to have the seat I now occupy. I'm getting on, my dear, and in a few years I will be retiring. I shall look forward to having someone replace me, maybe in time be on the board of directors. And it is Mr Clayton whom I have in mind – a brilliant man.'

There came a pause for her to digest this bit of information. Then he gave a great sigh. 'But there could always be a slip, just as there ever is in this world. Your Stephen Clayton could quite suddenly do something that could shock this firm. Something unforgivable . . . I don't know what – yet. But what if this unforgivable episode could cost him his job? Together with no reference, could he ever get employment on any newspaper ever again? Human beings can be so frail without realising it. That would be awful, a man expecting to marry and provide for a wife and family, to keep her in the luxury she has never known, instead reduced to scrimping and scraping, seeking any job that could bring him a living lower than any of his calibre would ever expect.'

At last he broke off, bestowing her with a smile. But it was a smile that would haunt her through all her years, his lips revealing his slightly uneven teeth while the eyes remained like those of a reptile, expressionless but for the cold evil that dwelt there. It was an expression that could make any man quake. It made her quake and she knew she'd be accepting the offer, for Stephen's sake. To walk out now would be to ruin his life. She was trapped.

She refused to meet the eyes of her jailer, and said in a small but determined voice, 'I shall do it for two weeks. I've my wedding to prepare for.'

'That's fine with me,' he said, sitting back in his chair.

'Then I shall leave to be married and Mr Clayton will go on working here for as long as he needs to.'

'Of course,' he replied amiably. 'And thank you so much, Miss Lovell, for your cooperation. I'm sure you will make a wonderful job of this most important assignment. I assure you, your name will go down in the history of this newspaper. There are war artists out there used by other papers but none with the same talent as you possess with a mere pencil and paper. You could even become famous, your name known around the art world.'

She didn't want to hear all this rubbish. She stood up sharply and said tersely: 'I leave you to make all the arrangements, Mr Mathieson.'

She left the office knowing that those arrangements had in fact already been executed, he well aware that she would have to accept in the end. In her throat, acid bile had gathered. Later she was sick, quietly, in the Ladies', the bile burning her lips.

Chapter Twenty-Eight

Connie knew she would have to come out with it eventually. But saying anything about it to Stephen too soon would have him storming up to Mathieson's office and God knows what would happen then. She could imagine a row, he forbidding her to be sent over there, even if only on the coast of northern France, away from the fighting.

And what if Mathieson told him it was all her idea? She wouldn't put that past him. Surely Stephen would know she'd never suggest such a thing, that all she wanted was to marry him and settle down.

The danger was of him getting hot under the collar and threatening the man. Mathieson in turn could threaten to report him for instigating a row with his superior and have him sacked. Even if he remained calm, the chief editor could lie that he had been rude and disruptive without provocation, resulting in Stephen losing his job. It was best to say nothing until it was too late to alter the arrangement.

But Stephen would have to know eventually even if she waited until her last evening to tell him. What might that do to their marriage plans? Unable to sleep for worrying about it, she knew Mathieson was deadly serious about getting rid of Stephen if she refused to comply. The powers-that-be would agree with their chief editor, viewing it as a wonderful scoop. She felt she had never hated anyone as much as she hated Mathieson, but what could she do? The whole thing was bizarre.

Time was creeping on and still she'd not been able to find the courage to speak of it to Stephen. It was beginning to feel like a ton weight on her shoulders. She told her parents the news on Monday evening, banking on them saying they wouldn't allow their daughter to go anywhere near France. But she made the mistake of saying she'd be miles away from danger and before she could remedy the mistake her mum, at least, was all for her going.

'Our own daughter picked out to do an important job like that for 'er paper,' her mum said, beaming and proud. 'Fancy that now. So long as you're not in any danger. And you'll be 'ome in a couple of weeks, you say. Your newspaper must be so proud of you, and so are we.'

'Sent overseas by your newspaper. Comin' up in the world – bit late, though, you and your Stephen getting married come autumn.' His tone seemed sarcastic, but he went on, 'Just 'ope they'll give you bigger wages because of it. Your mum could do wiv a bit more 'ousekeepin'.'

'No, love,' came Mum's reply. 'You need to put it towards the wedding.'

Connie feelings went out to her. How could she explain about the way Mathieson was blackmailing her?

'It's valuable experience, at least,' she finished lamely.

Her father looked at her, his eyes narrowing to slits. 'What valuable experience? You getting' married, ain't you? You won't need to work again, so what're you talkin' about?'

'I don't know.' Dad was no fool. Had he seen through this odd idea of her employers?

He gave a contemptuous snort. 'Valuable experience, my arse! Going out there to gawp at them what's 'ardly got nothink to live for any more. You've got one 'ere – your own poor bloody brother. What's 'e got to look forward to? I'd say what you're doin' ain't natural. Bloody macabre, I'd say.'

Getting up from the table and reaching for his tobacco pouch he began filling his pipe, tamping it down as he headed to the parlour for a quiet smoke.

'So when d'you expect to go, love?' Mum asked as she took the dinner she'd been warming in the oven and placed it on the kitchen table for Connie.

'Wednesday,' Connie said in a small voice as she sat down to eat.

Her father paused in the doorway. 'Bit quick, ain't it? Tryin' to get as much as they can out of you before you leave fer good.'

Connie ignored the slating remark. She was seeing Stephen tonight. They wouldn't be going out, instead spending the evening in his flat. They'd make love, but for the first time ever she felt no joy in seeing him. She knew what his response would be when she did tell him. He'd say flatly that she wasn't to go. If she inadvertently let it slip before the last moment, he would flatly state that he'd be telling Mathieson he wasn't willing to let his future wife embark on such an assignment. Stephen would then find himself out of a job, with little prospect of employment on any other newspaper, and where would their wedding be then, their new house, his certainty of a job for life?

She had no option but to comply with that slimy creature's wishes. But she wouldn't be in any danger, Connie reasoned, not in a hospital with efficient nursing staff tending those about to be sent home. She could very well be sketching faces full of hope for once.

What if Stephen blamed her for keeping it quiet all this time? She'd have to tell him but maybe it was best to wait until tomorrow night, too late for him to tackle Mathieson.

Tuesday crawled by, and they lay in their lovely double bed this last evening before he took her home. She found she could keep it to herself no longer. It had to be said. Trying to keep her voice even, she began to explain why their chief editor had called her up to his office. Lying side by side, his arm around her after having made love, she'd drawn a deep breath and, as gently as she could, began to explain what Mathieson had wanted of her. Dragging his arm from under her shoulders, almost painfully, he sat bolt upright. 'And you agreed to go? And you said nothing to me.'

'Stephen, I'm telling you now,' she began but he cut through her words, his voice harsh.

'How could you have agreed? You're not going. I'm going up there to sort it out first thing tomorrow morning.'

'It's tomorrow morning I'm going,' she said in a small voice. 'It's all arranged.'

'Arranged – behind my back? You and him—'

'He said if I didn't comply, you'd be out on your ear, with no references. I'd no option. I love you, darling. I couldn't do that to you.'

Maggie Ford

She found herself crying, and sought the comfort of his shoulder. But he leapt out of the bed to stand glaring down at her, unconscious of his nakedness. She gazed at him in terror, seeing their marriage plans dissolving into nothing.

'I couldn't tell you before,' she pleaded. 'You'd have gone up there and caused a scene. It would have been even worse for you. What could I do, darling? I had to agree to go. It'll only be a couple of weeks.'

'Damn a couple of weeks!' he burst out. 'You didn't see fit to tell me.'

'If I'd told you, you'd have only made things worse by going after him. He blackmailed me into agreeing. What was I to do?'

But he was no longer listening, turning away to clamber into his vest and pants, that in itself announcing in her mind that their relationship was over, despite her pleas. She watched him go over to the dressing table, gaze at his reflection in the mirror for a second, then turn and retrace his steps to stand at the side of the bed, staring down at her. She looked up at him, silently imploring him to see why she had kept her assignment from him.

In a low voice he said, 'It depends if you *want* to go.'

It sounded as though he really believed it to have been all her idea, the onus on her. It was unfair and her own anger rose.

'It'd be an experience,' she burst out, stupidly.

'Experience!' He frowned, his fine blue eyes boring into her. 'Come November we'd have been married.' His voice shook. 'You'd have been leaving this job for good and all these assignments you've been sent out on, all behind you. So why would you need more experience?'

He sounded just like her father at this point. 'You'd be my wife. You've just told me he was using me to blackmail you into going. So which is it? That you had no option or that you want the accolade?'

Finally she said in a lame voice, 'It'll only be for two weeks. I don't want to leave this place under a cloud. I'd rather leave . . . well, with everyone's good wishes.'

She expected him to bitterly challenge that last statement, say that, for her, she actually wanted to leave in a blaze of glory, but as she gazed at him, he seemed to droop.

'What time in the morning?' The flatness of his tone shocked her, as if he was talking to a stranger.

'I'm to be at London Docks by nine. There's a taxi picking me up from home.'

'Got it all sorted, haven't you?' he muttered. He sounded like a man defeated, which made her heart go out to him.

'Darling—' she began, but he interrupted her.

'Even so, I think I'll have a word with our chief editor in the morning – set things straight with him, insist he give those upstairs my opinion on this and—'

'No, Stephen, don't, please!' she cried out in panic. 'I'll be back before you know it.'

'Maybe I won't be here by then,' he said sharply. 'Better get dressed, Connie. I'll take you home.'

It was as if he was saying his final goodbyes, emphasising it by leaving the room for her to get dressed, find her handbag, comb her hair.

He was waiting for her in the lounge as she appeared, opening the door to the apartment. Without speaking, he took her arm to lead her down to the street. But it was a cold grasp, a grasp that spoke volumes.

They didn't speak in the taxi. She could find nothing more to say. Alighting, he saw her to her door, then without kissing her, turned and walked off, his last words: 'Take care of yourself.'

Not, 'I'll be waiting for you to be home again' just 'Take care of yourself' before walking away.

It was strange being on board a ship. Connie had never been to the seaside in her whole life, not even Southend-on-Sea, the destination of choice for those from the East End wealthy enough to afford a holiday.

Now she would soon be crossing the Channel. She should have felt excited but she didn't. Stephen's attitude last night had torn her apart, but what could she do? She'd told him she was doing this for his sake, but he hadn't seemed to have believed her.

Maybe she would come back with wonderful sketches to be put in the *London Herald* for the gawping eyes of its readers and be lauded by the newspaper, although Mathieson would make sure to reap most of the credit for having thought up this project. By the time she returned, would Stephen have seen the sense of it and propose to her afresh, would they get married, would she be a joyful housewife? Instead of being buoyed up by hope, she gazed over the grey empty sea, adding her poor offering of private tears to its expanse. The sea didn't care – a few tears meant nothing to it.

The ship was filled to overflowing with servicemen on their way to war, some returning after a spell of leave. She was almost the only woman aboard, except for some nurses going over to help the injured and bring them back home. The ship would bring the bodies home too, those that had been found, the rest to lie silently in no-man's-land. She prayed too that Albert and George would never be among them. At least praying helped take her mind off Stephen a little.

She was aware of the mass of servicemen ever moving back and forth behind her, their low-pitched voices filling the air, occasionally deep laughter and every now and again a group bursting into song.

A couple of the nurses came to stand beside her and asked what she was doing on board. They seemed impressed when she told them, but concerned. 'It'll take you some getting used to, some of the things you'll see,' one remarked. 'But keep your chin up.'

As the French coast loomed in front of her, for the first time, perhaps due to that nurse's remark, she felt a tremor in her stomach. To combat it she thought back to the passing scenery of the River Thames. She'd never been outside London before but had seen pictures of countryside, but this – the fresh smell of the river, the open air, the river widening, its banks receding to grow indistinct, finally seeming to merge with the horizon, eventually to disappear altogether – was something completely different. There was a different smell, a fresh salty tang that filled the nostrils as if opening up a powerful sense of freedom.

But there was something else she'd became aware of as they moved even further into the Channel: a rocking sensation up, down and sideways, making the stomach churn. She took a deep breath, fought for control, desperate not to be sick in front of strangers and risk them laughing at her.

Someone came up to her, leaned beside her on the rail, wrists crossed casually in front of him; a corporal, laden down with his kit.

'Feel it, do yuh?'

She glanced at him in alarm.

He smiled as he gazed over the rail into the water, not looking at her. 'Not nice. Don't look at the water, lass. Keep yuh eyes on the horizon. Helps calm yuh insides.' With that, he moved away as some mates hailed him.

She did as she'd been advised and began to feel a bit better, but lonely. She thought of Stephen, wished she wasn't here, wished she was at work. It was Wednesday, and they would have been preparing to go out for a dinner together this evening.

To quell the tears that had gathered in her eyes, she lifted them to the horizon. Some naval ships had joined them, their guns manned by the crew as protection from U-boats. This was a danger she had not expected. What if a U-boat got through the convoy? This, a troop carrier, was full of men sent to kill Germans – a target important enough to be hounded, sunk if possible.

She hadn't thought of that. What had Mathieson got her into? Anger swelled in her breast. When she got back home – *please God, let me get back home* – she would expose him for the self-seeking liar she now knew him to be. And she the stupid cow who'd let herself be so deceived – if Stephen only knew.

She was glad to finally land, file down the gangplank with the VAD nurses, followed by the troops. Whisked off to the hospital some half a mile away, she was met by a nursing sister. Tall, thin, straight-faced, of maybe forty years, she regarded her with what looked like disdain.

'You are . . .?' she began in a full-blooded tone.

'Miss Lovell. From the *London Herald*. I've been sent here to—'

'I have already been informed of the reason, Miss Lovell,' she broke in, turning to lead the way into the hospital, a low, one-storied building that appeared to have been built some hundred years ago. 'I do not feel that you should be here,' she went on, leading the way down a long, low corridor, clean but not very well lit, that opened at intervals on to long, narrow wards. 'But now you are here, I'll thank you not to get in the way of my nurses and to make yourself as invisible as possible. Do what you have to do and leave my nurses to do what they have to.' She stopped beside a closed door and turned to face her, a cold, stiff expression on her face. 'Do you understand, Miss Lovell?' As Connie nodded, the woman went on, 'I am Sister Connally. You will address me as Sister.' She indicated the door beside which she now stood. 'Your room. Not exactly the Ritz but it will serve for the short time you are here. I leave you to sort out your belongings.' Connie nodded, but Sister Connally had more to say. 'When you are ready, go to the desk at the end of this corridor. They will inform you where you are to go. I'll not have you going about the hospital without supervision. Do you understand, Miss Lovell?'

Again Connie nodded. The woman turned on her heel to march with amazing speed along the corridor, disappearing around a corner to her right.

So much for her first introduction to this place. She had been asked to sit more or less out of sight and not get in the way of overworked staff, which made it much harder to sketch the patients themselves.

Not that she'd any heart in it after her first glimpse of the appallingly shattered bodies and faces of the once handsome young men, their features torn to shreds, parts missing altogether. Those choking from or blinded by poison gas, maybe lost for ever in darkness. The sight made her cringe from the first moment so that she found herself totally unable to sketch any of it. If Mathieson could see what she was seeing, would he have been so keen to put such sights in his paper? She didn't think so.

She did manage to draw something. The lucky ones – blighty ones – seemed to count their own injuries as fortunate, getting them out of the war for good. Many with lost limbs did look traumatised, others relieved, glad to be done with the war and going home, even calling lost limbs a good wound in getting the sufferer home away from all this.

These she did sketch: that look of utter relief, despite the often hideous pain of the wounds, was something to see. She was sure her newspaper's readers would gain hope from such sketches. As for the others, she could hardly bring herself to depict that look in their eyes. She'd begun having disturbed sleep; each time her eyes closed, some frightful sight would invade her brain. Wide awake she would still see it – think though she might of other things.

She couldn't get Ronnie out of her mind as she sat to one side one day observing one stricken man unable to keep a single limb still. An officer at that, his temple bandaged, he must have felt he had no hope left of the life he'd once enjoyed. Shell shock. She thought of Ronnie with that same staring, vacant look; there was nothing one could do.

Ronnie had improved. Connie had got used to seeing a slight twitch to his head every now and again, and his hands hardly shook now. Dolly, sweet Dolly, trusted him to hold his daughter. His small family had done more for him than any hospital could. In Connie's opinion, no one could have done any better job on him than that little girl.

But not every man in this hospital would get that luck. And here she was, little more than an intruder as she sat half-concealed, trying to convey these tortured souls on paper, while attempting to stop her pencil from shaking. Her heart hardened towards the man who had tricked her into coming out here, the man who wanted sketches of traumatised men in order to increase the paper's readership.

After a week she'd had enough. Trauma, loss of sleep – all for a bloody newspaper, so it could sell even more – a feather in its cap! And there was something else too; a letter had arrived, and its contents called her home.

She sought out Sister Connally. 'I've done all I can,' she lied. 'I think I should go home now.'

'I think you should, Miss Lovell.' The woman's tone was cold. Connie had seen the compassionate look Sister Connally gave her patients, and saw herself as the woman must see her – an interloper – intruding into the private lives of men whose lives had been changed for ever, and all so her paper could sell more copies.

It was good to board the boat, now full of wounded returning home. Not once did she feel seasick though the sea reared up, the ship careering like a broken rocking horse. All she could think of was the letter she'd got yesterday. It had been from Stephen.

She had been certain that their wedding was off even before she'd read it. She'd wept, unable even to slit open the flap. A nurse had found her crying silently, the envelope on her lap. 'Bad news?' she'd asked, and when Connie hadn't replied, had gently taken it from her, saying, 'You haven't even opened it, dear. How can you think it bad news? Shall I open it for you?' she had offered. She'd said nothing as the single sheet was taken out and handed to her. 'Do you want me to stay while you read it?' she'd asked. 'It may be good news.' She'd shaken her head, watching the nurse leave to go about her duties.

The letter, written in short terms, had her in fresh tears, this time with joy and relief.

So angry. Wish you'd told me the facts. Confronted Mathieson, seems he had no authority to force you into going. None of the directors were aware of it. All he wanted was to feather his own nest. Had a meeting with the board of directors and they're appalled, want you back immediately, said there's no reason to send any woman unless she's a nurse able to deal with cases she'd come upon, or a volunteer. Mathieson will be dismissed prior to a hearing and I've arranged for you to come home straight away. I love you, Stephen.

P.S. By the way, I've been looking for a really nice house for us to move in to as soon as we're married, and intend on putting a deposit down as soon as you've seen it.

Suddenly Connie could see a life of comfort stretching on for ever for them both. Hastily she had scribbled a note to him saying indeed she would be coming home immediately.

Chapter Twenty-Nine

Stephen was at the London Docks to meet her. As she stepped on to the gangplank ahead of the stream of battle-torn men, she saw him standing there below her. He had seen her too, and was waving. Her heart soared. By the time she had stepped on to home soil, he was hurrying towards her to wrap his arms about her.

'Thank God you're safe!'

'I was always safe,' she laughed, almost smothered by his embrace. 'But all the suffering I saw. I could never be a nurse. I can't begin to praise them enough. I—'

'Well, you're home now, my love,' he broke in.

'I'm so sorry about all that business. I was so frightened of you losing your job. I had no other choice but to—'

'That's all behind us now,' he cut in again. 'Come on, my love, I've a cab waiting. I'm taking you straight home.'

In the taxi he explained how he had gone up to Mathieson's office, demanding he recall Connie and telling the man that he knew about the blackmail. Mathieson had threatened to make it bad for him with the powers-that-be. But Stephen had called his bluff and taken it further. It transpired that the board knew nothing of what had been going on.

'So he's gone,' Stephen concluded, cuddling her to him in the taxi. 'Dismissed. Where he goes to from there, I don't care one hoot! And I'm going upstairs – being promoted to the position of chief editor. I was informed that I've been here for enough years and doing good enough work to deserve the promotion.' He laughed. 'More like relieving the guilty consciences, I reckon.'

'I think it's more you having the strength to expose him,' she said.

'Or trying to make amends for all that's happened,' he insisted, his arm around her drawing her closer.

'Well, I don't think it matters any more,' she said, turning her face to his to have him kiss her long and ardently, not caring whether the cabbie was watching or not.

'And also,' he whispered as they reluctantly broke away, 'I think it has a lot more to do with my settling down and getting married again. A soberly married man is seen as a more reliable employee.' He ended with a chuckle then suddenly grew serious. 'What I want is to have you out of that office as soon as possible. No more of your being sent out on tasteless jobs just to gain the paper even more prestige. What I'd like to do is bring our wedding forward.'

Connie felt a tingle of excitement go through her. 'When?' she asked.

He thought for a moment. 'September, early September like we had planned, before all the trees start thinking of losing their leaves,' he mused poetically.

'What trees?' She gave a silly laugh, feeling suddenly giddy with joy. 'How many trees do you see in this part of London?'

'In all the London parks,' he answered, and she laughed again, but he had grown serious. 'I'd like it to be even sooner but it takes time to make all the arrangements – the church, the ceremony, the honeymoon, your wedding dress, my wedding suit.' He sounded like a small boy excited at the prospect of Christmas. 'I need to marry you, my dearest love, as soon as possible. I want to feel normal again, you and I travelling together through this world, everything else way behind us.'

She knew what he meant. Those years of loneliness, brooding on what he had lost, had changed him. Married, he could be a normal person again.

Connie knew that she never would have met Stephen if not for working at the paper, and while at times her work had been exciting, she hated producing work that ran against her finer feelings, invading the privacy of people's shattered lives by sketching them at their lowest moments. She wanted to be an ordinary married woman in love with her husband, cooking for him, keeping their home clean and tidy, maybe join a small group of like-minded women. She and Stephen would love each other and go through life together into old age, loving and content.

The taxi had turned into her road. Stephen indicated Connie's house and the vehicle slowed noisily to a stop. Stephen whispered laughingly, 'When this war's over I shall be able to return to using my own car again.'

As they alighted, Stephen paying off the driver, her front door opened and she saw her parents framed in the doorway. Mum had her arms held out as Connie mounted the two steps. Dad was standing back a little.

'Oh, love,' were her mother's first words, and she held Connie to her. 'You're 'ome at last, safe and sound. Oh, love, I was so worried.'

'I was fine, Mum,' she said, breaking away from the embrace.

She saw her father turn and retrace his steps into the parlour where he'd come from and a dull anger gripped her heart.

Leaving her mother to kiss Stephen's cheek and bring him into the house, she followed her father into the parlour. 'Me and Stephen have decided to bring our wedding forward to the beginning of September,' she said almost rebelliously, 'and he's been looking for a house for us.'

She wanted to add 'and there's nothing you can do about it', when she noticed a faint change to his expression. Shock – astonishment – deference? At that moment she could have done with paper and pencil to sketch what she was seeing, but she was finished with that; she never wanted to sketch anyone's feelings ever again. If she wanted to draw and paint, she'd paint pretty little scenes and put all that traumatic stuff behind her.

'Do you understand what I am saying, Dad?' she challenged.

His voice came low and gruff, as always. 'Yeh, I know what you're sayin', and I expect you want my congrat-ulations. Well, congratulations. You've done well fer yourself, and you ain't brought trouble 'ome, cos for a long time I did fear you would. But, he's proved a good man, so congratulations.'

Connie knew that this brusque admission was the nearest her father would ever get to praise but, with a springing of her heart, she knew that he meant what he said.

When Stephen followed her mother into the room, she saw her father move towards him. He wiped his right hand down the side of his trousers before holding it out to him. 'Evenin', and by the way, congratulations.'

'About us getting married in September,' Connie said.

Her mother gasped. 'Oh, my goodness, that's . . . you're not . . .?'

Connie smiled. 'No, Mum. I just can't wait to leave work, that's all. I've had enough.'

She *had* had enough. The moment Stephen got his promotion she'd hand in her notice, leaving herself free to deal with the wedding preparations.

After all she had been through it would be lovely to spend the rest of their evening lying together in his bed, *their bed*, being made love to. Feeling his naked body against hers, thrilling to their climax, knowing if they did make a mistake, in five weeks' time they'd be married. But for now she had to think of Mum and Dad's feelings, of Stephen getting her back home again by eleven.

'Stephen's taxi is waiting,' she said. 'We'll be going out for a few hours. Won't be late.' But her glowing cheeks had surely revealed to her mother that it would be more than a quiet nightcap. But her mother kissed her goodnight and said she was off upstairs now, the look in her ageing hazel eyes telling her daughter that she knew more than she let on. But Connie didn't care. Soon she would leave the paper and become Stephen's wife.

Lying with him this evening, his hands on her naked skin, she in turn lovingly exploring his nakedness, it had been easy to blot from her mind all the terrible sights she'd witnessed in France. One week of it and she'd had enough. Now that could all be put behind her and she be his again.

She undressed slowly as she reflected on her evening, knowing that in a month's time there'd be a lovely new bedroom of their own, a lovely house to wander around in the morning, naked if she wanted. She could see herself making Stephen's breakfast, just the two of them eating in a lovely large breakfast room. What bliss that would be.

Slipping into bed, she gazed up at the darkened ceiling of the back bedroom and listened to someone from next door visiting their outside toilet. Sighing contentedly, she turned over on to her side and let her eyelids droop, lovingly conjuring up Stephen's face.

Almost immediately there came other faces. Quickly she opened her eyes and stared into the darkness in an effort to sweep them away. For a few minutes she remained still, chiding her overactive imagination, finally letting the lids again drop gently, cosily tired, ready for sleep.

Seconds later she was sitting bolt upright, her breath escaping her in short gasps as she stared into the darkness, needing to see light – any light that would shoo away the sights that had appeared behind her closed lids: eyes filled with fear, panic, staring, haunted by what their owners had seen, and other eyes belonging to faces, no, half faces above bandages that covered a jaw shot away, a cheek torn to the bare bone, bone gone to reveal a gaping hole instead of a mouth, instead of a nose.

She had glimpsed it all as the VAD nurses came to change bandages, too busy with their helpless patients to hardly notice her sitting silently a small distance away. She fought to concentrate on the eyes of those ravaged soldiers rather than their injuries. Those that hadn't been blinded, stared above the bandages with despair and the silent wish to die rather than be sent home to face the world, grotesquely mutilated for life. She had been filled with horror for the pain they had experienced, and with pity for the lives that they would have to reconstruct when they were sent home.

As she lay in her bed, a retinue of maimed soldiers marched before her eyes each time she closed them. Unable to bear it, she finally leapt from her bed to turn the gaslight on and remained staring out of the window at the moonlit night – anything not to have those harrowing sights repeated each time she attempted to sleep.

Was this what her poor brother Ronnie was still suffering from despite Dolly's every effort to help him? How long then would these awful visitations go on for her? She only hoped it was just a single reaction from what she'd seen and would fade in a day or two.

The next morning she felt fit for nothing. Her mum looked at her with a bewildered expression though she didn't ask what the matter was. She was glad to leave for work. It was a help seeing Stephen. He'd not yet moved to the upper office and for that she was grateful.

'Are you all right?' he asked when he came over to speak to her. 'You look positively worn out. You're not worrying about the wedding?' He smiled. 'Nothing for you to do. I'll be doing all the arranging.'

'The thing is I'd rather not be asked to go out on any more assignments for the time being. I don't think I could face any more of it, at least not for a while.'

He smiled again, tenderly. 'You won't have to. I've already had a word with them up there. I've told them you need to get yourself ready to marry me. They appreciate very much that you've brought back some amazing work, all of which they intend to use, but they do understand it must have been traumatic for you and think you might need a rest for a month or two. By that time you'll be Mrs Stephen Clayton.'

She said nothing, unable to bring herself to speak in case her voice trembled, prompting him to ask what was wrong. Nor could she bring herself to tell him.

Maybe she should have told him. Her sleep continued to be disturbed. She continued to be haunted by eyes hollow with despair above bandages concealing hideous injuries. Those eyes had etched themselves against her closed lids, and she saw them each time she tried to sleep. When had they become filled with condemnation, blaming her?

The dream when it did come was always the same: Stephen fleeing across no-man's-land, she trying to reach him, to rescue him. She'd wake up hearing herself calling out, crying his name.

That first time, the bedroom door had burst open, jerking her awake. Mum hurried in. 'Connie, love, what in Gawd's name is it? We 'eard you callin' out like you was being murdered. It must of been a nightmare you was having, love? What was it?'

Finding herself being rocked gently back and forth in her mother's arms, Connie had managed to pull away. 'It was just a dream – a silly dream.'

'Well, you try and go back to sleep, love, and if you want anything, just call me, all right?'

'All right,' she echoed in a small voice.

There were no more dreams that night but only because she now refused to sleep. The faces of those she had sketched were ever accusing her the moment she closed her eyes. Taking the chair from the little dressing table, she spent the rest of the night sitting by the window, dressing gown wrapped around her, the gaslight turned on just a glimmer, to be turned off at the first light of dawn so no one would know she had not slept. But she could see by her mother's face that she was becoming a little concerned about her drained looks.

'You mustn't start worrying so much about the wedding, love,' she'd say. 'You need to look lovely when you walk down that aisle.' She would nod and promise not to worry. But her disturbed sleep was taking its toll.

Slumped in that chair, she'd still find herself having drifted off without knowing it, waking with a start to realise by the clock on the wall that she'd been asleep for an hour or so. At least this way there were no nightmares. But still, when consciously closing her eyes, those stricken ones of the poor disfigured victims would assail her. She would often try reading a book to take her mind off other things until a jerk of her head falling forward pulled her awake to realise she'd nodded off.

301

Almost a week with hardly any sleep was beginning to leave a big impact, and sitting upright on the old dressing-table chair pulled up to the window was not the best place for proper rest. She'd drag herself to work only half-awake at times.

Stephen was becoming concerned. 'You look all in, my love,' he said as they lunched together the Thursday after her return. 'Are you sleeping properly?'

Connie couldn't help a smile. Sleeping properly? If only he knew.

'You're not worrying about the wedding, though, are you, darling? You mustn't. Leave it all to me.'

Of course she was worrying about the wedding, worrying about their marriage, worrying about awakening him in the night by crying out. Would she find a way to explain those dreams? Could she even bring herself to talk about their content? Would he understand or would he become cross? She felt as if she was falling to pieces. And where would their marriage be then?

She had no fear of sharing their bed the evenings they came back to his flat because after they'd made wonderful love, lying naked in each other's arms, feeling married already, she would say she must go home, and he understood that she didn't want her parents frowning upon her.

This way she limped through another month, saying nothing to anyone, just that she wasn't feeling well, might be going down with a cold.

Stephen was naturally worried. 'You've got to look your best for the wedding,' he'd remarked as they sat at the restaurant dinner table one evening. It had sounded like an order.

A Girl in Wartime

'I know!' she'd shot back at him. If this was how he was going to behave whenever she was out of sorts, she almost felt she didn't *want* to marry him. It was an unreasonable thought, born from the trauma she'd experienced. Then came another unreasonable thought: had he shown his first wife the sympathy he should have? A moment later she hated herself for such thoughts, blaming it on her sleepless nights.

303

Chapter Thirty

September 1917

'Stephen, I want to postpone our wedding,' Connie said.

They were in his flat. He looked at her, half amazed, half angry. 'But we've booked the church. And the reception. And the honeymoon.' He'd planned to take her to Wales. 'And then there's the guest list . . . '

It wasn't much of a guest list. In wartime, wedding receptions were frugal affairs, what with the food shortages growing tighter by the week. And as she intended to leave work very soon in preparation for her wedding, she wouldn't be inviting anyone from the paper either. Stephen had no one on his side, at least not anyone he cared to invite, and it came to her that she knew nothing of what family he had. In all their time together he'd never taken her to visit any of his kin – if he had any – he had never spoken of them and she had never asked. So there was really only her family, a few friends of hers and a couple of people he wanted to be there.

'You can't expect to postpone it at such short notice,' he added.

She was going to have to tell him, but prevaricated instead. 'Why can't we have it sometime in late November, nearer my birthday? Stephen, darling, I'm not well.'

'Then you must see a doctor,' he said firmly. She suddenly hated him for his firmness. But it was the state she was in doing that.

'I don't want to see a doctor,' she snapped.

It would mean divulging what was wrong with her and that would be an admission of cowardice, a lack of grit, such as the ordinary traumatised soldier was often accused of, such as Ronnie himself might have been, for what little treatment he was getting.

She felt an affinity with her brother. What if she were to speak to him? But that might undo all the hard work that his wife had put into making him better, could even make him worse, and Dolly didn't deserve that. She had been a tower of strength – something no one would have ever credited her with when she first came to live with his family. Dolly, who was holding him together, she and his little daughter Violet, who was now eighteen months and toddling, even saying a few words: 'Dada', 'Mumma', 'ball', 'door', 'me'. The word Dada always made Ronnie straighten with pride and cease twitching for a moment.

Even so, she needed to speak to him, ask his advice: should she go ahead with the present arrangements or be brave and postpone it?

Ronnie seldom came out of his and Dolly's room. Connie knew that their mum and dad were relieved that he didn't as his presence made them feel awkward, being forced to watch him struggling with his crutches, hearing his stammer, trying to ignore his inability to keep his hands from shaking. But he was the only person Connie felt she could talk to, being more or less in the same boat.

Waiting until Dolly had taken little Violet out shopping with Mum, she tapped on his door.

'Who – who is it?' came the halting voice.

'It's Connie,' she whispered. 'Can I come in?'

'Oh . . .' There was a moment's hesitation, then, 'Y-yes, c-c-come in.'

It seemed to her that it was said reluctantly and she suddenly felt like an intruder. She nearly replied that it didn't matter, but she was beginning to feel desperate. She wondered how deeply desperation must have gripped him at times. What must he have gone through to end up as he was? And here she was looking to bother him with her own petty affliction, with not spine enough to cast her own devils aside. Yet as she told him of her problems, of the line of disfigured men she saw each time she closed her eyes, he sat quietly, nodding from time to time with understanding, and she noticed that he had stopped twitching as he listened, his hands becoming unexpectedly still.

'Bite the bullet,' he said in an amazingly even voice as hers died away, not a trace of a stutter. 'Put your cards on the table, Sis, say you want to postpone it cos you ain't feeling up to it, ain't feeling well. Don't 'ave to tell him why, cos he won't understand. He ain't never bin in the thick of it all, ain't seen the slaughter, felt what it's like seeing dead bodies, comrades drowning in mud and . . . well, it don't matter. But the way you are,

306

Sis, you can't go through with any wedding in your state. Don't try to explain. Just say no.'

'But I could lose him that way,' she said.

'No you won't,' Ronnie said firmly, his voice so steady it was unbelievable. But a few hours later he could be seen shaking and twitching again. Connie felt that it might have been her fault for burdening him with her own problems.

Today, she tried again to tell Stephen how she felt, saying she was sure she'd collapse at the very altar if he insisted on keeping it as it was, but it wasn't so easy putting it as Ronnie had told her to.

In his flat she found herself fighting not to cry and this time it must have been the sheer desperation on her face, her halting words pleading for more time, that finally he conceded, her beseeching expression seeming to alarm and confuse him at the same time.

'I do love you,' she whispered as he held her to him. 'I love you more than anything in this world. But—'

'But?' He cut through her words, his voice flat, alarming her such that she expected him to add, 'It isn't working, is it?'

'I *do* love you, darling,' she burst out. 'So very, very much. It's just this wedding. I've not been well and it's too close. I shall never get better in that short time.' She looked up at him as he continued to hold her close. 'Darling, all I'm asking is can we put it off for a little while longer – give me time to get better.'

How could she tell him about those torn faces, those phantom eyes that appeared each time she closed hers? Would he understand? As Ronnie had said, he'd never had to face the war, never knew what it could do to some

307

people. She could imagine Stephen telling her that she must pull herself together and put it all behind her – as if it was as easy as that! And if she couldn't . . .

It had even started to affect their love making. The moment she closed her eyes as he fondled her, those faces would flash across her brain, making her unable to respond, leaving her to draw away and say she still wasn't feeling well enough. He'd ask what was wrong and had become annoyed as she made feeble excuses for her actions. He even asked if she still loved him. She'd say of course she did, with all her heart, just that not having felt all that well she still wasn't quite herself just now.

She was ruining everything they had. She felt as if she was going mad. Perhaps she was?

That night as he drew her to him, clasping her tightly, he whispered, 'We can't go on like this,' and for a moment she was horrified; her worst fears, it seemed, were being realised. But seconds later, his arms had tightened about her and he asked, 'Would it make you feel better, darling, if we did postpone the wedding to November – nearer your birthday, or maybe leave it until spring when the weather is better, whatever you feel more comfortable with.'

It was such a kind thought. Why then did she in her sensitive state feel that it more resembled a wish not to get married at all – maybe a wish to be free of her, this unbalanced woman?

Fighting a second of panic, she clung to him. 'Oh, darling, let it be November. Let it be November! I'll feel so much better then and everything will be so different.'

She was on the verge of telling Stephen about her visions but would he understand? She needed to talk to

Ronnie again. Going through it himself, he understood, could even help her in a way. She fervently hoped so as Stephen passionately kissed her, saying, 'November, then, darling,' between kisses.

She could have clung to him so tightly that all her breath was gone out of her, knowing how lucky she was to have such a wonderful man.

So it was arranged. The wedding would be held in November, just before her birthday in December, when she'd be twenty. And it would give him more time to find another really nice house for them instead of this rush that he'd seemed to have been in with nothing completed. A house was still to be found, but it had shown how eager he was to marry her. She was more than a little surprised he'd given in so easily. But by November perhaps her strange visitations would have subsided, with Ronnie's help.

Ronnie had spoken words of wisdom, had said of himself when she spoke to him a week later, 'You feel you can't move forward and it makes you depressed as if you've got nothink to live for. At least that's how I felt.'

He'd said 'felt', speaking of it in past tense, and if he could move on, though still a long way from total recovery, then there was hope for her. He had even endorsed it by saying only the other day, 'You know, Sis, I'm beginning to feel a lot better since I've bin talking to you.'

Yes, she had seen how one could let the sense of depression take hold. Ronnie had shown her by his own example that she wasn't to let it do that. And yes, she would go through with her wedding in November, become Stephen's wife, and live a happy and contented life.

Meantime she would go on having chats with Ronnie, taking courage from him enough to face her own demons, spending whatever few moments they could find, which wasn't often in a house full of people and she having to go to work. But few as their moments together were, it was helping both of them. He'd improved amazingly and Connie felt she was more a help to her brother and he to her than any doctor could have been, and that made her feel good.

This Saturday morning while Dolly and their mother were out shopping, Dad on his Saturday coal round, Ronnie had leaned forward, taken both her hands in his, and, in a remarkably steady voice, had said, 'I know 'ow it is with you, Sis. It takes one miserable sod to know another, as they say. We can be miserable sods together and maybe in time we'll cure each other.' He took a deep breath. 'Dolly's done a lot fer me – knows 'ow things are – but I need something more, and doctors ain't the answer, not fer me anyway. Me 'elping you is helping me. Bit selfish, eh?'

All that long speech without one stammer. Ronnie had a cheeky grin she hadn't seen since before he'd volunteered when war broke out.

That Monday she went into work after having had two good nights of sleep, amazingly, and only once assaulted by flashes of those anguished eyes, after which, while considering the need to get up, sit by the window, she'd fallen into a dreamless sleep without knowing it. She couldn't bless Ronnie enough.

Everything seemed to be speeding up, Connie and Stephen's wedding day seeming to be racing towards them. Connie felt ready for it this time and could hardly wait. Stephen had found a house for them in Victoria Park Road, a wonderful large house, he told her – though he didn't want her to see it until they were married – with a lovely, low-walled front garden and flowering trees, though bare this time of year, the rear of the house overlooking the park itself. The two of them would have lots of room to spare, it being all theirs, with no one tripping over each other's feet as in her parents' home.

As October passed she was beginning to feel that the devils in her head had begun spiriting themselves away; only now and again one would plant itself on her eyelids as she closed them but it was nothing like it had been and she was beginning to feel she could deal with them as any normal person might. In fact, she felt she could look forward to a normal life again.

There was only one fly in the ointment: air raids had begun to be stepped up and Connie prayed that nothing would drop on their new home or any of her families' homes for that matter. Squadrons of German aeroplanes now flew overhead and London was being bombed indiscriminately, especially in the East End, leaving Connie to add to her prayers that there'd be no raid on the day of her wedding. She couldn't begin to say how relieved she was to have left work – no more of those traumatic visits to sketch the faces of devastated victims. She didn't think the paper missed her. The idea finally was dropped; the paper's readers had lost interest in her sketches of distraught people. Nor did she care any more. In a month's time she'd be married and the paper would have lost her anyway.

Chapter Thirty-One

November 1917

It was now the day before Connie's wedding and where had the time gone? Preparations were stepping up, excitement was mounting; Connie had no time to think of the past. All she wanted was to lie in Stephen's arms, be made love to and not have to worry about rules.

Albert had come home on leave in time to see her be married. He looked worn out, hollow-cheeked, dull-eyed. She who'd caught and sketched many such expressions knew now what he had been going through, and felt for him that he would have to return to the front line when his leave was up. She was already praying for his safety.

George hadn't come home. Maybe he thought it best not to try to wangle leave for his youngest sister's wedding and risk spoiling her day knowing how he might be received by his father, whom he was well aware still held a grudge.

Others missing from the wedding would be Elsie's Harry and Lillian's Jim, who were both in France. She was deeply concerned for them all, her sisters without their husbands, their boys growing up, their dads not seeing it. Elsie took it all in her stride, stoically, soldiering on as it were, but Lillian was forever lamenting her husband's absence until Mum lost patience with her and told her to pull herself together: she was doing no one, much less herself and little James, any good.

But it was lovely Albert being back, even though he and Edie were living at her parents' home, married but with no place of their own. There was no chance with the war going on and he overseas. Connie smiled as she got into bed. Tomorrow she would be married and able to start a family too – as soon as possible.

Mum crept in just after she'd laid down. 'Make sure you get a good night's sleep, love,' she whispered. 'You've got to be nice and fresh for the morning.' Bending, she kissed her on forehead. 'Don't let excitement keep you awake. I'll be needin' to wake you up early tomorrow mornin'.'

Connie nodded, her mother dropping yet another a tender kiss on her forehead before creeping out of the room as if she was already asleep and fearing to wake her, turning at the door to whisper, 'Night-night, love.'

Mum had done a lovely spread for the wedding breakfast, as far as her and everyone else's bits of ration and a few hoarded extras could contribute.

Excitement thrilling deep in her stomach, Connie drifted off into sleep. It seemed like just seconds later that she was jerked awake to the shrill blowing of police whistles warning of yet another air raid. The police warning was hardly needed. Planes could already be heard piercing the hitherto quiet night air, their engines roaring above the East End.

313

Connie shot upright in bed as the house suddenly shook as if hit by some giant fist, the crash of an explosion almost instantaneous. Leaping out of bed, she ran for the bedroom door, met her parents coming out of theirs, and ran with them downstairs.

Ronnie and Dolly's door was wide open as if flung by some invisible hand, and Connie saw Dolly clutching little Violet to her. Ronnie was sitting on the edge of their bed, desperately searching for his crutches. A strange smell was filling the house – a dusty, burning smell.

Dad was now at the street door, still in his combinations. People were running by in all sorts of nightwear, the street full of cloying smoke. It was impossible to see more than two yards in any direction.

'What 'appened?' he was yelling. 'Where did it come down?'

Someone running by was shouting over his shoulder as he ran: 'Over the road – 'ouse over the road bin 'it. Down the street a bit.'

Mum was at the door, dragging Connie's father's outdoor coat from its peg to throw over his shoulders. 'Best go and see whose 'ouse it is,' she cried, but he was already off, pushing his arms into the sleeves of the coat as he went.

Left standing there, fingers to her lips in horror, the rest of the family gathered behind her, Connie heard her mother whisper, 'Oh Gawd, we know everyone in this street.'

Dolly was on the front doorstep. 'Our windowpanes is broken,' she said. 'Blackout curtains might be torn. Hope Ron ain't put our gas lamp on.'

A flicker of annoyance rippled through Connie. Ronnie may be an invalid but he wasn't a fool. But her annoy-

314

ance was only momentary; people were now running everywhere.

'Someone ought to see what your father's doing,' her mother was saying, her voice shaking. 'In case he's in any danger.'

Why she leapt to the call, Connie didn't know, but grabbing her own winter coat from its hook, she found herself running down the street after her father. What she thought she could do she'd no idea but the struck tenement was only a few doors down the street to hers and already she had a sick feeling.

The once nice house had been wrecked, its upper storey collapsed, rubble strewn from one side of the street to the other. The house opposite had lost all its windows. But already Connie felt a cold grip around her heart. It was Doris Copeland's house, her friend she'd been to school with. They'd often go out of an evening, would spend evenings in her house or she in hers, still friends even after she'd met Stephen. Doris was herself going steady with a boy.

Two people lay in the road and neighbours were covering them with coats. Other people stood around helplessly. Who were those covered by coats?

'Mrs Copeland,' she was told. 'Didn't stand a chance – and her poor daughter too.' Connie felt a wave of faintness pass across her brain. 'And 'er old man away fightin' in France,' the woman was going on. 'What's he goin' to do when they give 'im the news? He ain't got no one else, the poor bugger. That's if he lives long enough out there. Poor things – it's cruel!'

Connie hardly heard her. She wanted to sink to the ground, give way to tears. Instead, she looked at the woman, seeing in those faded eyes the hollow look of despair for the bereaved man, and she knew that if she had been ordered to sketch them she would have cried out, 'NO! No – no – no!'

Turning away, she ran blindly back along the rubble-strewn street to collapse into her mother's arms.

'It's Doris,' she sobbed. 'Her and her mum – dead! Oh, Mum . . . oh, Mum . . .'

With no strength left in her she felt herself helped into the dust-laden back parlour, carefully assisted to sit in her father's wooden armchair. In shock and grief she closed her eyes. Seconds later they shot open, behind the lids the despairing eyes of one so full of sorrow for her neighbour and the daughter that they seemed to pierce right through her eyelids to her brain.

The rest of the night was ruined for sleep. Dawn had yet to come up upon her wedding day. There would be no wedding. How could there be? Cancelled, at the last moment. People would understand. One look at the bombed home across the road, people would understand.

It wasn't only their road that had suffered terrible damage; during the night they heard that factories and warehouses south of Commercial Road had also been hit. Now, still a long time to morning, Dad had gone to tell Albert what had happened, bringing him back to see whether he could help.

'You'll 'ave to go and give the news to her Stephen,' Dad had said to him. 'I can't go. I'm wanted 'ere.' Albert had nodded and Dad ploughed on, 'Tell 'im she's too deep in shock and grief over what's 'appened to 'er best friend to have any wits about her, let alone go through wiv the wedding. He'll 'ave to understand there just can't possibly be a wedding 'ere, not now, not after all what's 'appened.'

Stephen was with them well before dawn and sat with Connie in her bedroom, the only private place in the house. Sitting on the edge of her bed, he cuddled her to him.

'I do understand, darling,' he said gently, she in tears. 'After what you've been through, of course you can't possibly face going through with it. I'll sort everything out, don't worry.'

'I'm so sorry,' was all she could manage and she felt his arm about her tighten.

'That state you're in,' he said, 'I think you should come back with me. Leave the family to sort out things here. You need rest – time to recover.'

He hadn't mentioned her friend and she silently blessed him for his gentle understanding as she lay against him, crying quietly.

'Meantime you should come back with me,' he said again. 'And as soon as it is light, I shall go and explain the situation to the church. You mustn't worry on that score, my love. What you need is rest and quiet, away from all this.'

Soothed by his steady tone, she felt him gently kiss her, ease her down on her bed, and kiss her again. He asked her if she was all right, at which she nodded silently. She closed her eyes as he quietly left and heard him talking to her parents, the parlour door closing, muffling what they were saying.

She lay for a moment, thinking of him. Seconds later Doris's round face filled her vision; her brown eyes were staring at her, yet it wasn't the Doris she knew – more

317

a face, torn and bleeding and burnt, and tormented eyes that horrified her.

Leaping up from the bed, she ran to the door and down the stairs to burst into Ronnie's room. He was sitting on the edge of his bed, his crutches by his side. He caught her as she flung herself against him. He held her tightly and she heard him saying to Dorothy, 'It's all right. She'll . . . she'll be okay.'

As Dorothy left the room, she gave her a concerned look. The pair of them left alone, Ronnie said in a low, steady voice. 'I've seen so much death.' It was as if he was talking to himself. 'You never get used to it, though you sort of form a wall around yourself and hold on to that wall like it's a part of you. That's how it's been with me, but you mustn't let it be. I'm beginning to learn that now. It's tragic. And still fresh. But you've got to let go of the wall. Maybe not yet. But your poor friend's death – you'll always cherish her memory and of course you'll mourn for 'er. Only natural. But you can't let it rule you. That's what I've bin doin' but I know now you 'ave to let go or you'll end up going potty, like me.'

'You're not potty,' she murmured, surprised at the evenness of her voice when moments before it had been on the brink of hysteria.

Ronnie shrugged. 'It's a terrible thing for you, I know. But you've got a good man in that Stephen and you can't spoil that. You can't let thoughts of youself spoil that. Life goes on, Sis.' He gave a dry chuckle that sounded full of cynicism. 'It does, you know. It has to, else you'll go off your rocker and be no good to anyone. And you can't do that to your Stephen. He's a good bloke.'

He gave her a little push with his shoulder. He was grinning – that old grin she remembered when he'd come back to say he'd joined up.

'Now you go back upstairs, get yourself ready to go back 'ome with him, where you can both 'ave a quiet chat about when you both intend to get married. That's the important thing. Go on now.'

Feeling a sudden strength, she hugged her brother and took herself into the parlour, ignoring her family's anxious faces. 'I'm going back with Stephen to his flat,' she said, surprised by the steadiness of her voice.

'Connie—' her mum began, but Connie interrupted her.

'Sorry, Mum, I can't stay here.' She wanted to say not with what had happened over the road but instead said, 'I need to be with him, the two of us on our own, away from here.'

As her parents stood silent, Albert said quietly, 'That's the best thing, Sis.'

It was still dark and cold when she left. Stephen carried a change of clothing for her in a small suitcase. It was awful thinking she'd have to pass that shattered house; she could see that those poor victims had been borne away by ambulance, but there were a few neighbours still standing in groups, talking and comforting each other.

She dreaded the thought of passing the house but Stephen turned left instead. 'We'll go through the alley,' he said quietly, and she blessed him for his forethought.

That way was longer and few ever used this route, having to walk down two more roads to get to the high street. But not now, not in the early hours of the morning after her friend had died. She clung to Stephen's arm, head bent against the cold breeze, huddled into her coat,

319

collar up, scarf tied over her hat and under her chin, he firmly holding her up.

In his cosy apartment she lay beside him in the safe peace of their bed as a watery dawn came up, the weather having begun a drizzle.

She had him make love to her, which helped to take away the horror of those recent events, and what did it matter if this time in her need for him they'd overlooked the use of protection? But now, lying here beside him, fulfilled, his arm around her, it was all beginning to pile back on her, thoughts of poor Doris, the senseless loss hitting her again.

'Stephen,' she said suddenly.

'Hmm?' He was almost half-asleep.

'I don't want to go back home. I don't want to live there any more.'

He sat up slowly, looking down at her, his blue eyes querying. 'You can't just walk out, my darling. They'll be worried sick. We'll have breakfast, then I'll take you home.'

'No!' She could hear the panic in her own voice. 'If I go back, each time I pass that house where my friend . . . I don't think I could face it.'

'But you must tell them about your decision, darling,' he said finally, very quietly. 'You can't just stay away and leave it at that. They'll be worried for you.'

'I can't go back!' she cried in desperation, sitting bolt upright. For a moment she stared at him then said in a small voice, 'It's the dreams I have. I've had them on and off ever since I came back from France. I see the eyes of those poor stricken men looking at me, their faces all torn and—'

She stopped, unable to describe her devils – the only way she could think of them as being. Stephen was gazing at her, slow realisation spreading across his features.

'I didn't know,' he said quietly. 'I thought you were simply having bad dreams. I thought they were just a passing thing, and would go away in time.'

'I used to have the dreams but when I close my eyes I see things like they're printing themselves on my eyelids, looking at me, accusing me of prying into their private pain. I can't go through all that again. I told Ronnie. He knew exactly what I was going through. We'd talk and it helped. And I think it helped him too. Some of those awful jerking movements of his seem to have stopped and he doesn't stutter as much. I think we've helped each other, though I still get those faces, those eyes, looking at me accusingly whenever I close mine.' She paused. 'But if I have to go back home,' she went on, 'and be forced to pass my poor friend's bombed house, knowing I'll never see her again, it'll all come back. I know it will. And I don't think I could stand it.'

He was silent for a moment or two, then said, 'I'll go and see your parents this morning. Explain about your dreams—'

'No, Stephen, don't!' she interrupted in panic. 'I don't want them to know. Just say we intend to live together and will be making fresh arrangements for our wedding. Let them think what they like.'

For a while longer he gazed at her, then smiled, very tenderly. 'Very well, my sweet, so when would you like to marry me?'

All her fears suddenly seemed to melt away. All she could say, very stupidly, was, 'Whenever you like.'

Maggie Ford

He conjured up a playful smile. 'Well, Christmas, next month is too busy a time to think about weddings, and January's a rotten month, so how about February? We'll make it a quiet one, just family, no frills or fripperies.'

She was in his arms, crying, 'Oh, yes, yes! Oh darling, yes!'

Living with him, her lover, appalled her parents but it wasn't up to them.

'Livin' in sin, I ain't 'aving them two anywhere near this 'ouse,' her father had said. But Mum, so Connie discovered from Dolly when they met up for lunch, had apparently belted him with her tongue, saying who the hell did he think he bloody-well was, this war was changing everything and with these bloody air raids who could say if they might not all be dead tomorrow, so shut his ranting and see a bit of sense!

But it was the first Christmas Connie had ever had away from home – she and Stephen spending it quietly together in his apartment. The arrangement was strange and unsettling for them all, but by January it had come to be accepted, especially when they told Mum there would be a quiet wedding in February, with just the family invited – if they wanted to be there.

'Of course we want to be there,' Mum said, cuddling her to her bosom. 'Whatever gave you the idea we wouldn't be?'

Ronnie was thrilled and congratulated her. She wrote to Albert. He replied saying 'good for you', and lamented the fact that he wouldn't be given leave to be there to give her away if their father felt disinclined to. Ronnie

322

had also offered but Dad had decided to call a truce and do the honours as any father should.

Connie had written to George as soon as the new date of her wedding in February had been set and he'd replied, but to her alone, a short note saying that he wished her well on her day, that he was okay, up to his knees in mud, of course, when going out with a stretcher to pick up the wounded, but that was all.

Reading it, knowing him at risk, Connie prayed for him with all her heart. Her eldest brother was a brave man, despite what they'd all said.

Come February, and the wedding was quiet and sedate, just as Connie wanted. Her whole family – those who could make it – beamed with happiness as her father walked her down the aisle. She and Stephen went straight from the wedding to the house he'd had redecorated and furnished. Until then he hadn't wanted her to see it before it was complete. 'I want you to see it for the first time on the day I carry you across the threshold,' he had said.

'And another thing,' he went on as they lay together, man and wife at last. 'I have your Ronnie to thank for bringing you back to life, to me.'

She knew what he meant, but insisted, 'It was you too, my love.'

She felt him shake his head. 'He was the one who knew what you were going through. I didn't. No one did. And in a strange way I think he cured himself as well to some extent without realising it.'

It was true. They had helped each other more than any institution or doctor could have. He was getting around more on his crutches, even venturing outside the house with Dolly at his side, wheeling their daughter in her pram.

'I feel I owe your brother something,' Stephen went on. 'And to that end I've spoken to a few contacts and found a small firm that has dedicated itself to employing men like him. He'll earn a small wage and I'm also looking to find him and his little family a rented tenement not far from your parents so he can be independent.'

Too overwhelmed to speak, she threw herself at him as he lay there. But there was something else she needed to tell him, unsure whether she should or not.

Finally she whispered, 'I think I'm pregnant, Stephen.'

She saw him turn his head to look at her with concern.

'Are you sure?' And when she nodded against his chest, he went on, 'How far are you?'

'It should be around August, if I'm right.'

'If you're right?' he asked. He sounded worried, but she smiled.

'It must have been that night I walked out to live with you. I've not seen any of my usual visits since then, so it must have been then.'

She felt him draw a huge intake of breath, her head rising a little on his chest. 'Good God,' he murmured. 'But when you start to show, they'll all be counting on their fingers.' That struck her as funny.

'Let them,' she laughed, pleased with herself now. 'I don't care.'

He laughed with her. 'Neither do I,' he said and kissed her. She had never felt so fulfilled. She'd got to the altar, pregnant, with no one aware of it. By the end of August or maybe early September, they'd be three. It was the most wonderful feeling she'd ever known.

Chapter Thirty-Two

May 1918

Connie had a lovely home. They had only to step out of their front door, walk a few yards along the avenue to stroll in the park at their leisure on a Sunday. Life was idyllic, and damn the war! Even so, she prayed it would have ended by the time the baby arrived.

The war, however, seemed to be going on for ever, even appearing to be getting worse. Russia had collapsed and there were even more German troops to face now. She worried for Albert, and for George.

True, America was making an impact, with their fit young men fresh from good living as opposed to battle-weary Allied troops. When they'd entered the war, hopes had risen and they cheered all the way.

Now, nearly a year later, those hopes were beginning to die, just like those thousands of young American boys as well as Canadians, Australians, New Zealanders and others from all parts of the Commonwealth, yet nothing seeming to have been achieved. How much longer? It looked as if her baby could easily be born into a war-torn world, the Allies advancing only to be pushed back, advancing again, again to be pushed back, over and over, more lives lost, endless, senseless slaughter.

And how was Albert? And George? Albert wrote frequently to Edie saying he was fine, fed up but fine, writing the same to his parents and sisters. George wrote not at all. No one knew how he was and Connie knew it hurt her mother. Whether it hurt Dad, the man never let on.

It was late May and Connie thought of Albert stuck in Flanders with no hope of leave for the time being. Literally stuck, according to his last letter to Edie, as most of his time was spent battling mud. It not having stopped raining for months, they were up to their knees in it. He wrote identical letters to his parents, they, as always, worried for him. At home it had also been a wet winter and spring so heaven knew what it was like out there with everything churned up.

Albert added that the trenches were these days tending to cave in from lack of use. Fighting, he wrote, was mostly in the open these days. A sort of tit-for-tat business, the Bosch pushed back a few miles only to gain what ground they'd lost, to be pushed back again and so on and so on. Behind the lines there were observation posts, medical-aid posts, areas of cooking, officers headquarters, repair shops. 'That's until shells bugger it all up and we have to start repairs all over again. Home from home!' he'd added wryly. 'I'm in one of the trenches now, helping to board up the sides where they've gone and collapsed. This one's called Piccadilly.'

He wrote the same to Connie and Stephen. On the face of it they were light-hearted letters but reading between the lines made their hearts bleed.

There was nothing from George – it was worrying. 'But if something bad had happened,' Mum had said more than once, 'we'd've been informed straight away. They do, don't they?'

George had hardly contacted any of his family, as if, having proved he was no coward, he had washed his hands of them.

She prayed for her brothers, constantly. They all did. Everyone did, for their boys, their husbands, brothers, cousins. Sometimes prayers were not enough. Since Russia's collapse, German forces had been piling in on the Western Front, in places shattering the Allied lines, though the Allies still fought hard to hold on to what they'd won. Even with the weight of the Americans, it was frightening and this spring was not a happy time.

Everywhere she went, she saw drawn faces, creeping fear that Germany with its larger weight of troops could win this war, all those millions of lads and men killed for nothing. If she still had her sketch book she could have done an amazing job recording those bleak, harrowing expressions, but she had thrown her sketch book away. She was – thank God – no longer an employee of the *London Herald*, though Stephen remained a valued asset to them. She had enough of those harrowed expressions in her head from her experience in France to last a lifetime.

It had been hard for Connie to return to her street, to walk past the tenement where Doris had lived – and died – but she had to, otherwise she'd never see her family. In any case, the baby inside her gave her the strength she needed to confront her fears. She knew she'd do anything for the little being she was carrying, and would not deny her son or daughter the chance to know her family. Besides, she reasoned to herself, her child had been conceived the night Doris had died, restoring – in Connie's mind, at least – some balance to the world.

Even Mum had looked very down when Connie had gone there to see her yesterday. 'Poor Mrs Daly next door,' she said over a cup of tea. 'She got a telegram yesterday morning telling her that her son's missing, believed killed – ain't that just terrible? It makes me worry for our Bertie. She looked so awful. That young Allen's all she had.'

That was true. The woman's husband had passed away just before the war and she had only one sister living up north.

'Poor thing,' Mum had gone on, stirring her tea, a faraway look in her eyes. 'What if that was to 'appen to my Albert? Or our George?'

'It won't, Mum,' Connie soothed, wishing her mother would stop stirring her tea, a sign of her concern. She felt herself shudder.

It was then she became aware of her mother staring at her – not her face, but her midrift, eventually to lift her eyes to Connie's face.

'You puttin' on weight, gel?'

The question was loaded with connotation. Connie shrank a little.

'I . . . it's probably good living.' She laughed, then ceased. Her mother hadn't laughed. She continued to gaze, narrow-eyed at Connie's middle.

Connie felt herself shrink a little. So far she had told no one other than Stephen, but very soon she would have to tell Mum. Mum was sharp-eyed, and even though at six months she was able to disguise her swelling belly, her mum wouldn't be slow in counting on her fingers. Having had four children herself, she was well aware of the stages and would know that conception had taken place well before her daughter's February wedding.

She sat here at the table, eyeing her mother, not really sure how to begin. She heard her mother say, 'When's it due, then, love?' in a quiet, even tone.

There was nothing else for it but to say, 'I'm not sure, really.'

Mum smiled slowly. 'Yes you are, love. You can count, can't you? At least up to nine!'

Connie took a deep breath, replied slowly. 'Well, it could be end of August or early September, I'm not sure. I've not been to the doctors yet.'

'Then you should go, love, just to make sure everything's orright.'

No condemnation; Mum understood. Probably no one else would – would begin to count on their fingers and mutter among themselves. Especially her sisters. Their men fighting in France, and they having to look after their children on their own, they would probably glow at the knowledge of what she'd been up to before marriage. To be honest they still looked sideways at Stephen not being in the forces, partially deaf or not. The added slight would suit them down to the ground, Connie thought with a wry, uncharitable smile.

But Mum would take it in her stride, and only pray her new grandchild would be born safe and sound; when the time came she would be by her side. She deeply blessed her mum for her quiet understanding. And Mum would deal with when and how her dad was told too.

Looking to get her family on her side, she told Ron and Dolly and got both their congratulations and joy for her. She wrote to George, who sent back his usual short remark: 'Good for you' but did add that he was fine at present, though his job could be a bit horrific. She knew what he meant from her own experience in France. He wrote that he'd been given leave a couple of times but felt it best not to come home and had instead spent it in Paris; that he had met a Parisian girl there, was learning French, and the two of them were corresponding. But he said not to tell Mum and Dad as they'd get all riled up.

She also wrote to Albert, he too congratulating her and wishing he'd be home for when his niece or nephew was born, that by that time the war might be over. On that point he didn't sound that sure. He said things were even worse than at the start of the conflict. Somewhat poignantly, he wrote that he hoped Ronnie was coming along okay, and that he missed him terribly.

Albert had never missed anyone so much in all his life as he missed Ron. In fact, rather than getting used to it, it was getting worse. This morning he'd been holed up in some trench eating bully beef, wishing there was a bit of bread to go with it, but bread wasn't often on the menu these days.

At the moment the shelling was relentless and made him feel as if there'd never been any other life but this. The bombing seemed to have been going on for hours, sometimes his own side, other times the enemy's. When it finally ceased it would usually herald orders to attack, with tanks now as added protection, tanks that could clear barbed wire and formed some sort of cover. But the German had tanks too. The full weight of the whole German army was now concentrated on the Western Front since the collapse of Russia. It often left him wondering what hope there was of ever winning this war, but it didn't do to think like that.

Maybe it was this sense of loneliness, of isolation amid masses. These days most were strangers to him, those he'd known either killed and left behind, wounded and taken away, or captured and taken God knows where. If only he had Ronnie here with him still. But he must not think like that. Ronnie was alive and safe in England. Here, where they had more or less started three, or was it four, years ago – it like a lifetime, in any case – Ronnie could be dead.

Beneath the bombardment, he crouched alongside a host of strangers in a hastily dug trench at the edge of some wood. Here he scribbled off a quick letter to Edie, hurriedly written in pencil on paper torn from his notebook. He wrote that he hoped she was fine and asked how everyone was at home, especially Ronnie, and how was Connie doing, near the end of her time now. He hoped the baby would be born okay. He ended by giving Edie all his love and wishing he was with her.

By the time he'd received Edie's reply saying everyone was well, he and his comrades had been ordered forward.

The next few days were full of advancing, retreating, advancing – almost like a game of push and shove, though here it was no game. Even less so on this particular advance, as leaping into an enemy dugout, his bayonet stabbing blindly at those defending it, he felt a searing pain rip through his shoulder, knocking him backwards.

A German stood over him, his bayonet on its way towards his throat. Instinctively he tried to deflect the thrust, missed, but seconds later the man had collapsed on top of him, bayoneted through the back by someone else, his own blood and that of the German mingling together as the unknown lifesaver leapt on towards yet another target.

Trod on by others piling into the German defence, Albert felt his senses leaving him, his mind telling him that the bayonet thrust had gone on into his lung, leaving him to bleed to death. He saw Edie leaning over him, her face blurred by tears.

Regaining consciousness, he was still aware of the face above him. Edith? Not Edith. Edith was blonde and pretty. This person was dark-haired and not pretty. Nor was it a she. The man wore a medical officer's uniform.

'Feeling better, soldier?' came the deep voice. Without waiting for a reply, he went on, 'You're doing fine, man. A pretty deep wound in the shoulder though not that serious. But it'll take you out of the advance for the time being, might even get you a bit of leave.'

And he'd thought he been about to bleed to death from a pierced lung. Who was it who'd saved him by stabbing his attacker? He'd never know. But the man had saved his life and he hoped whoever he was would not lose his.

Connie and her mum were sipping tea in the kitchen, talking about the baby. Just under three weeks off being born, she guessed now. She was feeling ungainly, short of breath, cumbersome and far from pretty, though Stephen seemed to think she was Venus herself. If her calculations were right, it was overdue, but Mum had said the first one nearly always was. So it looked like it might arrive the second week in September, hopefully stopping the looks from her sisters who were already counting up on their fingers and smirking.

Connie was just draining her tea when the back door burst open and a frantic Lillian almost fell into the kitchen, startling the two of them.

Leaping up despite her bulk, Connie caught her as she fell against the kitchen table, almost knocking it side-ways, in a flood of tears. She seemed about to collapse, having run all the way from her house, two streets away, apron still on, her hair in curlers, no coat despite a rather cold day.

Mum was up from her chair too. 'Whatever's the matter, love?'

'My Jim! They believe he's been killed!'

'Dear God . . .'

Lillian was holding out a telegraph, crumpled from her shaking grip. 'He's dead! I've lost my poor Jim . . .' Mum guided her to her chair, Lillian breaking down in sobs. Her arms flung across the table, nearly knocking over her mother's cup of half-finished tea, and she let her head fall in her arms.

'He might only be missin',' Mum was saying, her own voice choked as she leaned over her, trying to cuddle her as the girl sobbed. 'They'll find 'im. They will, love. Or he might of bin taken prisoner.'

Connie's head was swimming. She was unable to find words to say to her sister. Unable to do anything, Connie

Maggie Ford

ordered herself a taxi to take her home to Victoria Park
Road on her mother's advice that she mustn't exert or
worry herself with the baby so near. Mum had decided to
go back with Lillian to collect little James from the neighbour Lillian had left him with and bring them back here.

That evening, lying in bed, Stephen breathing softly
beside her, Connie tried to sleep, but there was no sleep
in her. In her mind she was filled with images of a face
bandaged where a chin had been blown away, another
with a deep hole where a nose should have been, above
the bandages, the eyes filled with despair.

She made herself speak to the images in her mind,
reassure them it was all right. But it wasn't all right.
There were artificial face parts now, made to look like
noses or parts of cheeks or parts of chins, but nowhere
near the real thing. They would still be disfigured for
life. There was little anyone could do. These men were
destined to be noticed and then turned hastily away from,
eyes averted. Once handsome, light-hearted youths had
become things of revulsion or even, God forbid, pity.
Pity was far worse than revulsion.

In her mind she sought to heal those young men; she
took herself through endless scenes in her head, talking
to those blinded by bursting shells or choking from
creeping poison gas; trying to comfort, endlessly telling
the blinded that they'd never have to see that look of
pity in the eyes of others: a ghastly play inside her head
that she seemed never able to escape.

In her womb the baby kicked, bringing her awake. It
was not as hard as it usually was, and quickly settled
down. There came a small but nagging pain too as if she
should be visiting the toilet, but she didn't. Getting up,

334

she crept downstairs to her lovely kitchen and began making herself a cup of tea. So long as she kept busy the scenes that played out in her head would be given no room. But she felt she was going slowly mad. There was no other way to see it. And she felt helpless for it.

As she waited for the kettle to boil she sank down on one of the chairs in her lovely big kitchen, her chin in her cupped hands, and stared at the pale blue walls. Instantly the things in her head began again to conjure up deplorable scenes. What in God's name was wrong with her? In anger, part fear, part frustration, she leaped up to scream at the top of her voice.

Instantly the scene vanished. But she had awoken Stephen. He was downstairs in seconds, holding her to him as she broke down in a flood of tears. She let herself collapse against his firm body. 'Stephen – I think I'm going mad!'

'You're not going mad, darling,' he whispered against her cheek. 'I have been consulting certain medical people and they think it could be a form of shell shock.'

'Shell shock?' She leaned away to stare at him. 'I was nowhere near the fighting.'

'I know, but—'

'And what were you doing discussing me with some stranger?'

'The man's a doctor, a psychiatrist.'

'A psychiatrist?' she stormed, furious now. 'Whatever he is, he's still a stranger, nothing to do with this family. How dare you, Stephen!'

He remained calm. 'I feel we should consult someone who is familiar with the affliction. We've got to get you cured, my love.'

335

Maggie Ford

'I'm not going to anyone like that. It never did Ronnie any good.' It was she who helped him, no one else.

'Well you can't go on like this, my darling, tearing yourself apart,' he soothed, holding her to him again.

Of course she couldn't go on like this. She was tearing the both of them apart, even possibly ruining her marriage.

'All right, I'll see this . . . whoever he is,' she consented in a small voice.

Seconds later she was calling out from a sudden sharp pain, an urgent wish to visit the toilet, but instinct told her it was not that.

'Stephen, I think it's started,' she gasped. 'The baby, I think it's on its way!'

Chapter Thirty-Three

Two days of sheer agony. She had never felt such pain. Such an effort to push, gasping, wanting only to give up, bullied by the nurses not to. But finally in the early hours, the baby was born, the pain it had caused her in coming into the world seeming to fly away as if by magic.

'You've a lovely little girl,' the midwife said proudly. A girl! And she had so wanted to given Stephen a son.

Connie had intended to call her baby Stephen after his father. Instead she decided to compromise and name the baby Stephanie, and he was in complete agreement with that.

'I'm sorry it's a girl,' she said when he came in the following morning after the birth.

He'd paid for the best care; private hospital, the luxury of a private room with attentive nurses and the best doctor he could find. She couldn't have felt better treated, and all she could do was present him with a daughter who, when she grew up and married, wouldn't even carry on his name. Maybe the next time she would give him a boy?

He smiled down at her. 'I'm glad it's a girl, my darling,' he said gently. 'She will never have to be sent off to war, like your brothers.'

She knew he was thinking of Albert, who was home on seven days' leave, his arm still in a sling.

His features were pale and drawn and he looked old. He saw himself as fortunate to be alive but after his leave he'd be sent back to France to finish recuperating in some hospital there, readying him to be sent back to the trenches, possibly to receive an even more serious wound or maybe even worse – a mortal one.

She could see it written on Albert's face when he and Edie came to see her and the baby. He had come to the hospital to say goodbye as he was off to France the next day. She wanted to cry for him but all she could say was, 'I'm so glad you were home for the birth of your little niece. It's so lovely to see you. And Bertie, take good care of yourself – very good care.'

'Don't worry, I will,' he answered with what she knew was forced cheerfulness as she kissed him farewell, Edie at his side pushing back her tears. The two bent down to kiss the baby, then straightened up to shake Stephen's hand and be wished good luck, Edie to peck her brother-in-law's cheek and be told to keep her chin up.

Watching, Connie felt a small surge of guilt. Her three brothers had all been in the thick of it, George even going against his so-called religion, yet Stephen was still a civilian, kept out of the forces by a mere stone-deaf right ear and a responsible job. Did he ever feel the weight of it?

In all honesty she had never given it thought before, merely thanked her lucky stars that she'd never had to go through what Edie and Dolly had to, or what her sisters were going through, Lillian seeing herself a widow.

His last leave three months behind him, Albert was glad his wound had healed nicely. It had been good to see Edie and his family, visit Connie and Stephen and their baby, and he had been overjoyed to hear she had asked him to be godfather to little Stephanie.

But this made it all the more hellish to have to come back to the muck and the mud – it rained here constantly – and the horrific slaughter, all over again.

It was the first day of November. The war seemed to be going on for ever. As fast as they got the enemy on the run, things would turn to begin all over again. They tried to advance in yet another attack across rain-soaked, bomb-cratered ground, through a fog of choking smoke from bomb and shell, hoping not to fall into one of the many craters that were everywhere, to be swallowed up, never to be found. Most of what was in front of them was so obliterated that one occasionally tripped over an unseen dead body, or would hear a moan of pain as a boot unavoidably connected with the still conscious wounded. They had been warned against pausing to help as they'd become a target themselves. It was enough to make a man feel he might go suddenly berserk.

Except being weighed down by full kit and rifle, boots sinking to the ankles in soft mud to impede every step, gave one little chance to go berserk and run off. All a man could do was trudge on.

His lungs filled with smoke and the foul air of rotting corpses; he hoped it wasn't also heavy with gas. He had his mask at the ready just in case.

339

Hand-to-hand combat was raging as he finally reached the enemy lines. Moments later, hands were being lifted into the air and from those around him came cheers.

And around him there were exultant shouts: 'It's ours!' 'We got the buggers!' 'Come on – keep your bloody 'ands up, you bleedin' Gerry swinehund!'

Standing ineffectually to one side, rifle levelled though there seemed little need for it now with the few they'd captured – the rest having fled with their hands above their head – all Albert could think about was the men he'd seen fall on the way.

Who were they? Someone's sweetheart, husband, son, father – all of them comrades of his. There came a strange thought. He might have known some of them, some of them quite closely. But in a few days, when the roll was called, he probably wouldn't recall a single one of their names. Or if he did, there'd be a moment of sorrow, then it would pass. Rather like being at a gathering, making the acquaintance of some of them, feeling close for a while, then as everyone began to leave, the party over, unable to recall any one of them, much less wonder who they were or where they came from. Death here was for him something like that. And suddenly he felt ashamed.

But this was no time to feel ashamed. When he went to what passed for a bed, he'd slept like a log. This morning his section, along with several other sections, stood by in readiness to go over the top to push Gerry even further back towards his homeland. It was twelve midday, the sun was still trying to come out – one could just glimpse it through thin cloud – helping to lift their spirits, although behind that was the knowledge that by tomorrow they could be pushed back again, especially if Gerry had a weight of extra numbers behind them. Intelligence said not. But who trusted intelligence?

They waited. The sun finally broke through. The waiting continued. Still nothing happened. Breakfast had been doled out ages ago. Would they get a midday meal? Albert thought. He felt hungry. Then came the idiotic prayer: don't let me die feeling hungry. He almost laughed but felt too keyed up to.

Officers were pushing their way along the crumbling trench, easing themselves between clustered soldiers. In their wake was an odd sound. Cheering? What was there to cheer about?

Two officers had reached where Albert stood. 'At ease, men.' They were smiling. 'You can all grin if you want, lads. At eleven o'clock this morning, Germany agreed to an armistice, signed, sealed and delivered. We are at peace. The war is over.'

'Who won?' come a shout, half insolent, half stunned.

'We did,' replied the major.

'Can't you 'ear the cheering, you daft soldier?' Their sergeant bawled, but no one heard him, his parade ground voice drowned out by their own outburst of cheering.

But there were some who didn't cheer, who stood in reflective silence, remembering lost comrades, good comrades, close comrades; others were silent in a prayer of relief, thanksgiving, sadness for those who'd gone, but glad not to have been one of them. Albert too felt himself go through a depth of reaction like a fist slowly burying itself in his diaphragm.

Yet self-awareness had begun to surface: he would be going home. He and Edie would be together. He would go back to his milk round, they would rent a nice little

Maggie Ford

house and they would live happily ever after. There'd
never again be a war like this – the war to end all wars,
someone had said – and he believed it. The whole world
fighting each other, fighting itself to a standstill; such a
war could never be allowed to happen again. He felt
suddenly very philosophical as he stared at the quiet
faces around him. It was all over.

In another part of France, George was listening to the
same news.

Standing with the others in the hospital tent as the
news was given out, there was no cheering, no singing.
All around him lay the wounded on their beds, each one
in need of attention. There was no time for celebrating,
though he suspected each doctor, nurse, orderly, was
offering up quiet thanks.

Some patients took the wonderful news silently, no
doubt weighing up their relief against the life they would
lead from now on, seeing themselves as no good for
anything. But some cheerfully lifted a thumb into the
air, grinning like Cheshire cats, trusting to be cured
enough to go home and begin living again.

As for George going home, he didn't think so. He had
another destination in mind and was beginning to feel
that life for him would be taking a wonderful turn.

No, he wouldn't be going home. As soon as he was
out of this RAMC uniform, he'd be straight off to Paris
to a future he'd never have dreamed of having, had there
not been a war.

Chapter Thirty-Four

The whole of London, the whole country in fact, was going wild with relief and excitement at the wonderful news of an armistice having been signed. It had more or less taken everyone by surprise. The war was over. After four years of combat, the fighting had stopped. Joy was uncontrollable. People – in places, a great crush of people – were dancing in the streets, clutching at each other with joy. Soldiers who had been brought home earlier were being kissed and cuddled by outright strangers, others lifted shoulder-high to be borne along, laughing down at their handlers.

Flags, banners, streamers and Union Jacks had appeared as if from nowhere, to be waved, hung up on washing lines, nailed to windows and door frames; beer too seemed to have appeared as if by magic, mugs of it being drank, spilling down shirt fronts every time someone knocked into someone else, almost every working man and woman having downed tools to join in the celebrations.

Yet there were windows that had curtains drawn, street doors that had not opened, windows and doors behind which grieving families sat mourning the loss of a son, a father, a husband, like Mrs Daly, Mum's next-door neighbour.

Connie would bet her Mum would have gone in there to be with her for a while, unless Mrs Daly had preferred to mourn alone. But Connie's first thought had been for Lillian. Her Jim was still missing assumed killed, nothing yet to confirm or deny it. 'I ought to try and get round there to see how she is,' Connie told Stephen.

Monday, he had been at work, but as the wonderful news spread most of the newspaper's staff left the premises, some to gather news, others to be with their families. Most shops and businesses had closed, the streets jam-packed.

Connie would have gone to comfort her sister earlier but had held back in case Stephen might come home. She was glad when she heard his key turn in the lock, having struggled through the madness on the streets.

'I didn't think I'd ever get through,' Stephen said, surveying the scene below from an upstairs window, just below them a new crush of people already dancing and singing in this normally quiet avenue. 'They're going wild,' he went on as he took off his coat and trilby. 'Sheer strangers, dancing, singing, kissing, going completely mad.' There was a lot of drinking going on, he told her. 'Seems the pubs decided to stay open. They know where the money is. You've no idea what it was like in all the main thoroughfare. You'd stand no chance of getting to your sister's.'

But Connie felt anxious for the bereaved girl. 'They're probably all on their own, her and little Jamie. She must be feeling so terribly lonely.'

'So are a lot of people,' he said, his tone soft with sympathy, but she ignored him.

'I can't help about other people. She's my sister and she really ought to have someone with her.'

'Maybe your sister Elsie's with her. They only live a couple of streets away from each other.'

'And there's Mum and Dad. I ought to go see if they're all right. And there's Ron and Dolly and their Violet.'

'They're with your parents. They're probably fine. Do you really want to drag little Stephanie around the streets as they are?'

'If I went, you could keep an eye on her.'

'If you go, I'm going with you, Connie. I'm not letting you loose at the mercy of that excited mob, you and our child.'

She gathered up her coat, hat, gloves, handbag, together with the baby's outdoor things, leaving him with no choice but to humour her.

'We'll cut across the park,' he said as they left, holding Stephanie in his arms. 'And we'll go straight to your sister's. Your parents have got each other, and Ronald's got them. We might even chance to find a taxi.'

They took the back streets, no taxi to be seen, and still full of people. People were celebrating to the full and by the time they reached Lillian's, Connie too felt the elation, her face hot from walking, as well as aching from a constant grin. She strove to control herself as Stephen knocked on the door of the little tenement house.

Instantly it was jerked open, as if her sister had seen them coming. Connie expected her to throw herself into her arms, her face reddened from crying, her eyes

Maggie Ford

inflamed. But her face was wreathed in smiles as she flung her arms around Connie's neck.

'Oh, Con! Mum 'n' Dad's here. We've had such wonderful news! Early this morning a telegram came – they've found my Jim! He was taken prisoner weeks ago and no one knew. No one informed. Oh, Connie, ain't it just wonderful?'

She was crying now, still grasping Connie to her. 'He's all right. He's fine. They'll be sending 'im home any time. Ain't it wonderful?'

Trooping up the gangplank on to a ship already crowded with war-weary men all looking to go home and to stay there, Albert felt himself heave a great sigh as they began to move. He was leaving France for ever, never to return as far as he was concerned, never to set eyes on the Continent ever again.

A smooth crossing on this windless if overcast November day, but it wouldn't have mattered if there'd been a full-force gale. Each man was on deck, each with a grin on his face. The wounded were safe below. Albert was going home – going home for good.

He watched the white cliffs of Dover come into sight, growing in height as they sailed nearer until he felt he was so close he could touch them as the vessel manoeuvred into the docks which were already full of English ships bearing men home from the war.

While docking, Albert found himself practically shoved off the ship amid an orderly crush, each man eager to feel home soil under his feet. Most packed into trains, each bound for home, but Albert's train was totally stuffed to the doors. Among scores of others he was

346

forced to stand all the way, but it didn't matter. In a couple of hours he'd be embracing Edie.

With the change of trains, he finally alighted at Bethnal Green Station, and began to walk the rest of the way, kitbag over his good shoulder, the other shoulder having had the stitches removed and healing well, although still tender. He could hardly wait to get out of uniform. Three days had passed since the news had broke, but he still found himself twice kissed on the cheek by two different women he happened to pass, clapped on the back from a middle-aged man he'd never met in his life before, and his hand shaken by another even older man, who rasped, 'Well done, son, welcome 'ome!'

It was wonderful to have Edie throw herself into his arms in tears of joy. Tonight they would lie in bed and make slow but passionate love, no longer with just a few days before being sent back. Tomorrow they'd have the joy of each other without haste.

'I want a big family,' she said quietly that night. Yes, a big family, none of his children ever to be caught up in war, a teenager as he had been.

On Saturday his mum had planned a homecoming party for him, a family get-together. Edie's parents were invited too. After a few days' rest, he felt he would be ready for it.

It was good to see them all together, furniture cleared from the room ready for a party, Connie's old downstairs bed gone for good. Mum's front room had also been reinstated to her best room, Ronnie having mastered his crutches and insisting on manoeuvring himself upstairs to his old bedroom. And soon, he said, he was to be fitted with a false leg. Stephen was paying. He'd also been employed by a little company Stephen had found that took on men incapacitated by war. On top of that he'd soon be moving into a little house Stephen had got for him. Albert smiled. Connie had done well for herself marrying such a generous man.

The family was all here: Connie and Stephen and their little Stephanie; Ron and Dolly with their little'un, Ronnie quiet, greatly changed from the buoyant lad he'd once been but better than he was; Elsie's Harry home, looking pretty well. Lillian's Jim was also back looking haggard: evidently, prisoners of war had got the rough end of the stick when it came to being fed. Mum promptly handed him a plateful of food despite the meagre feast she'd managed to get together, no one begrudging him.

Dad's parents had come, Granddad still playing the mouth-organ for all his age. Connie's grandmother having confined herself to a chair in the corner and being helped to food, saying her old legs wouldn't let her dance. Not that there was much room to dance in, some of the neighbours having been invited, swelling the numbers but thankfully contributing to the table with whatever they'd found suitable in their larders to compensate for extra mouths. Not that it was a lot, rationing nowhere near being lifted, in fact worsening, yet very acceptable.

But in all this, one face was missing – George's. Mum said nothing but Connie knew she felt it keenly.

One week of peace had gone by. It was wonderful yet odd too – as if people were waiting for something to happen and wreck everything. One pitiful reminder was all the crippled who were jobless, with little so far seeming to have been done for them. They lined the kerbsides at intervals, cap placed on the ground in the hopes of the odd copper being dropped into it. But with so many having fought for their country, who had even the odd copper to spare?

Seeing them, Ronnie could think himself lucky, thought Connie as she and Stephen paid her parents a visit that Sunday, and she felt embarrassingly indebted to her wonderful husband for his generosity to her brother.

Alone in the kitchen, her mother's rounded face was creased with concern when they entered, which prompted Connie to ask what was wrong.

'It's our George,' she said quietly.

Mum reached into her apron pocket and brought out a letter still in its envelope but the envelope flap already opened.

'Came yesterday but I've not shown your dad yet,' she whispered. 'I don't know what he'll say about it.'

'Can I read it?' asked Connie, she too feeling the need to whisper.

Her mother handed it to her. 'I really don't know what to make of it. I don't want your dad going off the handle. What if he throws it straight in the fire?'

'Maybe it would be best if I read it out aloud to him. He can't do anything then.'

'What about your Stephen, him there to witness if your dad does throw it in the fire. I'm not keen on other people seeing what goes on between our George and your dad.'

'Stephen is family, Mum,' Connie reminded her, and saw her mother nod slowly.

'I suppose he is.' She lifted her head in sudden determination. 'All right, love, get it over and done with and see what 'appens. But I'm not 'aving your dad show us up. I'll warn 'im to take care, in no uncertain terms.' Connie couldn't help but smile at her set expression. When she wanted, Mum could have her way in her own quiet manner.

But what she'd read was no laughing matter. She felt suddenly empty at what she'd read, but her brother George was his own master – he'd proved that long ago.

The others hardly looked up as she and her mother entered the room, Dolly sitting with Violet on her lap; Stephen with his little daughter on his, talking to Ronnie; Dad listening. Ronnie and Dad were puffing away, filling the room with both pipe and tobacco smoke.

Mum took one sniff and went and lifted up the lower sash window a fraction. 'All this stink. It can't be good for the kiddies,' she said sharply. Connie was only grateful that Stephen hadn't been included in her disapproval. Stephen had never smoked as far as Connie knew. If he ever had it would probably have been after losing his first wife.

'Bloody 'ell!' Dad exploded, catching the full force of cold November air, his chair backing straight on to the window despite the lower sash having been lifted not much more than half an inch. 'You shut the bloody thing, woman!'

If there was to be a row, thought Connie, best it be over the letter she held rather than over a small waft of draught.

Going to her father, she said loudly, 'A letter came yesterday. It's for you and Mum. It's important.'

He looked at his wife, his moustache bristling visibly, the draught forgotten. 'Then why didn't you say yesterday?'

'She couldn't,' Connie said sharply. 'It should be read while there are people here.'

People here could stop him throwing it straight into the fire in temper.

He held his hand out for it but Connie held it away from him. Ignoring him, she began reading aloud:

Sorry if this is only a short letter but I'm on my way to Paris. I shan't be coming home, at least not for quite a while. It depends. I know how Dad feels, but that's not why I won't be coming home, at least not just yet. I need to tell you why.

While in France I spent a few leaves in Paris – no point in coming home. You understand why. In Paris I met a girl. Her name is Camille. She's Parisian and has been teaching me French. We got serious and I asked her if we might become engaged and she said yes, so I'll be living in France and we plan to get married in a couple of months' time. It'll be a quiet affair. She has no family so only a few friends of hers are invited, and as I say, I won't be home. So you don't have to concern yourself on that score, Dad. Maybe one day we'll come and visit or maybe Connie and her husband might like to come and see us.

Connie paused. She had written to him regularly while the war raged, telling him of her coming marriage and the birth of her daughter. But somehow she had felt it best to keep this exchange of correspondence secret from her parents for the time being. Her brief pause was met by utter silence, she bent her head to continue reading:

I know Dad won't care to read this but hope you'll read it out to him, Mum, whether he likes it or not. I don't hold him any grudges. The war's over. It's behind us and there's no use looking back into the past. It solves nothing. I know I was a fool. At least I admit it. But now I'm well and happy and hope all of you are too, including you, Dad.

Connie folded the letter and handed it back to her mother, not once taking her eyes off her father.

She saw him slowly tap out the glowing tobacco from the bowl of his pipe into the fire, replacing the empty pipe on the mantelpiece, a sign that he was divorcing his mind from what he had heard.

Then just as slowly he retrieved the pipe and, reaching for his old black leather tobacco pouch, began refilling the bowl, tamping it down as the others watched, taking a taper from the holder by the side of the fire, holding it to the flames until it ignited and applying it to the fresh tobacco.

Puffing steadily, he leaned back in his wooden armchair.

'Well, I'm buggered,' he rumbled quietly and slowly, almost like someone in awe. 'Our George gettin' married. Well, bugger me!'

Acknowledgements

In the process of writing *A Girl in Wartime* I got some valuable info from the War Office who were very obliging. I also gained a good deal of general information from a very heavy tome called *Chronicle of the Twentieth Century* which gives really valuable help on anything one needs to look up, including pieces from newspapers.

Read on for a sneak peek at

THE FACTORY GIRL

Also by Maggie Ford

Available from Ebury Press

EBURY
PRESS

Chapter One

February, a raw Saturday afternoon – not a day to choose to go up to the West End, more one for huddling by a nice, warm fire, with her nose in the romance she was currently reading, *Drifting Petals*.

Today, though, Geraldine Glover had a purpose in mind. Time was running out, cold weather or no. In four weeks her older sister, Mavis, was getting married to Tom Calder. Three months had passed since the Armistice. Young men were still coming home, couples were making up for lost time and all a man wanted after maybe four years of hell in the trenches was to get married to the girl who had waited for him. Mavis and Tom wanted the same thing: to get married, settle down and forget the war.

It wasn't as easy as it sounded. Men coming home in droves to no jobs, and with little money to find the rent for somewhere to live, usually ended up living in one room in a parent's house. This was what Tom and Mavis were going to have to do. With no room at home with Mum and Dad, who had two sons and three daughters crammed in a shabby East End terraced two-up two-down in Burgoyne Road off Grove Road, they'd go to his parents' house.

It would be a frugal wedding with no frills or flounces. With food shortages the wedding breakfast would be made up of whatever the family could bring. At least Dad had work at the docks and there was the promise of a job there for Tom if Dad could pull strings, so Mavis would have her trousseau.

Even so, Geraldine envied her sister, wishing it was she who was getting married and leaving her cramped home where three girls had to share one bed, while her brothers, one older, one younger, shared a single bed in the back room where the family ate. It meant they couldn't go to bed until everyone else did or went off into the front room, normally kept for best.

Some families around here had even more kids and heaven knows how they coped. But all Geraldine ever dreamed of was one day having her own room to do what she liked in, as Mavis would four weeks from now. But as yet she didn't even have a regular boyfriend, let alone one to marry. There were plenty who fancied her and whom she'd been out with, but none she'd want to marry. The only one – Alan Presley from Medway Road – was married although going through a divorce and had no interest in other girls these days – a case of once bitten twice shy.

When she was fifteen and he was seventeen they'd gone around together in a group and he'd been sweet on her, but they'd lost touch when he went into the Army in 1917. Writing letters was a chore and later she heard that he'd found a girl from the next street to hers while home on leave. The girl had got pregnant and on his next leave they had to marry, but a year later he'd come home from France to find her in bed with another bloke and that was it. Even so, you can't start making eyes at someone still married, if separated and waiting for a divorce. Wouldn't be appropriate. But he was a handsome-looking bloke and her heart still went pitter-pat for him.

Standing in the bus queue outside Mile End Station, Geraldine eyed the clock outside a watchmaker's opposite: ten to two. If a Number 25 didn't arrive soon she'd end up frozen stiff. Huddling deeper into her thick jacket with the wind pressing her heavy hobble skirt against her ankles, she sighed.

The queue was growing steadily as there had been no bus for nearly fifteen minutes. The first one along would no doubt be full by now, not even standing room, and would probably sail right by, though it might be followed by another after all this delay – buses seemed to love keeping each other company.

Geraldine turned her mind to signs of life from the London & General Omnibus Company. She was partially correct about buses keeping each other company as finally two 25s appeared, the first doing exactly as she'd expected, the driver looking smug as it trundled straight by.

Crinkling her pretty face into a wry grin as she took her turn boarding the second bus, she managed to find a seat on top where at least she could have a smoke. Lots of girls doing men's jobs during the war had learned to smoke and it had become accepted. She didn't smoke all that much herself, but the odd puff helped a girl of eighteen get through a humdrum week as a machinist on piecework in a clothing factory where utility dresses, blouses and skirts offered very little variety of design. Anyway, she was tired having worked like mad all Saturday morning and a cigarette helped to perk her up.

Today, however, she felt perky enough, eagerly looking forward to what she had in mind to do once she'd alighted on Oxford Street. She'd done it many times before but today was special for she needed to look good at her sister's wedding, and for someone on a meagre wage there was only one way to do it.

She found little in Oxford Street to tempt her even though London's West End had all the newest fashions. Moving on to Regent Street, there was nothing there either that really caught her eye. Disappointment growing, she found herself wandering down New Bond Street. If there was nothing here she'd be properly stuck. There was such a scarcity of fabrics even though the war was over, and unless you could afford to pay something like ten or twelve guineas, which for her represented nine to ten weeks' earnings, a really stunning dress was out of the question. But what she was looking for had to be extra special to make her stand out at this wedding, though she always aimed to stand out anywhere.

True, for most of the time she and her fifteen-year-old sister Evelyn would be wearing bridesmaid's dresses – skimpy things in cheap rose-pink cotton that would make them look like a pair of candlesticks following the bride up the aisle. Tom's six-year-old cousin Lily, in pale blue, to Geraldine's mind would just about put the kybosh on the whole ensemble. Though it was all Mavis could do on so little money, she'd never had any dress sense.

How they could have ever been sisters was beyond Geraldine.

'Let me make the dresses,' she'd implored. 'I'm a good dressmaker, as good as anyone.'

But Mavis had been adamant. 'I want ter buy them ready-made. That way I can be certain of 'em.'

'I could make them all at half the price.'

'I want proper ones.'

'And I don't know how to make proper dresses, I suppose!' she had stormed at Mavis, getting angry. 'Look at what I make for meself – everyone thinks they've been bought. And I save loads of money.'

'I don't care!' Mavis had stormed back. 'It's my day. And I decide what I want and 'ow I want it.'

'And end up makin' a pauper of yerself!'

'No I won't! Cos I've bin puttin' by fer ages for a decent weddin' dress.'

Mavis and Tom had been saving for this for two years but still hadn't much to show for it, with Tom away in the Army while she had got herself a job in a munitions factory, though now she worked in a local bread shop.

'All I want is a decent wedding,' she'd gone on. 'And I'm buyin' me own dresses.'

'Sewn tergether with cheap cotton what breaks as soon as you stretch a seam by accident, you wait and see. And, I'm sorry, Mave, but I think that rose pink you want us to wear is an 'ideous colour.'

Mavis had yelled at her again that she liked pink and it was her day and she'd do what she liked, walking off close to tears, leaving Geraldine to give up on her. Mavis was getting more uppity and highly strung the nearer her big day came and was best left alone. She would put up with the horrible colour as best she could and anyway, it would only be for a couple of hours.

Thinking of it, Geraldine wandered on down New Bond Street, gazing in the shop windows she passed. Moments later all other thoughts were swept from her mind at the sight of the most beautiful dress she had ever seen.

Mesmerised, she stared at it through the window. Draped tastefully on a graceful papier-mâché manikin was an ankle-length afternoon gown in pale-blue silk with separate dark-blue velvet panels. It had a square neckline and was cut in the latest barrel line, loose panels of velvet falling from the waist back and front with a square, tabard-like silk overbodice from shoulders to hips.

Real silk! It could be seen at a glance. She could never afford *real silk*. But artificial silk like Courtauld's Luvisca and a cheaper velvet would look every bit as good.

It took some courage to push open the boutique door. Usually she'd aim her sights lower. Big London stores held no fears for her, nor did most high-class shops. But this place – the opulence of it, the perfume wafting out of it crying, 'Nothing under fifteen guineas!' She was stepping on hallowed ground.

Clenching her teeth and trying to look as though fifteen guineas was nothing to her, although her beret decried all that, she approached another manikin draped in an identical dress to that in the window. So at least the outfit wasn't exclusive. Even so, she needed time to browse, to study the garment and make mental notes of every stitch, the cut, to see how the material fell. Real silk always fell beautifully. Would cheaper artificial silk do the same?

'May I be of assistance, madam?' The measured, almost sarcastic, cultured tone right behind her nearly made her leap out of her skin, as though she was already being accused of stealing.

Gathering her wits, she turned to the voice, immediately aware of the haughty, intimidating frigidness on the face of a woman neatly clad in a black dress with white collar and cuffs, her hair pulled back from her brow and not a trace of powder on her face. There was no warmth in her enquiry such as she might have used to a valued customer. The way it was couched practically screamed her opinion of a common working girl trespassing on her domain, riff-raff needing to be got out as quickly as possible and without fuss.

Steeling herself, Geraldine stood her ground, putting on her best high-class accent, which she could do when needed. 'I am browsing at the moment.'

She knew immediately that the sort of patron who entered here did not *browse* but would make straight towards an assistant to state what they had in mind and request to be conducted and advised.

The woman's face was vinegary. 'I should not imagine we have here anything that would suit madam.' In reality she was saying that would suit her pocket. 'Perhaps if madam tried one of the large stores.'

Geraldine ignored the broad hint. 'No, thank you,' she replied in her best West End voice, though even she was aware that to an ear accustomed to such there was no disguising a trace of flattened East End vowels.

'This caught my eye,' she went on, 'and I felt I needed to decide as to whether it would suit me or not.' She was overdoing the accent a bit.

The woman, thin, middle-aged and no doubt a spinster, was shorter than her, which gave Geraldine some feeling of advantage.

'I will let you know what I decide,' she dismissed her as haughtily as she could.

But still the woman hovered, saying nothing, her mien one that announced she would be keeping her eye on this intruder. It was humiliating but there was nothing Geraldine could do except turn back to the garment on the pretence of being deeply interested in buying it. All the time she could feel those eyes boring into the back of her neck lest she made off with something without paying for it. Suspicious old crow, trying to make her feel she was the lowest of the low.

There was no ticket on the gown – a place like this would never stoop to such practice. The type of customers who frequented here probably took it for granted that they'd be able to afford it whatever the price. Rude even to ask and she for one wasn't going to lower herself to ask either.

How exactly did they handle themselves, these people who frequented places like this? She could still feel those eyes burning into the back of her neck.

But there, it was done – every stitch, every fold and tuck, every line committed to memory. Turning back to the hovering assistant, she smiled.

'Thank you for your assistance, but I don't think this will suit me after all.'

How delightful, seeing the look on that prim face at being robbed of its triumph of catching her out for a tea leaf or turning her out as a common time-waster.

Even so, it was a relief to be away from those peering eyes. What she had selected was etched in her brain as clearly as though she still circled it – now to find the material as near a match to those lovely blues as possible.

A week perhaps to make it, meticulously copying the design now fixed in her mind, and then on the evening of the wedding, once out of that awful bridesmaid's gown, she'd have all eyes on her. And on her the next day too, compliments from all the family at Mum's – aunts and uncles, cousins and grandparents – as they gathered around the big table in the front room for Sunday dinner to round off the celebration, the newly-weds having gone off on honeymoon to Eastbourne.

In her fifteen-guinea outfit – it had to be at least that, though hers would cost not much more than fourteen shillings at the most, still a whole two weeks' pay – she'd be the talk of the family. She could hardly wait to seek out just the right stuff that would make her look like a lady of means.

It was in triumph, if very wearily, that she made her way back home, the parcel she clutched containing material from Selfridges in nearly identical colours to those she'd seen in New Bond Street, together with poppers and buttons that nearly matched, a spool of light-blue cotton and one of dark blue.

She'd need a nice row of beads to set it off, stones of rich sapphire blue – not the real gems of course. And she knew just where she could get something exactly like that, made and strung especially for her at nothing like what the real gems would cost.

Perhaps she would put in her order right now. Oddly, the thought of doing that, of going into the shop and speaking to its proprietor, made her heart step up a beat, and not just because of a mere necklace.

Chapter Two

It was well dark by the time she reached home, walking through the streets from the bus stop. Ten to five. The jewellers near the corner of Grove Road and Burgoyne Road where she lived was already closed. She'd have to wait until Monday, calling in on her way home from work, which was a nuisance.

Geraldine itched to secure just the right sort of necklace for the gown she would make. On the other hand she ought not be too impatient – better to finish it properly before looking for jewellery. She'd know by then what she really wanted and it would only take three or four days to do. Best to wait until then. But it would have been nice to pop in there now, if only to tell the proprietor what she was looking for.

She'd been in there a couple of times for cheap Christmas presents for her mother and sisters. The goods being cheap were an attraction and she'd found him very polite and helpful; being young and nice-looking was an even greater attraction to someone her age. The name above the shop said Hanfords and she assumed he was the Hanford who ran it but she didn't know his first name and she longed so much to know, especially as just lately she'd been seeing him in her dreams.

He'd only set up in the shop a couple of weeks before Christmas. Before that the place had been a store for clothing until the small factory renting it had closed a year ago. Its windows gradually became begrimed from neglect and it had stood there all forlorn among other busy shops.

Then last December there had been signs of work being done on it. Some evenings as she cycled home from work, she'd seen the young man supervising the refurbishment, her mind already rushing ahead of her.

As soon as the shop had opened she had gone in on the pretext of looking for Christmas presents, but while busily inspecting affordable trinkets laid out on the counter and in glass cabinets, her eyes had been on him. He'd seemed more interested in selling than returning her gaze, which was a pity, but after her third foray – she making sure to buy only one present at a time – he appeared to recognise her and she was sure there had been apprasial in those dark-grey eyes. She hoped so. It hadn't progressed any further so probably she was wrong. Since Christmas, though, she'd not had cause to go in there. She was not so well off that she could go buying things willy-nilly, even to get a glimpse of the proprietor who'd had the ability of making her heart do a little flip when he'd looked at her.

She noticed that he always closed his shop a little earlier than most on Saturdays. Perhaps he could afford to. He did seem to take more satisfaction from making jewellery than selling it. Even coming up to Christmas,

a busy time, he'd never been in the shop when she'd
gone there, the tinkle of the doorbell bringing him
hurrying from the back, dragging off a heat-soiled blue
apron as he came. And he sold only jewellery made by
himself. That wasn't any way to make a living unless
he was well off. Perhaps he'd find out soon enough and
close up and go away and she would never see him
again. Geraldine's heart sank at the thought.

Not all that many people appeared to go into his shop
despite what he sold being cheap. Not cheap and nasty
– cheap and nice, attractive, different. The stones were
only semi-precious – garnets, tiger eye, moonstones, that
sort of thing – and the metal was silver rather than gold,
but his workmanship was wonderful, delicate and
unusual, attractive to those with little money to spend
on expensive stuff. It was still early days of course.
Surely in time he would make a real living and stay on.
Life would be bleak if he were to pack up and go.

She spent as much time as she could gazing through
the tiny window at rings, pendants and brooches, always
hoping for a glimpse of him. Not earning enough to keep
forking out on jewellery, she couldn't keep on going in
on the pretext of buying, but next week she'd have a
legitimate excuse to be there, wouldn't she?

The Glover family always used the back door of the
house. The passage from the front door was an assault
course, with bicycles, tools, household bits and pieces
not immediately needed, and what her younger brother
Fred called *his stuff* – old toys mostly, toys he'd grown
out of as he was now thirteen and due to leave school
soon, but was still loath to part with. So with no access

by the front door everyone went round to the back to get in.

Every house in Bow, like everywhere in the East End, was identical to the next – row upon row of two-up two-downs in an unbroken terrace, back to back but for a small backyard; every street was the same, in a grid pattern without a tree or one touch of greenery, not even a bend in any of them to break the monotony.

The streets were playgrounds for the kids – cobbles, broken kerbs, bucked pavements, scuffed doorways and the peeling paintwork of windows bravely cleaned of East London's incessant smoke and grime were witness to every game a child could devise.

Of course there was always Victoria Park, that huge expanse of open space that was the nearest East London dwellers got to accessible countryside. But that was quite a traipse up Grove Road. It was easier playing in the street where a kid could be home in a second if hurt or upset, or wanting a wee or a skipping rope, or whatever. Victoria Park was for Sundays. Take sandwiches, a bottle of drink and spend a whole afternoon there feeling as though it was miles away from London.

Geraldine's house being an end terrace on the corner of Burgoyne Road and Conyer Street had an opening dividing it from the backyard of the end house in the adjoining street. But to come in by the back way had its unsavoury moments. As she came in, Geraldine wrinkled her nose in distaste at the smell of pee that wasn't coming from the outside lavatory. Each house had its outside lav. Mum kept hers scrupulously clean; some didn't. Brick-built, it was stuck on the back of the house, had a concrete floor and a wooden door, was dark, cold, uninviting and noisy when the chain was pulled, enough for all to know every time someone went, so that their next-door neighbours were starkly aware of Dad's weak bladder.

'Mum, it stinks out there!'

In the kitchen Mum was unwrapping newspaper containing fish and chips bought on the way home from the flicks. She, Dad and Fred went off regularly on Saturday afternoons no matter what films were being shown. Mum, not being much of a reader, had young Fred read the words out loud to her while the pianist gave it his all as drama or comedy unfolded.

Young Fred was hovering with his mouth watering but the walk from the fish shop on a cold evening had taken the heat out of the food and it needed to be rewarmed for a few minutes while Dad was upstairs taking off his suit and getting into something more comfortable.

'Mum, has Dad been peeing outside the door again?'

Her mother looked up from inserting plates into the warm gas oven, her face registering defence of her husband. 'Yer dad was busting and Fred was in the lav, taking 'is time as usual.'

'It weren't me,' protested Fred. 'It was 'im in there and me what was bustin'. I 'ad ter go.'

'Then you're a dirty little sod!' his mother rounded on him.

Young Fred looked belligerent. 'If 'e can do it, why can't I?'

'Because yer dad's got a weak bladder. He can't always wait, that's why.'

'But 'e does it in the night too, an' no one's in there.'

Ignoring the fact that as a mum she ought not let herself be drawn into argument with a thirteen-year-old, she said, 'I don't like yer dad usin' a po and it stinking the bedroom out all night. I'd sooner 'e goes downstairs. But sometimes 'e can't hold it and 'as ter go as soon as 'e gets out the back door.'

'It's only a couple of blooming yards away,' retorted Fred. 'It ain't the other end of London! It ain't the other end of Timbuctoo, is it?' he added, pleased with himself at the extent of his geographic knowledge.

Now she was cross. 'You mind your lip!' she shot at him. 'And wipe that grin off your face or I'll wipe it off for yer.'

'Don't matter who did it,' cut in Geraldine, 'it still stinks out there.'

Mum ignored her, her glare riveted on her son. 'What your dad does ain't nothink ter do with you, yer cheeky little bugger. He's excused if he can't make it to the lav in time with 'is waterworks. He's got an affliction – you ain't. An' I won't 'ave you piddling anywhere yer fancy. I don't care if you are leavin' school soon, I won't 'ave that sort of behaviour in me own house.'

Another slow grin spread across young Fred's face despite her earlier warning. 'I didn't do it in the '*ouse*,' he sniggered, the snigger sharply cut off by an aggrieved yelp as a clout caught him across the back of his head.

'Get up them stairs,' his mother exploded, and as he made his escape she yelled after him, 'Gettin' backchat from you – a bloody kid! And don't come down again till I say. I might even sling your fish and chips away.'

'Aw, Mum?' came the protest from the top of he stairs. 'I'm starvin'.'

'Then serves yer right fer being so cheeky,' she called up then, turning to Geraldine, now taking off her jacket in the warmth of the kitchen, added angrily, 'He's a little sod, that Fred. I won't 'ave him takin' after 'is dad. Yer dad's got trouble.' There was apology in her tone now. 'I'd sooner 'e do it out there than the chain going a dozen times a night and the neighbours 'earing it. He can't 'elp leaking, there's somethink wrong with 'im. He should see the doctor but that costs and we can't afford ter fork out just to 'ear he's got a weak bladder. Poor bugger, it's rotten fer 'im at work. Them dockers can be cruel and if they noticed it they'd be the first to take the piss out of him.'

Geraldine ignored the unwitting pun and went to hang her jacket in the passage, negotiating the four bicycles leaning one against the other to do so.

They all used bicycles – she to get to the clothing factory, Fred to get around with his mates, and a battered, second-hand old thing it was too, Dad to go to work at the docks, and Wally her older brother also to the docks, Dad being fortunate enough to have got him a job there after coming home from the war.

Reaching over them to get to the coat hooks on the wall, she heard Mum call to her, 'While you're there, Gel, call your dad down for 'is tea.'

She hated being called Gel. Her workmates called her Gerry, which wasn't too bad. But Gel! It was East End practice to shorten a long name. You couldn't do much with Fred, but Mavis was Mave and young Evelyn was Evie. Dad called Mum, Hild. But why give someone a decent name if it was going to be shortened to something horrible or ridiculous? Saying Hilda in full wouldn't take all that much more energy, but no, it was Hild. She called him Jack, because not even God Himself could shorten that name any more.

Dutifully she yelled up the stairs to Dad. 'Mum says your fish 'n chips is ready.' His okay floated down from behind the bedroom door.

Fred adding his plaintive voice to it called, 'Can I come down too?'

'I don't know. Better asked Mum.'

'M . . . u . . . m!'

'You stay where you are, you little bugger,' came the responding yell. 'I don't want no dirty little devil sittin' at my table.'

Mum, skilfully carrying cutlery, salt, vinegar, a jar of pickled onions and several large, white, somewhat chipped plates passed her on the way from the tiny kitchen where you couldn't swing a cat, let alone feed a family, to the back room. The flap-leaf of the table had been raised to accommodate them all, a cloth spread over it, a loaf waiting to be cut into slices and spread with dollops of margarine.

The back room was where the family ate, despite Fred and Wally's bed in one corner. With just two bedrooms it was the only place for them, the main one being Mum and Dad's, with the girls in the other one, it being unthinkable for them to sleep downstairs and their brothers accidentally seeing them in their nightdresses or worse, in their underclothes. Boys were different – sharing a bed downstairs, it didn't matter them being seen in their vests.

Even upstairs all three sisters shared one bed, it practically taking up the whole room with just enough space for the wardrobe, chest of drawers and a board they called a dressing table that housed a sewing machine belonging to Geraldine, but shared by all three. How families with even more children managed was a mystery to Geraldine, though friends had at times mentioned four or more to a bed. After evening meals, if not going out, everyone would end up in the front room, most of which were spent around the gramophone, allowing the boys to go to bed when they were ready.

'Mum, let Fred come down,' pleaded Geraldine, following her mother into the back room.

'It'll do 'im good ter stew up there for a bit,' said Mum, laying out plates. 'Teach 'im a lesson.' By this, she knew Mum would relent before the meal was finished.

Mum turned to her as Dad came creaking downstairs. Every stair creaked, as did the beds, chairs and cupboard doors. There were no secrets in this house.

'I didn't get you any fish 'n chips, Gel. Didn't know when you'd be 'ome. I could take a bit off each of ours if you like.'

'No, I'm fine, Mum. We 'ad a big dinner, remember. I'd much sooner 'ave a sandwich. Fish and chips make you fat.'

Her mother smiled, glancing at her daughter's slim figure, still in the best dress she'd put on for going up West, one she'd made herself in slate grey some while back. Geraldine had more dresses than most, being skilled on the sewing machine, artistic. She was proud of her.

'I got some in for Evie. She's at 'er friend's 'ouse down the street – should be 'ome any minute now. You could 'ave a bit of 'ers.'

'No thanks, Mum.'

'Well if yer don't want any there's some cheese in the larder. Yer could 'ave that. I weren't sure when you'd be 'ome, that's why I didn't get yer any.'

She eyed the parcel Geraldine had put down on a chair on coming in. 'Is that what yer went up the West End for? Spending yer 'ard-earned money on more stuff ter make. What yer goin' ter make now, as if you ain't got enough?'

This at least was a secret. No secret that she'd gone off up the West End – it was a rule of Mum's that her family always said where they were going in case they were needed urgently at home or had an accident out. Though how they'd have contacted each other if there had been any trouble had never been explained. The police coming round, she supposed, or some messenger from a hospital.

But the dress was a secret, at least until she had it all finished or the moment she started treadling away on the machine, the noise rumbling all over the house and Mum coming up to see what it was she was doing. She'd want to know all the ins and outs of what she was making, and in the end when it finally came out, she would inevitably say, 'Yer'll be wearing a bridesmaid dress, so why make somethink else? Yer'll upset Mavis thinking yer don't like what she got yer.' Though Mavis knew that already. She'd told her so, that she hated rose pink.

'Did yer go with a friend then?' Mum was asking.

Geraldine shrugged. 'No, on me own.'

Her mother moved past her to get the food from the oven as Dad went into the back room to seat himself at the table. ''Bout time you got yerself a boyfriend,' she said.

'I've got boyfriends.'

'I mean a real boyfriend, someone steady. You'll find yourself left on the shelf if you ain't careful.'

'Mum, I'm only eighteen. I've got time.'

Not bothering to reply to that, Mum hurried off into the back room, each hand now carrying a loaded plate, a tea towel protecting her skin from the oven's heat. 'Fred!' she called out as she went. 'Yours is on the table.'

As Fred came thumping down the stairs, all forgiven, the back door burst open to admit Evie. 'Blimey!' exploded the twelve-year-old. 'It don't 'alf stink out there!'

Her mother gave her a warning look as she returned to the kitchen to get two more plates from the oven. 'That's your sweet brother!' she said, her tone sharp. ''Cos he's leaving school this summer, he's feeling 'is feet and thinks he can get away with murder. I wish you lot wouldn't keep blaming yer dad for everything.'

'I never even mentioned Dad,' protested Evie hotly, dropping her coat on a kitchen chair and following her mother into the back room.

Left alone in the kitchen, Geraldine heard her mother call out one more request. 'You sure yer don't want some of ours divided up for yer?'

'No, Mum,' she called back. 'I'm getting meself a sandwich. I'm going out again in a little while.'

In fact she was seeing Eileen Moss, who she worked with. They were going to see the films her parents had seen this afternoon. They'd sit eating peanuts as fast as they could shell them and stare at the silent drama of Gloria Swanson's *Male and Female* and laugh at Charlie

Chaplin's slapstick comedy, *Sunnyside*, both of which Mum had said were very good.

Though it was nice going to the pictures, she'd have rather stayed at home this evening to start on her dress, itching to see how it would turn out, but she'd promised to go with Eileen, and anyway, there were too many at home tonight no doubt wanting to know what she was doing, what she was making, and what for.

THE FACTORY GIRL

By Maggie Ford

From rags to riches . . .

With the Armistice only a few months passed, times
are hard for eighteen-year-old Geraldine Glover.
A machinist at Rubins clothing factory in the
East End, she dreams of a more glamorous life.

When she meets Tony Hanford, the young and handsome proprietor of a small jeweller's shop in Bond
Street, Geraldine is propelled into a new world –
but it comes at a heavy price . . .

EBURY
PRESS